Maigret Victorious

By the same author

*

MAIGRET RIGHT AND WRONG
(*Maigret in Montmartre* and *Maigret's Mistake*)
MAIGRET AND THE YOUNG GIRL
MAIGRET AND THE BURGLAR'S WIFE
MAIGRET'S REVOLVER
MY FRIEND MAIGRET
MAIGRET GOES TO SCHOOL
MAIGRET'S LITTLE JOKE
MAIGRET AND THE OLD LADY
MAIGRET'S FIRST CASE
MAIGRET HAS SCRUPLES
MAIGRET AND THE RELUCTANT WITNESS
MADAME MAIGRET'S FRIEND
MAIGRET TAKES A ROOM
MAIGRET IN COURT
MAIGRET AFRAID
MAIGRET IN SOCIETY
MAIGRET'S FAILURE
MAIGRET'S MEMOIRS
MAIGRET AND THE LAZY BURGLAR
MAIGRET'S SPECIAL MURDER
MAIGRET AND THE SATURDAY CALLER
MAIGRET LOSES HIS TEMPER
MAIGRET SETS A TRAP
MAIGRET ON THE DEFENSIVE
MAIGRET AND THE HEADLESS CORPSE
THE PATIENCE OF MAIGRET
MAIGRET AND THE NAHOUR CASE
MAIGRET'S PICKPOCKET
MAIGRET HAS DOUBTS
MAIGRET TAKES THE WATERS
MAIGRET AND THE MINISTER
MAIGRET HESITATES
MAIGRET'S BOYHOOD FRIEND
MAIGRET AND THE WINE MERCHANT
MAIGRET AND THE KILLER
MAIGRET AND THE FLEA
MAIGRET AND MONSIEUR CHARLES
MAIGRET AND THE DOSSER
MAIGRET AND THE MILLIONAIRES
MAIGRET AND THE GANGSTERS
MAIGRET AND THE LONER
MAIGRET AND THE MAN ON THE
BOULEVARD

GEORGES SIMENON

Maigret Victorious

A SIXTH OMNIBUS

comprising

MAIGRET'S MEMOIRS
MAIGRET AND THE HEADLESS CORPSE
MAIGRET AND THE SATURDAY CALLER

HAMISH HAMILTON
LONDON

First published in Great Britain 1975
by Hamish Hamilton Ltd
90 Great Russell Street, London WC1

Copyright © 1975 by Georges Simenon

SBN 241 89164 7

Printed in Great Britain by
Western Printing Services Ltd, Bristol

CONTENTS

Maigret's Memoirs

MAIGRET'S MEMOIRS
(*Les Mémoires de Maigret*)
was first published in France in 1950
and in Great Britain in 1963

Translated from the French by Jean Stewart

CHAPTER ONE

Which affords me a welcome opportunity of explaining my relations with Monsieur Simenon

It was in 1927 or 1928. I have no memory for dates and I am not one of those who keep a careful record of their doings, a habit which is not uncommon in our profession and which has proved of considerable use and even profit to some people. And it was only quite recently that I remembered the notebooks in which my wife, for a long time without my knowledge and indeed behind my back, had stuck any newspaper articles that referred to me.

Because of a certain case that gave us some trouble that year—I could probably discover the exact date, but I haven't the courage to go and look through those notebooks.

It doesn't matter. At any rate I remember quite clearly what the weather was like. It was a nondescript day at the beginning of winter, one of those colourless grey and white days that I am tempted to call an administrative day, because one has the impression that nothing interesting can happen in so drab an atmosphere, while in the office, out of sheer boredom, one feels an urge to bring one's files up to date, to deal with reports that have been lying about a long time, to tackle current business ferociously but without zest.

If I stress the unrelieved greyness of the day it is not from any desire to be picturesque, but in order to show how commonplace the incident itself was, swamped in the trivial happenings of a commonplace day.

It was about ten o'clock in the morning. We had finished making our reports about half an hour ago, for the conference had been short.

Nowadays even the least well-informed members of the public know more or less what's involved in the conferences at Police Headquarters, but in those days most Parisians would have found it hard to say even which Government Service was housed in the Quai des Orfèvres.

At nine o'clock sharp a bell summons the various heads of departments to the Chief's big office, whose windows overlook the Seine. There is no glamour about these gatherings. You go there smoking your pipe or your cigarette, usually with a file tucked under your arm. The day hasn't got going yet, and is still vaguely redolent, for most people, of café au lait and croissants. You shake hands. You gossip, leisurely, waiting for everybody to turn up.

Then each in turn informs the Chief about what has been happening in his sector. A few remain standing, sometimes looking out of the window to watch the buses and taxis crossing the Pont Saint-Michel.

3

Contrary to general belief, we don't talk exclusively about crime.

'How's your daughter, Priollet? her measles?'

I remember hearing cookery recipes being knowledgeably set forth.

More serious problems are also discussed, of course; for instance, that of some deputy's or minister's son who has been behaving foolishly, who wilfully persists in his folly, and whom it is imperative to bring back to his senses without causing a scandal. Or that of a rich foreigner who has recently taken up residence in some Grand Hotel in the Champs-Elysées, and about whom the Government has begun to worry. Or of a little girl picked up in the street a few days previously, whom no relative has claimed, although her photograph has appeared in all the newspapers.

This is a gathering of professional people, and events are considered from a strictly professional point of view, without useless talk, so that everything becomes very simple. It's all in the day's work, so to speak.

'Well then, Maigret, haven't you arrested your Pole in the Rue de Birague yet?'

Let me hasten to say that I've nothing against Poles as such. If I happen to speak of them fairly often, it's not that I consider them a particularly aggressive or delinquent set of people. The fact is merely that at that time France, being short of labour-power, imported Poles by the thousand and settled them in the mines in the North. They were collected haphazardly in their own country, whole villages at a time, men, women and children, and piled into trains rather as negro labour was once recruited.

The majority of them have proved to be first-class workers, and many of them have become respected citizens. Nevertheless there was a certain proportion of riffraff, as was only to be expected, and for some time this riffraff gave us a good deal of trouble.

I am trying to convey the atmosphere to the reader by talking thus, somewhat disconnectedly, about the things that were preoccupying me at that time.

'I should like to keep him on the run for two or three days longer, Chief. So far he's led us nowhere. He's sure to end up by meeting some accomplices.'

'The Minister's getting impatient because of the Press ...'

Always the Press! And always, among the powers that be, that dread of the Press, of public opinion. No sooner has a crime been committed than we are urged to find a culprit immediately, at all costs.

We are practically told, after a few days: 'Put somebody or other in jail in the meantime, just to satisfy public opinion.'

I shall probably revert to this point. In any case it was not the Pole that we were discussing that morning, but a burglary that had recently been committed according to a new technique, which is an uncommon thing.

Three days earlier, on the Boulevard Saint-Denis, in the middle of the day, just as most of the shops had closed for the lunch-hour, a van had stopped in front of a small jeweller's. Some men had unloaded an enormous packing-case, which they had put down close to the door, and had gone off again with the van.

Hundreds of people had passed in front of that case without thinking twice about it. As for the jeweller, when he came back from the restaurant where he had been lunching, he knit puzzled brows.

And when he had shifted the case, which had now become very light, he discovered that a hole had been cut in the side that touched the door, and another hole in the door itself, and that of course all his shelves had been ransacked and his safe as well.

This was the sort of unsensational enquiry that is liable to take months and requires the largest number of men. The burglars had not left a single fingerprint, nor any compromising object.

The fact that the method was a new one made it impossible for us to hunt in any known category of thieves.

We had nothing but the packing-case, an ordinary case although a very large one, and for the past three days a round dozen of detectives had been visiting all manufacturers of packing-cases, and all firms making use of the largest size of packing-case.

I had just returned to my office, where I had begun to draw up a report, when the house telephone rang.

'Is that you, Maigret? Will you come to my room for a moment?'

Nothing surprising about that either. Every day, or almost every day, the Big Chief used to send for me at least once to his office, apart from the conference; I had known him since my childhood, he had often spent his holidays close to our home in the Allier, and he had been a friend of my father's.

And this particular Chief was, in my eyes, the real Chief in the fullest sense of the word, the chief under whom I had served my first term at Police Headquarters, who, without actually protecting me, had kept a discreet eye on me from above, and whom I had watched, in his black coat and bowler hat, walking alone under fire towards the door of the house in which Bonnot and his gang had for two days been resisting police and gendarmes.

I am referring to Xavier Guichard, with his mischievous eyes and his white hair, as long as a poet's.

'Come in, Maigret.'

The daylight was so dull that morning that the lamp in its green shade was alight on his desk. Close by, in an armchair, I saw a young man who rose to offer me his hand when we were introduced to one another.

'Chief-Inspector Maigret. Monsieur Georges Sim, who's a journalist. . . .'

'Not a journalist, a novelist,' the young man protested smilingly.

Xavier Guichard smiled too. And he had a whole range of smiles which could express all the various shades of what he was thinking. He also had at his disposal a sort of irony, perceptible only to those who knew him well and which, to others, sometimes made him appear a simpleton.

He spoke to me with the utmost seriousness, as if we were concerned with an important affair, a prominent personality.

'For his novel-writing, Monsieur Sim needs to know how Headquarters functions. As he has just explained to me, a good many dramatic stories wind up in this house. He has also made it clear that it's not so much the workings of the police machine that he wants to study in detail, for he has been able to get information about these elsewhere, but rather the atmosphere in which these operations take place.'

I merely glanced at the young man, who must have been about twenty-four and who was thin, with hair almost as long as the Chief's, and of whom the least I can say is that he seemed to have no lack of confidence about anything, least of all about himself.

'Will you show him round, Maigret?'

And just as I was moving towards the door I heard the fellow Sim remark:

'Excuse me, Monsieur Guichard, but you've forgotten to mention to the Chief-Inspector . . .'

'Oh yes, you're quite right. Monsieur Sim, as he has reminded us, is not a journalist. So there's no danger of his reporting to the newspapers things that ought to remain unpublished. He has promised me, without being asked, to use only in his novels whatever he may see or hear amongst us, and that in a form sufficiently altered to create no difficulties for us.'

I can still hear the Chief adding gravely, as he bent forward to look at his mail:

'You needn't worry, Maigret. He has given me his word.'

All the same, Xavier Guichard had let himself be led astray, I felt that already and my feeling was subsequently confirmed. Not only by the youthful audacity of his visitor, but on account of something that I only discovered later. The Chief, apart from his profession, had one passion: archaeology. He belonged to several learned societies and had written a fat book (which I have never read) about the remote origins of Paris and its surroundings.

Now young Sim had discovered this, whether or not by chance, and had made a point of talking to him about it.

Was it on this account that I had been sent for personally? Almost every day somebody at Headquarters gets the job of showing round visitors. Generally these are distinguished foreigners, or those connected in some way with the police force of their country, or sometimes merely influential voters, come up from the provinces and proudly exhibiting a card from their Deputy. It has become a routine. There is practically a little lecture that everybody has more or less learnt by heart, like guides to historical monuments.

But usually a sergeant serves the purpose, and the visitor has to be somebody very important for the head of a department to be disturbed.

'If you like,' I proposed, 'we'll go first to the anthropometrical department.'

'If it isn't too much bother, I'd rather begin with the waiting-room.'

This was my first surprise. He said it quite nicely, too, with a disarming glance, explaining:

'You understand, I should like to follow the route that your clients usually follow.'

'In that case you ought to start at the Police Station, for most of them spend the night there before being brought to us.'

He replied, calmly:

'I visited the Police Station last night.'

He took no notes. He had neither notebook nor fountain pen. He stayed for several minutes in the waiting-room with its tall windows, where are displayed, in black frames, the photographs of members of the Force killed on duty.

'How many casualties each year, on an average?'

Then he asked to see my office. Now it so happened that at that period the workmen were busy refitting it. I was provisionally installed on the mezzanine, in a disused office in the oldest administrative style, thick with dust, with black wooden furniture and a coal-burning stove of the sort you can still see in certain provincial railway stations.

This was the office in which I had started my professional life, in which I had worked as Detective-Sergeant for some fifteen years, and I must admit that I harboured a certain fondness for that huge stove, whose iron bars I loved to see glowing red in winter, and which I used to stoke up to the brim. This was not so much an inveterate habit as a trick to keep myself in countenance. In the middle of a difficult interrogation I would get up and poke the fire lengthily, then throw in noisy shovelfuls of coal, looking quite bland, while my client stared at me in bewilderment.

And the fact is that when at last I had a modern office at my disposal, equipped with central heating, I missed my old stove, but I was never allowed, nor ever even made the request—which would not have been granted—to take it with me into my new premises.

I must apologize for lingering over these details, but I know more or less what I'm getting at.

My guest looked at my pipes, my ashtrays, the black marble clock on the chimney-piece, the little enamel basin behind the door, and the towel that always smells like a wet dog.

He asked me no technical questions. The files did not seem to interest him in the slightest.

'This staircase takes us to the laboratory.'

7

There, too, he stared at the ceiling, which was partly glazed, at the walls, at the floor, and at the dummy which is used for certain reconstructions, but he paid no attention either to the laboratory itself with its complicated apparatus or to the work which was going on there.

Out of habit, I tried to explain:

'By magnifying several hundred times any written text, and comparing it . . .'

'I know. I know.'

And then he asked me, casually:

'Have you read Hans Gross?'

I had never heard the name mentioned. I have since learnt that it was that of an Austrian magistrate who, in the 1880s, held the first chair of scientific criminology at the University of Vienna.

My visitor, however, had read Hans Gross' two fat volumes. He had read everything, quantities of books of whose very existence I was ignorant and whose titles he quoted at me in an offhand manner.

'Follow me along this passage, and I'll show you the Records Office, where we keep the files of . . .'

'I know. I know.'

I was beginning to find him irritating. It looked as if he had put me to all this bother solely in order to stare at walls and ceilings and floors, to stare at us all, as if he were drawing up an inventory.

'We shall find a crowd in the anthropometric department just now. They'll have finished with the women by now. It'll be the men's turn . . .'

There were some twenty of these, stark naked, who had been rounded up during the night, and were waiting their turn to be measured and photographed.

'In short,' the young man said to me, 'all I've still got to see is the Special Infirmary of the Police Station.'

I frowned.

'Visitors are not admitted.'

It is one of the least-known places, where criminals and suspects are put through a number of mental tests by police doctors.

'Paul Bourget used to watch the proceedings,' my visitor calmly replied. 'I shall ask for permission.'

The fact is that I retained a wholly uninteresting memory of him, as uninteresting as the weather itself that day. If I made no effort to cut short his visit, it was primarily on account of the Chief's recommendation, and also because I had nothing important to do, and that it was, after all, a way of killing time.

He happened to pass through my office again, sat down and held out his tobacco pouch to me.

'I see you're a pipe smoker too. I like pipe smokers.'

There were, as usual, a good half dozen pipes lying about, and he examined them with a connoisseur's eye.

'What case are you on at the moment?'

In my most professional tone I told him about the robbery where the packing-case had been left at the door of the jeweller's shop, pointing out that this was the first time this technique had been used.

'No,' he said to me. 'It was used eight years ago in New York, at a shop in Eighth Avenue.'

He must have been pleased with himself, but I must admit that he did not seem to be boasting. He was smoking his pipe gravely, as if to add ten years to his age and put himself on an equal footing with the mature man that I already was.

'You see, Chief-Inspector, I'm not interested in professionals. Their psychology offers no problems. They are just men doing their own job, and that's all.'

'What are you interested in?'

'The others. Those who are made like you and me, and who end up one fine day by killing somebody without being prepared to do so.'

'There are very few of those.'

'I know.'

'Apart from crimes of passion . . .'

'There's nothing interesting about them either.'

That's all I remember of that encounter. I must have spoken to him incidentally of a case on which I had been busy a few months earlier, just because professionals were not involved in it, a case concerning a young girl and a pearl necklace.

'Thank you, Chief-Inspector. I hope I shall have the pleasure of meeting you again.'

Privately, I said to myself: 'I sincerely hope not.'

*

Weeks passed, then months. Once in the middle of winter I thought I recognized the fellow Sim in the main corridor of Police Head-quarters, pacing up and down.

One morning I found on my desk, beside my mail, a little book in a revolting illustrated cover, such as are displayed on newspaper stalls and read by shop girls. It was called: *The Girl with the Pearl Necklace*, and the author was called Georges Sim.

I hadn't even the curiosity to read it. I read few books, and no popular novels. I don't even know where I put the book, a paperback printed on cheap paper, probably in the wastepaper basket, and I thought no more about it for several days.

Then one morning I found an identical book in the same place on my desk, and thenceforward each morning a fresh copy appeared beside my mail.

It was some time before I noticed that my Inspectors, particularly Lucas, were glancing at me with amusement. At last Lucas said to me, after beating about the bush for a long time, as we made our way to the Brasserie Dauphine one day for a drink before lunch:

'So you're a character in a novel now, Chief.'

He pulled the book out of his pocket.

'Have you read it?'

He confessed that it was Janvier, the youngest member of the squad at that time, who had been putting a copy of the book on my desk each morning.

'It's quite like you in some ways, you'll see.'

He was right. It was like me to the extent that a sketch scribbled on the marble top of a café table by an amateur caricaturist is like a flesh-and-blood human being.

It made me bigger and clumsier than life, peculiarly ponderous, so to speak.

As for the story, it was unrecognizable, and I was made to use some quite unexpected methods, to say the least.

That same evening I found my wife with the book in her hands.

'The woman in the dairy gave it me. Apparently it's about you. I haven't had time to read it yet.'

What could I do? As the man Sim had promised, no newspaper was involved. The book concerned was not a serious work, but a cheap publication to which it would have been absurd to attach any importance.

He had used my real name. But he might have replied that there are quite a number of Maigrets in the world. I merely promised myself to receive him somewhat coldly if I happened to meet him again, convinced meanwhile that he would avoid setting foot in Police Headquarters.

In which I was mistaken. One day when I knocked at the Chief's door without having been sent for, to ask his advice on some point, he said:

'Come in, Maigret. I was just going to call you. Our friend Sim is here.'

No signs of embarrassment about our friend Sim. On the contrary, complete self-confidence and a bigger pipe than ever in his mouth.

'How are you, Chief-Inspector?'

And Guichard explained:

'He's just been reading me a few passages from something he has written about our place.'

'I know about it.'

Xavier Guichard's eyes were full of laughter, but this time it was of me that he seemed to be making fun.

'Then he told me some rather relevant things which may interest you. He'll repeat them to you.'

'It's quite simple. Hitherto, in France, in books, with very few exceptions, the sympathetic character has always been the offender, while the police have been exposed to ridicule, if not worse.'

Guichard was nodding approvingly.

'Quite true, isn't it?'

And it was, in fact, quite true. Not only in books but in daily life. I was reminded of a rather painful episode in my early days, when I was serving in the Public Highways Squad. I was on the point of arresting a pickpocket outside a Métro station when the fellow began yelling something—possibly 'Stop thief!'

Instantly a score of people fell upon me. I explained to them that I was a policeman, that the man now making his escape was a habitual criminal. I am convinced that they all believed me. They none-the-less managed to delay me by every possible means, thus allowing my pick-pocket time to get away.

'Well,' Guichard went on, 'our friend Sim is proposing to write a series of novels in which the police will be shown in their true light.'

I pulled a face, which the Chief did not fail to notice.

'More or less in their true light,' he corrected himself. 'You follow me? His book is only a rough draft of what he plans to do.'

'He has made use of my name.'

I thought the young man would be covered with confusion and would apologize. Not a bit of it.

'I hope you weren't offended, Chief-Inspector. I couldn't help it. When I have imagined a character under a particular name I find it quite impossible to change it. I tried out all possible combinations of syllables to replace those of the name Maigret, but in vain. In the end I gave it up. It wouldn't have been *my* character any longer.'

He said *my* character, quite calmly, and the amazing thing was that I never turned a hair, possibly on account of Xavier Guichard and the mischievously twinkling eyes he kept fixed on me.

'He is thinking this time not of a popular series but of what he calls . . . What did you call it, Monsieur Sim?'

'Semi-literature.'

'And you're counting on me to . . .'

'I should like to know you better.'

I told you at the beginning: his self-assurance was complete. I really believe that was the secret of his strength. It was partly through this that he had already succeeded in winning over the Chief, who was interested in every type of human being and who announced to me, without a smile:

'He is only twenty-four.'

'I find it hard to construct a character unless I know how he behaves at every moment of the day. For instance, I shan't be able to talk about millionaires until I have seen one in his dressing-gown eating his boiled egg for breakfast.'

This happened a long time ago and I wonder now for what mysterious reason we listened to all this without bursting out laughing.

'In short you'd like . . .'

'To know you better, to watch you living and working.'

Of course, the Chief gave me no orders. I should no doubt have rebelled. For quite a time I felt uncertain whether he wasn't playing a practical joke on me, for he had retained a certain Latin Quarter streak in his character, from the days when the Latin Quarter still went in for hoaxes.

It was probably in order not to seem to be taking the whole affair too seriously that I said, shrugging my shoulders:

'Whenever you like.'

Then young Sim jumped up delightedly.

'Right away.'

Once more, in retrospect, it may seem ridiculous. The dollar was worth I don't know what fantastic sums. Americans used to light their cigars with thousand-franc notes. Montmartre was teeming with negro musicians, and rich, middle-aged ladies let themselves be robbed of their jewellery by Argentinian gigolos at *thés dansants*.

The sale of *La Garçonne* was reaching astronomical figures, and the Vice Squad was overwhelmed by orgiastic parties in the Bois de Boulogne, which they scarcely dared interrupt for fear of disturbing Consular personalities having their fun.

Women had short hair and short skirts, and men wore pointed shoes and trousers tight round the ankles.

This explains nothing, I know. But everything is interconnected. And I can still see young Sim coming into my office next morning, as if he were one of my Inspectors, remarking kindly: 'Don't let me disturb you . . .' and going to sit down in a corner.

He still took no notes. He asked few questions. He tended rather to make assertions. He explained to me subsequently—and it doesn't follow that I believed him—that a man's reactions to an assertion are more revealing than his replies to a specific question.

One day at noon when we went for a drink to the Brasserie Dauphine, Lucas, Janvier and I, as was our frequent custom, he followed us.

And one morning, at the conference, I found him installed in a corner of the Chief's office.

This went on for several months. When I asked him if he was writing, he answered:

'Popular novels, still, to earn my living. From four to eight in the morning. By eight o'clock I've finished my day's work. I shall only start on semi-literary novels when I feel ready for it.'

I don't know what he meant by that, but, after I had invited him to lunch one Sunday in the Boulevard Richard-Lenoir and had introduced him to my wife, he suddenly stopped coming to the Quai des Orfèvres.

It seemed odd not to see him in his corner, getting up when I got up, following me when I went out and accompanying me step by step through the offices.

During that spring I received an invitation that was, to say the least, unexpected.

Georges Sim has the honour of inviting you to the christening of his boat, the Ostrogoth, *which will be performed by the Curé of Notre-Dame on Tuesday next, at the Square du Vert-Galant.*

I did not go. I learnt from the police of the district that for three days and three nights a rowdy gang kept up a tremendous din on board a boat moored right in the middle of Paris and flying all its flags.

Once, as I crossed the Pont-Neuf, I saw the aforesaid boat and, at the foot of the mast, somebody sitting at a typewriter, wearing a master-mariner's cap.

The following week the boat had gone, and the Square du Vert-Galant had resumed its usual appearance.

More than a year later I received another invitation, written this time on one of our fingerprint cards.

Georges Simenon has the honour of inviting you to the Anthropo-metrical Ball which will be held at the Boule Blanche *to celebrate the launching of his detective stories.*

Sim had turned into Simenon.

More precisely, feeling himself now fully adult, perhaps, he had resumed his real name.

I did not bother about it. I did not go to the ball in question and I learned next day that the Prefect of Police had been present.

Through the newspapers. The same newspapers that informed me, on the front page, that Chief-Inspector Maigret had just made his sensational entry into detective fiction.

That morning, when I arrived at Headquarters and climbed the great staircase, I was met with sly smiles and amused averted faces.

My inspectors did their utmost to keep straight faces. My colleagues, at the conference, pretended to treat me with unwonted respect.

Only the Big Chief behaved as if nothing had happened and asked me with an absent-minded air:

'And what about you, Maigret? How are things going?'

In the shops of the Richard-Lenoir district, there was not a tradesman who failed to show my wife the paper with my name in large letters, and ask her, full of wonderment:

'It *is* your husband, isn't it?'

It was myself, alas!

CHAPTER TWO

*In which it is argued that the naked truth is often
unconvincing and that dressed-up truths may
seem more real than life*

When the news got round that I was writing this book, and then that
Simenon's publisher, without having read it, before I had even finished
the first chapter, had offered to publish it, I was conscious of the somewhat dubious approval of my friends. They were saying, I'm convinced
of it: 'So Maigret's having a go too!'

The fact is that during the last few years, at least three of my former
colleagues, men of my own generation, have written and published
their memoirs.

Let me hasten to point out in so doing they were following an old
tradition of the Paris police, to which we owe, among others, the
memoirs of Macé and those of the great Goron, each in his time chief of
what was then called the Sûreté. As for the most illustrious of them all,
Vidocq, he unfortunately left no recollections written by himself which
we might compare with the portraits drawn of him by novelists, often
under his real name, or else, as in the case of Balzac, under that of
Vautrin.

It is not my business to defend my colleagues, but nevertheless I take
this opportunity of replying to an objection which I have frequently
heard raised.

'According to their writings,' I have been told, 'at least three of them
consider themselves responsible for the solution of every famous case.'

And people would quote, in particular, the Mestorino case, which
made a great sensation in its time.

Now I might make a similar claim myself, for a case of that scope
demands the collaboration of every branch of the Force. As for the final
interrogation, that famous twenty-eight-hour-long interrogation that
is cited as an example nowadays, there were not four but at least six of
us taking it in shifts, going over the same questions one by one in every
conceivable fashion, gaining a little bit of ground each time.

Under these conditions, it would have been hard to say which of us
at a given moment had pulled the trigger that provoked a confession.

I wish to assert, moreover, that the title of *Memoirs* was not chosen
by myself and was finally tacked on because we couldn't think of a
better word.

The same is true (I make this point as I correct the proofs) of the
subtitles, of what it seems are called chapter-headings, which the
publisher asked me to let him add as an after-thought, for typo-

graphical reasons, he told me kindly; in actual fact, I suppose, to give a touch of lightness to my text.

Of all the tasks I fulfilled at Headquarters, the only one I ever shirked was the writing up of reports. Was this due to an atavistic desire for accuracy, to scruples with which I have seen my father wrestling before me?

The joke has been made so often that it is almost a classic:

'Maigret's reports consist largely of parentheses.'

Probably because I try to explain too much, to explain everything, and because nothing seems to me clear or definite.

If *memoirs* implies the story of events in which I have been involved in the course of my career, I'm afraid the public will be disappointed.

In the space of almost half a century I don't think there have been more than a score of really sensational cases, including those to which I have already referred: the Bonnot case, the Mestorino case, plus the Landru case, the Sarrat case and a few others.

Now my colleagues, my former Chiefs in some cases, have spoken about these at length.

As for the other investigations, those which were interesting in themselves but hit no headlines in the newspapers, Simenon has dealt with them.

This brings me to what I wanted to say, what I've been trying to say ever since I started this manuscript, namely the real justification for these memoirs which are not proper memoirs, and now I know less than ever how I am to express myself.

I once read in the papers that Anatole France, who must at any rate have been an intelligent man and who was fond of indulging in irony, having sat for the painter Van Dongen for his portrait, not only refused to accept the picture once it was finished but forbade it to be shown in public.

It was at about the same period that a famous actress brought a sensational lawsuit against a caricaturist whose portrait of her she thought insulting and injurious to her career.

I am neither an Academician nor a stage star. I don't consider myself unduly susceptible. Never, during the course of my professional life, have I sent any single correction to the newspapers, although these have never been slow to criticize my activities and my methods.

Nowadays everyone cannot have his portrait painted, but at least we have all had the experience of being photographed. And I suppose everyone is familiar with that discomfort we feel when confronted with a picture of ourselves which is not quite a true likeness.

Is my meaning quite clear? I am rather ashamed of insisting on this. I know I am dealing with a vital, ultra-sensitive point, and I feel suddenly afraid of appearing ridiculous, a thing which rarely affects me.

I think I should scarcely mind if I were depicted under an appearance completely different from my own, even libellously so.

But let me revert to the comparison with photography. The lens does not permit of complete inaccuracy. The image is different without being different. Faced with the print, you are frequently incapable of putting your finger on the detail that offends you, of saying exactly *what* isn't you, *what* you don't recognize as belonging to yourself.

Well, for years this was my position when faced with Simenon's Maigret, whom I watched growing day by day beside me, so that some people ended by asking me quite seriously whether I had copied his mannerisms, and others whether my name was really my father's name or whether I had borrowed it from the novelist.

I have tried to explain more or less how the thing began, quite innocently on the whole and seemingly without importance.

The very youthfulness of the fellow whom worthy Xavier Guichard had introduced to me one day in his office inclined me rather to shrug my shoulders than to harbour suspicions.

And then, a few months later, I was properly caught up in a mesh from which I have never managed to escape and from which the pages I am now scribbling will not completely rescue me.

'What are you grumbling about? You're famous!'

I know! I know! It's easy to say that when you've not experienced it. I even admit that at certain moments, in certain circumstances, it's not disagreeable. Not merely because it flatters one's vanity. Often for practical reasons. For instance, merely to secure a good seat in a crowded train or restaurant, or to avoid having to queue.

For so many years I never protested, any more than I corrected misstatements in the newspapers.

And I'm not suddenly going to claim that I was boiling inwardly, or chafing at the bit. That would be exaggerating, and I detest exaggeration.

None the less I promised myself that one day I would say what I've got to say, quite quietly, without rancour or ill-feeling, and once for all put things in their true perspective.

And that day has come.

Why is this book called *Memoirs*? I'm not responsible for that, as I said before, and the word is not of my choosing.

I'm not really concerned here with Mestorino or Landru or with that lawyer in the Massif Central who exterminated his victims by plunging them into a bath full of quicklime.

I'm concerned, more simply, with setting one character against another, one truth against another truth.

*

You shall soon see what some people understand by truth.

It was at the beginning, at the time of that anthropometrical ball which, together with certain other somewhat spectacular affairs in questionable taste, served to launch what people were already beginning to call 'the first Maigrets', two volumes entitled: *The Hanged Man of Saint-Pholien* and *The Late Monsieur Gallet.*

Those two, I frankly admit, I read immediately. And I can still picture Simenon appearing in my office the next morning, pleased at being himself, even more self-assured than before if that were possible, but none the less with a trace of anxiety in his eyes.

'I know what you're going to say to me!' he flung at me as soon as I opened my mouth.

Pacing up and down, he began to explain:

'I'm quite aware that these books are crammed with technical inaccuracies. There's no need to count them up. Let me tell you they're deliberate, and this is why.'

I didn't take note of the whole of his speech, but I remember the essential point in it, which he often repeated to me subsequently with an almost sadistic pleasure:

'Truth never seems true. I don't mean only in literature or in painting. I won't remind you either of those Doric columns whose lines seem to us strictly perpendicular and which only give that impression because they are slightly curved. If they were straight, they'd look as if they were swelling, don't you see?'

In those days he was still fond of displaying his erudition.

'Tell someone a story, any story. If you don't dress it up, it'll seem incredible, artificial. Dress it up, and it'll seem more real than life.'

He trumpeted out those last words as if they implied some sensational discovery.

'The whole problem is to make something more real than life. Well, I've done that! I've made you more real than life.'

I remained speechless. For a moment I could find nothing to say, poor unreal policeman that I was.

And he proceeded to demonstrate, with an abundance of gestures and the hint of a Belgian accent, that my investigations as told by him were more convincing—he may even have said more accurate—than as experienced by myself.

At the time of our first encounters, in the autumn, he had not been lacking in self-confidence. Thanks to success, he was brimming over with it now, he had enough to spare for all the timid folk on earth.

'Follow me carefully, Inspector . . .'

For he had decided to drop the *monsieur le commissaire.*

'In a real investigation there are fifty of you, if not more, busy hunting for the criminal. You and your detectives aren't alone on the trail. The police and gendarmerie of the whole country are on the alert. They are busy in railway stations and ports and at frontiers. Not to mention the informers, let alone all the amateurs who take a hand.

'Just try, in the two hundred or two hundred and fifty pages of a novel to give a tolerably faithful picture of that swarming activity! A three-decker novel wouldn't be long enough, and the reader would lose heart after a few chapters, muddling everything, confusing everything.

'Now who is it that in real life prevents this confusion from taking place, who is there every morning putting everyone in his right place and following the guiding thread?'

He looked me up and down triumphantly.

'It's you yourself, as you know very well. It's the man in charge of the investigation. I'm quite aware that a Chief-Inspector from Central Police Headquarters, the head of a special squad, doesn't roam the streets in person to interview concierges and wine merchants.

'I'm quite aware, too, that, apart from exceptional cases, you don't spend your nights tramping about in the rain in empty streets waiting for some window to light up or some door to open.

'None the less things happen exactly as if you were there yourself, isn't that so?'

What could I reply to this? From a certain point of view it was a logical conclusion.

'So then, let's simplify! The first quality, the essential quality of truth is to be simple. And I have simplified. I have reduced to their simplest form the wheels within wheels that surround you, without altering the result in the slightest.

'Where fifty more or less anonymous detectives were swarming in confusion, I have retained only three or four, each with his own personality.'

I tried to object:

'The rest won't like it.'

'I don't write for a few dozen police officials. When you write a book about schoolmasters you're bound to offend tens of thousands of schoolmasters. The same would happen if you wrote about station-masters or typists. What were we talking about?'

'The different sorts of truth.'

'I was trying to prove to you that my sort is the only valid one. Would you like another example? One doesn't need to have spent as long as I have in this building to know that Central Police Headquarters, which belongs to the Prefecture of Police, can only operate within the perimeter of Paris and, by extension, in certain cases, within the Department of the Seine.

'Now in *The Late Monsieur Gallet* I described an investigation which took place in the centre of France.

'Did you go there, yes or no?'

It was yes, of course.

'I went there, it's true, but at a period when . . .'

'At a period when, for a certain length of time, you were working not for the Quai des Orfèvres but for the Rue des Saussaies. Why bother the reader's head with these administrative subtleties?

'Must one begin the account of every case by explaining: This took place in such and such a year. So Maigret was seconded to such and such a department.

'Let me finish . . .'

He had his idea and knew that he was about to touch a weak point.

'Are you, in your habits, your attitude, your character, a Quai des Orfèvres man or a Rue des Saussaies man?'

I apologize to my colleagues of the Sûreté Nationale, who include many of my good friends, but I am divulging no secret when I admit that there is, to say the least, a certain rivalry between the two establishments.

Let us admit, too, as Simenon had understood from the beginning, that, particularly in those days, there existed two rather different types of policeman.

Those of the Rue des Saussaies, who are directly answerable to the Ministry of the Interior, are led more or less inevitably to deal with political jobs.

I don't blame them for it. I simply confess that for my own part I'd rather not be responsible for these.

Our field of action at the Quai des Orfèvres is perhaps more restricted, more down to earth. Our job, in fact, is to cope with malefactors of every sort and, in general, with everything that comes under the heading 'police' with the specific limitation 'judiciary'.

'You'll grant me that you're a Quai des Orfèvres man. You're proud of it. Well, that's what I've made of you; I've tried to make you the incarnation of a Quai des Orfèvres man. And now, for the sake of minutiae, because of your mania for accuracy, have I got to spoil the clarity of the picture by explaining that in such and such a year, for certain complex reasons, you provisionally changed your department, which enabled you to work in any part of France?'

'But . . .'

'One moment. The first day I met you, I told you I was not a journalist but a novelist, and I remember promising Monsieur Guichard that my stories would never involve indiscretions that might prove awkward for the police.'

'I know, but . . .'

'Wait a minute, Maigret, for God's sake!'

It was the first time he had called me that. It was the first time, too, that this youngster had told me to shut up.

'I've changed the names, except for yours and those of two or three of your colleagues. I've been careful to change the place-names too. Often, for an extra precaution, I've changed the family relationship between the characters.

'I have simplified things, and sometimes I've described only one cross-examination where there were really four or five, and only two or three trails to be followed where, to begin with, you had ten in front of you.

'I maintain that I am in the right, that my truth is the right one.

'I've brought you a proof of it.'

He pointed to a pile of books which he had laid on my desk when he arrived and to which I had paid no attention.

'These are the books written by specialists on matters concerning the police during the last twenty years, true stories, of that sort of truth that you like.

'Read them. For the most part you're familiar with the investigations which these books describe in detail.

'Well! I'm willing to bet that you won't recognize them, precisely because the quest for objectivity falsifies that truth which always is and which always *must* be simple.

'And now . . .'

Well! I'd rather admit it right away. That was the moment when I realized where the shoe pinched.

He was quite right, dammit, on all the heads he had mentioned. I didn't worry in the least, either, because he'd reduced the number of detectives or made me spend nights in the rain in their stead, or because he had, deliberately or not, confused the Sûreté Nationale with Central Police Headquarters.

What shocked me, actually, although I scarcely liked to admit it to myself, was . . .

Good Lord, how hard this is! Remember what I said about a man and his photograph.

To take merely the detail of the bowler hat. I may appear quite ridiculous, but I must confess that this silly detail hurt me more than all the rest.

When young Sim came to Headquarters for the first time, I still had a bowler hat in my cupboard, but I only wore it on rare occasions, for funerals or official ceremonies.

Now it happened that in my office there hung a photograph taken some years earlier on the occasion of some congress or other, in which I appeared wearing that cursed hat.

The result is that even today, when I am introduced to people who've never seen me before, I hear them say:

'Why, you're wearing a different hat.'

As for the famous overcoat with the velvet collar, it was with my wife that Simenon had to have it out one day, rather than with myself.

I did have such a coat, I admit. I even had several, like all men of my generation. It may even have happened that, round about 1927, on a day of extreme cold or driving rain, I took down one of those old overcoats.

I'm not a dressy man. I care very little about being smart. But perhaps for that very reason I've a horror of looking odd. And my little Jewish tailor in the Rue de Turenne is no more anxious than I am to have me stared at in the street.

'Is it my fault if that's how I see you?' Simenon might have answered, like the painter who gives his model a crooked nose or a squint.

Only in that case the model doesn't have to spend his whole life in front of his portrait, and thousands of people aren't going to believe ever after that he has a crooked nose or a squint.

I didn't tell him all this that morning. I merely averted my eyes and said modestly:

'Was it absolutely necessary to simplify *me*?'

'To begin with, it certainly was. The public has to get used to you, to your figure, your bearing. I've probably hit on the right expression. For the moment you're still only a silhouette, a back, a pipe, a way of talking, of muttering.'

'Thanks!'

'The details will appear gradually, you'll see. I don't know how long it will take. Little by little you'll begin to live with a more subtle, more complex life.'

'That's reassuring.'

'For instance, up till now, you've had no family life, whereas the Boulevard Richard-Lenoir and Madame Maigret actually take up a good half of your existence. You've still only rung up your home, but you're going to be seen there.'

'In my dressing-gown and slippers?'

'And even in bed.'

'I wear nightshirts,' I said ironically.

'I know. That completes the picture. Even if you were used to pyjamas I'd have made you wear a nightshirt.'

I wonder how this conversation would have ended—probably with a regular quarrel—if I hadn't been told that a young informer from the Rue Pigalle wanted to speak to me.

'On the whole,' I said to Simenon, as he held out his hand, 'you're pleased with yourself.'

'Not yet, but it'll come.'

Could I really have announced to him that henceforward I forbade him to use my name? I was legally entitled to do so. And this would have given rise to a typically Parisian lawsuit which would have covered me with ridicule.

The character would have acquired a different name. But he would still have been myself, or rather that simplified myself who, according to the author, was going to grow progressively more complex.

The worst of it was that the rascal was quite right and that every month, for years, I was going to find, in a book with a photograph on its cover, a Maigret who imitated me more and more.

And if it had only been in books! The cinema was shortly to take it up, and the radio, and later television.

It's a strange sensation to watch on the screen, coming and going, speaking and blowing his nose, a fellow who pretends to be yourself, who borrows certain of your habits, utters sentences that you have uttered, in circumstances that you have known, through which you have lived, in settings which have sometimes been reconstructed with meticulous care.

Actually the first screen Maigret, Pierre Renoir, was tolerably true to life. I had become a little taller, a little slimmer. The face was different, of course, but certain attitudes were so striking that I suspect the actor of having observed me unawares.

A few months later I grew some six inches shorter, and what I lost in height I gained in stoutness, becoming, in the shape of Abel Tarride, obese and bland, so flabby that I looked like an inflated rubber animal about to float up to the ceiling. Not to mention the knowing winks with which I underlined my own discoveries and my cunning tricks!

I couldn't sit the film out, and my tribulations were not yet over.

Harry Baur was no doubt a great actor, but he was a full twenty years older than myself then, with a cast of features that was flabby and tragic at the same time.

Let's pass over that!

After growing twenty years older, I suddenly grew almost that much younger again, a good deal later, with a certain Préjean, about whom I have no complaint to make—any more than about the rest of them— but who looks far more like certain young detectives of the present generation than those of my own.

And finally, quite lately, I have been made to grow stout again, almost to bursting point, while I have begun, in the shape of Charles Laughton, to use English as my native tongue.

Well! of all those, there was one at least who had the good taste to cheat Simenon and to consider my truth more valid than his.

It was Pierre Renoir, who did not clap a bowler hat on to his head but wore a perfectly ordinary felt hat, and the sort of clothes worn by any civil servant, whether or not attached to the police.

I see that I have spoken only of trivial details, a hat, an overcoat, a stove, probably because those details were what first shocked me.

You don't feel any surprise at growing up first, then at growing old. But let a man so much as cut off the tips of his moustaches and he won't recognize himself.

The truth is that I'd like to have finished with what I consider as trivial defects before confronting the two characters on essential points.

If Simenon is right, which is quite possible, my own character will appear odd and involved by the side of that famous simplified—or dressed-up—truth of his, and I shall look like some peevish fellow trying to touch up his own portrait.

Now that I've made a beginning, with the subject of dress, I shall have to go on, if only for my own peace of mind.

Simenon asked me the other day—actually, he has changed too, from the young fellow I met in Xavier Guichard's office—Simenon asked me, with a touch of mockery:

'Well, what about the new Maigret?'

I tried to answer him in his former words.

'He's taking shape! He's still nothing but a silhouette. A hat, an overcoat. But it's his real hat. His real overcoat! Little by little, perhaps the rest will come, perhaps he'll have arms and legs and even a face, who knows? Perhaps he'll even begin to think by himself, without the aid of a novelist.'

Actually, Simenon is now just about the age I was when we met for the first time. In those days he tended to think of me as a middle-aged man and even, in his heart of hearts, as an elderly one.

I did not ask him what he thought about that today, but I couldn't help remarking:

'D'you know that with the course of time you've begun to walk and smoke your pipe and even to speak like *your* Maigret?'

Which is quite true and which, you'll agree, provided me with a rather piquant revenge.

It was rather as if, after all these years, he had begun to take *himself* for *me*!

CHAPTER THREE

In which I shall try to talk about a certain bearded doctor who had some influence on the life of my family and perhaps, all things considered, on my choice of a career

I don't know if I am going to be able to hit the right tone this time, for I've already filled my wastepaper basket this morning with the pages I've torn up one after the other.

And last night I almost gave the whole thing up.

While my wife was reading what I had written during the day, I watched her, pretending to read my paper as usual, and at a certain point I had the impression that she was surprised, and from then on to the end she kept glancing up at me in astonishment and almost in distress.

Instead of speaking to me immediately, she went to put the manuscript back in the drawer in silence, and it was some time before she said, trying to keep her remark as light as possible:

'Anyone would think you didn't like him.'

I did not need to ask of whom she was speaking, and it was my turn to be perplexed, to stare at her in wide-eyed surprise.

'What are you talking about?' I exclaimed. 'Since when has Simenon ceased to be a friend of ours?'

'Yes, of course . . .'

I wondered what could be at the back of her mind, and tried to recollect what I had written.

'I may be mistaken,' she added. 'Of course I must be mistaken, since you say so. But I had the impression, while reading certain passages, that you felt really resentful about something, and were having your revenge. I don't mean a big, open resentment. Something more secretive, more . . .'

She did not add the word—but I did so for her—'. . . more shameful . . .'

Now Heaven knows how far that was from my mind while I wrote. Not only have I always been on the most cordial terms with Simenon, but he quickly became a family friend of ours, and on the few occasions when we have travelled in the summer holidays it has almost always been to visit him in his various homes, while he was still living in France: in Alsace, at Porquerolles, in the Charente, the Vendée and so forth. More recently, when I agreed to go on a semi-official tour of the U.S.A. it was mainly because I knew I should meet him in Arizona, where he was then living.

'I give you my word . . .' I began gravely.

'I believe you. But perhaps your readers won't.'

It's my own fault, I'm convinced of it. I am not accustomed to using irony and I realize that I'm probably heavy-handed about it. Whereas on the contrary I had tried, out of diffidence, to treat this difficult subject with a light touch, since it caused me a certain personal embarrassment.

What I am trying to do, in short, is nothing more or less than to size up one image against another image, one character against its double, rather than against its shadow. And Simenon was the first to encourage me in this undertaking.

I add, to pacify my wife, who is fiercely loyal in her friendships, that Simenon, as I said yesterday in other terms, jokingly, is quite different now from the young man whose aggressive self-confidence occasionally made me wince; that on the contrary he himself is inclined to be taciturn nowadays, and speaks with a certain hesitancy, particularly about any subject on which he feels strongly, reluctant to make assertions and, I'd take my oath, seeking my approval.

Having said that much, am I to go on teasing him? Just a little, after all. This'll be the last time, no doubt. It's too good an opportunity, and I cannot resist it.

In the forty-odd volumes he has devoted to my investigations, there are perhaps a score of allusions to my origins, to my family, a few words about my father and his profession as estate-manager, one mention of the Collège de Nantes where I was partly educated, and other brief allusions to my two years as medical student.

And this was the same man who took over four hundred pages to tell the story of his own childhood up to the age of sixteen. It makes no difference that he did so in fictional form, and that his characters may or may not have been true to life, the fact remains that he did not consider his hero complete without the company of his parents and grandparents, his uncles and aunts, whom he describes with all their failings and complaints, their petty vices and their ulcers, while even the neighbour's dog is allotted half a page.

I am not objecting to this, and if I comment on it, it's an indirect way of forestalling any accusation that could be levelled at me of being too longwinded about my own family.

To my mind, a man without a past isn't a whole man. In the course of certain investigations, I have sometimes spent more time over the family and background of a suspect than over the suspect himself, and this has often provided the key to what might otherwise have remained a mystery.

It has been said, quite correctly, that I was born in Central France, not far from Moulins, but I don't think it has ever been specified that the estate of which my father was manager was one of seven and a half thousand acres and included no less than twenty-six small farms.

Not only was my grandfather, whom I remember, one of these tenant farmers, but he followed at least three generations of Maigrets who had tilled the same soil.

An epidemic of typhus, while my father was still young, had decimated his family, which included seven or eight children, and left only two survivors, my father and a sister who was later to marry a baker and settle at Nantes.

Why did my father go to the lycée at Moulins, thus breaking with such old traditions? I have reason to believe that the village priest took an interest in him. But it did not mean a break with the land, for after two years at an agricultural school he came back to the village and joined the staff at the château as assistant estate-manager.

I always feel a certain embarrassment when speaking about him. I have the impression, indeed, that people think:

'He has retained a child's picture of his parents.'

And for a long time I wondered whether possibly I was mistaken, whether my critical sense were not failing me.

But I have had occasion to meet other men of the same type, particularly among those of his generation, mostly from the same social class, which might be described as an intermediary one.

For my grandfather, the family at the château, their rights, their privileges, their behaviour were not subjects for discussion. What he thought of them in his heart of hearts I never discovered. I was quite a youngster when he died. I'm convinced none the less, when I remember certain looks of his, certain silences particularly, that his approval was not always passive, was not even always approval, nor yet resignation, but that it proceeded, on the contrary, from a certain pride and above all from a highly developed sense of duty.

This was the feeling that persisted in men like my father, mingled with a reserve, a sense of propriety which may have looked like resignation.

I can picture him very well. I have kept some photographs of him. He was very tall, very thin, his thinness emphasized by narrow trousers, bound in by leather gaiters to just below the knee. I always saw my father in leather gaiters. They were a sort of uniform for him. He wore no beard, but a long sandy moustache in which, when he came home in winter, I used to feel tiny ice-crystals when I kissed him.

Our house stood in the courtyard of the château, a pretty house of rose-coloured brick, one storey high, overlooking the low buildings in which lived several families of farm-hands, grooms and gamekeepers, whose wives for the most part worked at the château as laundresses, needle women or kitchen helps.

Within that courtyard my father was a kind of ruler to whom men spoke respectfully, cap in hand.

About once a week he used to drive off at nightfall, sometimes at dusk, with one or more farmers, to go and buy or sell livestock at some distant fair from which he only returned at the end of the following day.

His office was in a separate building, and on its walls hung photographs of prize oxen or horses, calendars of fairs and, almost invariably, the finest sheaf of wheat harvested on the estate, shrivelling up as the months went by.

About ten o'clock he used to cross the courtyard and go into a private part of the grounds. He would walk round the buildings until he came to the big flight of steps up which the peasants never went, and remained closeted for a time behind the thick walls of the château.

It was for him, in a word, what our morning conferences are for us at Headquarters, and as a child I felt proud to see him, very upright, without a trace of servility, as he climbed that awe-inspiring flight of steps.

He spoke little, and he seldom laughed, but when this did happen it was a surprise to discover how young, almost childish, his laugh was, and to see how much simple pleasantries amused him.

He never drank, unlike most of the people I knew. At each meal a small decanter was set aside for him, half filled with a light white wine harvested on the estate, and I never saw him drink anything else, even at weddings or funerals. And at fairs, where he was obliged to stay at inns, he had a cup of his favourite coffee sent up from the kitchen.

I thought of him as a grown man, and even as a middle-aged one. I was five when my grandfather died. As for my mother's parents, they lived over fifty miles away, and we only visited them twice a year, so that I never knew them well. They were not farming folk. They kept a grocer's shop in a largish village, with a café attached to it, as is often the case in country places.

I am not sure, in retrospect, that this was not the reason why our relations with our in-laws were not closer.

I was not quite eight years old when I finally realized that my mother was pregnant. By remarks overheard by chance, by whispers, I more or less grasped that the thing was unexpected, that after my birth the doctors had declared that she was unlikely to have any more children.

I reconstructed all this later, bit by bit, and I suppose this is always the case with childhood memories.

There was at this time in the neighbouring village, which was bigger than ours, a doctor with a pointed red beard whose name was Gadelle —Victor Gadelle if I am not mistaken—about whom people talked a great deal, almost always with an air of mystery, and, probably on account of his beard, and also on account of all that was said about him, I was almost inclined to take him for a kind of devil.

There was a drama in his life, a real drama, the first I ever came across and one which impressed me deeply, particularly as it was to have a profound influence on our family, and thereby on my whole existence.

Gadelle drank. He drank more heavily than any peasant in the neighbourhood, not only from time to time but every day, beginning in the morning and only stopping at night. He drank so much that, in a warm room, the atmosphere would be pervaded by a smell of alcohol which I always sniffed with disgust.

Moreover he was careless of his person. In fact you might have called him dirty.

How, under these conditions, could he have been my father's friend? That remained a mystery to me. The fact remains that he often came to see him and chat with him at our home and that there was even a ritual, which consisted of taking out of the glass-fronted sideboard, as soon as he arrived, a small decanter of brandy that was kept for his exclusive use.

About the original drama I knew almost nothing at the time. Doctor Gadelle's wife was pregnant, and this must have been for the sixth or seventh time. I thought of her as an old woman already, whereas she was probably about forty.

What had happened on the day of her confinement? Apparently Gadelle came home more drunk than usual, and, while waiting for his wife's delivery, went on drinking at her bedside.

As it happened, the first stages of her labour were unusually prolonged. The children had been taken to some neighbour's. Towards morning, as nothing seemed to be happening, the sister-in-law who had spent the night at the house went off to see to things at her own home.

Then, apparently, a great noise was heard in the doctor's house, with cries, and footsteps coming and going.

When people got there, they found Gadelle weeping in a corner. His wife was dead. So was the child.

And for a long time after I would overhear the village gossips whispering in each other's ears, with expressions of indignation or horror:

'A real shambles!'

*

For months the case of Doctor Gadelle was the main topic of conversation, and, as was to be expected, the neighbourhood was split into two factions.

Some people—and there was a good number of them—went into town, which was quite a journey in those days, to consult a different doctor, while others, through indifference or because they still trusted him, went on sending for the bearded doctor.

My father never took me into his confidence on this subject. I am therefore reduced to conjecture.

Gadelle, at any rate, never stopped coming to see us. He called on us as he had always done, in the course of his rounds, and the familiar gilt-edged decanter was put before him as usual.

He was drinking less, however. People said they never saw him tipsy now. One night he was sent for to the remotest of the farms for a confinement, and he acquitted himself with honour. On his way home he called at our house, and I remember he was very pale; I can still see my father clasping his hand with unwonted persistence as though to encourage him, as though to tell him: 'You see, things weren't so hopeless after all.'

For my father never gave up hope of people. I never heard him utter an irrevocable judgment, even when the black sheep of the estate, a foul-mouthed farmer of whose malpractices he had had to complain to the landlord, had accused him of some dishonest trick or other.

It's quite certain that if, after the death of Gadelle's wife and child, there had been nobody to stretch out a helping hand to the doctor, he would have been a lost man.

My father did so. And when my mother was pregnant, a certain feeling which I find hard to explain, but which I understand, obliged him to see the thing through.

He took precautions, none the less. Twice, during the last stage of her pregnancy, he took my mother into Moulins to consult a specialist.

When her time came, a stable lad went on horseback to fetch the doctor in the middle of the night. I wasn't sent away from home, but stayed there shut up in my own room, in a great state of agitation, although like all country lads I had acquired a certain knowledge of these things at an early age.

My mother died at seven in the morning, as day was breaking, and when I went downstairs the first thing that caught my eye, in spite of my emotion, was the decanter on the dining-room table.

I was left an only child. A local girl was brought in to look after the house and take care of me. I never saw Doctor Gadelle cross our threshold since that day, but neither did I ever hear my father say one word about him.

A blurred and colourless period followed this drama. I went to the village school. My father spoke less and less. He was thirty-two, and only now do I realize how young he was.

I did not protest when, on completing my twelfth year, I was sent as a boarder to the lycée at Moulins, since it was impossible to take me there every day.

I only stayed there a few months. I was unhappy there, an utter stranger in a new world that felt hostile to me. I said nothing about it to my father, who fetched me home every Saturday evening. I never complained.

He must have understood, for during the Easter holidays his sister, whose husband had opened a bakery at Nantes, suddenly came to see us, and I realized that they were discussing a plan already sketched out by letter.

My aunt, who had a very high colour, had begun to put on weight. She was childless and this grieved her.

For several days she hovered round me anxiously, telling me about the house at Nantes with its good smell of new bread.

She seemed very cheerful. I had guessed. I was resigned. Or, more precisely, since that's a word I don't care for, I had accepted.

My father and I had a long talk together as we walked through the countryside one Sunday morning after Mass. It was the first time he had talked to me as if I were a man. He was considering my future, the impossibility of studying if I stayed in the village, and if I remained at Moulins as a boarder the absence of normal family life.

I know now what he was thinking. He had realized that the company of a man like himself, who had withdrawn into himself and lived mainly with his own thoughts, was not desirable for a young boy who still had everything to hope for from life.

I went off with my aunt, a big trunk jolting behind us, in the cart that took us to the station.

My father did not shed a tear. Neither did I.

*

That's more or less all I knew about him. For years, at Nantes, I was the nephew of the baker and the baker's wife, and I almost got used to the man whom I saw every day with his shaggy chest glowing in the red light of his oven.

I used to spend all my holidays with my father. I won't go so far as to say we were strangers to one another. But I had my own private life, my ambitions, my problems.

He was my father, whom I loved and respected, but whom I'd given up trying to understand. And it went on like that for years. Is this always the case? I'm inclined to think so.

When my curiosity reawakened, it was too late to ask the questions which I so longed to ask then, and which I reproached myself for not asking when he was still there to answer me.

My father had died of pleurisy at the age of forty-four.

I was a young man, I had begun my medical studies. On my last visits to the château I had been struck by the flush on my father's cheekbones and the hectic glitter of his eyes at night.

'Has there ever been any tuberculosis in our family?' I asked my aunt one day.

She said, as though I had spoken of some shameful taint:

'Good heavens, no! All of them were as tough as oak-trees! Don't you remember your grandfather?'

I did remember him, precisely. I remembered a certain dry cough which he put down to smoking. And as far back as I could remember I always pictured my father with the same cheekbones under which a fire seemed to be glowing.

My aunt had the same pink flush too.

'It's from always living in the heat of a bakery,' she would retort.

She died, none the less, from the same illness as her brother, ten years later.

As for myself, when I got back to Nantes to collect my belongings before starting on a new life, I hesitated for a long while before calling on one of my professors at his private house and asking him to examine me.

'No danger of anything like that,' he reassured me.

Two days later I took the train to Paris.

*

My wife will forgive me this time if I hark back to Simenon and his picture of me, for I want to discuss a point raised by him in one of his latest books, which concerns me very closely.

It is indeed one of the points that vexed me most—and I'm not referring to such petty questions as dress, which I raised as a joke.

I should not be my father's son if I were not somewhat touchy about all that concerns my job, my career, and that's precisely the question.

I have sometimes had an uneasy feeling that Simenon was somehow trying to apologize for me to the public for entering the Police Force. And I am sure that in some people's eyes I only took up this profession as a last resort.

Now it is certainly a fact that I had begun my medical studies and that I chose that profession of my own free will, without being pushed into it by somewhat ambitious parents, as often happens.

I had not thought about the matter for years, and it had never occurred to me to ask myself any questions about it, when, precisely on account of something that had been written about my vocation, the problem gradually forced itself upon me.

I spoke to nobody about it, not even to my wife. Today I have to overcome certain feelings of diffidence to put things in their true light, or try to do so.

In one of his books, then, Simenon has spoken of 'a man who mends destinies', and he did not invent the phrase, which was one of my own, which I must have uttered one day when we were chatting together.

Now I wonder if it didn't all spring from Gadelle, whose tragic story, as I subsequently realized, must have struck me far more than I supposed.

Because he was a doctor, because he had failed, the medical profession had acquired in my eyes an extraordinary prestige, it seemed almost a sort of priesthood.

For years, without realizing it, I tried to understand the drama of this man at grips with a destiny that was too great for him.

And I remembered my father's attitude towards him. I wondered whether my father had understood the same thing that I had, whether that was why, at whatever cost to himself, he had let the man try his luck.

From Gadelle I went on instinctively to consider the majority of the people I had known, almost all of them simple folk with apparently straightforward lives, who none the less had had at one time or another to measure themselves against destiny.

Don't forget that I am trying to set down here not the reflections of a mature man but the workings of a boy's mind, then of a youth's.

My mother's death seemed to me so stupid a drama, so unnecessary.

And all the other dramas that I knew, all these failures plunged me into a sort of furious despair.

Could nobody do anything about them? Might there not be, somewhere, some man wiser or more experienced than the rest—whom I pictured more or less in the shape of a family doctor, of a Gadelle who was not a failure—capable of telling them gently, firmly:

'You're taking a wrong turn. By acting thus you're heading for disaster. Your right place is here rather than there.'

I think that was it; I felt dimly that too many people were not in their right places, that they were striving to play parts that were beyond their capacities, so that the game was lost for them before they started.

Above all, please don't imagine that I ever dreamed of becoming that sort of God-the-Father-figure myself.

After trying to understand Gadelle, and then to understand my father's attitude towards him, I went on looking around me asking the same questions.

One example may raise a smile. There were fifty-eight of us in my class one year, fifty-eight pupils with different social backgrounds, different qualities, ambitious and failings. Now I had amused myself working out the ideal destiny of all my fellow-pupils and, in my mind, I called them: 'the lawyer . . . the tax-collector . . .'

For quite a while, too, I exercised my wits in guessing what the people I came across would eventually die of.

Is it clearer now why I wanted to become a doctor? The word police, for me, suggested at that time merely the constable at the street corner. And if I had heard speak of the secret police, I had not the least conception what it could be.

And then suddenly I had to earn my living. I arrived in Paris without even the vaguest notion of what career I was to choose. In view of my unfinished studies I could at best hope for some office job, and it was with this in mind that, without enthusiasm, I started reading the 'small ads' in the newspapers. My uncle had in vain offered to teach me his trade and keep me at the bakery.

In the little hotel where I was staying, on the Left Bank, there lived on the same landing as myself a man who aroused my curiosity, a man of about forty who, Heaven knows why, reminded me somewhat of my father.

Physically, indeed, he was as different as possible from the fair, lean, slope-shouldered man whom I had always seen wearing leather gaiters.

He was rather short and squat, dark-haired, with a prematurely bald patch which he concealed by carefully combing his hair forward, and black moustaches with curled tips.

He was always neatly dressed in black, wore an overcoat with a velvet collar, which accounts for a certain other overcoat and carried a stick with a solid silver knob.

I think the likeness to my father lay in his bearing, in a certain way of walking without ever hurrying, of listening, of watching, and then, somehow, of withdrawing within himself.

I met him by chance in a homely restaurant in the neighbourhood; I discovered that he took his evening meal there almost every day and I began, for no definite reason, to want to get to know him.

In vain did I try to guess what his occupation in life might be. He must be unmarried, since he lived alone at the hotel. I used to hear him get up in the morning and come back at night at irregular hours.

He never had any visitors and, the only time I met him with a companion, he was standing at the corner of the Boulevard Saint-Michel talking to an individual of such unprepossessing appearance that one might unhesitatingly have described him, at that period, as an *apache*.

I was on the point of taking a job in a firm that made *passementerie*, in the Rue des Victoires. I was to call there next day with references for which I had written to my former teachers.

That evening at the restaurant, moved by some instinct or other, I decided to rise from table just as my hotel neighbour was replacing his napkin in his pigeonhole, so that I happened to be there to hold the door open for him.

He must have noticed me. Perhaps he had guessed that I wanted to speak to him, for he gave me a long look.

'Thank you,' he said.

Then, as I was standing still on the pavement:

'Are you going back to the hotel?'

'I think so . . . I don't know . . .'

It was a fine late-autumn night. The river bank was not far off, and the moon was visible rising behind the trees.

'Alone in Paris?'

'I'm alone, yes.'

Without asking for my company, he accepted it, he took it for granted as a *fait accompli*.

'You're looking for work?'

'How do you know?'

He did not even trouble to answer and slipped a cachou between his lips. I was soon to understand why. He was afflicted with bad breath and knew it.

'You're from the provinces?'

'From Nantes, but I come from the country originally.'

I spoke freely to him. It was practically the first time since I had come to Paris that I had found a companion, and his silence did not embarrass me at all, no doubt because I was used to my father's friendly silences.

I had told him almost the whole of my story when we reached the Quai des Orfèvres, on the other side of the Pont Saint-Michel.

He stopped in front of a great door that was standing ajar, and said to me:

'Will you wait a moment for me? I shall only be a few minutes.'

A policeman in uniform was on duty at the door. After pacing up and down for a moment I asked him:

'Isn't this the Palais de Justice?'

'This is the entry to Police Headquarters.'

My hotel neighbour was called Jacquemain. He was, in fact, unmarried, as I learned that evening while we were walking up and down the Seine, crossing the same bridges over and over again, with the massive Palais de Justice almost continuously towering over us.

He was a Detective-Inspector and he told me about his profession, as briefly as my father would have done of his, with the same underlying pride.

He was killed three years later, before I had myself acquired access to those offices in the Quai des Orfèvres which had come to hold such glamour for me. It happened in the neighbourhood of the Porte d'Italie, during a street fight. A bullet which was not even intended for him hit him right in the chest.

His photograph still hangs among the rest in one of those black frames surmounted by the inscription: 'Died in the performance of his duty.'

He didn't talk to me much. He chiefly listened to me. This did not restrain me from asking him, towards eleven o'clock that night, in a voice quivering with impatience:

'Do you really think it's possible?'

'I'll give you an answer tomorrow evening.'

Of course there was no question of my going straight into the Sûreté. The age of diplomas had not yet arrived, and everyone had to start in the ranks. My only ambition was to be accepted, in any capacity, in one of the Paris police stations, and to be allowed to discover for myself an aspect of the world of which Inspector Jacquemain had merely given me a glimpse.

Just as we were parting on the landing of our hotel, which has since been pulled down, he asked:

'Would you very much dislike wearing uniform?'

I felt a slight shock, I must admit, a brief hesitation which did not escape his notice and which can scarcely have pleased him.

'No . . .' I replied in a low voice.

And I wore it, not for long, for seven or eight months. As I had long legs and was very lean, very swift, strange as that may seem today, they gave me a bicycle and, in order that I might get to know Paris, where I was always losing my way, I was given the job of delivering notes to the various police stations.

Has Simenon talked about all this? I don't remember. For months, perched on my bicycle, I threaded my way between cabs and double-decker buses, still horse-drawn, of which I was horribly frightened, particularly when they were tearing down from Montmartre.

Officials still wore frock-coats and top-hats and, above a certain rank, they sported morning-coats.

Policemen were mostly middle-aged men with reddish noses who were to be seen drinking at bar-counters with coachmen and of whom song-writers made relentless fun.

I was unmarried. I felt shy of going courting in uniform, and I decided that my real life would only begin on the day when I should enter the house in the Quai des Orfèvres as a detective, using the main staircase, and not merely as a messenger carrying official notes.

When I mentioned this ambition to my hotel neighbour, he did not smile, but looked at me reflectively and murmured:

'Why not?'

I did not know that I was so soon to attend his funeral. My forecasts about human destiny were still not entirely adequate.

How I ate petits fours *at Anselme and Geraldine's, thereby shocking the Highways and Bridges*

Did my father or my grandfather ever wonder whether they might have become something other than what they were? Had they ever had other ambitions? Did they envy a different lot from their own?

It's strange to have lived with people for so long and yet to know nothing of what nowadays would seem essential. I have often asked myself the question, with the feeling that I was straddling two worlds, totally foreign to one another.

We talked about it not long ago, Simenon and I, in my flat in the Boulevard Richard-Lenoir. I think it may have been on the eve of his departure for the United States. He had paused to stare at the enlarged photograph of my father, although he had seen it for years hanging on the dining-room wall.

While he studied it with particular attention, he kept casting searching glances at me, as if he were trying to make comparisons, and this set him pondering.

'The fact is,' he finally remarked, 'you were born in an ideal milieu, Maigret, at the ideal moment in a family's evolution, to become a top-rank official.'

I was struck by this comment because I had already thought about it, in a less precise and above all a less personal fashion; I had noticed how many of my colleagues came from peasant families having quite recently lost direct contact with the land.

Simenon went on, almost regretfully and as though he envied me:

'I'm a whole generation ahead of you. I have to go back to my grandfather to find the equivalent of your father. My own father had already reached the civil servant stage.'

My wife was gazing at him attentively, trying to understand, and he added in a lighter tone:

'In the normal course of events I'd have had to make my way up from the bottom in some profession, and work hard to become a G.P. or a lawyer or an engineer. Or else . . .'

'Or else what?'

'To become an embittered rebel. Of course that's what usually happens. Otherwise there'd be a plethora of doctors and lawyers. I think I come from the stock that has provided the greatest number of misfits.'

I don't know why this conversation has suddenly recurred to me.

Probably because I'm recollecting my early years and trying to analyse my frame of mind at that period.

I was all alone in the world. I had just landed in an unfamiliar city in which wealth was flaunted more blatantly than today.

Two things struck one: that wealth on the one hand, and that poverty on the other; and I belonged to the second group.

A whole social set, in full view of the masses, lived a life of sophisticated leisure, and the newspapers reported all the doings of these people who had no other preoccupation than their own pleasures and vanities.

Now not for one moment did I feel tempted to rebel. I did not envy them. I did not hope to be like them one day. I did not contrast my lot with theirs.

For me they belonged to a world as different from mine as if it had been another planet.

I remember that in those days I had an insatiable appetite, which had already been legendary when I was a child. At Nantes my aunt used often to tell how she had seen me eat a four-pound loaf when I got back from school, which did not prevent me from having dinner a couple of hours later.

I earned very little money, and my great concern was to satisfy that hunger of mine; I looked for luxury not on the terraces of the famous boulevard cafés, nor in the shop-windows of the Rue de la Paix, but more prosaically on pork-butchers' counters.

In the streets through which I usually passed I had discovered a number of pork-butchers' shops, which fascinated me, and in the days when I still travelled about Paris in uniform, perched on a bicycle, I used to calculate my time so as to save the few minutes necessary to buy a piece of sausage or a slice of pâté, and devour it, with a roll from the nearby bakery, while standing on the pavement outside.

When my stomach was appeased I felt happy and full of self-confidence. I did my job conscientiously. I attached importance to the slightest tasks entrusted to me. And there was no question of overtime. I considered that all of my time belonged to the police, and it seemed to be quite natural that I should be kept at work for fourteen or fifteen hours at a stretch.

If I mention this it is not that I want to take any credit for it, but rather, on the contrary, because as far as I can remember it was a common attitude at that time.

Very few police constables had more than a primary education. On account of Inspector Jacquemain, the authorities knew—although I myself didn't then know who knew, or even that anyone knew—that I had begun advanced studies. After a few months I was greatly surprised to find myself appointed to a post which I had never dared to hope for: that of secretary to the Station Officer of the Saint-Georges district.

And yet the job had an unglamorous name at the time. It was called 'being the Station Officer's dog'.

My bicycle, my cap and my uniform were taken away from me. So was my chance of stopping at pork butchers' on my way through the Paris streets.

I was particularly grateful for the fact of being in plain clothes when one day, walking along the pavement of the Boulevard Saint-Michel, I heard a voice hailing me.

A tall fellow in a white overall was running after me.

'Jubert!' I cried.

'Maigret!'

'What are you doing here?'

'And you?'

'Listen. I daren't stop out just now. Come and pick me up at seven o'clock at the door of the chemist's shop.'

Jubert, Felix Jubert, was one of my fellow students from the medical school at Nantes. I knew he had broken off his studies at the same time as myself, but, I believe, for different reasons. Without actually being a dunce, he was slow-witted, and I remember they used to say about him:

'He works so hard he comes out in spots, but he's no wiser next day.'

He was very tall and bony, with a big nose, coarse features, red hair, and as long as I'd known him his face had always been covered, not with those small acne pimples that are the bane of young men's lives, but with big red or purple spots which he spent hours smothering in medicated ointments and powders.

I went along to wait for him that same evening at the chemist's shop where he had been working for some weeks. He had no relatives in Paris. He was living in the Cherche-Midi district with people who took in two or three lodgers.

'And what are you doing yourself?'

'I'm in the Police Force.'

I can still picture his violet eyes, clear as a girl's, trying to conceal their incredulity. His voice sounded quite odd as he repeated:

'The Police Force?'

He was staring at my suit, instinctively looking for the constable on duty at the corner of the boulevard as though to make a comparison.

'I'm secretary to the Station Officer.'

'Oh, good, I understand.'

Whether from conventional pride, or, more likely, because of my own inability to explain myself and his inability to understand, I did not confess that three weeks earlier I had still been wearing uniform, and that my ambition was to join the detective force.

In his opinion and in that of a great many people, a secretary's was a good, respectable job; I sat at a desk, nice and clean, with books in front of me and a pen in my hand.

'Have you many friends in Paris?'

Apart from Inspector Jacquemain I really knew nobody, for at the police station I was still a novice and people had to watch me before they would make friends with me.

'No girl friend either? What do you do with all your spare time?'

In the first place I hadn't much of that. And in the second, I spent it studying, for in order to reach my aim faster I had resolved to pass the examinations which had just been instituted.

We dined together that evening. Towards the end of the meal he told me, as if promising me a treat:

'I shall have to introduce you.'

'To whom?'

'To some very nice people. Friends of mine. You'll see.'

He gave no further explanation that first day. And I don't know why, it was several weeks before we saw each other again. I might quite well never have seen him again. I had not given him my address. I had not got his. It never occurred to me to go and wait for him outside the chemist's shop.

Chance, once again, brought us face to face at the door of the Théâtre Français, where we were both queuing.

'Isn't it silly,' he said. 'I thought I'd lost you. I don't even know at which police station you're working. I mentioned you to my friends.'

He had a way of talking about these friends which suggested that they were a very special set of people, almost a mysterious sect.

'You've got a dress suit, I hope?'

'I've got one.'

It was pointless to add that it had been my father's dress suit, which was somewhat old-fashioned, since he had worn it at his wedding, and which I'd had cut to fit me.

'I'll take you there on Friday. You must manage to be free without fail on Friday evening at eight o'clock. Can you dance?'

'No.'

'It doesn't matter. But it would be better if you took a few lessons. I know a good school that's not expensive. I've been to it myself.'

This time he had made a note of my address and even of the little restaurant where I used to have dinner when I was not on duty, and on Friday evening he was in my room sitting on my bed, while I dressed.

'I must explain to you, so that you don't drop any bricks. We shall be the only people there, you and I, who aren't connected with the Highways and Bridges Department. A distant cousin of mine, whom I happened to run into, introduced me. Monsieur and Madame Léonard are charming people. Their niece is the loveliest girl in the world.'

I gathered at once that he was in love with her and that it was in order to show me the object of his passion that he was dragging me off with him.

'There'll be others, you needn't worry,' he promised me. 'Very nice girls.'

As it was raining and we didn't want to arrive covered with mud, we took a cab, the first cab I had ever taken in Paris except on duty. I can still picture our white shirt-fronts as we passed under the gas lamps. And I can picture Felix Jubert stopping the cab in front of a florist's shop so that we might decorate our buttonholes.

'Old Monsieur Léonard,' he explained. 'Anselme they call him, retired about ten years ago. Before that he was one of the top officials in the Highways and Bridges Department, and even now his successors still come to consult him sometimes. His niece's father is in Highways and Bridges too, on the administrative side. And so is all their family, so to speak.'

To hear him talk of this Government service you realized that for Jubert it was Paradise Lost, that he would have given anything not to have wasted those precious years studying medicine, so that he too could have made a start on such a career.

'You'll see!'

And I saw. It was in the Boulevard Beaumarchais, not far from the Place de la Bastille, in an oldish but comfortable and fairly well-to-do block. All the windows were lit up on the third floor, and Jubert's upward glance as we got out of the cab showed me clearly that the party in question was being held there.

I felt rather ill at ease. I began to wish I hadn't come. My stiff collar hurt me; I was convinced that my tie was getting twisted and that one of the tails of my coat tended to curl up like a cock's crest.

The stair was dimly lit, the steps covered with a crimson carpet that seemed to me sumptuous. And the landing windows were filled with stained glass which for a long time I considered the last word in refinement.

Jubert had smeared his spotty face with a thicker coat of ointment, which for some reason gave it a purplish sheen. He reverently pulled a big tassel which hung in front of a door. Within, we could hear the buzz of conversation, with that touch of shrillness in voices and laughter which suggests the excitement of a social gathering.

A maid in a white apron opened the door to us, and Felix, as he held out his overcoat, was delighted to show himself a regular frequenter of the house by remarking:

'Good evening, Clémence.'

'Good evening, Monsieur Felix.'

The drawing-room was fairly big, rather dimly lighted, with a great deal of dark upholstery, and in the next room, visible through a wide glass partition, the furniture had been pushed against the wall so as to leave the floor free for dancing.

With a protective air Jubert led me up to an old white-haired lady sitting by the fireside.

'May I introduce my friend Maigret, about whom I had the honour of telling you, and who was most anxious to pay you his respects in person.'

No doubt he had been rehearsing his sentence all the way there, and was watching to see if I was making a proper bow, did not seem too ill at ease, and in short was doing him credit.

The old lady was charming, tiny, with delicate features and a lively expression, but I was disconcerted when she said to me with a smile:

'Why don't you belong to the Highways and Bridges? I'm sure Anselme will be sorry.'

Her name was Géraldine. Anselme, her husband, was sitting in another armchair, so still that you'd have thought he had been carried in bodily and set down there to be displayed like a waxwork figure. He was very old. I learned later that he was well over eighty and Géraldine just that age.

Somebody was playing the piano softly, a podgy youth in a tight coat, while a girl in a pale blue dress turned the pages for him. I could only see her from the back. When I was introduced to her I dared not look her in the face, so embarrassed did I feel at being there, not knowing what to say or where to stand.

Dancing had not yet begun. On a small table there stood a tray of *petits fours*, and a little later, as Jubert had left me to my fate, I went up to it, I still don't know why, certainly not out of greed, for I wasn't hungry and I have never liked *petits fours*, probably to keep myself in countenance.

I took one mechanically. Then a second. Somebody said:

'Hush!'

And a second girl, this time one in a pink dress, with a slight squint, began to sing, standing beside the piano, on which she leaned with one hand, while waving a fan with the other.

I kept on eating. I was not conscious of it. I was still less conscious that the old lady was watching me with stupefaction, than that others, noticing my performance, couldn't take their eyes off me.

One of the young men made some remark to his neighbour and once again somebody said: 'Hush!'

You could count the girls by the light-coloured patches they made against the men's black coats. There were four of them. Jubert apparently was trying to attract my attention without success, in great distress at seeing me pick up *petits fours* one by one and eat them conscientiously. He later admitted that he had felt sorry for me, being convinced I had had no dinner.

Others must have thought the same thing. The song ended. The girl in pink bowed, and everybody clapped; and then I noticed that I was the centre of all attention as I stood there beside the little table, my mouth full and a biscuit in my hand.

I was about to disappear without apologies, to beat a retreat, to run away, literally, from the room and the lively crowd that was so utterly foreign to me.

Just then, in a shadowy corner, I caught sight of a face, the face of the girl in blue, and on that face a gentle, reassuring, almost friendly expression. It looked as if she had understood me and was encouraging me.

The maid came in with refreshments, and after having eaten so much at the wrong time I dared not take a glass when it was offered me.

'Louise, won't you pass round the *petits fours?*'

That was how I learned that the girl in blue was called Louise and that she was the niece of M. and Mme Léonard.

She waited on everybody before coming up to me, and then, pointing to some cake or other on which there was a small preserved fruit, she said to me with an air of complicity:

'They've left the nicest. Just taste those.'

The only answer I could find was:

'Really?'

Those were the first words that passed between Madame Maigret and myself.

*

Presently, when she reads what I've been writing, I know she'll shrug her shoulders, murmuring:

'What's the good of telling all that?'

Actually, she's delighted with Simenon's picture of her, the picture of a good housewife, always busy cooking and polishing, always fussing over her great baby of a husband. It was even on account of that picture, I suspect, that she was the first to become his staunch friend, to the extent of considering him as one of the family and of defending him when I haven't dreamed of attacking him.

Now this portrait, like all portraits, is far from being strictly accurate. When I met her on that memorable evening she was a rather plump young girl with a very fresh face and a sparkle in her eyes that was lacking in her friends'.

What would have happened if I hadn't eaten those cakes? It's quite possible that she would never have noticed me among the dozen or so young men there who all, except my friend Jubert, belonged to Highways and Bridges.

Those three words, Highways and Bridges, have retained an almost comic significance for us, and if either of us utters them it sets us both smiling; if we hear the words spoken somewhere we cannot, even now, help casting a knowing glance at one another.

To do things properly I ought here to insert the whole genealogy of the Schöllers, Kurts and Léonards, which I found most confusing for a long time, and which represents my wife's side of the family.

If you go anywhere in Alsace between Strasburg and Mulhouse you'll probably hear speak of them. I think it was a Kurt from Scharrachbergheim who first, under Napoleon, founded the almost dynastic tradition of Highways and Bridges. Apparently he was quite famous in his day, and he married into the Schöller family, who were in the same Government service.

The Léonards in their turn entered the family, and since then, from father to son, from brother to brother-in-law or cousin, practically everybody has belonged to the same organization, to such an extent that it was considered a comedown for a Kurt to become one of the biggest brewers in Colmar.

I only guessed at all this that first evening, thanks to the few hints that Jubert had given me.

And when we went out into the driving rain, not bothering this time to take a cab, which, in any case, we'd have had difficulty in finding in that district, I had almost begun to feel regretfully that I'd chosen the wrong career myself.

'What d'you think of that?'

'Of what?'

'Of what Louise did! I'm not going to scold you. But it was a very awkward situation. Did you see how tactfully she put you at your ease, without showing it? She's an amazing girl. Alice Perret may be more brilliant, but . . .'

I didn't know who Alice Perret was. The only person who had made any impression on me that whole evening was the girl in pale blue, who, between dances, had come to chat with me.

'Alice is the one who sang. I think she's going to get engaged to the boy who came with her, Louis, whose parents are very rich.'

We parted very late that night. At every fresh downpour we went into some bistro that was still open, to take shelter and drink a cup of coffee. Felix would not let me go, talking unceasingly about Louise, trying to make me admit that she was the ideal girl.

'I know I don't stand much chance. It's because her parents want to find her a husband in Highways and Bridges that they've sent her to stay with her uncle Léonard. You see, there are no more available at Colmar or at Mulhouse, or else they're in the family already. She's been here two months now. She's to spend the whole winter in Paris.'

'Does she know?'

'What?'

'That she's supposed to marry into Highways and Bridges.'

'Of course. But she doesn't care. She's a most independent girl, far more so than you might think. You didn't have time to appreciate her. Next Friday you must try and talk to her more. If you could dance, it would make things easier. Why don't you take two or three lessons in the meantime?'

I took no dancing lessons. Which was just as well. For Louise, contrary to the worthy Jubert's belief, disliked nothing so much as gliding round in the arms of a dancing partner.

A fortnight later there occurred a trivial incident which, at the time, seemed of great moment to me—and which perhaps was so, but in a different way.

The young engineers who used to visit the Léonards were an exclusive clique and affected the use of words which had no meaning for anyone outside their own set.

Did I detest them? Most likely. And I objected to their insistent habit of calling me 'the Police Inspector'. It had become a wearisome game.

'Hi, Inspector . . .' they would call to me from one end of the drawing-room to the other.

Now, that particular evening, while Jubert and Louise were chatting in one corner, close to a green plant which I can still picture, a young fellow in glasses went up and whispered something to them, with a laughing glance in my direction.

A few minutes later I asked my friend:

'What was he saying?'

Visibly embarrassed, he said evasively:

'Nothing.'

'Something spiteful?'

'I'll tell you when we're outside.'

The spectacled boy repeated his performance with other groups, and everybody seemed to be having a good laugh at my expense.

Everybody except Louise, who refused a good many dances that evening and spent the time talking to me.

Once outside, I questioned Felix.

'What did he say?'

'Tell me frankly first. What did you do before you became the Station Officer's secretary?'

'Well . . . I was in the police . . .'

'In uniform?'

So that was the great sensation. The spectacled fellow must have recognized me from having seen me in my policeman's outfit.

Just imagine a policeman among the gentlemen from Highways and Bridges!

'What did she say?' I asked, with a lump in my throat.

'She was wonderful. She's always wonderful. You won't believe me, but you'll see . . .'

Poor old Jubert!

'She told him that you must certainly have looked better in uniform than he would.'

Nevertheless, I kept away from the Boulevard Beaumarchais the following Friday. I avoided meeting Jubert. A fortnight later, he came himself to hunt me out.

'Well, they were asking after you on Friday.'

'Who was?'

'Madame Léonard. She asked me if you were unwell.'

'I've been very busy.'

I felt sure that if Madame Léonard had spoken of me it was because of her niece . . .

Now then! I don't think there's any point in going into all these details. It's going to be hard enough to make sure that what I've written already doesn't get thrown into the wastepaper basket.

For nearly three months Jubert played his part without suspecting anything, and indeed without our making any effort to deceive him. It was he who used to come and fetch me at my hotel and tie my bow-tie for me on the pretext that I didn't know how to dress. It was he, again, who used to tell me when he saw me sitting by myself:

'You ought to pay some attention to Louise. You're not being polite.'

And when we left, it was always he who insisted:

'You're quite wrong to suppose that she's not interested in you. On the contrary, she's very fond of you. She's always asking me about you.'

Towards Christmas, the girl friend with the squint got engaged to the pianist, and they stopped coming to the Boulevard Beaumarchais.

I don't know if Louise's attitude was beginning to discourage the rest, if we were perhaps less discreet than we imagined. The fact remains that there were gradually fewer guests every Friday at Anselme and Géraldine's.

Jubert finally had it out with me in February, in my room. That Friday, he was not wearing evening dress, as I noticed immediately. He had that look of resigned bitterness that the Comédie Française actors wear in certain famous roles.

'I've come to tie your bow-tie, in spite of everything!' he said with a forced smile.

'You're not free tonight?'

'I'm utterly free, on the contrary, free as the air, freer than I've ever been.'

And standing before me with my white tie in his hand, and his eyes boring into mine:

'Louise has told me all.'

I was dumbfounded. For so far she'd told *me* nothing. And I had told her nothing either.

'What are you talking about?'

'About you and her.'

'But . . .'

'I put the question to her. I went to see her on purpose yesterday.'

'But what question?'

'I asked her if she would marry me.'

'And she said no?'

'She said no, that she was very fond of me, that I should always be her best friend, but that . . .'

'Did she mention me?'

'Not exactly.'

'Well then?'

'I've understood! I ought to have understood that first evening, when you ate those *petits fours* and she looked at you indulgently. When a woman looks so indulgently at a man who's behaving as you were ...'

Poor Jubert! We lost sight of him almost immediately, just as we lost sight of all the Highways and Bridges gentlemen, apart from Uncle Léonard.

For years we never knew what had become of him. And I was getting on for fifty when one day, on the Canebière at Marseilles, I went into a chemist's shop to buy some aspirin. I hadn't read the name on the shop front. I heard an exclamation:

'Maigret!'

'Jubert!'

'What's been happening to you? Silly of me to ask, since I've known all about you from the newspapers for a long time. How is Louise?'

Then he told me about his eldest son who, by a nice irony of fate, was preparing for the Highways and Bridges examination.

*

With Jubert missing from the Boulevard Beaumarchais, the Friday soirées became even more sparsely attended, and often, now, there was nobody to play the piano. On such occasions Louise would play and I would turn over for her, while one or two couples danced in the dining-room, which had now grown too big.

I don't think I asked Louise if she was willing to marry me. Most of the time we talked about my career, about the police, about a detective's job.

I told her how much I should earn when I was at last appointed to Headquarters, adding that this would take at least three years and that until then my salary would scarcely be adequate to set up house with properly.

I told her, too, about the two or three interviews I had had with Xavier Guichard, who was already our Big Chief, who had not forgotten my father and had more or less taken me under his wing.

'I don't know if you like Paris. For, you see, I shall have to spend all my life in Paris.'

'You can live there as quietly as in the provinces, can't you?'

Finally, one Friday, I found no guests there, only Géraldine who came to open the door to me herself, in her black silk dress, and who said to me in a rather solemn voice:

'Come in!'

Louise was not in the drawing-room. There were no trays of cakes and no refreshments. Spring had come, and there was no fire burning in the hearth. I felt I had nothing to cling on to, and I kept my hat in my hand, ill at ease in my dress suit and patent leather pumps.

'Tell me, young man, what are your intentions?'

That was probably one of the most painful moments in my life. The voice sounded to me hard and accusing. I dared not raise my eyes, and I could see nothing but the edge of a black dress against the flower-patterned carpet, with the tip of a very pointed shoe showing. My ears turned scarlet.

'I swear . . .' I stammered.

'I'm not asking you to swear, I'm asking you if you intend to marry her.'

I looked at her at last and I don't think I have ever seen an old woman's face expressing so much affectionate mischief.

'But of course!'

Apparently— I've been told so often enough since—I jumped up like a jack-in-the-box and repeated, still louder:

'Of course!'

And I almost shouted a third time:

'Why, of course!'

She did not even raise her voice to call:

'Louise!'

And Louise, who was standing behind a half-open door, came in awkwardly, blushing as much as myself.

'What did I tell you?' said her aunt.

'Why?' I broke in. 'Didn't she believe it?'

'I wasn't sure. It was auntie . . .'

Let's skip the next scene, for I'm sure my wife would censor it.

Old Léonard, for his part showed much less enthusiasm, I must admit, and he never forgave me for not belonging to Highways and Bridges. He was very old, almost a centenarian, and riveted to his arm-chair by his infirmities; he would look at me and shake his head, as if something had gone badly wrong with the way of the world.

'You'll have to take leave to visit Colmar. What about the Easter holidays?'

Old Géraldine wrote herself to Louise's parents, a series of letters—to prepare them for the shock, as she said—breaking the news to them.

At Easter I was allowed barely forty-eight hours' leave. I spent most of it in trains, which were less rapid then than today.

I was given a perfectly proper reception, without rapture.

'The best way to find out if both of you are serious is to keep apart from one another for some time. Louise will spend the summer here. In the autumn you can come back to see us.'

'May I write to her?'

'Within reason. Once a week, for instance.'

It seems funny today. It was not at all funny at the time.

I had promised myself, without a trace of secret spite, to choose

Jubert as best man. When I went to try and find him at the chemist's in the Boulevard Saint-Michel he had left, and nobody knew what had become of him.

I spent part of the summer hunting for a flat and I found the one in the Boulevard Richard-Lenoir.

'Until we find something better, you understand? When I'm promoted Inspector . . .'

CHAPTER FIVE

Dealing somewhat haphazardly with hobnailed socks,
apaches, *prostitutes, radiators, pavements and*
railway stations

A few years ago some of us talked of founding a sort of club, more likely
a monthly dinner, which was to be called 'The Hobnailed Socks Club'.
We got together for a drink, in any case, at the Brasserie Dauphine. We
argued about who should and who shouldn't be admitted. And we wondered quite seriously whether the chaps from the other branch, I mean
from the Rue des Saussaies, should be considered eligible.

Then, as was only to be expected, things got no further. At that time
there were still at least four of us, among the Inspectors in the Detective Force, who were rather proud of the nickname 'hobnailed socks'
formerly given us by satirical song-writers, and which certain young
detectives fresh from college sometimes used amongst themselves when
referring to those of their seniors who had risen from the ranks.

In the old days, indeed, it took a good many years to win one's
stripes, and exams were not enough. A sergeant, before hoping for
promotion, had to have worn out his shoe-soles in practically every
branch of the Force.

It is not easy to convey the meaning of this with any sort of precision
to the younger generation.

'Hobnailed shoes' and 'big moustaches' were the terms that sprang
naturally to people's lips when they spoke of the police.

And in fact, for years, I wore hobnailed shoes myself. Not from
preference. Not, as caricaturists seemed to imply, because we thought
such footwear was the height of elegance and comfort, but for more
down-to-earth reasons.

Two reasons, to be exact. The first, that our salary barely enabled
us to make ends meet. I often hear people talk of the gay, carefree
life at the beginning of this century. Young people refer enviously to
the prices current at that time, cigars at two sous, dinner with wine and
coffee for twenty sous.

What people forget is that at the outset of his career a public servant
earned somewhat under a hundred francs a month.

When I was serving in the Public Highways Squad I would cover
during my day, which was often a thirteen or fourteen hour day, miles
and miles of pavement in all weathers.

So that one of the first problems of our married life was the problem
of getting my shoes soled. At the end of each month, when I brought

back my pay-packet to my wife, she would divide its contents into a number of small piles.

'For the butcher ... For rent ... For gas ...'

There was hardly anything left to put in the last pile of small silver.

'For your shoes.'

Our dream was always to buy new ones, but for a long time it was only a dream. Often I went for weeks without confessing to her that my soles, between the hobnails, absorbed the gutter water greedily.

If I mention this here it is not out of bitterness but, on the contrary, quite lightheartedly, and I think it is necessary to give an idea of a police officer's life.

There were no such things as taxis, and even if the streets had been crowded with them they'd have been beyond our reach, as were the cabs which we used only in very special circumstances.

In any case, in the Public Highways Squad, our duty was to keep walking along the pavements, mingling with the crowd from morning till night and from night until morning.

Why, when I think of those days, do I chiefly remember the rain? As if it had rained unceasingly for years, as if the seasons had been different then. Of course, it is because the rain added a number of additional ordeals to one's task. Not only did your socks become soaked. The shoulders of your coat gradually turned into cold compresses, your hat became a waterspout, and your hands, thrust into your coat pockets, grew blue with cold.

The roads were less well lighted than they are today. A certain number of them in the outskirts were unpaved. At night the windows showed as yellowish squares against the blackness, for most of the houses were still lighted with oil lamps or even, more wretchedly still, with candles.

And then there were the *apaches*.

All round the fortifications, in those days, their knives would come into play, and not always for gain, for the sake of the rich man's wallet or watch.

What they wanted chiefly was to prove to themselves that they were men, tough guys, and to win the admiration of the little tarts in black pleated skirts and huge chignons who paced the pavements under the gas jets.

We were unarmed. Contrary to the general belief, a policeman in plain clothes has not the right to carry a revolver in his pocket and if, in certain cases, a man takes one, it's against the regulations and entirely on his own responsibility.

Junior officers could not consider themselves entitled to do so. There were a certain number of streets, in the neighbourhood of La Villette, Ménilmontant and the Porte d'Italie, where one ventured reluctantly and sometimes trembled at the sound of one's own footsteps.

For a long time the telephone remained a legendary luxury beyond the scope of our budgets. When I was delayed several hours there was no question of ringing up my wife to warn her, so that she used to spend lonely evenings in our gas-lit dining-room, listening for noises on the stairway and warming up the same dish four or five times over.

As for the moustaches with which we were caricatured, we really wore them. A man without a moustache looked like a flunkey.

Mine was longish, reddish brown, somewhat darker than my father's, with pointed ends. Later it dwindled to a toothbrush and then disappeared completely.

It is a fact, moreover, that most police inspectors wore huge jet-black moustaches like those in their caricatures. This is because, for some mysterious reason, for quite a long time, the profession attracted chiefly natives of the Massif Central.

There are few streets in Paris along which I have not trudged, watchful-eyed, and I learned to know all the rank and file of the pavements, from beggars, barrel-organ players and flower-girls to cardsharpers and pickpockets, including prostitutes and the drunken old women who spend most of their nights at the police station.

I 'covered' the Halles at night, the Place Maubert, the quays and the reaches beneath the quays.

I covered crowded gatherings too, the biggest job of all, at the Foire du Trône and the Foire de Neuilly, at Longchamps races and patriotic demonstrations, at military parades, visits from foreign royalties, carriage processions, travelling circuses and second-hand markets.

After a few months, a few years at this job one's head is full of a varied array of figures and faces that remain indelibly engraved on one's memory.

I should like to try—and it's not easy—to give a more or less accurate idea of our relations with these people, including those whom we periodically had to take off to the lock-up.

Needless to say, the picturesque aspect soon ceases to exist for us. Inevitably, we come to scan the streets of Paris with a professional eye, which fastens on certain familiar details or notices some unusual circumstance and draws the necessary conclusion from it.

When I consider this subject, the thing that strikes me most is the bond that is formed between the policeman and the quarry he has to track down. Above all, except in a few exceptional cases, the policeman is entirely devoid of hatred or even ill-will.

Devoid of pity, too, in the usual sense of the word.

Our relations, so to speak, are strictly professional.

We have seen too much, as you can well imagine, to be shocked any longer by certain forms of wretchedness or depravity. So that the latter does not arouse our indignation, nor does the former cause us that distress felt by the inexperienced spectator.

There is something between us, which Simenon has tried to convey without success, and that is, paradoxical as it may seem, a kind of family feeling.

Don't misunderstand me. We are on different sides of the barricade, of course. But we also, to some extent, share the same hardships.

The prostitute on the Boulevard de Clichy and the policeman who is watching her both have bad shoes and both have aching feet from trudging along miles of asphalt. They have to endure the same rain, the same icy wind. Evening and night wear the same hue for both of them, and they see with almost identical eyes the seamy side of the crowd that streams past them.

The same is true of a fair where a pickpocket is threading his way through a similar crowd. For him a fair, or indeed any gathering of some few hundreds of people, means not fun, roundabouts, Big Tops or gingerbread, but merely a certain number of purses in unwary pockets.

For the policeman too. And each of them can recognize at a glance the self-satisfied country visitor who will be the ideal victim.

How many times have I spent hours following a certain pickpocket of my acquaintance, such as the one we called the Artful Dodger! He knew that I was on his heels, watching his slightest movements. He knew that I knew. While I knew that he knew that I was there.

His job was to get hold of a wallet or a watch in spite of it all, and my job was to stop him or catch him in the act.

Well, it sometimes happened that the Dodger would turn round and smile at me. I would smile back. He even spoke to me sometimes, with a sigh:

'It's going to be hard!'

I was well aware that he was on his beam-ends and that he wouldn't eat that night unless he was successful.

He was equally well aware that I earned a hundred francs a month, that I had holes in my shoes and that my wife was waiting impatiently for me at home.

Ten times at least I picked him up, quite kindly, telling him:

'You've had it!'

And he was almost as relieved as I was. It meant that he'd get something to eat at the Police Station and somewhere to sleep. Some of them know the lock-up so well that they ask:

'Who's on duty tonight?'

Because some of us let them smoke and others don't.

Then, for a year and a half, the pavements seemed to me an ideal beat, for my next job was in the big stores.

Instead of rain and cold, sunshine and dust, I spent my days in an overheated atmosphere reeking of tweed and unbleached calico, linoleum and mercerized cotton.

In those days there were radiators at intervals in the gangways between counters, which sent up puffs of dry, scorching air. This was fine when you arrived soaking wet. You took up your position above a radiator, and immediately you gave out a cloud of steam.

After a few hours, you chose rather to hang about near the doors which, each time they opened, let in a little oxygen.

The important thing was to look natural. To look like a customer! Which is so easy, isn't it, when the whole floor is full of nothing but corsets, lingerie or reels of silk?

'May I ask you to come along with me quietly?'

Some women used to understand immediately and followed us without a word to the manager's office. Others got on their high horse, protested shrilly or had hysterics.

And yet here, too, we had to deal with a regular clientèle. Whether at the Bon Marché, the Louvre or the Printemps, certain familiar figures were always to be found, usually middle-aged women, who stowed away incredible quantities of various goods in a pocket concealed between their dress and their petticoat.

A year and a half, in retrospect, seems very little, but at the time each hour was as long drawn out as an hour spent in the dentist's waiting-room.

'Shall you be at the Galeries this afternoon?' my wife would ask me sometimes. 'I've got a few little things to buy there.'

We never spoke to one another. We pretended not to recognize each other. It was delightful. I was happy to watch her moving proudly from one counter to the next, giving me a discreet wink from time to time.

I don't believe that she ever asked herself either whether she might have married anyone other than a police inspector. She knew the names of all my colleagues, spoke familiarly about those whom she had never seen, of their fads, of their successes or their failures.

It took me years to bring myself, one Sunday morning when I was on duty, to take her into the famous house in the Quai des Orfèvres, and she showed no sign of amazement. She walked about as if she were at home, looking for all the details which she knew so well from hearsay.

Her only reaction was:

'It's less dirty than I'd expected.'

'Why should it be dirty?'

'Places where men live by themselves are never quite so clean. And they have a certain smell.'

I did not ask her to the Police Station, where she'd have got her fill of smells.

'Who sits here on the left?'

'Torrence.'

'The big fat one? I might have guessed it. He's like a child. He still plays at carving his initials on his desk.

'And what about old Lagrume, the man who walks so much?'

Since I've talked about shoes I may as well tell the story that distressed my wife.

Lagrume, Old Lagrume as we called him, was senior to all of us, although he had never risen above the rank of sergeant. He was a tall, melancholy fellow. In summer he suffered from hay-fever and, as soon as the weather turned cold, his chronic bronchitis gave him a hollow cough that sounded from one end of Headquarters to the other.

Fortunately he was not often there. He had been rash enough to say one day, referring to his cough:

'The doctor recommends me to keep in the open-air.'

After that, he got his fill of open-air. He had long legs and huge feet, and he was put in charge of the most unlikely investigations through the length and breadth of Paris, the sort that force you to travel through the town in all directions day after day, without even the hope of getting any results.

'Just leave it to Lagrume!'

Everybody knew what was involved, except the old fellow himself, who gravely made a few notes on his pad, tucked his rolled umbrella under his arm and went off, with a brief nod to all present.

I wonder now whether he was not perfectly well aware of the part he was playing. He was one of the meek. For years and years he had had a sick wife waiting for him to do the housework in their suburban home. And when his daughter married, I believe it was he who got up at night to look after the baby:

'Lagrume, you still smell of dirty nappies!'

An old woman had been murdered in the Rue Caulaincourt. It was a commonplace crime that made no sensation in the Press, for the victim was an unimportant small *rentière* with no connections.

Such cases are always the most difficult. I myself, being confined to the big stores—and particularly busy as Christmas drew near—was not involved in it, but, like everybody else at our place, I knew the details of the investigation.

The crime had been committed with a kitchen knife, which had been left on the spot. This knife provided the only evidence. It was quite an ordinary knife, such as are sold in ironmongers' shops, chain stores or the smallest local shops, and the manufacturer, who had been contacted, claimed to have sold tens of thousands within the area of Paris.

The knife was a new one. It had obviously be bought on purpose. It still bore the price written on the handle in indelible pencil.

This was the detail which offered a vague hope of discovering the tradesman who had sold it.

'Lagrume! You deal with that knife.'

He wrapped it up in a bit of newspaper, put it in his pocket and set off.

He set off for a journey through Paris which was to last for nine weeks.

Every morning he appeared punctually at the office, to which he would return in the evening to shut away the knife in a drawer. Every morning he was to be seen putting the weapon in his pocket, seizing his umbrella and setting out with the same nod to all present.

I learned the number of shops—the story has become a legend—which might possibly have sold a knife of this sort. Without going beyond the fortifications, and confining oneself to the twenty arrondissements of Paris, the number makes your head reel.

There was no question of using any means of transport. It meant going from street to street, almost from door to door. Lagrume had in his pocket a map of Paris on which, hour after hour, he crossed out a certain number of streets.

I believe that in the end his chiefs had even forgotten what task he had been set.

'Is Lagrume available?'

Somebody would reply that he was out on a job, and then nobody bothered any more about him. It was shortly before Christmas, as I have said. It was a wet, cold winter, the pavements were slimy, and yet Lagrume went to and fro from morning till night, with his bronchitis and his hollow cough, unwearying, never asking what was the point of it all.

During the ninth week, well into the New Year, when it was freezing hard, he turned up at three o'clock in the afternoon, as calm and mournful as ever, without the slightest gleam of joy or relief in his eyes.

'Is the Chief there?'

'You've found it?'

'I've found it.'

Not in an ironmonger's, nor a cheap store, nor a household goods shop. He had gone through all those unavailingly.

The knife had been sold by a stationer in the Boulevard Rochechouart. The shopkeeper had recognized his handwriting, and remembered a young man in a green scarf buying the weapon from him more than two months previously.

He gave a fairly detailed description of him, and the young man was arrested and executed the following year.

As for Lagrume, he died in the street, not from his bronchitis but from a heart attack.

*

Before discussing stations, and in particular that Gare du Nord with which I always feel I have an old score to settle, I must deal briefly with a subject of which I am not very fond.

I have often been asked, with reference to my early days and my various jobs:

'Have you been in the Vice Squad too?'

It isn't known by that name today. It is modestly called the 'Social Squad'.

Well, I've belonged to that, like most of my colleagues. For a very short period. Barely a few months.

And if I realize now that it was necessary, my recollections of that period are nevertheless confused and somewhat uneasy.

I mentioned the familiarity that grows up naturally between policemen and those on whom it is their job to keep watch.

By force of circumstances, it exists in that branch as much as in the others. Even more so. Indeed, the clientèle of each detective, so to speak, consists of a relatively restricted number of women who are almost always found at the same spots, at the door of the same hotel or under the same street lamp, or, for the grade above, at the terrace of the same brasseries.

I was not then as stalwart as I have grown with the passing years, and apparently I looked younger than my age.

Remember the *petits fours* incident at the Boulevard Beaumarchais and you will understand that in certain respects I was somewhat timid.

Most of the officers in the Vice Squad were on familiar terms with the women, whose names or nicknames they knew, and it was a tradition when, during the course of a raid, they packed them into the Black Maria, to vie with one another in coarseness of speech, to fling the filthiest abuse at one another with a laugh.

Another habit these ladies had acquired was to pick up their skirts and show their behinds in a gesture which they considered, no doubt, the last word in insults, and which they accompanied with a torrent of defiance.

I must have blushed to begin with, for I still blushed easily. My embarrassment did not pass unnoticed, for the least one can say of these women is that they have a certain knowledge of men.

I promptly became, not exactly their *bête noire*, but their butt.

At the Quai des Orfèvres nobody ever called me by my first name, and I'm convinced that many of my colleagues did not know it ... I shouldn't have chosen it if I'd been asked my opinion. I'm not ashamed of it either.

Could it have been some sly revenge on the part of some detective who was in the know?

I was specially in charge of the Sébastopol district which, particularly in the Halles area, was frequented at that time by the lowest class of women, particularly by a number of very old prostitutes who had taken refuge there.

It was here, too, that young servant girls newly arrived from Brittany or elsewhere served their apprenticeship, so that one had the two extremes: kids of sixteen, over whom the pimps quarrelled, and ancient harpies who were very well able to defend themselves.

One day the catchphrase started—for it quickly became a catchphrase. I was walking past one of these old women, stationed at the door of a filthy hotel, when I heard her call out to me, showing all her rotten teeth in a smile:

'Good evening, Jules!'

I thought she'd used the name at random, but a little further on I was greeted by the same words.

'Hullo, Jules!'

After which, when there was a group of them together, they would burst out laughing, with a flood of unrepeatable comments.

I know what some officers would have done in my place. They'd have needed no further inducement to pick up a few of these women and lock them up at Saint-Lazare to think things over.

The example would have served its purpose, and I should probably have been treated with a certain respect.

I didn't do it. Not necessarily from any sense of justice. Nor out of pity.

Probably because this was a game I didn't want to play. I chose rather to pretend I hadn't heard. I hoped they would tire of it. But such women are like children who have never had enough of any joke.

They made up a song about Jules which they began to sing or yell as soon as I appeared. Others would say to me, as I checked their cards:

'Don't be mean, Jules! You're so sweet!'

Poor Louise! Her great dread, during this period, was not that I might yield to some temptation, but that I might bring home an unpleasant disease. Once I caught fleas. When I got home she would make me undress and take a bath, while she went to brush my clothes on the landing or at the open window.

'You must have touched plenty today! Brush your nails well!'

Wasn't there some story that you could catch syphilis merely by drinking out of a glass?

It was not a pleasant experience, but I learned what I had to learn. After all, I had chosen my own career.

For nothing on earth would I have asked to be transferred. My chiefs did what was necessary of their own accord, more for the sake of results, I imagine, than out of consideration for myself.

I was put on stations. More precisely, I was posted to that gloomy, sinister building known as the Gare du Nord.

*

It had the advantage, like the big stores, that one was sheltered from the rain. Not from the cold nor from the wind, for nowhere in the world, probably, are there so many draughts as in the hall of a station, the hall of the Gare du Nord, and for months I had as many colds as old Lagrume.

Please don't imagine that I'm grumbling, or deliberately dwelling on the seamy side so as to get my own back.

I was perfectly happy. I was happy trudging along the streets and I was equally happy keeping an eye on so-called kleptomaniacs in the big stores. I felt that I was getting on a little each time, learning a job whose complexity was more apparent to me every day.

When I see the Gare de l'Est, for instance, I can never help feeling depressed, because it reminds me of mobilization. The Gare de Lyon, on the other hand, like the Gare Montparnasse, suggests holidays.

But the Gare du Nord, the coldest, the busiest of them all, brings to my mind a harsh and bitter struggle for one's daily bread. Is it because it leads towards mining and industrial regions?

In the morning, the first night trains, coming from Belgium and Germany, generally contain a certain number of smugglers, of illicit traders with faces as hard as the daylight seen through the glazed windows of the station.

It's not always a matter of small-scale fraud. There are the professionals in various international rackets, with their agents, their decoys, their right-hand men, people who play for high stakes and are ready to defend themselves by any method.

No sooner has this crowd dispersed than it's the turn of the suburban trains which come not from pleasant villages like those in the West or South, but from black, unhealthy built-up areas.

In the opposite direction, it's towards Belgium, the nearest frontier, that fugitives for the most varied reasons try to escape.

Hundreds of people are waiting there in the grey atmosphere redolent of smoke and sweat, moving restlessly, hurrying from the booking office to the waiting-rooms, examining the boards that announce arrivals and departures, eating or drinking, surrounded by children, dogs and suitcases, and almost always they are people who have not slept enough, whose nerves are on edge from their dread of being late, sometimes merely from their dread of the morrow which they are going elsewhere to seek.

I have spent hours, every day, watching them, looking amongst all those faces for some more inscrutable face with a more fixed stare, the face of a man or woman staking their last chance.

The train is there, about to leave in a few minutes. He's only got to go another hundred yards and hold out the ticket he's clutching. The minute hand jerks forward on the enormous yellowish face of the clock.

Double or quits! It means freedom or jail. Or worse.

I am there, with a photograph or a description in my wallet, sometimes merely the technical description of an ear.

It may happen that we catch sight of one another simultaneously, that our eyes meet. Almost invariably the man understands at once.

What follows will depend on his character, on the risk he's running, on his nerves, even on some tiny material detail, a door that's open or shut, a trunk that may happen to be lying between us.

Sometimes they try to run away, and then there's a desperate race through groups of people who protest or try to get out of the way, a race among stationary coaches, over railway lines and points.

I have come across two men, one of them quite young, who, at three months' distance, behaved in exactly the same way.

Each of them thrust his hand into his pocket as if to take out a cigarette. And next minute, in the thick of the crowd, with his eyes fixed on me, each of them shot himself through the head.

These men bore me no ill-will, nor did I bear them any.

We were each of us doing his job.

They had lost the game, and there was an end to it, so they were quitting.

I had lost it too, for my duty was to bring them into the courts alive.

I have watched thousands of trains leaving. I have watched thousands arriving too, each time with the same dense crowd, the long string of people hurrying towards something or other.

It's become a habit with me, as with my colleagues. Even if I'm not on duty, if by some miracle I'm going on holiday with my wife, my glance slips from one face to the next, and seldom fails to fall on somebody who's afraid, however he may try to conceal it.

'Aren't you coming? What's the matter?'

Until we're settled in our carriage, or rather until the train has left, my wife is never sure that we're really going to get our holiday.

'What are you bothering about? You're not on duty!'

There have been times when I've followed her with a sigh, turning round for a last look at some mysterious face vanishing in the crowd. Always reluctantly.

And I don't think it's only from professional conscientiousness, nor from love of justice.

I repeat, it's a game that's being played, a game that has no end. Once you've begun it, it's difficult, if not impossible, to give it up.

The proof is that those of us who eventually retire, often against their will, almost always end by setting up a private detective agency.

Moreover that's only a last resort, and I don't know one detective who, after grumbling for thirty years about the miseries of a policeman's life, isn't ready to take up work again, even unpaid.

I have sinister memories of the Gare du Nord. I don't know why, I always picture it full of thick, damp early-morning fog, with its drowsy crowd flocking towards the lines or towards the Rue Maubeuge.

The specimens of humanity I have met there have been some of the most desperate, and certain arrests that I have made there left me with a feeling of remorse rather than of any professional satisfaction.

If I had the choice, none the less, I would rather go on duty again tomorrow at the platform barrier than set off from some more sumptuous station for a sunny corner of the Côte d'Azur.

CHAPTER SIX

One staircase after another!

From time to time, almost always on the occasion of some political upheaval, troubles break out in the streets which are no longer merely the manifestation of popular discontent. It would seem that at a certain moment a breach is formed, invisible sluices are opened, and there suddenly appear in the wealthier districts creatures whose very existence is generally unknown there, who seem to have emerged from some haunt of beggars and whom the inhabitants watch from their windows as they might watch ruffians and cutthroats suddenly appearing from the depths of the Middle Ages.

What surprised me most, when this phenomenon occurred with notable violence after the riots on February 6th, was the astonishment expressed next day by most of the newspapers.

This invasion of the heart of Paris, for a few hours, not by demonstrators but by haggard individuals who spread as much terror around them as a pack of wolves, suddenly alarmed people who, by their profession, are almost as closely acquainted as ourselves with the underworld of a metropolis.

Paris was really frightened that time. Then, the very next day, once order was restored, Paris forgot that this rabble had not been destroyed, that it had simply gone to earth.

Of course, it's up to the police to keep it there.

Is it generally known that there is one squad solely concerned with the two to three hundred thousand North Africans, Portuguese and Algerians who live in the outskirts of the 20th arrondissement, who camp out there, one might rather say, scarcely knowing our language or not knowing it at all, obeying other laws, other reflexes than our own?

We have, at Headquarters, maps on which are marked little islands, as it were, in coloured pencil, the Jews of the Rue des Rosiers, the Italians of the Hôtel de Ville district, the Russians of Les Ternes and Denfert-Rochereau . . .

Many of them ask nothing better than to be assimilated, and our difficulties don't come from them, but there are some who, whether as a group or as individuals, keep deliberately on the fringe and lead their mysterious lives, unnoticed by the crowd around them.

Highly respectable people, whose petty frauds and meannesses are carefully camouflaged, are almost always the ones who ask me, with that slight quiver of the lips that I know so well:

'Aren't you sometimes disgusted?'

They aren't referring to any particular thing, but to the whole set of people we have to deal with. What they would like is to have us disclose really nasty secrets to them, unheard-of vices, a lot of filth at which they could express their horror while secretly relishing it.

Such people often use the term 'the dregs of society'.

'What dreadful things you must see among the dregs of society!'

I prefer not to answer them. I look at them in a certain way, without any expression on my face, and they must understand my meaning, for they generally look uncomfortable and don't ask any more.

I learned a great deal on the public highway. I learned much, too, on fairgrounds and in big stores, wherever crowds were gathered.

I have spoken of my experiences at the Gare du Nord.

But it was while I was in the Hotels Squad that I learned most about men, particularly those men who frighten the inhabitants of wealthy districts when the sluices happen to open.

Hobnailed shoes were no longer needed here, for one's job was not to cover miles of pavement but to trudge in a vertical direction, so to speak.

Every day I collected the index cards of some tens of hundreds of hotels, usually furnished apartment houses, where there was seldom a lift and one had to climb six or seven floors up a stifling staircase, amid a sickeningly acrid smell of poverty-stricken humanity.

Big hotels with revolving doors flanked by liveried servants have their own dramas too, their secrets into which the police pry daily.

But it's chiefly in thousands of hotels with unfamiliar names, inconspicuous from outside, that a certain floating population goes to earth, a population which is difficult to get hold of elsewhere and seldom law-abiding. We went in couples. Sometimes, in dangerous districts, we went in larger groups. We would choose the time at which most people were in bed, shortly after midnight.

Then a sort of nightmare would begin, with certain details always recurring, the night watchman, the landlord or his wife lying in bed behind the wicket and waking up unwillingly to try and forestall any accusation.

'You know quite well we've never had any trouble here . . .'

In the old days the names used to be written in registers. Later, when identity cards became compulsory, there were forms to be filled in.

One of us would stay below. The other went upstairs. Sometimes we were spotted in spite of all our precautions, and from the ground floor we would hear the house beginning to stir like a beehive, busy comings and goings in the rooms, furtive footsteps on the stairs.

Occasionally we would find a room empty, the bed still warm, and at the top of the house the skylight that gave on to the roofs would be open.

Usually we managed to reach the first floor without rousing the lodgers, and we would knock at the first door and be answered by grunts, by questions almost invariably in a foreign language.

'Police!'

That's a word they all understand. And then, in their underclothes or stark naked, men, women and children scurry about in the dim light, in the stench, unfastening unbelievable cases to hunt for a passport hidden under their belongings.

There's no describing the anxious look in those eyes, those sleep-walker's movements, and that particular brand of humility which is found only in the uprooted. A proud humility, shall I call it?

They did not hate us. We were the masters. We had—or they believed we had—the most terrible of all powers: that of sending them back across the frontier.

For some of them the fact of being here represented years of scheming or waiting. They had reached the promised land. They owned papers, real or forged.

And while they held them out to us, fearful lest we should thrust them in our pockets, they tried instinctively to win us with a smile, found a few words of French to stammer:

'Please, Mister Officer . . .'

The women rarely bothered about decency, and sometimes you would see a hesitant look in their eyes, and they would make a vague gesture towards the tumbled bed. Weren't we tempted? wouldn't we like to?

And yet all these people had their pride, a special pride that I cannot describe. The pride of wild animals?

Indeed, it was rather like caged beasts that they watched us pass, without knowing whether we were going to strike them or stroke them.

Sometimes you'd see one of them brandishing his papers, panic-stricken, and he'd start talking volubly in his own language, gesticulating, calling the rest to his aid, striving to make us believe that he was an honest man, that appearances were misleading, that . . .

Some would start weeping and others crouched sullenly in their corner as if they were about to spring, though actually resigned.

Identity check-up. That's what the operation is called in administrative language. Those whose papers are indisputably in order are allowed to stay in their rooms, where you hear them lock the door with a sigh of relief.

The others . . .

'Come downstairs!'

When they don't understand, you have to add a gesture. And they get dressed, talking to themselves. They don't know what they ought to take, or are allowed to take with them. Occasionally, as soon as our backs are turned, they slip back to get some hidden treasure and thrust it into their pockets or under their shirts.

They all stand about on the ground floor in a small silent group, each thinking only of his own case and how he's going to defend himself.

In the Saint-Antoine district there are certain hotels where I have found up to seven or eight Poles in a single room, most of them sleeping on the floor.

Only one was inscribed on the register. Did the landlord know? Did he exact payment for the additional sleepers? It's more than likely, but it's useless to try and prove such things.

The others' papers, needless to say, were not in order. What did they do when they had to leave the shelter of the room at daybreak?

For lack of work-cards, they could not earn a regular living. But they had not died of starvation. So they must have been eating somehow.

And there were, and still are, thousands, tens of thousands in the same case.

You may find money in their pockets, or hidden on top of some cupboard, or more frequently in their shoes. Then you have to discover how they procured it, and that's the most exhausting kind of cross-examination.

Even if they understand French they pretend not to understand it. Looking you in the eyes with an expression of good will, indefatigably reasserting their innocence.

It's useless to ask the others about them. They never betray one another. They will all tell the same story.

Now, on an average, sixty-five per cent of the crimes committed in the Paris area are due to foreigners.

Stairs, stairs and yet more stairs. Not only by night but by day, and tarts everywhere, professionals and others, some of them young and fine-looking, come, God knows why, from the depths of their own country.

I knew one of these, a Polish woman, who shared a hotel room in the Rue Saint-Antoine with five men, whom she used to send out on robberies, rewarding those who were successful in her own fashion, while the others fretted impatiently in the same room and afterwards usually fell savagely upon the exhausted winner.

Two of them were enormous powerful brutes, and she was not afraid of them, she could hold them in awe with a smile or a frown; while I was questioning them, in my own office, after some remark or other made in their own language I saw her calmly slap one of these giants in the face.

'You must see a queer lot of things!'

Well, we see men and women, all sorts of men and women in the most unbelievable situations, at every social level. We see them, we take note and we try to understand.

I don't mean understand some deep human mystery or other. That romantic idea is possibly the thing against which I protest the most earnestly, almost angrily. This is one of the reasons for this book, for these attempted corrections. Simenon has endeavoured to explain this, I admit. Nevertheless I have felt a certain embarrassment on seeing attributed to myself in his books certain smiles, certain attitudes which I have never assumed and which would have made my colleagues shrug their shoulders.

The person who has understood things best is my wife. And yet when I get back from work she never questions me with any curiosity, whatever the case with which I am concerned.

For my part, I don't deliberately take her into my confidence.

I sit down at table like any other official coming home from work. In a few words, as though for my own benefit, I may describe an encounter, an interview, or talk of the man or woman about whom I am making investigations.

If she puts a question, it's almost always a technical one.

'In which district?'

Or else:

'How old?'

Or again:

'How long has she been in France?'

For she has come to consider such details as revealing as we have ourselves.

She does not question me about sordid or pathetic side-issues.

And Heaven knows it's not for lack of feeling!

'Has his wife been to see him at the Police Station?'

'This morning.'

'Did she take the child with her?'

She takes a particular interest, for reasons on which I need not enlarge, in those who had children, and it would be a mistake to fancy that law-breakers, malefactors and criminals have none.

We had one of these in our own home, a little girl whose mother I had sent to prison for life, but we knew that the father would take her back as soon as he was restored to normal life.

She still comes to see us. She is a grown girl now, and my wife takes pride in going round the shops with her in the afternoon.

What I want to stress is that our behaviour towards those with whom we have to deal involved neither sentimentality nor hardness, neither hatred nor pity in the usual sense of the word.

Our job is to study men. We watch their behaviour. We take note of some of the facts. We try to establish others.

When, as a young man, I had to visit a disreputable lodging house from cellar to attic, exploring rooms like cells in a honeycomb, surprising people in their sleep, in their most elementary privacy, examining their papers through a magnifying glass, I could almost have foretold what would become of each of them.

For one thing, certain faces were already familiar to me, for Paris is not so big that one doesn't constantly come across the same individuals, in a given environment.

Certain cases, too recur almost identically, the same causes producing the same results.

The wretched Central European who had saved for months, if not years, to buy himself false passports from a clandestine agency in his own country, and who thought his troubles were over once he had safely crossed the frontier, will inevitably fall into our hands before six months, or twelve at most, are out.

Indeed, we could even follow him in our mind's eye from the frontier, and foretell in what district, in what restaurant, in what lodging house he will end up.

We know through whom he will try to procure the indispensable labour permit, genuine or forged; we shall merely have to go and pick him up in the queue that stretches out very morning in front of the big factories at Javel.

Why should we feel anger or resentment, when he lands up where he was bound to land up?

The same thing happens with the fresh-faced servant girl whom we see paying her first visit to a certain dance hall. Can we tell her to go back to her employers and keep away from that flashy companion of hers?

It would do no good. She'll come back. We shall meet her at other dance halls, then, one fine evening, outside the door of some hotel in the Halles or Bastille district.

Ten thousand go that way on an average, every year, ten thousand who leave their village and start off in domestic service in Paris, and who before a few months or a few weeks are out will have taken the plunge.

Is it so very different when a boy of eighteen or twenty, who has been working in a factory, begins to dress in a certain way, to adopt certain poses, to lean on the zinc counters of certain bars?

We shall see him presently in a new suit, wearing artificial silk socks and tie.

He'll end up in our hands too, looking shifty or crestfallen, after an attempted burglary or smash and grab raid, unless he has joined the car thieves' brigade.

There are certain signs you cannot mistake, and it was really these signs which were learning to recognize when we were sent to serve in every squad in turn, to cover miles of pavement on foot, climb up stair after stair and make our way into every sort of hovel and amidst every type of crowd.

That was why the nickname 'hobnailed socks' never annoyed us, quite the reverse.

There are few of us at Headquarters who, by the time they are forty, aren't well acquainted, for instance, with all the pickpockets. We even know where to find them on such and such a day, on the occasion of such and such a ceremony or festivity.

In the same way we know, for instance, that there will shortly be a jewel robbery, because a certain specialist who has seldom been caught redhanded has begun to run short of cash. He has left his hotel in the Boulevard Haussmann for a humbler one in the République district. He hasn't paid his bill for a fortnight. The woman with whom he's living has begun to have rows with him, and has bought no new hats for a long time.

We cannot follow him step by step; there would never be enough detectives to shadow every suspect. But we have him on the end of a string. The Public Highways Squad have been warned to keep a special eye on jewellers' shops. We know his way of working. We know he'll never work any other way.

It doesn't always come off. That would be too much to hope for. But it sometimes happens that he's caught in the act. It sometimes happens after a discreet interview with his girl friend, who's been given the hint that her future would be less problematic if she provided us with information.

The papers talk a great deal about gangs settling accounts with one another in Montmartre or the area round the Rue Fontaine, because there's always something exciting for the public about revolver shots by night.

But those are just the cases that worry us least at Headquarters.

We know the rival gangs, their interests and the points at issue between them. We also know their personal hatreds and resentments.

One crime calls forth another, by repercussion. If someone shoots down Luciano in a bar in the Rue de Douai, the Corsicans will inevitably take their revenge before very long. And almost always there's one amongst them who will give us the hint.

'Something's being plotted against Flatfooted Dédé. He knows it and he won't go out without a couple of killers as bodyguard.'

The day when Dédé gets his, it's ninety per cent certain that a more or less mysterious telephone call will put us in the picture about every detail of the story.

'There's one the less!'

We do arrest the guilty men, but it really makes little difference, for those people only exterminate one another, for reasons of their own, according to a certain code which they apply strictly.

It was to this that Simenon was alluding when, during our first interview, he declared so categorically:

'Professional crimes don't interest me.'

What he did not know then, but has learnt since, is that there are very few other sorts of crime.

I'm not including crimes of passion, which are straightforward for the most part, being merely the logical issue of an acute crisis between two or more individuals.

I'm not including those brawls where a couple of drunks knife one another one Saturday or Sunday night in the slums.

Apart from such accidents, the most frequent crimes are of two sorts:

The murder of some lonely old woman by one or more hooligans, and the murder of a prostitute in some piece of waste ground.

In the first case the culprit rarely escapes. Almost always he is one of those youngsters I mentioned before, who quit factory work a few months back, and is dying to show off his toughness.

He's had his eye on some tobacconist's or haberdasher's, some small shop in a quiet back-street.

Sometimes he's bought a revolver. At other times he makes do with a hammer or spanner.

Almost invariably he knows his victim and, in at least one case out of ten, she has done him a kindness at some time or another.

He has not planned to kill. He's put a scarf over his face so as not to be recognized.

The scarf slips, or else the old woman begins to scream.

He fires. He strikes. If he fires he empties the whole barrel, which is a sign of panic. If he strikes he strikes ten or twenty blows, savagely so it seems, but really because he's crazy with terror.

Does it surprise you that when we've got him in front of us, in a state of collapse and yet still trying to swagger, we merely say to him:

'You fool!'

They almost always pay with their lives. The least they can get away with is twenty years, when they're lucky enough to interest some first-rate counsel.

As for the murderers of prostitutes, it's only by a miracle that we lay hands on them. These investigations are the longest, the most discouraging, the most sickening I know.

They usually begin with a sack being fished up by some waterman on the end of his boathook, somewhere along the Seine, and containing, almost always, a mutilated body. The head is missing, or an arm, or both legs.

Weeks go by before identification is possible. Generally the victim is one of these elderly whores who don't even take their customers to a hotel or to their room, but make do with some doorway or the shelter of a railing.

She hadn't been seen lately in her neighbourhood, one of those districts which, as soon as night falls, becomes full of mystery and silent shadows.

The women who knew her are not anxious to get into contact with us. When we question them they give only the vaguest answers.

Eventually, by dint of patience, we manage, after a fashion, to discover some of her usual clients, lonely individuals themselves, solitary men of indefinite age who are remembered merely as shadowy figures.

Was she killed for her money? It's hardly likely. She had so little! Had one of these old fellows suddenly gone crazy, or did someone come from elsewhere, from another district, one of those maniacs who at regular intervals feel a fit coming on, know exactly what they will do and with incredible lucidity take precautions of which other criminals are incapable?

No one knows how many there are of these. There are some in every capital city, and, once the deed is done, they disappear once more, for a greater or less length of time, into anonymity.

They may be respectable people, fathers of families, model employees.

Nobody knows exactly what they're like, and when by chance we catch one of them it has almost always been impossible to establish a satisfactory conviction.

We possess more or less exact statistics for crimes of every sort.

Except one.

Poisoning.

And any rough guess would inevitably err in one direction or the other.

Every three months, or six months, in Paris or in the provinces, particularly in the provinces, in some very small town or in the country, a doctor may happen by chance to examine a dead body more closely than usual and be puzzled by certain symptoms.

I say chance, for the dead man is usually one of his patients, somebody he has known to be ill for a long time. The man has died suddenly, in his bed, in the bosom of his family, who display all the traditional signs of grief.

The relations dislike the suggestion of an autopsy. The doctor only insists on one if his suspicions are strong enough.

Or else, weeks after the funeral, an anonymous letter reaches the police, providing details which at first sight seem incredible.

I stress this to show all the circumstances that must be combined before such an investigation can be held. The administrative formalities are complicated.

The commonest case is that of a farmer's wife who has been waiting for years for her husband to die in order to set up house with the farm hand, and who has lost patience.

She has come to the help of Nature, as some people crudely put it.

Sometimes, though more rarely, a man will use the same method to get rid of an ailing wife who has become a dead weight in his home.

They are found out by chance. But how many other cases are there where chance does not play its part? We don't know. We can only risk hypotheses. There are some of us at Headquarters, as there are in the

Rue des Saussaies, who believe that of all crimes, particularly of those that go unpunished, this particular sort is the most frequent.

The others, those that interest novelists and so-called psychologists, are so unusual that they absorb only an insignificant part of our activities.

But that is the part with which the public is most familiar. These are the cases about which Simenon has written most and will, I suppose, go on writing.

I refer to those crimes which are committed suddenly in the most unlikely settings, and which are, as it were, the final outcome of something that has been brewing for a long time in secret.

Some well-kept, prosperous street in Paris or elsewhere. People who have a comfortable house, a family life, an honourable profession.

We have never had occasion to cross their threshold. Often the *milieu* is one to which we should normally not have access, where our presence would jar, where we should feel awkward, to say the least.

Now somebody has died a violent death, and so we come and ring at the door, and find ourselves confronted by inscrutable faces, by a family of which each member seems to have his own secret.

Here the experience acquired through years in streets, in stations, in lodging houses is no longer involved. Nor is that sort of instinctive respect felt by small fry towards authority, towards the police.

Nobody here is afraid of being sent back over the frontier. Nobody is going to be taken off to an office at Headquarters to be subjected for hours to a painstaking examination, gone over again and again.

The people we have before us are those highly respectable folk who in other circumstances would have asked us:

'Don't you sometimes feel disgusted?'

We do, in these very homes. Not immediately. Not invariably. For the task is a long and chancy one.

Even when a telephone call from some minister, some deputy, some important public figure doesn't try to divert us from our path.

There is a whole varnish of respectability to be peeled off little by little; there are family secrets, more or less repulsive, which they all combine to conceal from us and which have to be brought to light, regardless of protests and threats.

Sometimes five or six of them, or more, may have conspired to lie on certain points, while surreptitiously endeavouring to get the rest into trouble.

Simenon is apt to describe me as awkward and gruff, feeling ill at ease, with a furtive glance and a cantankerous way of barking out my questions.

It's in such cases as these that he has seen me thus, faced with what one might call amateur crimes, which one *invariably* discovers, in the end, to have been committed for motives of self-interest.

Not for money. I mean not crimes committed from an urgent need for money, as in the case of those petty ruffians who murder old women.

The interests involved behind these façades are more complicated, they are long-term interests, coupled with a concern for respectability. Often the thing goes back many years, concealing a whole lifetime of intrigue and dishonesty.

When these people, brought to bay, finally confess, the whole revolting story comes out, almost always with a panic fear of conseqences.

'Surely it's impossible for our family to be dragged in the mud? There must be some way out.'

That does happen, I'm sorry to say. Some people who should only have left my office for a cell at the Santé prison have disappeared from circulation, because there are certain influences against which a detective, even a chief-inspector, is powerless.

'Don't you sometimes feel disgusted?'

I have never done so when, as detective in the Hotels Squad, I spent my days or my nights climbing the stairs of squalid, overcrowded apartment houses, where every door disclosed some distressing or dramatic scene.

Nor does the word disgust convey my reaction to the thousands of professionals of every sort who have passed through my hands.

They have played their game and lost it. Almost all of them prided themselves on being good losers and some of them, after they had been sentenced, asked me to go and see them in prison, where we chatted like old friends.

I could mention several who have begged me to be present at their execution and saved their last dying look for me.

'I shall do all right, you'll see!'

They did their best. They were not always successful. I used to take away their last letters in my pocket, promising to send them off with a covering note of my own.

When I got home, my wife had only to look at me without asking questions to know how things had gone off.

As for the other cases, on which I prefer not to dwell, she was well acquainted with the meaning of certain angry moods of mine, a certain way of sitting down when I got home at night, and of filling my plate, and she never pressed me.

Which is ample proof that she was not destined for the Highways and Bridges!

CHAPTER SEVEN

*Describes a morning as triumphant as a cavalry trumpet
and a young fellow who was no longer thin, but who
had not yet grown really stout*

I can still recall the taste and the colour of the sunlight that morning.
It was in March. Spring had come early. I had already formed the
habit of going on foot, whenever I could, from the Boulevard Richard-
Lenoir to the Quai des Orfèvres.

I had no outside work that day, only files to classify in the Hotels
section, in which were probably the gloomiest offices in the whole
Palais de Justice, on the ground floor, with a little door leading into
the courtyard, which I had left open.

I kept as near to it as my work allowed. I remember the sun cutting
the courtyard exactly in two, and also cutting across a waiting police
van. From time to time its two horses stamped on the paving-stones,
and behind them there was a fine heap of gleaming dung, smoking in
the keen morning air.

I don't know why the courtyard reminded me of certain break-times
at school, at the same season of the year, when the air suddenly begins
to have a special fragrance and, when you've been running, your skin
smells of spring.

I was alone in the office. The telephone bell rang.

'Will you tell Maigret the Chief wants him?'

The voice of the old office clerk up there, who had been nearly fifty
years in his job.

'Maigret speaking.'

'Come up then.'

Even the great staircase, which was always full of dust, seemed gay,
with rays of sunlight slanting down as in churches. The morning
conference had just ended. Two Inspectors still stood talking, with
their files under their arms, by the Chief's door, on which I went to
knock.

And inside the office I could still smell the pipes and cigarettes of
those who had just gone out. A window was open behind Xavier
Guichard, who had plumes of sunlight in his silky white hair.

He did not hold out his hand to me. He seldom did so in the office.
And yet we had become friends, or, more precisely, he had been good
enough to honour my wife and me with his friendship. On one occasion,
the first, he had invited me alone to his flat in the Boulevard Saint-

71

Germain. Not the wealthy, fashionable part of the Boulevard. He lived, on the contrary, right opposite the Place Maubert, in a big new block that rose amidst rickety houses and squalid hotels.

I had gone back there with my wife. They had immediately got on very well together.

He was undoubtedly fond of her and of myself, and yet he has often hurt us without meaning to.

In the beginning, as soon as he saw Louise, he would stare insistently at her figure and, if we seemed not to understand, he would say with a little cough:

'Don't forget that I want to be godfather.'

He was a confirmed bachelor. Apart from his brother, who was Chief of the Municipal Police, he had no relatives in Paris.

'Come now, don't keep me waiting too long . . .'

Years had gone by. He must have misunderstood. I remember that when he told me of my first rise he had added:

'Perhaps that'll enable you to give me a godson.'

He never understood why we blushed, why my wife lowered her eyes, while I tried to touch her hand to comfort her.

He was looking very serious that morning, seen against the light. He left me standing, and I felt embarrassed by the insistent way in which he examined me from head to foot, as a sergeant-major looks over a recruit.

'D'you know, Maigret, you're putting on weight?'

I was thirty. Little by little I had stopped being thin, my shoulders had broadened, my chest had expanded, but I had not yet become really stout.

It was obvious. I must have seemed flabby in those days, with a somewhat babyish look. It struck me myself when I passed in front of a shop window and cast an anxious glance at my own silhouette.

It was too much or too little, and no clothes fitted me.

'I think I'm getting fatter, yes.'

I almost wanted to apologize and I had not yet realized that he was joking as he loved to do:

'I think I'd better transfer you to another department.'

There were two squads in which I had not yet served, the Sports Squad and the Finance Squad, and the latter was my nightmare, just as the trigonometry exam had long been the terror of my summer terms at school.

'How old are you?'

'Thirty.'

'The right age! That's fine. Young Lesueur will take your place in the Hotels Squad, from now on, and you shall put yourself at Inspector Guillaume's disposal.'

He deliberately said this in an unemphatic tone, as if it were something quite trivial, knowing that my heart was going to leap in my breast and that, as I stood before him there, I could hear triumphant clarion calls ringing in my ears.

Suddenly, on a morning that seemed to have been chosen on purpose —and I'm not sure that Guichard hadn't done so—the dream of my life was being realized.

At last I was to enter the Special Squad.

A quarter of an hour later I moved upstairs with my old office jacket, my soap and towel, my pencils and a few papers.

There were five or six men in the big room reserved for Detectives in the Homicide Squad, and before calling me, Inspector Guillaume let me settle down, like a new pupil.

'Stand us a drink on it?'

I wasn't going to say no. At midday I proudly took my new colleagues to the Brasserie Dauphine.

I had often seen them there, at a different table from the one I shared with my former pals, and we used to watch them with the envious respect felt by schoolboys for sixth formers who are as tall as their masters and treated by these almost on an equal footing.

The comparison was an apt one, for Guillaume was with us, and the Superintendent from the General Information Department came to join us.

'What'll you have?' I asked.

In our old corner we used to drink half-pints of beer, seldom an apéritif. Obviously that wouldn't do for this table.

Somebody said:

'A mandarin-curaçao.'

'Mandarins all round?'

As nobody objected, I ordered I don't know how many mandarins. It was the first time I had tasted one. In the intoxication of my triumph, it seemed to me barely alcoholic.

'Let's have another round.'

Wasn't this the moment, if ever, to show myself generous? We had three each, we had four. My new Chief insisted on paying his round too.

The town was full of sunlight. The streets were streaming with it. The women in their bright dresses were a delight. I threaded my way between pedestrians. I looked at myself in shop windows and thought I wasn't so fat after all.

I ran. I flew. I was exultant. As soon as I reached the foot of the stairs I began the speech I had prepared for my wife.

Going up the last flight, I came a cropper. I hadn't had time to get up again when our door opened, for Louise must have been getting anxious at my delay.

'Have you hurt yourself?'

It was a funny thing. At the precise moment when I stood up again I felt completely drunk and was amazed at it. The staircase was whirling round me. My wife's silhouette was blurred. She seemed to have at least two mouths and three or four eyes.

Believe it or not, it was the first time in my life that this had happened to me, and I felt so humiliated that I dared not look at her; I slunk into the flat like a guilty thing without remembering the triumphant phrases I had so carefully prepared.

'I think . . . I think I'm a bit drunk.'

I was painfully sniffling. The table was laid, with our two places opposite one another in front of the open window. I had promised myself to take her out to lunch at a restaurant, but I dared not propose it now.

So that it was in an almost gloomy tone that I announced:

'It's happened!'

'What's happened?'

Perhaps she was expecting me to tell her that I'd been flung out of the Force!

'I've been appointed.'

'Appointed what?'

Apparently I had great tears in my eyes, tears of vexation but also, no doubt, of joy, as I let fall the words:

'To the Special Squad.'

'Sit down. I'm going to make you a cup of strong black coffee.'

She tried to get me to lie down, but I was not going to desert my new post on the first day. I drank I don't know how many cups of strong coffee. In spite of Louise's insistence I couldn't swallow any solid food. I took a shower.

At two o'clock, when I went along to the Quai des Orfèvres, my cheeks had a peculiar rosy glow, my eyes were glittering. I felt limp and light-headed.

I went to sit down in my corner and spoke as little as possible, for I knew that my voice was unsteady and that I might get my syllables confused.

Next day, as though to put me to the test, they entrusted me with my first arrest. It was in the Rue du Roi de Sicile, in an apartment house. The man had been shadowed for five days already. He was responsible for several murders. He was a foreigner, a Czech if I remember rightly, a strongly-built fellow, invariably armed, invariably on the alert.

The problem was to immobilize him before he had time to defend himself, for he was the sort of man who would fire into the crowd, kill as many people as possible before letting himself be brought down.

He knew that he was at the end of his tether, that the police were on his heels but were still hesitating.

Out of doors he always managed to stay in the middle of a crowd, well aware that we could take no risks.

I was sent as assistant to Inspector Dufour, who had been following the man for several days and knew all his movements.

This was the first time, too, that I disguised myself. To have appeared in that sordid hotel dressed as we usually were would have provoked a panic under cover of which our man might have escaped.

Dufour and I put on old clothes and, to make things more convincing, went forty-eight hours without shaving.

A young detective, a skilled locksmith, had got into the hotel and had made us an excellent key of the man's bedroom.

We took a room on the same landing ourselves, before the Czech came back to bed. It was just after eleven when a signal from outside warned us that he was coming up the stairs.

The tactics we followed were not suggested by myself but by Dufour, an old hand at the game.

The man, not far away from us, had shut his door and was lying fully clothed on his bed, and he probably had a loaded revolver at least within reach.

We did not sleep. We waited for dawn. If you ask me why, I shall give the answer that my colleague, to whom I put the same question, gave me.

The murderer's first reflex, on hearing us, would undoubtedly have been to smash the gas burner in his room. We should thus have been in darkness, and he would have had an advantage over us.

'A man's resistance is always lower in the early morning,' Dufour told me, and I've confirmed this subsequently.

We crept into the passage. Everybody was asleep around us. Taking infinite care, Dufour turned the key in the lock.

As I was the tallest and the heaviest, it was my job to rush forward first, and I did so at one bound, and found myself on top of the man as he lay stretched out in bed, grabbing him by whatever I could get hold of.

I don't know how long the struggle went on, but it seemed to me interminable. I felt myself rolling on the ground with him. I could see a fierce face close to my own. I remember particularly a set of huge dazzling teeth. A hand, clutching my ear, was trying to wrench it off.

I was not conscious of what my colleague was doing, but I saw an expression of pain and rage on my opponent's face. I felt him gradually loosen his hold. When I was able to turn round, Inspector Dufour, sitting cross-legged on the floor, was holding one of the man's feet in his hand, and it looked as if he'd been giving it at least a double twist.

'Handcuffs,' he ordered.

I had already handcuffed less dangerous prisoners, such as refractory prostitutes. This was the first time I had carried out a forcible arrest, and the sound of handcuffs put an end for me to a fight which might have ended badly.

*

When people talk about a detective's flair, or his methods, his intuition, I always want to retort:

'What about your cobbler's flair, or your pastrycook's?'

Both of these have gone through years of apprenticeship. Each of them knows his job and everything concerned with it.

The same is true of a man from Police Headquarters. And that's why all the stories I have read, including those of my friend Simenon, are more or less inaccurate.

We sit in our office, drawing up reports. For this is also part of the job, a fact too frequently forgotten. I might even say that we spend far more time over administrative papers than on actual investigations.

We are told that a middle-aged gentleman is in the waiting-room, looking very nervous and asking to speak to the Chief immediately. Needless to say, the Chief hasn't time to receive all the people that turn up and want a personal interview because their little problem, to them, is the only important one.

There is one word which recurs so often that it has become like a refrain, and the office boy recites it like a litany: 'A matter of life and death.'

'Are you seeing him, Maigret?'

There is a little room next to the Inspectors' office for such interviews as these.

'Sit down. Cigarette?'

More often than not, before the visitor has had time to tell us his profession and his social status we have guessed them.

'It's a very delicate matter, quite personal.'

A bank cashier, or an insurance agent, a man with a quiet regular way of life.

'Your daughter?'

It's either his son or his daughter or his wife. And we can foretell almost word for word the speech he's going to pour forth to us. No. His son hasn't taken money out of the boss's cash box. Nor has his wife gone off with a young man.

It's his daughter, a very well-brought-up young girl about whom there has never been a word of criticism. She saw nobody, lived at home and helped her mother with the housework.

Her girl friends were as serious-minded as herself. She practically never went out alone.

And yet she's vanished, taking some of her belongings with her.

What can you tell him? That six hundred people disappear every month in Paris and that about two-thirds of them are found?

'Is your daughter very pretty?'

He has brought several photographs, convinced that they'll be useful for our search. If she's pretty, so much the worse, for the number of chances is lessened. If she's ugly, on the contrary, she'll probably come back in a few days or a few weeks.

'You can rely on us. We'll do what's necessary.'

'When?'

'Right away.'

He's going to ring us up every day, twice a day, and there is nothing to tell him, except that we haven't had time to look for the young lady.

Almost always a brief enquiry reveals that a young man living in the same block of flats, or the grocer's assistant, or the brother of one of her girl friends has disappeared on the same day as herself.

You cannot go through Paris and France with a fine tooth-comb for a runaway girl, and her photograph will merely go next week to join the collection of prints sent to police stations, to the various branches of the Force and to frontier posts.

*

Eleven o'clock at night. A telephone call from the Emergency Office, over the way, in the building of the Municipal Police, where all calls are centralized and inscribed on a luminous board that takes up the whole breadth of a wall.

The Pont de Flandre station has just heard that there's been trouble in a bar in the Rue de Crimée.

It's right the other side of Paris. Nowadays Headquarters has a few cars at its disposal, but formerly, you had to take a cab, or later a taxi, for which you couldn't be sure you'd be refunded.

The bar, at a street corner, is still open, with a broken window, figures standing prudently at some distance, for in that district people prefer not to attract the attention of the police.

Uniformed constables are there already, an ambulance, sometimes the Station Officer or his secretary.

On the ground, amidst the sawdust and spittle, a man lies crumpled up, one hand on his breast, from which a trickle of blood is flowing to form a pool.

'Dead!'

Beside him, on the floor, a small suitcase, which he was holding when he fell, has burst open, letting drop some pornographic postcards.

The anxious barkeeper tries to put himself in the right.

'Everything was quiet, as usual. This is a respectable house.'

'Had you seen him before?'

'Never.'

The answer was inevitable. He probably knows him very well, but he'll go on asserting to the end that it was the first time the man had set foot in his bar.

'What happened?'

The dead man is a drab figure, middle-aged or rather of indeterminate age. His clothes are old, of doubtful cleanliness, his shirt collar is black with grime.

Useless to hunt for relatives or a home. He must have been staying in the lowest type of furnished lodgings, on a weekly rate, and set off thence to hawk his wares in the neighbourhood of the Tuileries and the Palais-Royal.

'There were three or four customers . . .'

No point in asking where they are. They've flown away, and will not come back to give evidence.

'Did you know them?'

'Vaguely. By sight only.'

Of course! We could give his answers for him.

'A stranger came in and sat down at the other side of the bar, just opposite this chap.'

The bar is horseshoe-shaped, with overturned glasses on it and a strong smell of cheap spirits.

'They didn't speak to one another. This chap looked frightened. He put his hand into his pocket to pay . . .'

That is so, for he had no weapon on him.

'The other chap never said a word, but pulled out his gun and fired three times. He'd have gone on probably if his revolver hadn't jammed. Then he calmly pulled his hat down over his eyes and went out.'

That's clear enough. No need of flair. The *milieu* in which we have to hunt is a particularly restricted one.

There aren't so many of them who peddle dirty pictures. We know nearly all of them. Periodically they pass through our hands, serve a short sentence in gaol and then begin again.

The dead man's shoes—his feet are dirty and there are holes in his socks—bear the mark of a Berlin firm.

He is a newcomer. He must have been given the hint that there was no room for him in the district. Or else he was a subordinate to whom the goods were entrusted and who had kept the money for himself.

It'll take three days, four perhaps. Hardly longer. The Hotels Squad will promptly be called upon to help and, before the next night, will know where the victim was staying.

The Vice Squad, armed with his photograph, will pursue their separate enquiry.

This afternoon, in the neighbourhood of the Tuileries, they'll arrest some of those individuals who all offer passers-by the same trash with an air of mystery.

They won't be very nice to them. In the old days they were even less so than they are today.

'Have you ever seen that fellow?'

'No.'

'Are you sure you've never seen him?'

There's a certain little cell, very dark, very narrow, a sort of cupboard rather, on the mezzanine floor, where people like that are helped to remember, and it seldom happens that after a few hours they don't start banging on the door.

'I think I've caught sight of him . . .'

'His name?'

'I only know his first name: Otto.'

The skein will unwind slowly, but it will unwind to the end, like a tapeworm.

'He's a queer!'

Good! The fact that a homosexual is involved restricts the field of enquiry still further.

'Didn't he often go to the Rue de Bondy?'

It was almost inevitable. There's a certain little bar there frequented by practically all homosexuals of a certain social level—the lowest. There's another in the Rue de Lappe, which has become an attraction for sightseers.

'Whom have you seen him with?'

That's about all. It only remains, when we get the man between four walls, to make him confess and sign his confession.

*

All cases aren't as simple as that. Some investigations take months. And certain criminals are eventually arrested only after long years, and then sometimes by pure chance.

In practically every case, the process is the same.

You have to *know*.

To know the *milieu* in which a crime has been committed, to know the way of life, the habits, morals, reactions of the people involved in it, whether victims, criminals or merely witnesses.

To enter into their world without surprise, easily, and to speak its language naturally.

This is as true whether we are concerned with a bistro in La Villette or the Porte d'Italie, or with the Arabs in the Zone, with Poles or Italians, with the streetwalkers of Pigalle or the young delinquents of Les Ternes.

It's still true if we are concerned with the racing world or the gambling world, with safe-breaking specialists or jewel thieves.

That is why we aren't wasting our time when we spend years pacing the pavements, climbing stairs or spying on pilferers in big stores.

Like the cobbler, like the pastrycook, we are serving our apprenticeship, with this difference, that it goes on for practically the whole of our lives, because the number of different circles is almost infinite.

Prostitutes, pickpockets, cardsharpers, confidence tricksters or specialists in cheque forgery recognize one another.

One might say the same of policemen after a certain number of years on the job. And it's not a matter of hobnailed shoes or moustaches.

I think it's the look in our eyes that gives us away, a certain reaction —or rather lack of reaction—when confronted with certain creatures, certain states of destitution, certain abnormalities.

With all due deference to novelists, a detective is, above all, a professional. He is an *official*.

He's not engaged in a guessing game, nor getting worked up over a relatively thrilling chase.

When he spends a night in the rain, watching a door that doesn't open or a lighted window, when he patiently scans the pavement cafés on the boulevards for a familiar face, or prepares to spend hours questioning a pale, terrified individual, he is doing his daily job.

He is earning his living, trying to earn as honestly as possible the money that the Government gives him at the end of every month in remuneration for his services.

I know that my wife, when she reads these lines presently, will shake her head and look at me reproachfully, murmuring maybe:

'You always exaggerate!'

She will probably add:

'You're going to give a wrong idea of yourself and your colleagues.'

She's quite right. I may possibly be exaggerating somewhat in the contrary direction. It's by way of reaction against the ready-made ideas which have so often irritated me.

How many times, after the publication of one of Simenon's books, have my colleagues looked at me mockingly as I went into my office!

I could read in their eyes what they were thinking: 'Well, here comes God the Father!'

That is why I insist on the term official, which others consider derogatory.

I have been an official almost all my life. Thanks to Inspector Jacquemain, I became one on the threshold of manhood.

Just as my father, in his day, became estate-manager at the château. With the same pride. With the same concern to know everything about my job and to carry out my task conscientiously.

The difference between other officials and those of the Quai des Orfèvres is that the latter are, as it were, balanced between two worlds.

By their dress, by their education, by their homes and their way of life, they are indistinguishable from other middle-class people and share their dream of a little house in the country.

Most of their time is spent none the less in contact with the underworld, the riffraff, the dregs, often with the enemies of organized society.

This has often struck me. It's a strange situation about which I have sometimes felt uneasy.

I live in a bourgeois apartment, where the savoury smells of my carefully-prepared dinner await me, where everything is simple and neat, clean and comfortable. Through my windows I see only homes like my own, mothers walking with their children along the Boulevard, housewives going to do their shopping.

I belong to that social group, of course, to what are known as respectable people.

But I know the others too, I know them well enough for a certain contact to exist between myself and them. The tarts at the Brasserie in the Place de la République, when I go by, know that I understand their language and the meaning of their attitudes. So does the street-arab threading his way through the crowd.

And all the others whom I have met and still meet every day, under the most intimate conditions.

Isn't this enough to make some sort of bond?

It's not my business to make excuses for them, to justify or absolve them. It's not my business, either, to adorn them with some sort of halo, as was the fashion at one time.

It's my business simply to consider them as a fact, to look at them with the eye of one who knows them.

Without curiosity, because curiosity is quickly dulled.

Without hatred, of course.

To look as them, in short, as creatures who exist and who, for the well-being of society, for the sake of the established order, have got to be kept, willy nilly, within certain bounds and punished when they overstep them.

They are well aware of this themselves! They bear us no grudge for it. They often say:

'You're doing your job.'

As for what they think of that particular job, I'd rather not try to find out.

Is it surprising that after twenty-five or thirty years in the Force we walk with a rather heavy step, and have in our eyes an even heavier look, sometimes a blank look?

'Don't you sometimes feel disgusted?'

No, I don't! And it's probably through my job that I have acquired a fairly unshakeable optimism.

Paraphrasing a saying of my first religious instructor, I should like to say: a little knowledge turns one away from man, a great deal of knowledge brings one back to man.

It's because I have witnessed depravities of every sort that I have come to realize that they were compensated by a great deal of simple courage, good will or resignation.

Utterly rotten individuals are rare, and most of those I have come across, unfortunately, functioned out of my reach, out of our sphere of action.

As for the rest, I tried to prevent them from doing too much harm and to see to it that they paid for the harm they had already done.

After which, surely, we've settled our acocunts.

That chapter is closed.

CHAPTER EIGHT

The Place des Vosges, a young lady's engagement and some little notes from Madame Maigret

'On the whole,' Louise said, 'I don't see all that much difference.'

I always look rather anxiously at her when she's reading what I have just been writing, trying to forestall her criticisms.

'Difference between what?'

'Between what you say about yourself and what Simenon says about you.'

'Oh!'

'Perhaps I'm wrong to give my opinion.'

'No, no, of course not!'

All the same, if she is right, I've given myself needless trouble. And it's quite possible that she is right, that I haven't known how to go about it, how to set things out as I had promised myself.

Or else the famous tirade about made-up truths being truer than naked truths is not a mere paradox.

I have done my best. Only there are heaps of things that struck me as essential at the beginning, points I had determined to develop and which I have abandoned on the way.

For instance, one shelf of the bookcase is full of Simenon's books, which I have patiently stuffed with blue pencil marks, and I was looking forward to correcting all the mistakes he's made, either because he didn't know, or else for the sake of picturesqueness, often because he hadn't the courage to ring me up to verify some detail.

What's the use? I should look like a fussy fellow, and I'm beginning to believe myself that these things are not so very important.

One of his habits that irritated me most sometimes was that of mixing up dates, of setting at the beginning of my career investigations that took place much later on, and vice versa, so that sometimes my detectives are described as being quite young, whereas they were really staid fathers of families at the period in question, or the other way round.

I had even thought seriously, I confess it now that I've given up the idea, of establishing, thanks to the files of newspaper cuttings which my wife has kept up to date, a chronology of the principal cases in which I've been involved.

'Why not?' Simenon replied. 'Excellent idea. They'll be able to correct my books for the next edition.'

He added, without irony:

'Only, Maigret old fellow, you'll have to be kind enough to do the job yourself, for I've never had the courage to re-read my own books.'

I have said what I had to say, on the whole, and it cannot be helped if I've said it badly. My colleagues will understand, and everyone who's more or less connected with the Force, and it's chiefly for them that I was anxious to put things right, to speak not so much of myself as of our profession.

It looks as if some important question had escaped me. I hear my wife carefully opening the door of the dining-room where I am working, and tiptoeing forward.

She has just put a scrap of paper on the table before withdrawing in the same fashion. I read these pencilled words:

'Place des Vosges.'

And I can't resist smiling with private satisfaction, for this proves that she too has details to put right, one at least, and, actually, for the same reason as myself, out of loyalty.

In her case it's out of loyalty to our flat in the Boulevard Richard-Lenoir, which we have never deserted, which still belongs to us today, although we only use it a few days a year, now that we're living in the country.

In several of his books Simenon described us as living in the Place des Vosges without offering the slightest explanation.

I'm giving my wife's message then. It's quite true that for a number of months we lived in the Place des Vosges. But we were not in our own home.

That year our landlord had at last decided to get the building re-faced, which it had been needing for some time. In front of the house, workmen had set up scaffolding which surrounded our windows. Others, inside, began making holes in the walls and floor to install central heating. We had been promised that it would take three weeks at most. After a fortnight they had got nowhere, and just at that time a strike was declared in the building trade and nobody knew how long it might last.

Simenon was just off for Africa, where he was to spend nearly a year.

'Why don't you move into my flat in the Place des Vosges until the job's finished?'

And so it happened that we went to live there, at No. 21 to be exact, without incurring the reproach of disloyalty to our dear old Boulevard.

There was one period, too, in which, without warning me, he made me retire when I still had several years' service to run.

We had just bought our house at Meung-sur-Loire and we used to spend all my free Sundays getting it ready. He came to visit us there. The place delighted him so much that in the next book he quite shamelessly anticipated events, made me several years older and settled me there for good.

'It makes a change of atmosphere,' he told me when I spoke to him about it. '*I was getting bored with the Quai des Orfèvres.*'

Allow me to underline that sentence, which seems to me outrageous. It's he, you notice, who was getting bored with the Quai, with my office, with the daily duties at Headquarters!

Which did not prevent him subsequently, and will probably not prevent him in future from relating earlier investigations, still giving no dates, making me sometimes sixty years old and sometimes forty-five.

Here's my wife again. I have no study at home. I don't need one. When I have to work I settle down at the dining-table, and Louise retires into the kitchen, which she's quite glad to do. I look at her, thinking she wants to tell me something. But it's another scrap of paper which she's got in her hand and has come to lay timidly in front of me.

This time it's a list, just like when I'm going to town and she writes down on a scrap torn out of her notebook what I've got to bring her back.

My nephew heads the list, and I understand why. He's her sister's son. I got him into the Police Force a long time ago, at an age when he was fired with enthusiasm about it.

Simenon mentioned him, then the boy suddenly disappeared from his books, and I can guess Louise's scruples. She's been thinking that for some readers this may have appeared suspicious, as though her nephew had committed some folly.

The truth is quite simple. He hadn't done as brilliantly as he had hoped. And he did not put up much resistance to his father-in-law's pressing offers of a place in his soap factory at Marseilles.

The name of Torrence comes next on the list, big noisy Torrence (I believe that somewhere or other Simenon makes him die in place of another detective who was in fact killed by my side in a Champs-Elysées hotel).

Torrence had no father-in-law in soap. But he had a terrific appetite for life, together with a business sense that was hardly compatible with the existence of an official.

He left us to found a private detective agency, a highly respectable agency, I hasten to add, for that is not always the case. And for a long time he kept on coming to the Quai to ask for our help, or for information, or merely to breathe the atmosphere of the place again.

He has a big American car which stops from time to time in front of our door, and each time he is accompanied by a pretty woman, always a different one, whom he introduces with unvarying sincerity as his fiancée.

I read the third name, little Janvier as we have always called him. He is still at the Quai. Probably they still call him little Janvier?

In his last letter he informs me, not without a certain melancholy, that his daughter is engaged to a young man from the École Polytechnique.

Finally Lucas who, at the present moment, is probably sitting as usual in my office, at my desk, smoking one of my pipes which he begged me, with tears in his eyes, to leave him as a souvenir.

There's one word at the bottom of the list. I thought at first it was a name, but I couldn't decipher it.

I have just gone into the kitchen, where I was quite surprised to see bright sunlight, for I had closed the shutters in order to work in a half-light which I find helpful.

'Finished?'

'No. There's one word I can't read.'

She was quite embarrassed.

'It doesn't matter at all.'

'What is it?'

'Nothing. Don't pay any attention to it.'

Of course I insisted.

'Sloe gin!' she admitted at last, averting her head.

She knew I should burst out laughing, as in fact I did.

When it was a question of my famous bowler hat, my velvet-collared overcoat, my coal stove and my poker, I was well aware that she thought I was being childish when I insisted on making corrections.

Nevertheless she has herself scribbled the words *sloe gin* at the bottom of the list, making them illegible on purpose, I'm convinced, out of a sort of shame, rather like when she adds to the list of errands to be done in town some very feminine article which she rather shamefacedly asks me to buy for her.

Simenon has mentioned a certain bottle which we always had in our sideboard in the Boulevard Richard-Lenoir—we still have it there—and of which my sister-in-law, according to a hallowed tradition, brings us a supply from Alsace on her annual visit there.

He has thoughtlessly described it as sloe gin.

Actually it is raspberry brandy. And for an Alsatian, apparently, this makes a tremendous difference.

'I've made the correction, Louise. Your sister will be satisfied.'

This time I left the kitchen door open.

'Nothing else?'

'Tell the Simenons I'm knitting socks for . . .'

'But I'm not writing them a letter, you know!'

'Of course. Make a note of it for when you do write. They're not to forget the photo they promised us.'

She added:

'Can I lay the table?'

That's all.

Meung-sur-Loire, Sept. 27, 1950.

85

Maigret and the Headless Corpse

MAIGRET AND THE HEADLESS CORPSE
(Maigret et le Corps sans Tête)
was first published in France in 1955
and in Great Britain in 1967

Translated from the French by Eileen Ellenbogen

CHAPTER ONE

The Fouled Propeller

In the faint, grey light of early dawn, the barge lay like a shadow on the water. Through the hatchway appeared the head of a man, then shoulders, then the great gangling body of Jules, the elder of the two Naud brothers. Running his hands through his tow-coloured hair, as yet uncombed, he surveyed the lock, the Quai de Jemmapes to his left, and the Quai de Valmy to his right. In the crisp morning air he rolled a cigarette, and while he was still smoking it, a light came on in the little bar on the corner of the Rue des Récollets.

The proprietor, Popaul, came out on to the pavement to take down his shutters. His hair, too, was uncombed, and his shirt open at the neck. In the half-light, the yellow façade of the bar looked more than usually garish.

Rolling his cigarette, Naud came down the gangplank and across the quay. His brother, Robert, almost as tall and lanky as himself, emerging from below deck in his turn, could see, through the lighted window, Jules leaning on the bar counter and the proprietor pouring a tot of brandy into his coffee.

It was as though Robert were waiting his turn. Exactly as his brother had done, he rolled a cigarette. As the elder brother left the bar, the younger came down the gangplank, so that they met half-way, in the road.

'I'll be starting the engine,' said Jules.

Often, in the course of a day, they would not exchange more than a dozen laconic sentences, all relating to their work. They had married twin sisters, and the two families lived on the barge, which was named *The Two Brothers*.

Robert took his elder brother's place at the bar, which smelt of coffee laced with spirits.

'Fine day,' said Popaul, who was a tubby little man.

Naud, without a word, glanced out of the window at the sky, which by now was tinged with pink. The slates and tiles of the rooftops and one or two paving stones below were still, after a cold night, coated with a translucent film of rime, which was just beginning to melt here and there. Nothing seemed quite real, except the smoking chimney pots.

The diesel engine spluttered. The exhaust at the rear of the barge spurted black fumes. Naud laid his money on the counter, raised the tips of his fingers to his cap, and returned across the quay. The lock-keeper, in uniform, was at his post, preparing to open the gates. Some

89

way off, on the Quai de Valmy, there were footsteps, but, as yet, not another soul in sight. Children's voices could be heard below deck on the barge, where the women were making coffee.

Jules reappeared on deck, and leaned over the stern, frowning. His brother could guess what the trouble was. They had taken on a load of gravel at Beauval from Wharf No. 48 on the Ourcq Canal. As usual, they were several tons overweight, and the previous night, as they were drawing away from the dock at La Villette, headed for the Saint-Martin Canal, they had churned up a good deal of mud.

As a rule, in March, there was no shortage of water. This year, however, there had been no rain for two months, and the Canal Authority was hoarding its reserves.

The sluice-gates opened. Jules took the wheel. His brother went ashore to cast off the moorings. The propeller began to turn, and, as they had both feared, thick mud, churned up by the blades, was soon bubbling to the surface. Leaning with all his weight on the boat-hook, Robert tried to head the barge towards the lock. It was as though the propeller were spinning in a vacuum. The lockkeeper, used to this sort of thing, waited patiently, clapping his hands together to keep warm.

The engine shuddered with a grinding sound. Robert looked at his brother, who switched off.

Neither of them could make out what had gone wrong. The propeller, protected by the rudder, could not have scraped the bottom. Something must have got caught in it, a loose cable, maybe, such as are frequently left lying about in canals. If that was the trouble, they were going to have a job disentangling it.

Robert went behind the boat, leaned over, and felt about in the muddy water with his hook, trying to reach the propeller. Jules, meanwhile, fetched a smaller boat-hook. His wife, Laurence, poked her head through the hatchway.

'What's up?'

'Dunno.'

Silently, the two men felt about with their boat-hooks, trying to reached the fouled propeller. After a few minutes of this, Dambois the lockkeeper, known to everyone as Charles, came down to the quay to watch. He asked no questions, but just stood by, silently puffing at his pipe, the stem of which was held together with string.

From time to time, people hurried past, office workers on their way to the Place de la République, nurses in uniform making for the Hospital of Saint-Louis.

'Got it?'

'I think so.'

'What is it? Rope?'

'I couldn't say.'

Jules Naud had certainly hooked something. He managed, after a time, to free the propeller. Bubbles rose to the surface.

Gently, hand over hand, he drew up the boat-hook and, with it, a strange-looking parcel, done up with string, and a few remnants of sodden newspaper.

It was a human arm, complete from shoulder to fingertips, which, through long immersion, was drained white and limp as a dead fish.

*

At Police Headquarters, 3rd Division, situated at the far end of the Quai de Jemmapes, Sergeant Depoil was just going off night duty, when he saw the lanky figure of the elder Naud standing in the doorway.

'I'm from the barge *The Two Brothers*, up near the lock at the Récollets. We were just pulling out when the propeller jammed. We've fished up a man's arm.'

Depoil had served fifteen years in the 10th Arrondissement. His first reaction, like that of all the other police officers to be involved in the case, was incredulity.

'A *man's* arm?' he repeated.

'Yes, a man's. Dark hair on the back of the hand, and ...'

There was nothing remarkable in the recovery, from the Saint-Martin Canal, of a corpse which had fouled someone's propeller. It had happened before, more than once. But as a rule it was a whole corpse, sometimes that of a man, some old tramp, most likely, who had taken a drop too much and stumbled into the water, or a young thug knifed by someone from a rival gang.

Dismembered bodies were not all that uncommon either. Two or three a year were about average, but invariably, in the Sergeant's long experience, they were women. One knew what to expect right from the start. Nine out of ten would be cheap prostitutes, the kind one sees loitering in lonely places at night.

One could safely conclude, in every case, that the killer was a psychopath.

There was not much one could teach the local police about their neighbours. At the Station, they kept up-to-date records of the activities of every crook, every shady character in the district. Few crimes were committed—from shoplifting to armed robbery—that were not followed in a matter of days by the arrest of the perpetrator. Psychopathic killers, however, were rarely caught.

'Have you brought it with you?' asked Depoil.

'The arm?'

'Where is it?'

'At the quay. Can we go now? There's this load we've got to deliver, Quai de l'Arsenal. They'll be waiting for it.'

The Sergeant lit a cigarette, and went to the telephone to notify the Salvage Branch. Next, he rang his Divisional Superintendent, Mangrin, at his home.

'Sorry to get you out of bed, sir. A couple of bargees have just fished a human arm out of the canal. No! A man's ... That's how it struck me too ... What's that, sir? ... Yes, he's still here ... I'll ask him.'

Holding the receiver, he turned to Naud:

'Would you say it had been in the water long?'

Jules Naud scratched his head.

'It depends what you mean by long.'

'Is it in a very bad state?'

'Hard to tell. Two or three days, I'd say.'

The Sergeant repeated into the instrument:

'Two or three days.'

Doodling on his note pad, he listened while the Superintendent gave his instructions.

'Can we go?' repeated Naud, when he had hung up.

'Not yet. As the Superintendent quite rightly says, we don't know what else you may have picked up, and if you moved the barge, we might lose it.'

'All the same, I can't stop there for ever. There are four others already, lined up to go through the lock. And they're beginning to get impatient.'

The Sergeant had dialled another number, and was waiting for a reply.

'Hullo! Victor? I hope I haven't woken you. Oh! You're having breakfast, are you? Good. I've got a job for you.'

Victor Cadet lived in the Rue du Chemin-Vert, not far from the Police Station, and it was unusual for a month to go by without some call upon his services from that quarter. He had probably retrieved, from the Seine and the canals of Paris, a larger and more peculiar assortment of objects, corpses included, than any other man.

'I'll be with you as soon as I've got hold of my mate.'

It was seven o'clock in the morning. In the Boulevard Richard-Lenoir, Madame Maigret, already dressed, as fresh as paint and smelling faintly of soap, was busy in the kitchen getting breakfast. Her husband was still asleep. At the Quai des Orfèvres, Lucas and Janvier had been on duty since six o'clock. It was Lucas who got the news first.

'There's a queer thing!' he muttered, turning to Janvier. 'They've fished an arm out of the Saint-Martin Canal, and it's not a woman's.'

'A man's?'

'What else?'

'It could have been a child's.'

There had, in fact, been one such case, the only one, three years before.

'What about letting the boss know?'

Lucas looked at the time, hesitated, then shook his head.

'No hurry. He may as well have his coffee in peace.'

By ten minutes to eight, a sizeable crowd had gathered on the quay where *The Two Brothers* was moored. Anyone trying to get too close to the thing lying on the ground covered with sacking was ordered back by the policeman on guard. Victor Cadet's boat, which had been lying downstream, passed through the lock and came alongside the quay.

Cadet was a giant of a man. Looking at him, one wondered whether his diving suit had had to be made to measure. His mate, in contrast, was undersized and old. He chewed tobacco even on the job, and stained the water with long brown streamers of spittle.

It was he who secured the ladder, primed the pump and, when everything was ready, screwed on Victor's huge, spherical diving helmet.

On deck, near the stern of *The Two Brothers*, could be seen two women and five children, all with hair so fair as to be almost white. One of the women was pregnant, and the other had a baby in her arms.

The buildings of the Quai de Valmy were bathed in sunshine, golden, heart-warming sunshine, which made it hard to credit the sinister reputation of the place. True, there was not much new paint to be seen. The white and yellow façades were streaked and faded. Yet, on this day in March, they looked as fresh as a scene by Utrillo.

There were four barges lined up behind *The Two Brothers*, with washing strung out to dry, and restless children who would not be hushed. A smell of tar mingled with the less agreeable smell of the canal.

At a quarter past eight, Maigret finished his second cup of coffee, wiped his mouth, and was just about to light up his morning pipe, when the telephone rang. It was Lucas.

'Did you say a *man's* arm?'

He, too, found it hard to believe.

'Have they found anything else?'

'We've got the diver, Victor, down there now. We'll have to let the barges through fairly soon. There's a bottleneck building up at the lock already.'

'Who's on duty there?'

'Judel.'

Inspector Judel, a young policeman of the 10th arrondissement, was conscientious if somewhat dull. He could safely be left in charge at this early stage.

'Will you be going yourself, sir?'

'It's not much out of my way.'

'Do you want one of us to meet you there?'

'Who have you got?'

'Janvier, Lemaire ... Hang on a minute, sir. Lapointe's just come in.'

Maigret hesitated. He was enjoying the sunshine. It was warm enough to have the windows open. Was this just a straightforward, routine case? If so, Judel was quite competent to handle it on his own. But at this stage, how could one be sure? If the arm had been a woman's, Maigret would have taken a bet that there was nothing to it.

But since it was a man's arm, anything was possible. And if it should turn out to be a tricky case, and he, the Chief Superintendent, should decide to take over, the day-to-day Headquarters routine would to some extent be affected by his choice of assistant, because, whoever it was, Maigret would want him to see the case through to the end.

'Send Lapointe.'

It was quite a while since he had worked in close collaboration with Lapointe. His youth, his eagerness, his artless confusion when he felt he had committed a *faux pas*, amused Maigret.

'Had I better let the Chief know?'

'Yes. I'm sure to be late for the staff meeting.'

It was March 23rd. The day before yesterday had been the first day of spring, and spring was in the air already—which was more than could be said in most years—so much so, in fact, that Maigret very nearly set off without his coat.

In the Boulevard Richard-Lenoir he hailed a taxi. There was no direct bus, and this was not the sort of day for shutting oneself up in the underground. As he had anticipated, he arrived at the Récollets Lock before Lapointe, to find Inspector Judel gazing down into the black waters of the canal.

'Have they found anything else?'

'Not yet, sir. Victor is still working under the barge. There may be something more there.'

Ten minutes later, Lapointe drove up in a small black police car, and it was not long before a string of glittering bubbles heralded Victor's return to the surface. His mate hurried forward to unscrew the metal diving helmet. The diver lit a cigarette, looked round, saw Maigret, and greeted him with a friendly wave of the hand.

'Found anything?'

'There's nothing more there.'

'Can we let the barge go?'

'It won't turn anything up except mud, that's for sure.'

Robert Naud, who had been listening with interest, walked across to his brother.

'Start the engine!'

Maigret turned to Judel.

'Have you got a statement from them?'

'Yes, they've both signed it. Anyway, they'll be at the Quai de l'Arsenal, unloading, for the best part of a week.'

The Quai de l'Arsenal was only a couple of miles downstream, between the Bastille and the Seine.

The overloaded barge was very low in the water, and it was a slow business getting it away. At last, however, it scraped along the bottom into the lock, and the gates closed behind it.

The crowd of spectators dispersed, leaving only a few idle bystanders who had nothing better to do, and would very likely hang around all day.

Victor was still wearing his diving suit.

'If there's anything else to find,' he explained, 'it'll be upstream. An arm's light enough to shift with the current, but the rest, legs, torso, head, would sink.'

There was not a ripple to be seen on the canal, and floating refuse lay, seemingly inert, on the surface.

'Of course, there's nothing like the current you get in a river. But each time the level is raised or lowered in the lock, there's movement, though you'd barely notice it, all along the reach.'

'In other words, the search ought to extend right up to the next lock?'

'He who pays the piper . . .,' said Victor, inhaling and blowing smoke through his nostrils. 'It's up to you.'

'Will it be a long job?'

'That depends on where we find the rest of the body—assuming, of course, it's in the canal at all.'

Why would anyone, getting rid of a body, dump part of it in the canal, and the rest somewhere else—say on some patch of waste ground?

'Carry on.'

Cadet signalled to his mate to move the boat a little way upstream, and indicated that he was ready to be screwed into his diving helmet.

Maigret moved away, followed by Judel and Lapointe. They formed a solitary little group on the quay, observed by the spectators with the instinctive respect accorded to authority.

'You'll have to search all rubbish dumps and waste ground, of course.'

'That's what I thought,' said Judel. 'I was only waiting for you to give the word.'

'How many men can you spare?'

'Two right away. Three by this afternoon.'

'Find out if there have been any gang-fights or brawls locally in the past few days, and keep your ears open for anyone who may have heard anything—screams, say, or someone shouting for help.'

'Very good, sir.'

Maigret left the local man on guard over the human arm, which lay covered with sacking on the flagstones of the quay.

'Coming, Lapointe?'

He made for the bar on the corner, with its bright yellow paint, and pushed open the glass door, noting the name *Chez Popaul*, inscribed on it. Several local workmen in overalls were having snacks at the counter.

The proprietor hurried forward.

'What can I get you?'

'Do you have a telephone?'

Before the words were out of his mouth, he saw it. It was on the wall next to the bar counter, not enclosed in a booth.

'Come on, Lapointe.'

He had no intention of making a 'phone call where it could be overheard.

'Won't you have something to drink?'

'We'll be back,' promised the Chief Superintendent, not wishing to give offence.

Along the quay there were blocks of flats and concrete office buildings, interspersed with one-storey shacks.

'There's bound to be a bistro with a proper telephone box somewhere round here.'

Walking along, they could see, across the canal, the faded flag and blue lamp of the Police Station and, behind it, the dark, massive Hospital of Saint-Louis.

They had gone about three hundred yards when they came to a dingy-looking bar. The Chief Superintendent pushed open the door. Two steps led down into a room with a tiled floor, dark red tiles of the kind commonly seen in Marseilles.

The room was empty except for a large ginger cat lying beside the stove. It got up, stretched lazily, and went out through an open door at the back.

'Anyone there?' called Maigret.

The staccato tick-tick of a cuckoo clock could be heard. The room smelt of spirits and white wine, especially spirits, and there was a faint whiff of coffee.

Someone was moving about in a back room. A woman's voice called out rather wearily, 'Coming!'

The ceiling was low and blackened with smoke, and the walls were grimy. Indeed the whole place was murky, but for faint patches of sunlight here and there. It was like a church lit only by stained-glass windows. A scribbled notice on the wall read: *Snacks served at all hours*, and another: *Patrons are welcome to bring their own food*.

There were, for the time being, no patrons to take advantage of these amenities. It was plain to Maigret and Lapointe that they were the first that day. There was a telephone box in a corner, but Maigret was waiting for the woman to appear.

When at last she did appear, she shuffled in, sticking pins in her dark, almost black hair. She was thin, sullen-faced, neither young nor old, perhaps in her early or middle forties. Her felt slippers made no sound on the tiles.

'What do you want?'

Maigret and Lapointe exchanged glances.

'Have you a good white wine?'

She shrugged.

'Two white wines. And a *jeton* for the 'phone.'

He went into the telephone box, shutting the door behind him, and rang the Public Prosecutor's office to make his report. The Deputy to whom he spoke was as surprised as everyone else to hear that the arm fished out of the canal was a man's.

'The diver is working upstream now. He says if there's anything more to find, that's where it will be. The next step, as far as I'm concerned, is to have Doctor Paul examine the arm as soon as possible.'

'I'll get in touch with him at once and ring you back, if that suits you.'

Maigret, having read out the number on the dial, went over to the bar. Two glasses of wine stood ready poured on the counter.

'Your very good health,' he said, raising his glass to the woman.

For all the interest she showed, he might not have spoken. She just stared vacantly, waiting for them to go, so that she might finish making herself presentable, or whatever it was she had been doing when they arrived.

She must have been attractive, once. She had, like everyone else, undoubtedly once been young. Now, everything about her, her eyes, her mouth, her whole body, was listless, faded. Was she a sick woman, anticipating a dreaded attack? Sometimes sick people who knew that, at a particular hour of the day, the pain would recur, wore that same look of apathy mixed with apprehension, like drug addicts in need of a shot.

'They're ringing me back,' murmured Maigret, sounding apologetic.

It was, of course, like any other bar or café, a public place, impersonal in a sense, yet both men had the feeling of being intruders who had blundered in where they had no right to be.

'Your wine is very good.'

It really was good. Most Paris bistros advertise a *petit vin du pays*, but this, as a rule, turns out to be a wholesale product, straight from Bercy. This wine was different. It had a distinctive regional flavour, though the Superintendent could not quite place it.

'Sancerre?' he ventured.

'No. It comes from a little village near Poitiers.'

That accounted for the slight flinty tang.

'Is that where you come from?'

She did not answer. She just stood there, motionless, silent, impassive. Maigret was impressed. The cat, which had come into the room with her, was rubbing its back against her bare legs.

'What about your husband?'

'He's gone there to get more.'

More wine, she meant. Making conversation with her was far from easy. The Superintendent had just signalled to her to refill the glasses when, much to his relief, the telephone rang.

'Yes, it's me. Did you get hold of Paul? When will he be free? An hour from now? Right, I'll be there.'

The Deputy talked. Maigret listened in silence, with an expression of deepening disapproval, as it sank in that the Examining Magistrate in charge of the case was to be Judge Coméliau. He was the most pettifogging, niggling man on the Bench, and Maigret's very own private and personal enemy.

'He says, will you please see to it that he's kept in the picture.'

'I know.'

Maigret knew all too well what he was in for: five or six 'phone calls a day from Coméliau, not to mention a briefing session every morning in the magistrate's office.

'Ah! well,' he sighed. 'We'll do our best.'

'Don't blame me, Superintendent. There just wasn't anyone else available.'

The sunlight had penetrated a little further into the room, and just reached Maigret's glass.

'Let's go,' he said, feeling in his pocket for change. 'How much?'

And, outside in the street:

'Have you got the car?'

'Yes, I left it over by the lock.'

The wine had put colour in Lapointe's cheeks, and his eyes were bright. From where they were, they could see a little group of onlookers watching the diver's progress from the edge of the quay. As Maigret and the Inspector came up to them, Victor's mate pointed to a bundle in the bottom of the boat. It was larger than the first.

'A leg and foot,' he called out, and spat into the water. This time, the wrapping was in quite good condition. Maigret saw no necessity to take a closer look.

'Shall we need a hearse?' he asked Lapointe.

'There's plenty of room in the boot, of course.'

The prospect did not commend itself to either of them, but they did have an appointment at the Forensic Laboratory, a large, bright, modern building overlooking the Seine, not far from the junction of the river and the canal. It would not do to keep the pathologist waiting.

'What should I do?' Lapointe asked.

Maigret could not bring himself to say. Repressing his revulsion, Lapointe carried the two bundles, one after the other, to the car, and laid them in the boot.

'Do they smell?' asked the Superintendent, when Lapointe rejoined him at the water's edge.

Lapointe, who was holding his hands out in front of him, nodded, wrinkling his nose.

*

Doctor Paul, in white overall and rubber gloves, smoked incessantly. He subscribed to the theory that there was no disinfectant like tobacco, and often, during a single autopsy, would smoke as many as two packets of *Bleues Gauloises*.

He worked briskly and cheerfully, bent over the marble slab, chatting between puffs.

'Naturally, I can't say anything definite at this stage. For one thing, there's not a great deal to learn from a leg and an arm on their own. The sooner you find the rest of the body, the better. Meanwhile, I'll do as many tests as I can.'

'What age would you say?'

'As far as I can tell at a glance, a man somewhere between fifty and sixty—nearer fifty than sixty. Take a look at this hand.'

'What about it?'

'It's a broad, strong hand, and it's done rough work in its time.'

'A labourer?'

'No. A farm worker, more likely. Still, it's a fair bet that that hand hasn't gripped a heavy implement for years. This was not a fastidious man. You can tell by the nails, especially the toe-nails.'

'A tramp?'

'I don't think so, but, as I say, I can't be sure till I have more to go on.'

'Has he been dead long?'

'Again, I can only hazard a guess—don't take my word for it. I may have changed my mind by tonight or tomorrow. But, for the time being, I'm fairly confident that he died not more than three days ago, at the very outside.'

'Not last night?'

'No, the night before that, possibly.'

Maigret and Lapointe were smoking too, and, as far as they could, they kept their eyes averted from the marble slab. As for Doctor Paul, he seemed to be enjoying his work, handling his instruments like a juggler.

He was changing into his outdoor clothes when Maigret was called to the telephone. It was Judel from the Quai de Valmy.

'They've found the torso!' he announced, sounding quite excited about it.

'No head?'

'Not yet. According to Victor, it won't be so easy. Because of its weight, it will probably be sunk in the mud. He's found an empty wallet and a woman's handbag, though.'

'Near the torso?'

'No, quite a long way off. There probably isn't any connection. As he says, every time he goes down, he finds enough junk to open a stall in the Flea Market. Just before he found the torso, he came up with a child's cot and a couple of slop pails.'

Paul, holding his hands out in front of him, was waiting before taking off his gloves.

'Any news?' he asked.

Maigret nodded. Then to Judel:

'Can you get it to me at the Forensic Lab?'

'I'm sure we can manage it.'

'Right. I'll be here, but be quick about it, because Doctor Paul . . .'

They waited outside the building, enjoying the fresh air, and watching the flow of traffic on the Pont d'Austerlitz. Across the Seine, several barges and a small sailing boat were unloading at the quayside opposite a warehouse. Paris, in the morning sun, was throbbing with youth and gaiety. It was the first real spring day. Life was full of promise.

'No tattoo-marks or scars, I suppose?'

'None on the arm or leg, at any rate. From the condition of the skin, I'd say he was not an outdoor type.'

'Hairy, though.'

'Yes. I have a fair idea of what he must have looked like. Dark, broad-shouldered, but below medium height, with well-developed muscles, and coarse dark hair on the arms, hands, legs and chest. A real son of the soil, sturdy, independent, stubborn. The countryside of France is full of men like him. It'll be interesting to see his head.'

'If we ever find it!'

A quarter of an hour later, two uniformed policemen arrived with the torso. Doctor Paul, all but rubbing his hands, got to work at the marble slab like a craftsman at his bench.

'As I thought,' he grumbled. 'This isn't a skilled job. What I mean to say is: this man wasn't dismembered by a butcher or a Jack-the-Ripper, still less by a surgeon! The joints were severed by an ordinary hack-saw. The rest of the job, I'd say, was done with a large carving knife. All restaurants have them, and most private kitchens. It must have been a longish job. It couldn't have been done all at once.'

He paused.

'Take a look at his chest. What do you see, and I don't mean hair?'

Maigret and Lapointe glanced at the torso, and looked away quickly.

'No visible scars?'

'I don't see any. I'm quite certain of one thing. Drowning wasn't the cause of death.'

It was almost comical. How on earth would a man found in pieces in a canal contrive to drown?

'I'll examine the organs next, and especially—in so far as its practicable—the contents of the stomach. Will you be staying?'

Maigret shook his head. He had seen quite enough. He could hardly wait to get to a bar and have a drink, not wine this time, but a drop of the hard stuff, to get rid of the foul taste in his mouth, which seemed to him like the taste of death.

'Just a minute, Maigret. What was I saying? D'you see this white line here, and these small white spots on the abdomen?'

The Superintendent nodded, but did not look.

'That's an old operation scar. Quite a few years old. Appendectomy.'

'And the spots?'

'Now there's an odd thing. I couldn't swear to it, but I'm almost sure they're grapeshot or buckshot wounds, which confirms my feeling that the man must have lived in the country at some time or other. A smallholder or gamekeeper, maybe. Who knows? A long time ago, twenty years or more, someone must have emptied a shotgun into him. There are seven, no, eight of these scars in a curve, like a rainbow. Only once before in the whole of my life have I ever seen anything like them, and they weren't so evenly spaced. I'll have to photograph them for the record.'

'Will you give me a ring?'

'Where will you be? At the Quai des Orfèvres?'

'Yes. In my office, and I'll probably lunch in the Place Dauphine.'

'As soon as I have anything to report, I'll let you know.'

Maigret led the way out into the sunshine, and mopped his forehead. Lapointe felt impelled to spit several times into the gutter. He, too, it seemed, had a bitter taste in his mouth.

'As soon as we get back to Headquarters, I'll have the boot fumigated,' he said.

On their way to the car park, they went into a bistro for a glass of marc brandy. It was so potent that Lapointe retched, held his hand to his mouth, and, for a moment, with eyes watering, wondered anxiously whether he was going to be sick.

When he felt better, he muttered:

'Sorry about that.'

As they went out, the proprietor of the bar remarked to one of the customers:

'That's another of them come from identifying a corpse. It always takes them that way.'

Situated as he was, directly opposite the mortuary, he was used to it.

CHAPTER TWO

Red Sealing-wax

When Maigret came into the great central lobby of the Quai des Orfèvres he was, for a second or two, dazzled, because even this lobby, surely the greyest and dingiest place on earth, was sunlit today, or at least gilded with luminous dust.

On the benches between the office doors, there were people waiting, some handcuffed. As Maigret went past, to report to the Chief of Police on the Quai de Valmy case, a man stood up and touched his hat in greeting.

With the familiarity born of daily meetings over many years, Maigret called out:

'Well, Vicomte, what have you to say for yourself? You can't complain this time that it's just another case of someone chopping up a whore.'

The man known to everyone as the Vicomte did not seem to object to his nickname, although he must have been aware of the innuendo. He was, in a discreet way, a homosexual. For the past fifteen years he had 'covered' the Quai des Orfèvres for a Paris newspaper, a press agency, and some twenty provincial dailies.

In appearance, he was the last of the Boulevard dandies, dressed with Edwardian elegance, wearing a monocle on a black ribbon round his neck. Indeed, it could well have been the monocle (which he hardly ever used) that had earned him his nickname.

'Have they found the head?'

'Not to my knowledge.'

'I've just spoken to Judel on the 'phone. He says, no. If you get any fresh news, Superintendent, spare a thought for me.'

He returned to his bench, and Maigret went into the Chief's office.

The window was open, and from there, too, one could see river craft plying up and down the Seine. The two men engaged in pleasant conversation for ten minutes or so.

The first thing Maigret saw when he went through the door of his own office was a note on his blotting pad. He knew at once what it was—a message from Judge Coméliau, of course, asking him to ring him as soon as he got in.

'Chief Superintendent Maigret here, Judge.'

'Ah! Good morning, Maigret. Are you just back from the canal?'

'From the Forensic Lab.'

'Is Doctor Paul still there?'

'He's working on the internal organs now.'

'I take it the corpse hasn't been identified yet?'

'With no head, there's not much hope of that. Not unless we have a stroke of luck . . .'

'That's the very thing I wanted to discuss with you. In a straight-forward case, where the identity of the victim is known, one can tell more or less where one is going. Do you follow me? Now, in this case, we haven't the faintest idea who may be involved. Within the next day or two, we may be in for a nasty shock. We must be prepared for the worst, the very worst, and therefore would do well to proceed with extreme caution.'

Coméliau enunciated every syllable, and liked the sound of his own voice. Everything he said or did was of 'extreme' importance.

Most examining magistrates were content to leave matters in the hands of the police until they had completed their enquiries. Not so Coméliau. He always insisted on directing operations from the outset, owing, no doubt, to his exaggerated dread of 'complications'. His brother-in-law was an ambitious politician, one of a handful of Deputies with a finger in every departmental pie. Coméliau was fond of saying:

'You must understand that, owing to his position, I am more vulnerable than my brother-magistrates.'

Maigret got rid of him eventually by promising to inform him immediately of any new development, however trivial, even if it meant disturbing him at his home in the evening. He looked through his mail, and then went to the Inspectors' Duty Room, to give them their orders for the day.

'Today is Tuesday, isn't it?'

'That's right, sir.'

If Doctor Paul had estimated correctly that the body had been in the Saint-Martin Canal about forty-eight hours, then the crime must have been committed on the Sunday, almost certainly during the evening or night, since it was hardly likely that anyone intent on getting rid of a number of bulky and sinister packages would be so foolhardy as to attempt it in broad daylight with the Police Station not five hundred yards away.

'Is that you, Madame Maigret?' he said playfully to his wife, when he had got her on the line. 'I shan't be home for lunch. What were we having?'

Haricot mutton. He had no regrets. Too stodgy for a day like this.

He rang Judel.

'What news?'

'Victor is having a snack in the boat. The whole body has been recovered, except the head. He wants to know if he's to go on looking.'

'Of course.'

'I've got my men on the job, but they haven't come up with any-thing much so far. There was a spot of trouble in a bar in the Rue des

Récollets on Sunday night. Not *Chez Popaul*. Further up towards the Faubourg Saint-Martin. A concierge has reported the disappearance of her husband, but he's been missing for over a month, and the description doesn't fit.'

'I'll probably be along some time this afternoon.'

On his way to lunch at the Brasserie Dauphine, he looked in at the Inspectors' Duty Room.

'Ready, Lapointe?'

He really did not need his young assistant just to share the table at which he always sat in the little restaurant in the Place Dauphine. This thought struck him as they walked along in companionable silence. He smiled to himself, remembering a question that had once been put to him on this subject. His friend, Doctor Pardon of the Rue Popincourt, with whom he and his wife dined regularly once a month, had turned to him one evening, and asked very earnestly:

'Can you explain to me, Maigret, why it is that plainclothes policemen, like plumbers, always go about in pairs?'

He had never thought about it, though, on reflection, he had to admit that it was a fact. He himself, when he was out on a case, almost always took an inspector with him.

He had scratched his head.

'I imagine it goes back to the days when Paris was a lawless city, and it wasn't safe to go into some districts alone, especially at night.'

It was not safe even today to make an arrest single-handed, or venture into the underworld on one's own. But the more Maigret had thought about it, the less this explanation had satisfied him.

'And another thing. Take a suspect who has reluctantly made some damaging admission, either in his own home or at Headquarters. If there had been only one police officer present at the time, it would be that much easier to deny everything later. And a jury will always attach more weight to evidence when there is a witness to corroborate it.'

All very true, but still not the whole truth.

'Then there's the practical angle. Say someone is being shadowed. Well, you can't watch him like a hawk and make a telephone call at the same time. And then again, more often than not, your quarry will go into a building with several exits.'

Pardon had smiled then as Maigret was smiling now.

'I'm always suspicious,' he said, 'of tortuous answers to simple questions.'

To which Maigret had retorted:

'Well, then, speaking for myself, I usually take an inspector along for company. I'm afraid I'd be bored stiff on my own.'

He did not repeat this conversation to Lapointe. One should never poke fun at the illusions of youth, and the sacred fire still burned in Lapointe. It was pleasant and peaceful in the little restaurant, with other police officers dropping in for a drink at the bar, and four or five lunching in the dining-room.

'Will the head be found in the canal, do you think?'

Maigret, rather to his own surprise, shook his head. To be honest, he had not given the matter much thought. His response had been instinctive. He could not have said why, he just had a feeling that the diver, Victor, would find nothing more in the mud of the Saint-Martin Canal.

'Where can it be?'

He had no idea. In a suitcase at a left-luggage office, maybe. At the Gare de l'Est, a few hundred yards from the canal, or the Gare du Nord, not much further away. Or it might have been sent by road to some address or other in the provinces, in one of the fleet of heavy, long-distance lorries that the Superintendent had seen lined up in a side street off the Quai de Valmy. These particular lorries were red and green, and Maigret had often seen them about the streets, heading for the motorways. Until today, he had had no idea where their depot was. It was right there in the Rue Terrage, next to the canal. At one time during the morning, he had noticed twenty or more of them strung out along the road, all inscribed: 'Zenith Transport. Roulers and Langlois.'

When Maigret directed his attention to details of this kind, it usually meant that he was thinking of nothing in particular. The case was interesting enough, but not absorbing. What interested him more, at the moment, was the canal itself and its surroundings. At one time, right at the beginning of his career, he had been familiar with every street in this district, and could have identified many a night prowler who slunk past in the shadow of the buildings.

They were still sitting over their coffee when Maigret was called to the telephone. It was Judel.

'I was in two minds about ringing you, sir. I wouldn't exactly call it a lead, but one of my men, Blancpain, thinks he may be on to something. I posted him near where the diver is working, and, about an hour ago, his attention was attracted by an errand boy on a carrier bicycle. He had a feeling he'd seen him before, earlier on, more than once, at regular intervals of about half an hour, in fact. People have been coming to the quay all day to watch the diver. Most of them stay for a bit and then wander away, but this character, according to Blancpain, kept himself to himself, and seemed to be drawn there by something more than curiosity. Errand boys, as a rule, work to a pretty tight schedule on their rounds, and don't have all that much time to waste.'

'Has Blancpain spoken to him?'

'He was intending to, but as soon as he made a move towards him—very casually, so as not to scare him off—the lad hopped on to his bicycle, and pedalled away at top speed towards the Rue des Récollets.

Blancpain did chase after him, but couldn't make much headway in a crowded street on foot—he had no transport—and finally lost him in the traffic of the Faubourg Saint-Martin.'

There was a brief silence. It was all very vague, of course. It might mean nothing. On the other hand, it could be a break-through.

'Was Blancpain able to describe him?'

'Yes. A lad of between eighteen and twenty—probably a country boy—very healthy complexion—fair—longish hair—wearing a leather jerkin and a turtle-neck sweater. Blancpain couldn't read the name of the firm on his carrier, but was able to see that one word ended in "ail". We're checking on all the local shopkeepers who employ an errand boy.'

'What news from Victor?'

'He says that as long as he's getting paid for it, he doesn't care whether he's under water or on dry land, but he's sure its a waste of time.'

'What about the rubbish dumps and waste ground?'

'Nothing so far.'

'I should be getting the pathologist's report shortly. I'm hoping that will tell us something about the dead man.'

At half-past two, when Maigret was back in his office, Paul rang to report his findings, which would later be confirmed in writing.

'Do you want it at dictation speed, Maigret?'

Maigret drew a writing pad towards him.

'I've had to rely on guess-work to some extent, but I think you'll find I'm not far out. First of all, here's a description of your man as far as one can be certain in the absence of the head. Not very tall, about five foot eight. Short, thick neck and, I feel sure, round face and heavy jowl. Dark hair, possibly greying a little at the temples. Weight: eleven and a half stone. I would describe him as thick-set, stocky rather than tubby, muscular rather than fat, though he did put on a bit of weight towards the end. The condition of the liver suggests a steady drinker, but I wouldn't say he was an alcoholic. More probably the sort who likes a glass of something, white wine mostly, every hour or even every half-hour. I did, in fact, find traces of white wine in the stomach.'

'Any food?'

'Yes. It was lucky for us that his last meal—lunch or dinner, which-ever it was—was indigestible. It consisted mainly of roast pork and haricot beans.'

'How long before he died?'

'Two to two-and-a-half hours, I'd say. I've sent scrapings from under his toenails and fingernails to the laboratory. Moers will be getting in touch with you direct about them.'

'What about the scars?'

'I can confirm what I told you this morning. The appendectomy was performed five or six years ago, by a good surgeon, judging from the quality of the work. The buckshot scars are at least twenty years old, and if you ask me, I'd say nearer forty.'

'Age?'

'Fifty to fifty-five.'

'Then he would have got the buckshot wound as a child?'

'In my opinion, yes. General health satisfactory, apart from the inflammation of the liver that I've already mentioned. Heart and lungs in good condition. There's a very old tuberculosis scar on the left lung, but it doesn't mean much. It's quite common for babies and young children to contract a mild form of TB which no one even notices. Well, that's about it, Maigret. If you want any more information, bring me the head, and I'll do my best to oblige.'

'We haven't found it, yet.'

'In that case, you never will.'

There, Maigret agreed with him. There are some beliefs in the Quai des Orfèvres which have been held for so long that they have come to be taken for granted. The belief, for instance, that, as a general rule, only the corpses of cheap prostitutes are found dismembered. And the belief that, although the torso is usually found, the head is not.

No one questions these beliefs, they are just accepted by everyone.

Maigret stumped off to the Inspectors' Duty Room.

'If I'm wanted, I shall be upstairs in the lab.'

He climbed slowly to the top floor of the Palais de Justice, where he found Moers poring over his test-tubes.

'Is that my corpse you're working on?' he asked.

'I'm analysing the specimens Paul sent up to us.'

'Found anything?'

The laboratory was immense, and full of pathologists absorbed in their work. Standing in one corner was the dummy used in the reconstruction of crimes, for instance, in a case of stabbing, to determine the relative positions of victim and assailant.

'It's my impression,' murmured Moers, who always spoke in a whisper, as though he were in church, 'that your man seldom went out of doors.'

'What makes you think that?'

'I've been examining the particles of matter taken from under his toe-nails. That's how I can tell you that the last pair of socks he wore were navy-blue wool. I also found traces of the kind of felt used for making carpet slippers, from which I conclude that the man practically lived in his slippers.'

'If you're right, Paul should be able to confirm it, because if one lives in slippers over a long period, one ends up with deformed feet, or so my wife always tells me, and . . .' He broke off in mid-sentence to telephone Doctor Paul at the Forensic Laboratory. Finding that he had already left, he rang his home.

'Maigret here. Just one question, Doctor. It's Moers' idea really. Did you get the impression that our man wore carpet slippers most of the time?'

'Good for Moers! I almost said as much to you earlier on, but it was just an impression, and I didn't want to set you on a false trail. It came into my mind, while I was examining the feet, that the man might have worked in a café or a bar. Barmen, like waiters and policemen—especially policemen on point duty—tend to get fallen arches, not because they do much walking, but because they stand for long hours.'

'You mentioned that the fingernails were not well kept.'

'That's true. It's not very likely that a hotel waiter would have black fingernails.'

'Nor a waiter in a large brasserie or a respectable coffee-house.'

'Has Moers found anything else?'

'Not so far. Many thanks, doctor.'

Maigret stayed in the laboratory for almost an hour, roaming about, and leaning over the benches to watch the technicians at their work.

'Would it interest you to know that there were also traces of soil mixed with potassium nitrate under the nails?'

Moers knew as well as Maigret where such a mixture was most often to be found: in a cellar, especially a damp cellar.

'Was there much of it?'

'That's what struck me. This was ingrained, occupational dirt.'

'In other words a man who regularly worked in a cellar?'

'That would be my guess.'

'What about the hands?'

'There are traces of the same mixture under the fingernails, and other things too, including minute splinters of red sealing-wax.'

'The kind used for sealing wine-bottles?'

'Yes.'

Maigret was almost disappointed. It was beginning to look too easy.

'In other words, a bistro!' he muttered grumpily.

Just then, in fact, it seemed to him more than likely that the case would be over that same evening. He saw, in his mind's eye, the thin, dark woman who had served him with a drink that morning. She had made a deep impression on him, and she had been in his mind more than once that day, not necessarily because he had associated her with the dismembered man, but because he had recognized her as someone out of the ordinary.

There was no lack of colourful characters in a district such as the Quai de Valmy. But he had seldom come across anyone as negative as this woman. It was hard to put it into words. As a rule, when two people look at one another, an interchange of some sort, however slight, takes place. A relationship is established, if only a hostile one.

Not so with this woman. Her face, when she had seen them standing

at the bar, had betrayed no trace of surprise or fear, no trace of anything, indeed, but a profound and seemingly habitual lassitude.

Or was it indifference?

Two or three times, between sips of wine, Maigret had looked her
straight in the eye, but there had been no response, not so much as the
flicker of an eyelash.

Yet, it was not the insensibility of a moron. Nor was she drunk, or
drugged, at least not at that moment. He had made up his mind, there
and then that he would pay her another visit, if only to discover what
kind of people her customers were.

'Are you on to something, sir?'

'Maybe.'

'You don't sound exactly overjoyed.'

Maigret did not care to pursue the subject. At four o'clock, he went
in search of Lapointe, who was catching up on his paper-work.

'Would you mind driving me over there?'

'To the canal?'

'Yes.'

'I hope they'll have had time to fumigate the car.'

There were brightly coloured hats in the streets already, with red
this year as the dominant colour, brilliant poppy-red. The awnings,
plain orange or candy-striped, were down over the street cafés. There
were people at almost every table, and there seemed to be a new air of
cheerful briskness about the passers-by.

At the Quai de Valmy, a small crowd was gathered near where
Victor was still searching the canal bed. Among them was Judel.
Maigret and Lapointe got out of the car and went over to him.

'Nothing more?'

'No.'

'No clothing?'

'We've been working on the string. If you think it would help, I'll
send it up to the lab. As far as we can tell, it's just the ordinary coarse
string most shopkeepers use. Quite a lot was needed for all those parcels.
I've got someone making enquiries in the local hardware shops, so far
without results. Then there's what's left of the newspapers that were
used for wrapping. I've had them dried out, and they're mostly last
week's.'

'What's the most recent date?'

'Saturday morning.'

'Do you know that bistro in the street just beyond the Rue Terrage,
the one next door to the surgical instruments place?'

'*Chez Calas?*'

'I didn't notice the name; it's a murky little place below street level,
with a big charcoal stove in the middle, and a zinc bar counter painted
black, stretching almost from end to end.'

'That's it, Omer Calas's place.'

When it came to local landmarks, the district police had the edge on the Quai des Orfèvres.

'What sort of place is it?' asked Maigret, watching the air bubbles which marked Victor's comings and goings under water.

'Quiet. They've never given us any trouble, as far as I know.'

'Would you say Omer Calas was a townsman or a countryman?'

'A countryman, I should think. I could look up his registration. It's always happening. A man comes to Paris as a personal servant or chauffeur, and ends up married to the cook and running a bistro in double harness.'

'Have they been there long?'

'Longer than I have. As far back as I can remember, its always been much the same. It's almost opposite the Police Station, and I occasionally drop in for a drink. They do a good white wine.'

'Who looks after the bar? The proprietor?'

'Most of the time—except for an hour or two every afternoon, when he's at a brasserie in the Rue La Fayette playing billards. He's mad keen on billards.'

'When he's away, does the woman look after the bar?'

'Yes, they have no staff. I seem to remember they did have a little waitress at one time, but I've no idea what became of her.'

'What sort of people go there?'

'It's hard to say,' said Judel, scratching the back of his head.

'All the bistros hereabouts cater for more or less the same class of customer, and yet no two are alike. Take *Chez Popaul*, opposite the lock. It's busy from morning to night. There it's neat spirits and rowdy talk, and there's always a blue haze of tobacco smoke about the place. Any time after eight at night you're sure to find three or four women in there, waiting for their regular fellows.'

'And Omer's place?'

'Well, for one thing it's a bit off the beaten track, and for another, it's dark and rather gloomy. You must have noticed the atmosphere yourself. They get dockers from round about dropping in for a drink in the morning, and a few take their sandwiches along at lunch-time, and order a glass of white wine. There's not much doing in the afternoon, and I daresay that's why Omer goes off for his game of billiards after lunch. As I said, there are no regulars at that time, just the occasional passer-by. Trade picks up again at the end of the day.

'I've been in myself once or twice of an evening. It's always the same. A hand of cards at one of the tables, and a couple of people, no more, drinking at the bar. It's one of those joints where, if one doesn't happen to be a regular, one is made to feel out of place.'

'Is the woman Omer's wife?'

'I've never thought to ask. I can easily find out, though. We can go over to the station now, if you like, and look them up in the records.'

'I'll leave that to you. You can let me know later. Omer Calas is away from home, it seems.'

'Oh? Is that what she told you?'

'Yes.'

By now, the Naud brothers' barge had docked at the Quai de l'Arsenal, and the cargo of gravel was being unloaded by crane.

'I should be grateful if you would compile a list of all the bistros in the district, drawing my attention to any whose proprietor or barman has been absent since Sunday.'

'Do you think? . . .'

'It's Moers' idea. He may be right. I'm going along there.'

'To Calas's?'

'Yes. Coming, Lapointe?'

'Shall we be needing Victor tomorrow?'

'We can't chuck the tax-payers' money out of the window. I have a feeling that, if there had been anything more to find, he'd have found it today.'

'That's what he thinks, too.'

'Tell him he can give up as soon as he feels like it, and not to forget to let me have his report by tomorrow.'

Maigret paused on his way, to take another look at the lorries in the Rue Terrage, and read the inscription, 'Roulers and Langlois', over the great archway of the depot.

'I wonder how many there are,' he murmured, thinking aloud.

'What?' Lapointe asked.

'Lorries.'

'I've never driven into the country without finding myself crawling along behind one. It's bloody near impossible to pass them.'

The chimney pots, which had been rose-pink that morning, were now a deepening red in the setting sun, and there were pale green streaks here and there in the sky, green streaks almost the same colour as the green sea at dusk.

'Do you really believe, sir, that a woman could have done it?'

He thought again of the thin, dark woman who had poured their drinks that morning.

'It's possible . . . I don't know.'

Perhaps Lapointe felt, as he did, that it was all too easy.

Confront the men of the Quai des Orfèvres with a thoroughly tangled and apparently insoluble problem, and you will have every one of them, Maigret most of all, fretting and grumbling over it. But give them something that, at first sight, seems difficult, and later turns out to be straightforward and commonplace, and those same men, Maigret included, will not be able to contain their disappointment.

They were at the door of the bistro. On account of its low ceiling, it was darker than most, and there was already a light switched on over the counter.

The same woman, carelessly dressed as she had been in the morning, was serving two men, office workers by the look of them. She must have recognized Maigret and his colleague, but she showed no sign of it.

'What will you have?' was all she said, without so much as a smile.

'White wine.'

There were three or four bottles with drawn corks in a bucket behind the counter. Presumably it was necessary to go down to the cellar from time to time to get more. The floor behind the bar was not tiled, and there was a trap door, about three foot square, leading, no doubt, to the cellar below. Maigret and Lapointe had not taken their drinks to a table. From the conversation of the two men standing beside them at the bar, they gathered that they were not, in fact, office workers, but male nurses on night-shift at the Hospital of Saint-Louis on the other side of the canal. From something one of them said to the woman, it was evident that they were regulars.

'When do you expect Omer back?'

'You know he never tells me anything.'

She replied unselfconsciously, and with the same indifference as she had shown when Maigret had spoken to her earlier in the day. The ginger cat was still stretched out beside the stove, with every appearance of having been there all day.

'I hear they're still searching for the head!' said the man who had asked about her husband. As he spoke, he glanced at Maigret and his companion. Had he seen them on the quay earlier in the day? Or was it just that he could tell by the look of them that they were policemen?

'It hasn't been found, has it?' he went on, addressing himself direct to Maigret.

'Not yet.'

'Do you think it will be found?'

The other man subjected Maigret to a long stare, and then said:

'You're Chief Superintendent Maigret, aren't you?'

'Yes.'

'I thought so. I've often seen your picture in the papers.'

The woman still did not bat an eyelid. For all one could tell, she had not even heard.

'It's weird, carving up a man like that! Coming, Julien? How much, Madame Calas?'

With a slight nod to Maigret and Lapointe, they went out.

'Do you get many of the hospital staff in here?'

'A few.'

She did not waste words.

'Has your husband been away since Sunday?'

She looked at him blankly and asked, as though it were a matter of indifference to her:

'Why Sunday?'

'I don't know. I thought I heard ...'

'He left on Friday afternoon.'

'Were there many people in the bar then?'

She seemed to be trying to remember. At times, she looked so with-drawn—or bored, was it?—that she might have been a sleep-walker.

'There are never many people in the afternoon.'

'Was there anyone at all? Try and think.'

'There may have been. I don't remember, I didn't notice.'

'Did he have any luggage?'

'Of course.'

'Much?'

'A suitcase.'

'What was he wearing?'

'A grey suit. I think. Yes.'

'Do you know where he is now?'

'No.'

'Didn't he say where he was going?'

'I know he must have taken the train to Poitiers. From there, he'll have gone on by bus to Saint-Aubin or some other village in the district.'

'Does he stay at the local inn?'

'As a rule.'

'Doesn't he ever stay with friends or relations? Or on one of the estates where he gets his wine?'

'I've never asked him.'

'You mean to say, that if you needed to get in touch with him urgently, to pass on some important message, for instance, or because you were ill, you wouldn't know where to find him?'

This too appeared to be a matter of indifference to her.

'Sooner or later he'd be bound to come back,' she said in her flat, monotonous voice. 'The same again?'

Both glasses were empty. She refilled them.

CHAPTER THREE

The Errand Boy

It was, all in all, one of Maigret's most frustrating interrogations. Not that one could call it an interrogation in the accepted sense, with life going on as usual around them. The Chief Superintendent and Lapointe stood at the bar for a long time, sipping their drinks like ordinary customers. And that was what they really were. True, one of the male nurses had recognized Maigret earlier on, and had addressed him by name, but the Superintendent, when speaking to Madame Calas, made no reference to his official standing. He would ask a question. She would reply, briefly. Then there would be a long silence, during which she completely ignored him.

At one point, she went out of the room through a door at the back, which she did not bother to shut behind her. The door presumably led to her kitchen. She was gone some time. They could hear her putting something on the stove. While she was away, a little old man came in and, obviously knowing his way about, made straight for a corner table, and took a box of dominoes from the shelf underneath. He tipped the dominoes on to the table and jumbled them up, as though intending to play on his own. The clink of the pieces brought the woman back from the kitchen. Without a word, she went to the bar, and poured a pink apéritif, which she slapped down on the table in front of him.

The man waited. A few minutes later, another little old man came in and sat down opposite him. The two were so much alike that they could have been brothers.

'Am I late?'

'No. I was early.'

Madame Calas poured an apéritif of a different sort, and carried it over to the table. On the way, she pressed a switch, and a light came on at the far end of the room. All without a word spoken, as in a mime.

'Doesn't she give you the creeps?' Lapointe whispered to Maigret. That was not the effect she had on the Superintendent. He was intensely interested in her, more so than in anyone he had met for a very long time.

Had he not in his youth dreamed of an ideal vocation for himself, a vocation which did not exist in real life? He had never told anyone, had never even given it a name, but he knew now what it was he had wanted to be: a guide to the lost.

In fact, curiously enough, in the course of his work as a policeman, he had often been able to help people back on to the right road, from which they had misguidedly strayed. More curiously still, recent years had seen the birth of a new vocation, similiar in many respects to the vocation of his dreams: that of the psychoanalyst, whose function it is to bring a man face to face with his true self.

To be sure, he had discovered one of her secrets, though secret was perhaps hardly the word for something that all her regular customers must be aware of. Twice more she had retreated to the back room and, the second time, he had clearly heard the squeaking of a cork in a bottle.

She drank. He was quite sure of one thing. She never got drunk, never lost her self-control. Like all true alcoholics, whom doctors are powerless to help, she knew her own capacity. She drank only as much as was needed to maintain her in the state of anaesthesia which had so puzzled him at their first meeting.

'How old are you?' he asked her, when she was back at her post behind the counter.

'Forty-one.'

There was no hesitation. She said it without a trace of either coquetry or bitterness. She knew she looked older. No doubt she had stopped caring years ago about other people and what they thought of her. She looked worn out, with dark shadows under her eyes, a tremor at the corner of her mouth and, already, slack folds under the chin. She must have lost a great deal of weight, judging by her dress, which was far too big, and hung straight down from her shoulders.

'Were you born in Paris?'

'No.'

She must know, he felt sure, what lay behind his questions. Yet she did not shrink from them. She was giving nothing away, but at least he got a straight answer to a straight question.

The two old men, behind Maigret, were playing dominoes, as no doubt they did every evening at this time.

What puzzled Maigret was that she did her drinking out of sight. What was the point, seeing that she did not care what people thought of her, of slinking off into the back room to have her swig of wine or spirits, or whatever it was, straight out of the bottle? Could it be that she still retained this one vestige of self-respect? He doubted it. It is only when they are under supervision that hardened alcoholics resort to subterfuge.

Was that the answer? There was the husband, Omer Calas. He might well object to his wife's drinking, in front of the customers at least.

'Does your husband go regularly to Poitiers for his wine?'

'Every year.'

'Once a year?'

'Sometimes twice. It depends.'

'On what?'

'On our trade.'

'Does he always go on a Friday?'

'I can't remember.'

'Did he say he was going on a business trip?'

'To whom?'

'To you.'

'He never tells me anything.'

'Would he have mentioned it to any of the customers, or a friend?'

'I've no idea.'

'Were those two here last Friday?'

'Not when Omer left. They never come in before five.'

Maigret turned to Lapointe.

'Ring the Gare Montparnasse, will you, and find out the times of the afternoon trains to Poitiers. Have a word with the stationmaster.'

Maigret spoke in an undertone. Had she been watching him, Madame Calas would have been able to lip-read the message, but she did not trouble to do so.

'Ask him to make enquiries among the station staff, especially in the booking office. Let him have the husband's description.'

The telephone box, unlike most, was not at the far end of the room, but near the entrance. Lapointe asked for a *jeton*, and moved towards the glass door. Night was closing in, and there was a bluish mist outside. Maigret, who had his back to the door, heard quickening footsteps, and turned to catch a glimpse of a young face which, in the half-light, looked blurred and very pale. Then he saw the dark outline of a man running in the direction of La Villette, followed by Lapointe, who had wrenched open the door to dash out and give chase. He had not had time to shut the door behind him. Maigret went outside, and stood on the pavement. He could now barely see the two running figures, but, even after they had disappeared from view, he could still hear their rapid footsteps on the cobbles.

Lapointe must have seen a face he recognized through the glass door. Maigret had not seen very much, but he could guess what must have happened. The fugitive fitted the description of the errand boy who, earlier in the day, had watched the diver at work in the canal, and fled when approached by a policeman.

'Do you know him?' he asked Madame Calas.

'Who?'

It was no use pressing the point. Anyway, she might well have been looking the other way when it all happened.

'Is it always as quiet as this in here?'

'It depends.'

'On what?'

'On the time of day. And some days are busier than others.'

As though to prove it, a siren sounded, releasing the workers at a nearby factory, and, a few minutes later, there was a noise in the street like a column on the march. The door opened and shut and opened and shut again, a dozen times at least. People sat down at the tables, and others, like Maigret, stood at the bar.

Most of them seemed to be regulars, as the woman did not ask what they wanted, but silently poured their usual drinks.

'I see Omer's not home.'

'No.'

She did not go on to say: 'He's out of town,' or 'He left for Poitiers on Friday.'

She merely answered the question, and left it at that. What was her background? He could not even hazard a guess. Life had tarnished her, and eroded some part of her real self. Through drink, she had withdrawn into a private world of her own, and her links with reality were tenuous.

'Have you lived here long?'

'In Paris?'

'No. In this café.'

'Twenty-four years.'

'Was your husband here before you?'

'No.'

He did some rapid mental arithmetic.

'So you were seventeen when you first met him?'

'I knew him before that.'

'How old is he now?'

'Forty-seven.'

This did not altogether tally with Doctor Paul's estimate of the man's age, but it was not far out. Not that Maigret was convinced he was on the right track. His questions were prompted more by personal curiosity than anything else. For it would surely be a miracle if, without the smallest effort on his part, he were to establish the identity of the headless corpse on the very first day of the enquiry.

There was a hum of voices in the bar, and a floating veil of tobacco smoke had formed overhead. People were coming and going. The two players, absorbed in their game of dominoes, seemed unaware that they were not the only people on earth.

'Have you a photograph of your husband?'

'No.'

'Not even a snapshot?'

'No.'

'Have you any of yourself?'

'No. Only the one on my identity card.'

Not one person in a thousand, Maigret knew from experience, can claim not to possess a single personal photograph.

'Do you live upstairs?'

She nodded. He had seen from the outside that the building was a single-storey structure. The space below street level comprised the café and kitchen. The floor above, he assumed, must consist of two or three rooms, more likely two, plus a lavatory or lumber room.

'How do you get up there?'

'The staircase is in the kitchen.'

Shortly after this exchange, she went into the kitchen, and this time he heard her stirring something in a saucepan. The door burst open noisily, and Maigret saw Lapointe, flushed, bright-eyed and panting, pushing a young man ahead of him.

The little fellow, as Lapointe was always referred to at the Quai des Orfèvres, not because he was undersized, but because he was the youngest and most junior of the Inspectors, had never looked so pleased with himself in his life.

'I didn't catch him until we were right at the end of the road!' he said, grinning broadly and reaching out for his glass, which was still on the counter. 'Once or twice I thought he'd given me the slip. It's just as well I was the five hundred metre champion at school!'

The young man, too, was panting, and Maigret could feel his hot breath.

'I haven't done anything,' he protested, appealing to Maigret.

'In that case, you have nothing to fear.'

Maigret looked at Lapointe.

'Have you seen his identity card?'

'Just to be on the safe side, I kept it. It's in my pocket. He works as an errand boy for the Maison Pincemail. And he's the one who was snooping on the wharf this morning, and made a quick getaway when he saw he'd been noticed.'

'What did you do that for?' Maigret asked the young man.

He scowled, as lads do when they want to show what tough guys they are.

'Well?'

'I've nothing to say.'

'Didn't you get anything out of him on the way?' he asked Lapointe.

'We were both so puffed we could hardly speak. His name is Antoine Cristin. He's eighteen, and he lives with his mother in rooms in the Faubourg Saint-Martin.'

One or two people had turned round to look at them, but not with any great interest. In this district, a policeman bursting into a bar was quite a common sight.

'What were you up to out there?'

'Nothing.'

'He had his nose pressed against the glass,' Lapointe explained. 'The minute I saw him, I remembered what Judel had said, and I nipped out to get him.'

'If you had done nothing wrong, why try to get away?'

He hesitated, took a quick look round to satisfy himself that there were at least a couple of people within earshot, then said, with a theatrical curl of the lip: 'Because I don't like rozzers.'

'But you don't mind spying on them through glass doors?'

'There's no law against it.'

'How did you know we were in here?'

'I didn't.'

'What did you come for, then?'

He flushed, and bit his fleshy lower lip.

'Come on, let's have it.'

'I was just passing.'

'Do you know Omer?'

'I don't know anyone.'

'Not even Madame?'

She was back in her place behind the bar, watching them. But there was no trace of fear or even anxiety in her face. Had she anything to hide? If so, her nerve was beyond anything Maigret had ever encountered in a criminal or accessory to a crime.

'Do you know her?'

'By sight.'

'Don't you ever come in here for a drink?'

'Maybe.'

'Where's your bicycle?'

'At the shop. I'm off at five.'

Maigret made a sign to Lapointe, one of the few secret signs used by plain-clothes detectives. Lapointe nodded. He went into the telephone box, and rang not the Gare Montparnasse, but the Police Station just across the road, and eventually he got hold of Judel.

'We've got the kid here, at Calas's place. In a minute or two, the boss will let him go, but he wants someone standing by in case he makes a run for it. Any news?'

'Nothing worth mentioning. Four of five reports of scuffles in bars on Sunday night; someone who thinks he heard a body being dropped in the water; a prostitute who claims she had her handbag snatched by an Arab ...'

'So long.'

Maigret, very bland, turned to the young man.

'What will you have, Antoine? Wine? Beer?'

'Nothing.'

'Don't you drink?'

'Not with rozzers, I don't. You'll have to let me go, you know.'

'You're very sure of yourself.'

'I know my rights.'

He was a broad-shouldered, sturdy country lad, with a wholesome complexion. Paris had not yet robbed him of his robust health. Maigret could not count the number of times he had seen kids just like him end up having coshed some poor old soul in a tobacconist's or draper's shop, to rob the till of a couple of hundred francs.

'Have you any brothers or sisters?'

'I'm an only child.'

'Where's your father?'

'He's dead.'

'Does your mother go out to work?'

'She's a cleaner.'

Maigret turned to Lapointe:

'Give him back his identity card. All in order, is it? The correct address, and so on?'

'Yes.'

The boy looked uncertain, suspecting a trap.

'Can I go?'

'Whenever you like.'

He went without a word of thanks or even a nod, but on his way out he winked furtively at the woman, a signal which did not escape Maigret.

'You'd better ring the station now.'

He ordered two more glasses of white wine. There were fewer people in the café now. Only three customers, other than Lapointe and himself, and the two old men playing dominoes.

'You don't know him, do you?'

'Who?'

'The young man who was here just now.'

Unhesitatingly, she said:

'Yes.'

It was as simple as that. Maigret was disconcerted.

'Does he come here often?'

'Quite often.'

'For a drink?'

'He drinks very little.'

'Beer?'

'And, occasionally, wine.'

'Does he usually come in after work?'

'No.'

'During the day?'

She nodded. Her unshakeable composure was beginning to exasperate the Superintendent.

'When he happens to be passing.'

'You mean when he's round this way on his bicycle? In other words, when he's out delivering?'

'Yes.'

'And what time of day would that be?'

'Between half-past three and four.'

'Does he have a regular round?'

'I think so.'

'Does he stand at the bar?'

'Sometimes he sits at a table.'

'Which one?'

'This one over here, next to the till.'

'Is he a particular friend of yours?'

'Yes.'

'Why wouldn't he admit it?'

'He was showing off, I expect.'

'Does he make a habit of it?'

'He does his best.'

'Do you know his mother?'

'No.'

'Are you from the same village?'

'No.'

'He just walked in one day, and you made a friend of him. Is that it?'

'Yes.'

'Half-past three in the afternoon. That's when your husband is out playing billiards in a brasserie, isn't it?'

'Most days, yes.'

'Is it just a coincidence, do you think, that Antoine should choose that particular time to visit you?'

'I've never thought about it.'

Maigret hesitated before asking his next question. The very idea shocked him, but he had a feeling there were even more shocking revelations to come.

'Does he make love to you?'

'It depends what you mean.'

'Is he in love with you?'

'I dare say he likes me.'

'Do you give him presents?'

'I slip him a note from the till, occasionally.'

'Does your husband know?'

'No.'

'Doesn't he notice that sort of thing?'

'He has done, from time to time.'

'Was he angry?'

'Yes.'

'Isn't he suspicious of Antoine?'

'I don't think so.'

Entering this dark room, two steps down from the street, they had stepped into another world, a world in which all the familiar values were distorted, in which even familiar words had a different meaning. Lapointe was still in the telephone box, talking to the stationmaster.

'Will you forgive me, Madame Calas, if I ask you a more intimate question?'

'If you want to, you will, whatever I say.'

'Is Antoine your lover?'

She did not flinch, or even look away from Maigret.

'It has happened from time to time,' she admitted.

'You mean to say you have had intercourse with him?'

'You'd have found out sooner or later, anyway. I'm sure he'll tell you himself before long.'

'Has it happened often?'

'Quite often.'

'Where?'

It was a question of some importance. Madame Calas, in the absence of her husband, had to be available to serve anyone who might happen to come in. Maigret glanced up at the ceiling. But could she be sure of hearing the door open, up there in the bedroom?

In the same straightforward manner in which she had answered all his questions, she nodded towards the open kitchen door at the back of the room.

'In there?'

'Yes.'

'Were you ever interrupted?'

'Not by Omer.'

'By whom?'

'One day, a customer wearing rubber-soled shoes came into the kitchen, because there was no one in the bar.'

'What did he do?'

'He laughed.'

'Didn't he tell Omer?'

'No.'

'Did he ever come back?'

It was intuition that prompted Maigret to ask. So far he had judged Madame Calas correctly. Even his wildest shots had hit the target.

'Did he come back often?' he pressed her.

'Two or three times.'

'While Antoine was here?'

'No.'

It would not have been difficult to tell whether or not the young man was in the café. Any time earlier than five o'clock, he would have to leave his delivery bicycle at the door.

'Were you alone?'

'Yes.'

'And he made you go into the kitchen with him?'

For a second, there was a flicker of expression in her eyes. Mockery? Perhaps he had imagined it. All the same, he believed he could read an unspoken message there:

'Why ask, when you know the answer?'

She understood him as well as he understood her. They were a match for one another. To be more precise, life had taught them both the same lesson.

It all happened so quickly that Maigret wondered afterwards whether he had imagined the whole thing.

'Are there many others?' he asked, lowering his voice. His tone was almost confidential now.

'A few.'

Then, standing very still, not bending forward towards her, he put one last question:

'Why?'

To that question, there was no answer but a slight shrug. She was not one to strike romantic attitudes or dramatize her situation.

He had asked her why. If he did not know, it was not for her to tell him.

The fact was that he did know. He had only wanted confirmation. He had got it. There was no need for her to say anything.

He now knew to what depths she had sunk. What he still did not know was what had driven her there. Would she be equally ready to tell him the truth about her past?

That would have to wait. Lapointe had joined him at the bar. He gulped down some wine and then said:

'There is a week-day train to Poitiers that leaves at four-forty-eight. The stationmaster says that neither of the booking-office clerks remembers anyone answering the description. He's going to make further enquiries, and ring us at Headquarters. On the other hand, he thinks we'd do better to ring Poitiers. It's a slow train, and it goes on south from Poitiers, so there would have been fewer people stopping there than had boarded the train at Montparnasse.'

'Put Lucas on to that. Tell him to ring Saint-Aubin and the nearest villages. Where there isn't a police station, let him try the local inn.'

Lapointe asked Madame Calas for some *jetons*, and she handed them over listlessly. She asked no questions. Being interrogated about her husband's movements might have been an everyday occurrence. Yet she knew what had been found in the Saint-Martin Canal, and could not have been unaware of the search that had been going on all day almost under her windows.

'Did you see Antoine last Friday?'

'He never comes on Friday.'

'Why not?'

'He has a different round that day.'

'And after five o'clock?'

'My husband is usually back by then.'

'So he wasn't here at any time during the afternoon or evening?'

'That's right.'

'You've been married to Omer Calas for twenty-four years?'

'I've been living with him for twenty-four years.'

'You're not married?'

'Yes. We were married at the Town Hall in the 10th arrondissement, but not until sixteen or seventeen years ago. I can't remember exactly.'

'No children?'

'One daughter.'

'Does she live with you?'

'No.'

'In Paris?'

'Yes.'

'How old is she?'

'She's just twenty-four. I had her when I was seventeen.'

'Is Omer the father?'

'Yes.'

'No doubt about it?'

'None whatever.'

'Is she married?'

'No.'

'Does she live alone?'

'She's got rooms in the Ile Saint-Louis.'

'Has she a job?'

'She's assistant to one of the surgeons at the Hôtel-Dieu, Professor Lavaud.'

For the first time, she had told him more than was strictly necessary. Could it be that, in spite of everything, she still retained some vestige of natural feeling, and was proud of her daughter?

'Did you see her last Friday?'

'No.'

'Does she ever come to see you?'

'Occasionally.'

'When was the last time?'

'Three or four weeks ago.'

'Was your husband here?'

'I think so.'

'Does your daughter get on well with him?'

'She has as little to do with us as possible.'

'Because she's ashamed of you?'

'Possibly.'

'How old was she when she left home?'

There was a little colour in her cheeks now, and a touch of defiance in her voice.

'Fifteen.'

'Without warning?'

She nodded.

'Was there a man?'

She shrugged.

'I don't know. It makes no difference.'

The room was empty now, except for the two old men. One was putting the dominoes back in their box, and the other was banging a coin on the table. Madame Calas got the message, and went over to refill their glasses.

'Isn't that Maigret?' one of them asked in an undertone.

'Yes.'

'What does he want?'

'He didn't say.'

Nor had she asked him. She went into the kitchen for a moment, came back to the bar, and said in a low voice:

'My meal is ready. Will you be long?'

'Where do you have your meals?'

'Over there.' She pointed to a table at the far end of the room.

'I won't keep you much longer. Did your husband have an attack of appendicitis several years back?'

'Five or six years ago. He had an operation.'

'Who did it?'

'Let me think. A Doctor Gran...Granvalet. That's it! He lived in the Boulevard Voltaire.'

'Where is he now?'

'He died, or so we were told by another of his patients.'

Had Granvalet been alive, he could have told them whether Omer Calas had a rainbow-shaped scar on his abdomen. Tomorrow, they would have to track down the assistants and nurses who had taken part in the operation. Unless, of course, they found Omer safe and well in some village inn near Poitiers.

'Was your husband ever, years ago, involved in a shotgun accident?'

'Not since I've known him.'

'Did he ever join a shooting party?'

'He may have done, when he lived in the country.'

'Have you ever noticed a scar, rather faint, on his stomach, in the shape of a rainbow?'

She frowned, apparently trying to remember, and then shook her head.

'Are you sure?'

'I haven't seen him undressed for a very long time.'

'Did you love him?'

'I don't know.'

'How long did you remain faithful to him?'

'For years.'

She said this with peculiar emphasis.

'Were you very young when you first knew each other?'

'We come from the same village.'

'What village?'

'It's really a hamlet, about midway between Montargis and Gien. It's called Boissancourt.'

'Do you go back there often?'

'Never.'

'You've never been back?'

'No.'

'Not since you and Omer came together?'

'I left when I was seventeen.'

'Were you pregnant?'

'Six months.'

'Was it generally known?'

'Yes.'

'Did your parents know?'

In the same matter-of-fact tone, about which there was a kind of nightmare quality, she said dryly:

'Yes.'

'You never saw them again?'

'No.'

Lapointe, having finished passing on Maigret's instructions to Lucas, came out of the telephone box, mopping his brow.

'What do I owe you?' asked Maigret.

For the first time, she had a question to ask.

'Are you going?'

And, taking his tone from her, he replied,

'Yes.'

CHAPTER FOUR

The Boy on the Roof

Maigret hesitated a long time before taking his pipe out of his pocket, which was most unlike him; and when he did, he assumed an absent-minded air, as though he had just got it out to keep his hands occupied while he was talking.

The staff meeting in the Chief's office had been short. When it was over, Maigret and the Chief stood for a few minutes talking by the open window, and then Maigret made straight for the little communicating door which led to the Department of Public Prosecutions. The benches all along the corridor in the Examining Magistrates' Wing were crowded, two police vans having driven into the courtyard a short while before. Maigret recognized most of the prisoners waiting handcuffed, between two guards, and one or two, apparently bearing him no ill-will, nodded a greeting as he went past.

By the time he had got back to his office the previous evening, there were several messages on his pad requesting him to ring Judge Coméliau. The judge was thin and nervy, with a little brown moustache that looked dyed, and the bearing of a cavalry officer. His very first words to Maigret were:

'I want to know exactly how things stand.'

Obediently Maigret told him, beginning with Victor's search of the Saint-Martin Canal, and his failure to find the head. Even at this early stage, he was interrupted.

'The diver will be continuing the search today, I presume?'

'I didn't consider it necessary.'

'It seems to me that, having discovered the rest of the body in the canal, it's logical to assume that the head can't be far away.'

This was what made him so difficult to work with. He was not the only meddling magistrate, but he was certainly the most pig-headed. He wasn't a fool, by any means. It was said by lawyers who had known him in his student days that he had been one of the most brilliant men of his year.

One could only suppose that he had never learnt to apply his intelligence to the hard facts of life. He was very much a man of the Establishment, guided by inflexible principles and hallowed taboos, which determined his attitude in all things. Patiently, the Chief Superintendent explained:

'In the first place, Judge, Victor is as much at home in the canal as you are in your office and I am in mine. He has gone over the bottom inch by inch, at least a couple of hundred times. He's a conscientious chap. If he says the head isn't there . . .'

'My plumber is a conscientious chap, too, and he knows his job, but that doesn't prevent him from assuring me, every time I send for him, that there can't possibly be any defect in my water system.'

'It rarely happens, in the case of a dismembered corpse, that the head is found near the body.'

Coméliau was making a visible effort, with his bright little eyes fixed on Maigret, who went on:

'It's understandable. It's no easy matter to identify a torso or a limb, especially when it's been some time in the water, but a head is easily recognizable. And, because it's less cumbersome than a body, it's worth taking the trouble to dispose of it further afield.'

'Yes, I'll grant you that.'

Maigret, as discreetly as he could, had got out his tobacco pouch and was holding it in his left hand, hoping that something might distract the magistrate's attention, so that he could fill his pipe.

He turned to the subject of Madame Calas, and described the bar in the Quai de Valmy.

'What led you to her?'

'Pure chance, I must admit. I had a 'phone call to make, and there was no telephone box in the first bar I went into, only a wall instrument, making private conversation impossible.'

'Go on.'

Maigret told him of Calas's alleged departure by train for Poitiers, and of the relationship between the proprietress of the bar and Antoine Cristin, the errand boy. And he did not forget to mention the crescent-shaped scar.

'Do you mean to tell me that you believed this woman when she said she didn't know whether or not her husband had such a scar?'

This infuriated the judge, because he could not understand it.

'To be perfectly frank, Maigret, I can't understand why you didn't have the woman and the boy brought in for questioning in the ordinary way. It's the usual practice, and generally produces results. I take it her story is a pack of lies?'

'Not necessarily.'

'But claiming she didn't know where her husband was or when he would return . . . Well, really! . . .'

Coméliau was born in a house on the Left Bank, with a view over the Luxembourg. He was still living in it. How could such a man be expected to have the smallest insight into the minds of people like Omer Calas and his wife?

At last! The flicker of a match, and Maigret's pipe was alight. Now for the disapproving stare. Coméliau had a perfect horror of smoking, and this was his way of showing it when anyone had the impudence to light up in his presence. Maigret, however, was determined to outface him.

'You may be right,' he conceded. 'She could have been lying to me. On the other hand, she could have been telling the truth. All we have is a dismembered corpse without a head. All we know for certain is that the dead man was aged between forty-five and fifty-five. So far, he has not been identified. Do you imagine that Calas is the only man to have disappeared in the past few days, or gone off without saying where? Madame Calas is a secret drinker, and her lover, the errand boy, is scared of the police. Does that give me the right to have her brought to Headquarters as a suspect? What kind of fools will we look, if, in the next day or so, a head is found, and it turns out not to be the head of Omer Calas at all?'

'Are you having the house watched?'

'Judel of the 10th arrondissement has a man posted on the quay, and I went back myself after dinner last night to take a look round.'

'Did you get any results?'

'Nothing much, I stopped one or two prostitutes in the street, and asked them a few questions. It's one of those districts where the atmosphere is quite different at night from what it is by day, and I was hoping that, if there was anything suspicious going on around the café on Sunday night, one of these women would have seen or heard it.'

'Did you discover anything?'

'Not much. I did get what may be a lead from one of them, but I haven't had time to follow it up.

'According to her, the woman Calas has another lover, a middle-aged man with red hair, who either lives or works in the district. My informant, it must be admitted, is eaten up with spite, because, as she put it, "that woman takes the bread out of our mouths". If she were a pro, she said, they wouldn't mind so much. But she does it for nothing. All the men, it seems, know where to go. They only have to wait till the husband's back is turned. No one is refused, I'm told, though, of course, I haven't put it to the test.'

In the face of such depravity, Coméliau could only heave a distressful sigh.

'You must proceed as you think fit, Maigret. I don't see any problem myself. There's no need to handle people of that sort with kid gloves.'

'I shall be seeing her again shortly. And I intend to see the daughter as well. As to identification, I hope we shall be able to clear that up through the nurses who were present at the operation on Calas five years ago.'

In that connection, one curious fact had emerged. The previous evening, while Maigret was wandering about the streets, he had suddenly remembered another question he wanted to put to Madame Calas, and had gone back to the bistro. Madame Calas was sitting half-asleep on a chair, and four men were playing cards at a table. Maigret had asked her the name of the hospital where her husband had been operated on.

He had formed an impression of Calas as a fairly tough character, not at all the sort to cosset himself, fret about his health, or fear for his life. Yet, when it came to undergoing a simple operation, without complications, virtually without risk, he had not chosen to go into hospital but, at considerable expense, to a private clinic at Villejuif. And not just any private clinic, but a religious establishment, staffed by nuns.

Maigret looked at his watch. Lapointe must be there by now. He would soon be telephoning to report.

'Be firm, Maigret!' urged Coméliau, as the Superintendent was leaving.

It was not lack of firmness that was holding him back. It was not pity either. Coméliau would never understand. The world into which Maigret had suddenly been plunged was so different from the familiar world of daily life that he could only feel his way, tentatively, step by step. Was there any connection between the occupants of the little café in the Quai de Valmy and the corpse thrown into the Saint-Martin Canal? Possibly. But it was equally possible that it was mere coincidence.

He returned to his office, feeling restless and disgruntled, as he nearly always did at this stage of any enquiry.

Last night, he had been collecting and storing information without stopping to consider where it was all leading. Now, he was faced with a jumble of facts which needed sorting out and piecing together.

Madame Calas was no longer simply a colourful character, such as he occasionally encountered in his work. She was his problem, his responsibility.

Coméliau saw her as a sexually promiscuous, drink-sodden degenerate. That was not how Maigret saw her. Just what she was, he could not say yet, and until he knew for sure, until he felt the truth in his bones as it were, he would be oppressed by this indefinable uneasiness.

Lucas was in his office. He had just put the mail on his desk.

'Any new developments?'

'Have you been in the building all the time, sir?'

'With Coméliau.'

'If I'd known, I'd have had your calls transferred. Yes, there has been a new development. Judel is in a fearful stew.'

It was Madame Calas who came at once into Maigret's mind, and he wondered what could have happened to her. But it had nothing to do with her.

'It's about the young man, Antoine. I think that was the name.'

'Yes, Antoine. What's happened? Has he vanished again?'

'That's it. It seems you left instructions last night that he was to be kept under observation. The young man went straight to his lodgings, at the far end of the Faubourg Saint-Martin, almost at the junction with the Rue Louis-Blanc. The man detailed to follow him had a word with the concierge. The boy lives with his mother, who is a cleaner, on the seventh floor of the building. They have two attic rooms. There's no lift. I got all this from Judel, of course. Apparently, the building is one of those ghastly great tenements, housing fifty or sixty families, with swarms of kids spilling out on to the stairs.'

'Go on.'

'That's about all. According to the concierge, the boy's mother is an estimable woman with plenty of guts. Her husband died in a sanatorium. She has had T.B. herself. She claims to be cured, but the concierge doubts it. Well, when he had heard all this, Judel's man rang the Station for further instructions. Judel, not wanting to take any chances, told him to stay where he was and watch the building. He stood guard outside until about midnight. All the tenants were in by then. He went in after the last of them, and spent the night on the stairs.

'This morning, just before eight, a thin woman went past the lodge, and the concierge called out to him that this was Antoine's mother. He saw no necessity to stop or follow her. It was not until half an hour later that, having nothing better to do, he thought of going up to the seventh floor, to have a look round.

'It did strike him as odd then that the boy hadn't yet left for work. He listened at the keyhole, but couldn't hear a sound. He knocked, and got no answer. In the end, after examining the lock and seeing that it was anything but secure, he decided to use his skeleton keys.

'The first room he came to was the kitchen. There was a bed in it, the mother's bed. In the other room there was a bed too, unmade. But there was no one there, and the skylight was open.

'Judel is furious with himself for not having foreseen this, and given instructions accordingly. It's obvious that the kid got out through the skylight during the night, and crawled along the rooftops looking for another open skylight. He probably got out through a building in the Rue Louis-Blanc.'

'They've checked that he's not hiding in the tenement, I take it?'

'They're still questioning the tenants.'

Maigret could imagine Judge Coméliau's sarcastic smile when he was told about this.

'Nothing from Lapointe?'

'Not yet.'

'Has anyone turned up at the mortuary to identify the corpse?'

'Only the regulars.'

There were about a dozen of these, elderly women for the most part, who, every time a body was found, rushed to the mortuary to identify it.

'Didn't Doctor Paul ring?'

'I've just put his report on your desk.'

'If you speak to Lapointe, tell him to come back here and wait for me. I won't be far away.'

He walked towards the Ile Saint-Louis. He skirted Notre-Dame, crossed a little iron footbridge, and soon found himself in the narrow, crowded Rue Saint-Louis-en-l'Ile. The housewives were all out doing their shopping at this time of day, and he had difficulty in pushing past them as they crowded round the little market stalls. Maigret found the grocer's shop above which, according to Madame Calas, her daughter Lucette had a room. He went down the little alley-way at the side of the shop, and came to a cobbed courtyard shaded by a lime tree, like the forecourt of a village school or country vicarage.

'Looking for someone?' shrilled a woman's voice from a window on the ground floor.

'Mademoiselle Calas.'

'Third floor, left hand side, but she's not at home.'

'Do you know when she'll be back?'

'She very seldom comes home for lunch. She's not usually back before half-past six in the evening. If it's urgent, you can get her at the hospital.'

The Hôtel-Dieu, where Lucette Calas worked, was not far away. All the same, it was no easy matter to find Professor Lavaud. This was the busiest time of the day. The corridors were crowded with hurrying men and women in white coats, nurses pushing trolleys, patients taking their first uncertain steps. There were doors opening on to other corridors leading Heaven knows where.

'Please can you tell me where I can find Mademoiselle Calas?'

They hardly noticed him.

'Don't know. Is she a patient?'

Or they pointed down a corridor.

'Along there.'

He was told to go first in one direction and then in another, until at last he reached a corridor where stillness and silence reigned. It was like coming into port after a voyage. Except for a girl seated at a table, it was deserted.

'Mademoiselle Calas?'

'Is it personal business? How did you manage to get this far?'

He must have penetrated one of those sanctums not accessible to ordinary mortals. He gave his name, and even went so far as to produce his credentials, so little did he feel he had any standing here.

'I'll go and see if she can spare you a minute or two, but I'm afraid she may be in the operating theatre.'

He was kept waiting a good ten minutes, and he dared not light his pipe. When the girl came back she was accompanied by a nurse, rather tall, with an air of self-possession and serenity.

'Are you the gentleman who wished to see me?'

'Chief Superintendent Maigret from Police Headquarters.'

The contrast with the bar in the Quai de Valmy seemed all the greater on account of the cleanliness and brightness of the hospital, the white uniform and starched cap of the nurse.

Lucette Calas seemed more astonished than distressed. Obviously, she had not the least idea what he had come about.

'Are you sure I'm the person you want to see?'

'You are the daughter of Monsieur and Madame Calas, of the Quai de Valmy, aren't you?'

It was gone in a flash, but Maigret was sure he had seen a spark of resentment in her eyes.

'Yes, but I . . .'

'There are just one or two questions I'd like to ask you.'

'I can't spare very long. The Professor will be starting his round of the wards shortly, and . . .'

'It will only take a few minutes.'

She shrugged, looked round, and pointed to an open door.

'We'd better go in there.'

There were two chairs, an adjustable couch for examining patients, and a few surgical instruments that Maigret could not identify.

'Is it long since you last saw your parents?'

She started at the word 'parents', and Maigret thought he knew why.

'I see as little of them as possible.'

'Why is that?'

'Have you seen them?'

'I've seen your mother.'

She was silent. What more explanation was needed?

'Have you anything against them?'

'What should I have, except that they brought me into the world?'

'You weren't there last Sunday?'

'I was out of town. It was my day off. I spent it in the country with friends.'

'So you can't say where your father is?'

'You really should tell me what this is all about. You turn up here and start asking questions about two people who admittedly are, in the strictly legal sense, my parents, but from whom I have been totally estranged for years. Why? Has something happened to him?'

She lit a cigarette, saying:

'Smoking is allowed in here. At this time of day, at any rate.'

But he did not take advantage of this opportunity to light his pipe.

'Would it surprise you to hear that something had happened to one or other of them?'

She looked him straight in the eye, and said flatly:

'No.'

'What would you expect to hear?'

'That Calas's brutality to my mother had gone too far for once.'
She did not refer to him as 'my father', but as 'Calas'.

'Does he often resort to physical violence?'

'I don't know about now. It used to be an almost daily occurrence.'

'Didn't your mother object?'

'She put up with it. She may even have liked it.'

'Have you any other possibilities in mind?'

'Maybe she put poison in his soup.'

'Why? Does she hate him?'

'All I know is that she's lived with him for twenty-four years, and
has never made any attempt to get away from him.'

'Is she unhappy, do you think?'

'Look, Superintendent, I do my best not to think about her at all.
As a child I had only one ambition—escape. And as soon as I could
stand on my own feet, I got out.'

'I know. You were just fifteen.'

'Who told you?'

'Your mother.'

'Then he hasn't killed her.'

She looked thoughtful, then, raising her eyes to his, said:

'Is it him?'

'What do you mean?'

'Has she poisoned him?'

'I shouldn't think so. We don't even know for sure whether anything
has happened to him. Your mother says he left for Poitiers on Friday
afternoon. He goes there regularly, it seems, to get his supplies of white
wine from the vineyards round about.'

'That's right. He did even when I lived with them.'

'A body has been recovered from Saint-Martin Canal. It may be
his.'

'Has no one identified it?'

'Not so far. The difficulty is that the head has not been found.'

Was it perhaps because she worked in a hospital that she did not
even blench?

'How do you think it happened?' she asked.

'I don't know. I'm feeling my way. There seem to be several men in
your mother's life, if you'll forgive my mentioning it.'

'You surely don't imagine it's news to me!'

'Do you know whether your father, in childhood or adolescence, was
wounded in the stomach by a shot-gun?'

She looked surprised.

'I never heard him mention it.'

'You never saw the scars, of course?'

'Well, if it was a stomach wound . . .' she protested, with the beginning of a smile.

'When were you last at the Quai de Valmy?'

'Let me think. It must be a month or more.'

'Was it just a casual visit, keeping in touch with home, as it were?'

'Not exactly.'

'Was Calas there?'

'I make it my business only to go there when he's out.'

'In the afternoon, was it?'

'Yes, he's always out then, playing billiards somewhere near the Gare de l'Est.'

'Was there a man with your mother?'

'Not on that occasion.'

'Had you any special reason for going to see her?'

'No.'

'What did you talk about?'

'I can't remember. One thing and another.'

'Was Calas mentioned?'

'I doubt it.'

'You wouldn't by any chance have gone to ask your mother for money?'

'You're on the wrong track there, Superintendent. Rightly or wrongly, I have too much pride for that. There have been times when I've gone short of money, and, for that matter, food, but I've never gone to them begging for help. All the more reason not to do so now, when I'm earning a good living.'

'Can't you recall anything that was said on that last occasion at the Quai de Valmy?'

'Nothing special.'

'Among the men you saw in the bar from time to time, do you remember a fresh-complexioned youth who rides a carrier-bicycle?'

She shook her head.

'Or a middle-aged man with red hair?'

This did strike a chord.

'With small-pox scars?' she asked.

'I don't know.'

'If so, its Monsieur Dieudonné.'

'Who is Monsieur Dieudonné?'

'I know very little about him. A friend of my mother's. He's been going to the café for years.'

'In the afternoon?'

She knew what he meant.

'Whenever I've seen him, it's been in the afternoon. But you may be wrong about him. I can't say for sure. He struck me as a quiet sort of man, the kind one thinks of as sitting by the fire after dinner in his slippers. Come to think of it, he always seems to be sitting by the stove, facing my mother. They behave like people who have known each other for a very long time. They take one another for granted, if you see what I mean. They could be mistaken for an old married couple.'

'Do you happen to know his address?'

'He's got a muffled kind of voice. I'd know it again if I heard it. I've known him to get up and say: "Time to get back to work." I imagine his place of work must be somewhere near there, but I don't even know what he does. He doesn't dress like a manual worker. He might be a book-keeper, or something of the sort.'

A bell sounded in the corridor. The girl sprang to her feet.

'It's for me,' she said. 'I'll have to go, I'm afraid.'

'I may have to take up a little more of your time. If so, I'll call on you in the Rue Saint-Louis-en-l'Ile.'

'I'm never there except in the evening. Please don't make it too late. I go to bed early.'

He watched her go down the corridor. She was shaking her head slightly, puzzled by what she had just heard.

'Excuse me, Mademoiselle. How do I get out of here?'

He looked so lost that the girl at the desk smiled, got up, and led him along the corridor to a staircase.

'You'll manage all right from here. Down the stairs, then left, and left again.'

'Thank you.'

He had not the temerity to ask her what she thought of Lucette Calas. He scarcely knew what he thought of her himself.

He stopped at the bar opposite the Palais de Justice for a glass of white wine. When, a few minutes later, he got back to his office, he found Lapointe waiting for him.

'Well, how did you make out with the nuns?'

'They couldn't have been nicer. I expected it to be rather an embarrassing experience, but they made me feel quite at home . . .'

'What about the scars?'

Lapointe was less enthusiastic on this subject.

'In the first place, the doctor who did the operation died three years ago, as Madame Calas told us. The sister in charge of records showed me the file. There's no mention of any scar, which isn't surprising. On the other hand, I did discover one thing: Calas had a stomach ulcer.'

'Did they operate?'

'No. Apparently they always do extensive tests before an operation, and record their findings.'

'There's no reference to any distinguishing marks?'

'None at all. The sister very kindly went and spoke to the nuns who were present at the operation. None of them remembered Calas very clearly. One thought she remembered his asking for time to say his prayers before they gave him the anaesthetic.'

'Was he a Catholic?'

'No, he was scared. That's the kind of thing nuns don't forget. They wouldn't have noticed the scars.'

They were back where they started, with a headless corpse that could not be identified with any certainty.

'What do we do next?' murmured Lapointe.

With Maigret in his present disgruntled mood, he judged it wiser to keep his voice down.

Perhaps Judge Coméliau was right after all. If the man found in the Saint-Martin Canal was Omer Calas, then it might indeed be true that there was no way of getting the evidence they needed except by subjecting his wife to cross-examination. A heart-to-heart with Antoine, the lad with the bicycle, if only they could lay their hands on him, would also be helpful.

'Come on.'

'Shall I get the car?'

'Yes.'

'Where are we going?'

'To the Canal.'

On his way out, he gave instructions to the Inspectors concerned to order a search in the 10th arrondissement for a red-haired man with a pock-marked face, Christian name: Dieudonné.

The car nosed its way between buses and lorries. When they came to the Boulevard Richard-Lenoir, and were almost at Maigret's own front door, he suddenly growled:

'Take me to the Gare de l'Est.'

Lapointe looked at him in bewilderment.

'There may be nothing to it, but I'd like to check all the same. We were told that Calas had a suitcase with him, when he left on Friday afternoon. Suppose he came back on Saturday. If he's the man, then whoever killed and dismembered him must have got rid of the suitcase somehow. I'm quite sure it isn't still in the house at the Quai de Valmy, and I bet you we won't find the clothes he's supposed to have been wearing there, either.'

Lapointe nodded agreement.

'No suitcase has been recovered from the canal, nor any clothes, in spite of the fact that the dead man was stripped before being carved up.'

'And the head hasn't been found!' exclaimed Lapointe, taking it a stage further.

There was nothing original about Maigret's reasoning. It was just a matter of experience. Six murderers out of ten, if they have anything incriminating to get rid of, deposit it in the left luggage office of a railway station.

And it was no distance from Quai de Valmy to the Gare de l'Est.

Lapointe eventually found somewhere to park the car, and he followed Maigret to the left luggage office.

'Were you on duty last Sunday afternoon?' he asked the clerk.

'Only up to six o'clock.'

'Did you take in a lot of luggage?'

'Not more than usual.'

'Have any cases deposited on Sunday not been claimed yet?'

The clerk walked along the shelves, where suitcases and parcels of all shapes and sizes were stacked.

'Two,' he said.

'Both left by the same person?'

'No. The ticket numbers aren't consecutive. The canvas holdall, anyway, was left by a woman, a fat woman. I remember her because of the smell of cheese.'

'Are there cheeses in it?'

'No, the smell has gone. Maybe, it was the woman herself.'

'What about the other one?'

'It's a brown suitcase.'

He pointed to a cheap, battered case.

'Is it labelled?'

'No.'

'Can you describe the person who handed it in?'

'I could be wrong, but I'd swear it was a country lad.'

'Why a country lad?'

'That's how he struck me.'

'Because of his complexion?'

'Could be.'

'What was he wearing?'

'A leather jerkin, if I remember rightly, and a peaked cap.'

Maigret and Lapointe exchanged glances. Antoine Cristin was in both their minds.

'What time would it have been?'

'Round about five. Yes. A little after five, because the express from Strasbourg had just come in.'

'If anyone comes to claim the case, will you please ring the Police Station at the Quai de Jemmapes immediately.'

'What if the chap takes fright and runs?'

'We'll be here, anyway, within minutes.'

There was only one way of getting the suitcase identified. Madame Calas would have to be brought to see it.

She looked up mechanically when the two men came in, and went to the bar to serve them.

'We won't have anything just now,' said Maigret. 'Something has been found which you may be able to identify. The Inspector will take you to see it. It's not far from here.'

'Had I better close the bar?'

'There's no need. It will only take a few minutes. I'll stay here.'

She did not put on a hat. She merely changed out of her slippers into shoes.

'Will you attend to the customers?'

'I doubt if it will be necessary.'

Maigret lingered for a moment on the pavement, watching Lapointe drive off with Madame Calas beside him. His face broke into a mischievous smile. He had never before been left all by himself in a bistro, just as if he owned it. He was so tickled by the notion that he went inside and slipped behind the bar.

CHAPTER FIVE

The Bottle of Ink

The patches of sunlight were exactly where they had been the morning before. One, on the rounded end of the zinc counter was shaped like an animal, another fell like a spotlight on a print of a woman in a red dress, holding a glass of foaming beer.

The little café, as Maigret had felt the previous day, like so many of the cafés and bars in Paris, had something of the atmosphere of a country inn, deserted most of the week, suddenly coming to life on market day.

Although he was tempted to help himself to a drink, he could not permit himself to give way to such a childish whim. Sternly, with his hands in his pockets and his pipe clenched between his teeth, he went over to the door at the back.

He had not yet seen what lay behind that door, through which Madame Calas was always disappearing. Not surprisingly, he found a kitchen, rather untidy, but less dirty than he would have expected. Immediately to the left of the door was a dresser, painted brown, on which stood an open bottle of brandy. So, wine was not her tipple, but brandy, which—since there was no glass to be seen—she presumably swigged straight out of the bottle.

A window looked on to the courtyard, and there was a glass door, which was not locked. He pushed it open. Stacked in a corner were barrels, discarded straw wrappers, and broken buckets. There were rust-rings everywhere. Paris seemed far away, so much so that it would not have surprised him to find a mass of bird-droppings, and hens scratching about.

Beyond the courtyard was a cul-de-sac, bounded on both sides by a blank wall, and presumably leading off a side road.

Mechanically, he looked up at the first floor windows of the bistro. They were very dirty, and hung with faded curtains. Was there a flicker of movement up here, or had he imagined it? It was not the cat, which he had left stretched out by the stove.

He went back into the kitchen, taking his time, and then up the spiral staircase which led to the floor above. The treads creaked. There was a faint musty smell, which reminded him of little village inns at which he had stayed.

There were two doors on the landing. He opened the first, and was in what must have been the Calas's bedroom. The windows looked out on to the Quai de Valmy. The double bed, of walnut, had not been made that morning, but the sheets were reasonably clean. The furniture was what one would expect in this sort of household, old, heavy stuff, handed down from father to son, and glowing with the patina of age.

A man's clothes were hanging in the wardrobe. Between the windows stood an arm-chair covered in red plush and, beside it, an old-fashioned radio set. The only other furniture was a round table in the middle of the room, covered with a cloth of indeterminate colour, and a couple of mahogany chairs.

No sooner had he come into the room than he felt that something was not quite as it should be. What was it? He looked searchingly about him. Once again, his glance rested on the table covered with a cloth. On it was a bottle of ink, apparently unopened, a cheap pen, and one of those blotters advertising an apéritif that are often put on café tables for the convenience of customers. He opened the blotter, not expecting to find anything of interest, and indeed he found nothing but three blank sheets of paper. Just then, he thought he heard a board creak. He listened. The sound had not come from the lavatory, which led off the bedroom. Returning to the landing, he opened the door to the other room, which was as large as the first. It was used as a lumber room, and was piled high with chipped and broken furniture, old magazines, glasses and other bric-à-brac.

'Is there anyone there?' he called loudly, almost certain that he was not alone in the room.

For a moment, he stood absolutely still, and then, without making a sound, shot out his arm and jerked open a cupboard.

'No tricks this time!' he said.

It did not greatly surprise him to discover that it was Antoine cowering there in the cupboard, like a trapped animal.

'I thought it wouldn't be long before I found you. Come on out of there!'

'Are you arresting me?'

The young man, terrified, was staring at the handcuffs which the Superintendent had taken out of his pocket.

'I haven't made up my mind yet what I'm going to do with you, but I'm not having any more of your Indian rope tricks. Hold out your hands.'

'You've no right. I haven't done anything.'

'Hold out your hands!'

He could see that the lad was only waiting for a chance to make a dash for it. He moved towards him, and leaning forward with all his weight, pinned him against the wall. When the boy had tired of kicking him in the shins, Maigret managed to fasten on the handcuffs.

'Now then, come along with me!'

'What has my mother been saying?'

'I don't know what she's going to say about all this, but, as far as we're concerned, we want to know the answers to a few questions.'

'I'm saying nothing.'

'You come along with me, just the same.'

He motioned him forward. They went through the kitchen and into the bar. Antoine looked round, startled by the emptiness and the silence.

'Where is she?'

'The proprietress? Don't worry, she'll be back.'

'Have you arrested her?'

'Sit down over there, and don't move!'

'I'm not taking orders from you!'

He had seen so many of them at that age, all more or less in the same plight, that he had come to expect the defiant posturing and backchat.

It would please Judge Coméliau, at any rate, that Antoine had been caught, though he himself did not believe that they would learn much from him.

The street door was pushed open, and a middle-aged man came in. He looked round in surprise, seeing Maigret very much in command in the middle of the room, and no Madame Calas.

'Is Madame not here?'

'She won't be long.'

Had the man seen the handcuffs and, realizing that Maigret was a police officer, decided that discretion was the better part of valour? At any rate, he touched his cap, muttered something like 'I'll come back later', and beat a hasty retreat.

He could not have got as far as the end of the road when the black car drew up at the door. Lapointe got out first, opened the door for Madame Calas, and then took a brown suitcase from the boot.

She saw Antoine at first glance, frowned, and looked anxiously at Maigret.

'Didn't you know he was hiding upstairs?'

'Don't answer!' urged the young man. 'He has no right to arrest me—I've done nothing. I challenge him to prove anything against me.'

Briskly, Maigret turned to Lapointe.

'Is the suitcase his?'

'She didn't seem too sure at first, then she said it was, then that she couldn't swear to it without seeing what was in it.'

'Did you open it?'

'I wanted you to be present. I signed for it, but the clerk was most insistent that he must have an official requisition as soon as possible.'

'Get Coméliau to sign it. Is the clerk still there?'

'I imagine so. I couldn't persuade him to leave his post.'

'Ring him. Ask him to try and get someone to take over from him for a quarter of an hour. That shouldn't be too difficult. Tell him to hop into a taxi and come here.'

'I understand,' said Lapointe, looking at Antoine. Would the baggage clerk recognize him? If so, it would make everything a lot easier.

'Ring Moers as well. I want him here too, with a search warrant. And tell him to bring the photographers.'

'Right you are, sir.'

Madame Calas who was standing in the middle of the room as though she were a stranger to the place, asked, as Antoine had done before her:

'Are you going to arrest me?'

'Why should I?' countered Maigret. She looked at him in bewilderment.

'Am I free to come and go?'

'In the house, yes.'

He knew what she wanted, and, sure enough she went into the kitchen and disappeared, making straight for the brandy bottle, no doubt. To lend colour to her presence there, she rattled the crockery, and changed out of her shoes—which must have been pinching her, since she so seldom wore them—into slippers.

When she returned to her place behind the counter, she was herself again.

'Can I get you anything?'

'Yes, a glass of white wine—and one for the Inspector. Perhaps Antoine would like a beer?'

His manner was unhurried, hesitant even, as though he had not quite made up his mind what to do next. He took a leisurely sip of wine, and then went over to the door and locked it.

'Have you the key of the suitcase?'

'No.'

'Do you know where it is?'

In 'his' pocket, she supposed.

In Calas's pocket, since, according to her, he had his suitcase with him when he left the house.

'Have you a pair of pliers or a wrench of some sort?'

She took her time getting the pliers. Maigret lifted the suitcase on to a table. He waited for Lapointe to come out of the 'phone box before forcing the flimsy lock.

'I've ordered a white wine for you.'

'Thank you, sir.'

The metal buckled and eventually broke. Maigret lifted the lid. Madame Calas had not moved from behind the counter. She was watching them, but did not seem greatly concerned.

In the suitcase were a grey suit of quite good quality, a pair of shoes, almost new, shirts, socks, razor, comb, toothbrush, and a cake of soap still in its wrapping.

'Are these your husband's things?'

'I suppose so.'

'Aren't you sure?'

'He has a suit like that.'

'And it's not in the wardrobe?'

'I haven't looked.'

She was no help, but, at the same time, she did not hinder them. As before, her answers to questions were curt and guarded, though, unlike Antoine, she was not on the defensive.

While Antoine was scared stiff, the woman gave the impression of having nothing to fear. The comings and goings of the police seemed to be a matter of indifference to her. They could carry on, as far as she was concerned, whatever they might discover.

'Anything strike you as odd?' Maigret said to Lapointe, while they were rummaging in the suitcase.

'You mean everything shoved in higgledy-piggledy like that?'

'Well, that's how most men would pack a suitcase. But there's something else. Calas, or so we're told, was setting out on a journey. He took a spare suit, and a change of shoes and underclothes. It's reasonable to assume that he packed the case upstairs in his bedroom.'

Two men in housepainters' overalls rattled at the door, peered in through the glass, mouthed inaudible words, and went away.

'If that is so, can you think of any reason why he should have taken his dirty washing with him?'

One of the two shirts had, in fact, been worn, as well as a pair of pants and a pair of socks.

'Do you mean you think someone else may have put the stuff in the suitcase?'

'He could have done it himself. The likelihood is that he did. But not at the start of his journey. He was packing to come home.'

'I see what you mean.'

'Did you hear what I said, Madame Calas?'

She nodded.

'Do you still maintain that your husband left on Friday afternoon, taking the suitcase with him?'

'I can only repeat what I have already told you.'

'You're sure you don't mean Thursday, Friday being when he came back?'

She shook her head.

'Whatever I say, you'll believe what you want to believe.'

A taxi drew up at the door. Maigret went to open it. As the station clerk got out, he said:

'It can wait. I won't keep you a minute.'

The Superintendent ushered him into the café. The man looked about him, taking his time over it, getting his bearings, wondering what it was all about.

His glance rested on Antoine, who was still sitting on a bench in the corner. Then he turned to Maigret, opened his mouth, and gave Antoine another searching look.

All this time, which seemed longer than it was, Antoine was scowling defiance at him.

'I really do believe,' began the man, scratching his head. He was conscientious, and there was some doubt in his mind.

'Well then! From what I can see of him, I'd say he was the one.'

'You're lying,' shouted the young man furiously.

'Maybe I ought to see what he looks like standing up.'

'Stand up.'

'No.'

'Stand up!'

Maigret heard Madame Calas's voice behind him.

'Get up, Antoine.'

The clerk looked at him thoughtfully.

'I'm almost sure,' he murmured. 'Does he wear a leather jerkin?'

'Go and have a look upstairs in the back room,' said Maigret to Lapointe.

They waited in silence. The station employee glanced towards the bar. Maigret could take a hint.

'A glass of white wine?' he asked.

'I wouldn't say no.'

Lapointe returned with the jerkin that Antoine had worn the previous day.

'Put it on.'

The young man looked to the woman for guidance, resigned himself grudgingly, and held out his wrists for the handcuffs to be removed.

'Can't you see, he's just trying to suck up to the rozzers? They're all the same. Mention the word "police", and they shake in their shoes. Well, what about it? Do you still say you've seen me before?'

'I think so, yes.'

'You're lying.'

The clerk addressed himself to Maigret. He spoke calmly, though it was possible to detect an undercurrent of feeling in his voice.

'This is a serious business, I imagine. I shouldn't like to get an innocent person into trouble. This boy looks like the one who deposited the suitcase at the station on Sunday. Naturally, not knowing that anyone was going to ask me about him, I didn't take much notice of him. Perhaps if I saw him in the same place, under the same conditions, lighting and so on . . .'

'I'll have him brought to you at the station some time today or tomorrow,' said Maigret. 'Thank you. Your very good health!'

He saw him to the door, and locked it after him. There was, in the Chief Superintendent's attitude to the case, a kind of diffidence that puzzled Lapointe. He could not have said when he had begun to notice it. Perhaps the previous day, right at the start of the enquiry, when they had come together to the Quai de Valmy, and pushed open the door of the Calas bistro.

Maigret was pursuing his investigations in the normal way, doing all that was required of him, but surely with a lack of conviction that was the last thing any of his subordinates would have expected of him? It was difficult to define. Half-heartedness? Reluctance? Disinclination? The facts of the case interested him very little. He seemed to be wrapped up in his thoughts, which he was keeping very much to himself.

It was particularly noticeable here in the café, especially when he was talking to Madame Calas, or furtively watching her.

It was as though the victim were of no account, and the dismembered corpse meant nothing to him. He had virtually ignored Antoine, and it was only with an effort that he was able to attend to the routine aspects of his work.

'Ring Coméliau. I'd rather you did it. Just give him a summary of events. You'd better ask him to sign a warrant for the arrest of the kid. He'll do it in any case.'

'What about her?' asked the Inspector, pointing to the woman.

'I'd rather not.'

'What if he insists?'

'He'll have to have his own way. He's the boss.'

He had not bothered to lower his voice, in spite of the presence of the other two, whom he knew to be listening.

'You'd better have a bite to eat,' he advised Madame Calas. 'It may not be long before you have to go.'

'For long?'

'For as long as the judge thinks fit to hold you for questioning.'

'Will they keep me in prison?'

'At the Central Police Station to begin with, I expect.'

'What about me?' Antoine asked.

'You too. But not in the same cell!' Maigret added.

'Are you hungry?' Madame asked the boy.

'No.'

She went into the kitchen just the same, but it was to have a swig of brandy. When she came back, she asked:

'Who will look after the place when I'm gone?'

'No one. Don't worry. It will be kept under supervision.'

He was still watching her with that same thoughtful expression. He could not help himself. It seemed to him that he had never encountered anyone so baffling.

He had experience of artful women, some of whom had stood up to him for a long time. In every case, however, he had felt from the first that he would have the last word. It was just a matter of time, patience and determination.

With Madame Calas, it was different. She did not fit into any category. If he were to be told that she had murdered her husband in cold blood, and had carved him up single-handed on the kitchen table, he would not have found it impossible to believe. But he would not have found it impossible to believe, either, that she simply did not know what had become of her husband.

There she was in front of him, a living creature of flesh and blood, thin and faded in her dark dress, which hung from her shoulders like a shabby window-curtain. She was real enough, with the fire of her inner life smouldering in her sombre eyes, and yet there was about her something insubstantial, elusive.

Was she aware of the impression she created? One would say so, judging from the cool, perhaps even ironic manner in which she, in her turn, appraised the Chief Superintendent.

This was the reason for Lapointe's uneasiness a little while back. The normal process of conducting a police enquiry with a view to apprehending a criminal was being overshadowed by the private duel between Maigret and this woman.

Nothing which did not directly concern her was of much interest to the Chief Superintendent. Lapointe was to have further proof of this when, a minute or two later, he came out of the telephone box.

'What did he say?' asked Maigret, referring to Coméliau.

'He'll sign the warrant and send it across to your office.'

'Does he want to see him?'

'He presumed you'd want to interrogate him first.'

'What about her?'

'He's signing two warrants. It's up to you what you do with the second one, but if you ask me . . .'

'I see.'

Coméliau was expecting Maigret to go back to his office, and have Antoine and Madame Calas brought to him there separately, so that he could grill them for hours, until they gave themselves away.

The head of the dead man had still not been found. There was no concrete proof that the man whose remains had been fished out of the Saint-Martin Canal was Calas. All the same, they did now have strong circumstantial evidence, namely the suitcase, and it was by no means unusual to obtain a full confession, after a few hours of interrogation, in cases where the cards were more heavily stacked against the police.

Judge Coméliau was not the only one to see the matter in this light. Lapointe was of the same opinion, and he could scarcely hide his astonishment when Maigret instructed him: 'Take him to Headquarters. Shut yourself up with him in my office, and get what you can out of him. Don't forget to order some food for him, and something to drink.'

'Will you be staying here?'

'I'm waiting for Moers and the photographers.'

Looking unmistakably put out, Lapointe motioned to the young man to stand up. As a parting shot, Antoine called to Maigret from the door:

'I warn you, you'll pay for this!'

At the Quai des Orfèvres, at about this time, the Vicomte, having poked his nose into most of the offices in the Palais de Justice, as he did every morning, had started on the Examining Magistrates.

'Any news, Monsieur Coméliau? Have they still not found the head?'

'Not yet. But I can tell you more or less officially that the identity of the victim is known.'

'Who is it?'

Coméliau graciously consented to give ten minutes of his time to answering questions. He was not altogether displeased that, for once, it was he and not Maigret whom the Press was honouring with its attentions.

'Is the Chief Superintendent still there?'

'I presume so.'

Thus it came about that news of the enquiries in progress at the Calas bistro and the arrest of a young man, referred to only by his initials, appeared in the afternoon editions of the newspapers, two hours after the Vicomte's interview with Coméliau, and the five o'clock news on the radio included an announcement to the same effect.

Left on his own with Madame Calas, Maigret ordered a glass of wine at the bar, carried it across to a table, and sat down. As for her, she had not moved. She had remained at her post behind the bar where, as proprietress, she had every right to be.

The factory sirens sounded the mid-day break. In less than ten minutes, at least thirty people were crowded round the locked door. Some, seeing Madame Calas through the glass, indicated by gestures that they wanted to speak to her.

Suddenly, Maigret broke the silence.

'I've seen your daughter,' he said.

She looked at him, but said nothing.

'She confirmed that she last came to see you about a month ago. I couldn't help wondering what you found to talk about.'

It was not a question, and she did not choose to make any comment.

'She struck me as a sensible young woman, who has done well for herself. I don't know why, but I had the feeling that she was in love with her boss, and might be his mistress.'

Still she did not flinch. Was it of any interest to her? Did she feel any affection for her daughter, even the smallest remnant?

'It can't have been easy at the beginning. It's tough going for a girl of fifteen, trying to make her own way, alone, in a city like Paris.'

She was still looking at him, but her eyes seemed to see through and beyond him. Wearily, she asked:

'What is it you want?'

What, indeed, did he want? Was Coméliau right after all? Ought he not to be engaged at this very moment in making Antoine talk? As for her, perhaps a few days in a police cell were just what was needed to bring about a change of heart.

'I'm wondering what made you marry Calas in the first place, and, even more, what induced you to stay with him all those years.'

She did not smile, but the corners of her mouth twitched, in contempt, perhaps, or pity.

'It was done deliberately, wasn't it?' went on Maigret, not quite sure himself what he meant.

He had to get to the bottom of it. There were times, and this was one of them, when it seemed to him that he was within a hair's breadth, not merely of solving the mystery, but of sweeping aside the invisible barrier that stood betwen them. It was just a question of finding the words which would evoke the simple, human response.

'Was *the other one* here on Sunday afternoon?'

This, at least, did get results. She started. After a pause, she was reluctantly compelled to ask:

'What other one?'

'Your lover. Your real lover.'

She would have liked to keep up the pretence of indifference, asking no questions, but in the end she yielded:

'Who?'

'A red-haired, middle-aged man, with small-pox scars, whose Christian name is Dieudonné.'

It was as though a shutter had come down between them. Her face became completely expressionless. What was more, a car had drawn up at the door. Moers, and three men with cameras, had arrived.

Once again, Maigret went to the door and unlocked it.

Admittedly, he had not triumphed. All the same, he did not consider that their tête-à-tête had been altogether a waste of time.

'Where do you want us to search, sir?'

'Everywhere. The kitchen first, then the two rooms and the lavatory upstairs. There's the courtyard as well, and, of course, the cellar. This trap door here presumably leads to it.'

'Do you believe the man was killed and dismembered here?'

'It's possible.'

'What about this suitcase?'

'Go over it thoroughly. The contents too, of course.'

'It will take us the whole afternoon. Will you be staying?'

'I don't think so, but I'll look in again later.'

He went into the telephone box and rang Judel at the Police Station opposite, to give him instructions about having the place watched.

When he had done, he said to Madame Calas:

'You'd better come with me.'

149

'Shall I take a change of clothing, and things for washing?'

'It would be advisable.'

She stopped on her way through the kitchen for a stiff drink. Soon, she could be heard moving about in the bedroom above.

'Is it safe to leave her on her own, sir?'

Maigret shrugged. If a crime had been committed here, steps must have been taken long before this to remove all traces of it, and dispose of anything incriminating.

All the same, it did surprise him that she should take so long getting ready. She could still be heard moving about, turning taps on and off, opening and shutting drawers.

She paused again in the kitchen, realizing no doubt that this was the last drink she would get for a long time.

When at last she reappeared, the men gaped at her in amazement, which in Maigret's case was mixed with a touch of admiration.

In the space of twenty minutes or less, she had completely transformed herself. She was now wearing a most becoming black coat. Under her carefully brushed hair and charming hat, her face seemed to have come to life. Her step was lighter, her carriage more upright. There was self-respect, even a hint of pride, in her bearing.

Was she aware of the sensation she was creating? Was there, perhaps, a touch of coquetry in her make-up? She did not smile, or show any sign of being amused at their astonishment. She looked inside her bag to make sure she had everything, and then, drawing on her gloves, said, almost in a whisper:

'I'm ready.'

She was wearing face-powder and lipstick. The scent of Eau de Cologne, mingled with the fumes of brandy on her breath, seemed somehow inappropriate.

'Aren't you taking a suitcase?'

She said no, almost defiantly. Would it not be an admission of guilt to take a change of clothing? At the very least, it would be an acknowledgement that there might be some justification for keeping her in custody.

'See you later!' Maigret called out to Moers and his assistants.

'Will you be taking the car?'

'No. I'll get a taxi.'

It was a strange experience, walking by her side, in step with her, there in the sunlit street.

'The Rue des Récollets would be the best place to find a taxi, I imagine?'

'I expect so.'

'I should like to ask you a question.'

'You surprise me!'

'When did you last take the trouble to dress as you are dressed now?'

She looked thoughtful, obviously trying to remember.

'Four years ago or more,' she said at last. 'Why do you ask?'

'No particular reason.'

What was the point of explaining, when she knew as well as he did? He managed to stop a taxi just as it was driving past. He opened the door for her, and got in beside her.

CHAPTER SIX

The String

The truth was that he had not yet made up his mind what to do with her. If anyone but Judge Coméliau had been in charge of the case, things would have been different. He would have been prepared to take a risk. With Coméliau, it was dangerous. Not only was he finicky, a stickler for the rules, scared of public opinion and parliamentary criticism, but he had always mistrusted Maigret's methods, which he considered unorthodox. It had come to a head-on collision between them more than once in the past.

Maigret was well aware that the judge had his eye on him, and would not hesitate to hold him responsible if he were to step out of line or if anything, however trivial, should go wrong.

He would have much preferred to leave Madame Calas at the Quai de Valmy until he had a clearer insight into her character, and some clue as to her connection, if any, with the case. He would have posted a man, two men, to watch the bistro. But then Judel had posted a constable outside the tenement in the Faubourg Saint-Martin, and what good had that done? The boy Antoine had got away just the same. And Antoine was just an overgrown kid, with no more sense than a thirteen-year-old. Madame Calas was a different proposition. The newspapers in the kiosks already carried the story of the little café and its possible connection with the crime. At all events, Maigret had seen the name Calas in banner headlines on the front pages. Suppose, for instance, that tomorrow morning the headlines read: '*Madame Calas disappears*'. He could just imagine his reception on arrival at the judge's office.

While pretending to look straight before him, he was watching her out of the corner of his eye. She did not seem to notice. She was sitting up very straight, and there was an air of dignity about her. As they drove through the streets, she looked out of the window with interest and curiosity.

Just now she had admitted that she had not worn her street clothes for at least four years. She had not told him what the occasion was on which she had last worn her black dress. Perhaps it was even longer since she had been in the centre of town, and seen the crowds thronging the Boulevards.

Since, on account of Coméliau, he was not free to do as he liked, he had had to adopt a different procedure.

As they were approaching the Quai des Orfèvres, he spoke for the first time.

'Are you sure you have nothing to tell me?'

She seemed a little taken aback.

'What about?'

'About your husband.'

She gave a slight shrug, and said confidently:

'I didn't kill Calas.'

She called him by his surname, as country women and shopkeepers' wives often call their husbands. But, in her case, it seemed to Maigret to strike a false note.

'Shall I drive up to the entrance?' the taxi-driver turned round to ask.

'If you will.'

The Vicomte was there, at the foot of the great staircase, in company with two other journalists and a number of photographers. They had got wind of what had happened, and it was useless to try and conceal the prisoner.

'One moment, Superintendent.'

Did she imagine that Maigret had tipped them off? She held herself erect, as they took photographs, even following her up the stairs. Presumably Antoine, too, had undergone this ordeal.

They were upstairs in his own domain, and still Maigret had not made up his mind. In the end, he made for the Inspectors' Duty Room. Lucas was not there. He called to Janvier.

'Take her into an empty room for a few minutes and stay with her, will you?'

She could not help hearing. The Superintendent felt oppressed by the mute reproach of her look. Was it reproach, though? Was it not rather disillusionment?

He walked away without another word, and went to his own office, where he found his desk occupied by Lapointe, in shirt-sleeves. Facing the window, Antoine was sitting bolt upright on a chair, very flushed, as though he were feeling the heat.

Between them was the tray sent up from the Brasserie Dauphine. There were dregs of beer in the two glasses, and a couple of half-eaten sandwiches on plates.

As Maigret's glance travelled from the tray to Antoine, he could see that the boy was vexed with himself for having succumbed. No doubt it had been his intention to 'punish' them by going on hunger-strike. They were familiar with self-dramatization in all its forms at the Quai des Orfèvres, and Maigret could not help smiling.

'How is it going?' he asked Lapointe.

Lapointe indicated, by a lift of the eyebrows, that he was getting nowhere.

'Carry on, lads.'

Maigret went across to Coméliau's office. The magistrate was on his way out to lunch.

'Well, have you arrested the pair of them?'

'The young man is in my office. Lapointe is dealing with him.'

'Has he said anything?'

'Even if he knows anything, he won't talk, unless we can prove something against him, and rub his nose in it.'

'Is he a bright lad?'

'That's exactly what he isn't. One can usually make an intelligent person see sense in the end, or at least persuade him to retract self-contradictory statements. An idiot will just go on denying everything, even in the teeth of the evidence.'

'What about the woman?'

'I've left Janvier with her.'

'Will you be dealing with her yourself?'

'Not for the moment. I haven't got enough to go on.'

'When do you expect to be ready?'

'Tonight, maybe. If not, tomorrow or the next day.'

'And in the meantime?'

Maigret's manner was so bland and amiable that Coméliau wondered what he was up to.

'I came to ask your advice.'

'You can't keep her here indefinitely.'

'That's what I think. A woman especially.'

'Wouldn't the best thing be to have her locked up?'

'That's up to you.'

'But you would prefer to let her go?'

'I'm not sure.'

Frowning, Coméliau considered the problem. He was furious. Finally as though he were throwing down a challenge, he barked:

'Send her to me.'

Why was the Chief Superintendent smiling as he disappeared down the corridor? Was it at the thought of a tête-à-tête between Madame Calas and the exasperated judge?

He did not see her again that afternoon. He merely went into the Inspectors' Duty Room, and said to Torrence:

'Judge Coméliau wants to see Madame Calas. Let Janvier know, will you?'

The Vicomte intercepted him on the stairs. Maigret shook him off firmly, saying:

'Coméliau's the man you want to see. He'll be making a statement to the Press, if not immediately then very shortly, you can take my word for it.'

He stumped off to the Brasserie Dauphine, stopping at a bar for an apéritif. It was late. Almost everyone had had lunch. He went to the telephone.

'Is that you?' he said to his wife.

'Aren't you coming home?'

'No.'

'Well, I hope you'll take time off for lunch.'

'I'm at the Brasserie Dauphine. I'm just about to have something.'

'Will you be home for dinner?'

'I may be.'

The brasserie had its own distinctive blend of smells, among which two were dominant: the smell of Pernod around the bar, and that of coq-au-vin, which came in gusts from the kitchen.

Most of the tables in the dining-room were unoccupied, though there were one or two of his colleagues lingering over coffee and Calvados. He hesitated, then went across to the bar and ordered a sandwich. The sun was still shining brilliantly, and the sky was clear, but for a few white clouds scudding across it. A sudden breeze had blown up, scattering the dust in the streets, and moulding the women's dresses against their bodies.

The proprietor, behind the bar, knew Maigret well enough to realize that this was not the time to start a conversation. Maigret was eating absent-mindedly, staring into the street with the mesmerized look of a passenger on board ship watching the monotonous and hypnotic motion of the sea.

'The same again?'

He said yes, probably not knowing what he had been eating, ate his second sandwich, and drank the coffee which was put in front of him before he had even ordered it.

A few minutes later, he was in a taxi, heading for the Quai de Valmy. He stopped it at the corner of the Rue des Récollets, opposite the lock, where three barges were lined up, waiting to go through. In spite of the filthy water whose surface was broken from time to time by unsavoury-looking bubbles, there were a few anglers, tinkering with their floats as usual.

As he walked past *Chez Popaul*, with its yellow façade, the proprietor recognized him, and Maigret could see him, through the window, pointing him out to the people at the bar. All along the road, huge long-distance lorries were parked, bearing the name 'Roulers and Langlois'.

On his way, Maigret passed two or three little shops, of the sort to be found in all densely populated, residential districts of Paris. In front of one a trestle, piled high with fruit and vegetables, took up half the pavement. A few doors further on, there was a butcher's shop which seemed to be empty, then, almost next door to *Chez Calas*, a grocer's shop, so dark that it was impossible to see into it.

Madame Calas must have had to go out sometimes, if only to do her shopping. These presumably were the shops she went to, wearing her slippers no doubt, and wrapped in the coarse, black, woollen shawl that he had noticed lying about in the café.

Judel must have interviewed the shopkeepers. The local police, being known to them, inspired more confidence than the men from the Quai des Orfèvres.

The door of the bistro was locked. He peered through the glass, but could see no one in the bar. Through the open kitchen door, however, he could see the flickering shadow of someone moving about out of sight. He rapped his knuckles on the glass, but had to knock several times more before Moers appeared, and seeing him there, ran to unlock the door.

'I'm sorry. We were making rather a lot of noise. Have you been waiting long?'

'It doesn't matter.'

It was he who remembered to lock the door again.

'Have you had many interruptions?'

'Most people try the door and then go away, but some are more persistent. They bang on the door, and go through a whole pantomime to be let in.'

Maigret looked round the room, then went behind the bar to see if he could find a blotting pad, like the one advertising an apéritif that he had seen on the table in the bedroom. There were usually several of these blotters dotted about in cafés, and it struck him as odd that here there was not even one, though the place was well supplied with other amenities, including three games of dominoes, four or five bridge cloths, and half-a-dozen packs of cards.

'You carry on,' he said to Moers. 'I'll be back shortly.'

He threaded his way through the cameras set up in the kitchen, and went upstairs, returning with the bottle of ink and the blotting-pad.

He sat down at a table in the café, and wrote in block capitals: 'CLOSED UNTIL FURTHER NOTICE.'

He paused after the first word, thinking perhaps of Coméliau closeted at this very minute with Madame Calas.

'Are there any drawing pins anywhere?'

Moers answered from the kitchen:

'On the left-hand side of the shelf under the counter.'

He found them, and went out to pin his notice above the door. Coming back, he felt something brush against his leg, something alive, and looked down to see the ginger cat gazing up at him and mewing.

That was something he had overlooked. If the place was going to be left unoccupied for any length of time, something would have to be done about the cat.

He went into the kitchen, and found some milk in an earthenware jug, and a cracked soup plate.

'Who can I get to look after the cat?'

'Wouldn't a neighbour take it? I noticed a butcher's shop on my way here.'

'I'll see about it later. Anything interesting, so far?'

They were going through the place with a fine tooth-comb, sifting through the contents of every drawer, searching every corner. First, Moers, examining things under a magnifying glass, or, when necessary, his portable microscope, then the photographers, recording everything on film.

'We began with the courtyard, because, with all the junk there is out there, it seemed the most likely place to choose if one had something to hide.'

'I take it the dustbins have been emptied since Sunday?'

'On Monday morning. All the same, we examined them thoroughly, especially for traces of blood.'

'Nothing?'

'Nothing,' repeated Moers, after a moment's hesitation.

Which meant that he thought he might be on to something, but was not sure.

'What is it?'

'I don't know, sir. It's just an impression that all four of us had. We were discussing it when you arrived.'

'Go on.'

'Well, there's something peculiar about the set up, at least as far as the courtyard and the kitchen are concerned. This isn't the sort of place you'd expect to find spotlessly clean. You only have to open a few drawers to see that everything is stuffed in anyhow, and most of the things are thick with dust.'

Maigret looked about him. He saw what Moers meant, and his eyes brightened with interest.

'Go on.'

'There was a three days' pile of dirty dishes on the draining-board, and several saucepans. There's been no washing up done since Sunday. An indication of slovenly habits, you might think. Unless it's just that the woman lets things slide when her husband's away.'

Moers was right. She wouldn't bother to keep the place tidy, or even particularly clean.

'In other words, one would expect to find dirt everywhere, dirt accumulated over a period of a week or ten days. In fact, in some drawers and inaccessible corners, we did find dirt that had been there even longer. In general, however, there was evidence that the place had been recently and extensively scrubbed, and Sambois found a couple of bottles of bleach in the courtyard, one of them empty and, judging from the condition of the label, recently bought.'

'When would you say this spring-cleaning had been done?'

'Three or four days ago. I can't be more definite until I've made one or two tests in the lab, but I should know for certain by the time I come to write my report.'

'Any finger-prints?'

'They bear out our theory. Calas's prints are all over the drawers and cupboard, only on the inside, though.'

'Are you sure?'

'Well, at any rate, they are the same as those of the body in the canal.'

Here, at last, was proof that the dismembered corpse was that of the proprietor of the bistro in the Quai de Valmy.

'What about upstairs?'

'Nothing on the surface, only inside the wardrobe door and so on. Dubois and I have only been up there to look round. We'll make a thorough job of it later. What struck us was that there wasn't a speck of dust on any of the furniture, and that the floor had been thoroughly scrubbed. As for the bed, the sheets were changed recently, probably three of four days ago.'

'Were there dirty sheets in a laundry basket, or anywhere else?'

'I thought of that. No.'

'Was the washing done at home?'

'I couldn't see any evidence of it. No washing machine or copper.'

'So they must have used a laundry?'

'I'm almost sure of it. So unless the van called yesterday or the day before ...'

'I'd better try and find out the name of the laundry. The neighbours will probably know.'

But before the words were out of Maigret's mouth, Moers had gone over to the dresser and opened one of the drawers.

'Here you are.'

He handed Maigret a bundle of bills, some of which bore the heading: 'Récollets Laundry'. The most recent was ten days old.

Maigret went into the telephone box, dialled the number of the laundry, and asked whether any washing had been collected from the bistro that week.

'We don't call at the Quai de Valmy until Thursday morning,' he was told.

So the last collection of laundry had been on the previous Thursday.

No wonder it had struck Moers as odd. Two people do not live in a house for almost a week without soiling some household linen. Where was it then, and in particular where were the dirty sheets? The ones on the bed had certainly not been there since Thursday.

He was looking thoughtful when he went back to join the others.

'What was it you were saying about the prints?'

'So far, in the kitchen, we have found prints belonging to three people, excluding yourself and Lapointe, whose prints I know by heart. The prints most in evidence are a woman's. I presume they're Madame Calas's.'

'That can easily be checked.'

'Then there are the prints of a man, a young man I should guess. There aren't many of them, and they are the most recent.'

Antoine, presumably, for whom Madame Calas must have got a meal in the kitchen, when he turned up in the middle of the night.

'Finally, there are two prints, half obliterated. Another man's.'

'Any more of Calas's prints inside the drawers?'

'Yes.'

'In other words, it looks as though very recently, on Sunday possibly, someone cleaned the place from top to bottom, but didn't bother with turning out drawers and cupboards?'

They were all thinking of the dismembered corpse, which had been recovered piecemeal from the canal.

The operation could not have been undertaken in the street or on open ground. It must have taken time, and each part had been carefully wrapped in newspaper, and tied with string.

What would any room look like, after being used for such a purpose?

Maigret's remorse at having delivered Madame Calas into the merciless clutches of Judge Coméliau was beginning to subside.

'Have you been down to the cellar?'

'We've been everywhere, just to get our bearings. At a glance, everything looked quite normal down there, but there again, we'll be going over it thoroughly later.'

He left them to get on with their work, and spent some time in the café roaming about, with the ginger cat following him like a shadow. The bottles on the shelf reflected the sun, and there were warm pools of light on the corner of the bar counter. He remembered the great stove in the middle of the room, and wondered whether it had gone out. He looked inside, and saw that there were still a few glowing embers. Mechanically, he stoked it up.

Next, he went behind the counter, studied the bottles, hesitated, and then poured himself a glass of Calvados. The drawer of the till was open. It was empty except for a couple of notes and some small change. The list of drinks and prices was posted near the window to his right.

He consulted it, took some loose change out of his pocket, and dropped the money for the Calvados into the till. Just then he caught sight of a figure beyond the glass door, and gave a guilty start. It was Inspector Judel peering in.

Maigret went to unlock the door.

'I thought you'd probably be here, sir. I rang Headquarters, but they didn't seem to know where you'd gone.'

Judel looked round, and seemed surprised at the absence of Madame Calas.

'Is it true, then, that you have arrested her?'

'She's with Judge Coméliau.'

Judel caught sight of the technicians at work in the kitchen, and jerked his chin in their direction.

'Have they found anything?'

'It's too early to say.'

And it would take too long to explain. Maigret could not face it.

'I'm glad I found you here, because I didn't want to take action without your authority. I think we've found the man with red hair.'

'Where?'

'If my information is correct, practically next door. Unless, that is, he's on night shift this week. He's a storeman with Zenith Transport, the firm . . .'

'Rue des Récollets. I know. Roulers and Langlois.'

'I thought you would wish to interview him yourself.'

Moers called from the kitchen:

'Can you spare a minute, sir?'

Maigret went over to the door at the back of the café. Madame Calas's black shawl was spread out on the kitchen table, and Moers, having already examined it through his magnifying glass, was focusing his microscope.

'Take a look at this.'

'What is it I'm supposed to see?'

'You see the black wool fibres, and those brownish threads like twigs, interwined with them? Well in fact, those are strands of hemp. It will have to be confirmed by analysis, of course, but I'm quite sure in my own mind. They're almost invisible to the naked eye, and they must have rubbed off on to the shawl from a ball of string.'

'The same string that . . . ?'

Maigret was thinking of the string used to parcel up the remains of the dismembered man.

'I could almost swear to it. I don't imagine Madame Calas very often had occasion to tie up a parcel. There are several kinds of string in one of the drawers, thin white string, red string and twine, but not a scrap of string anything like this.'

'I'm much obliged to you. I take it you'll still be here when I get back?'

'What are you going to do about the cat?'

'I'll take it with me.'

Maigret picked up the cat, which did not seem to mind, and carried it outside. He considered entrusting it to the grocer, but decided that it would probably be better off with the butcher.

'Isn't that Madame Calas's cat?' asked the woman behind the counter, when he went in with it.

'Yes. I wonder if you'd mind looking after it for a few days?'

'So long as it doesn't fight with my own cats.'

'Is Madame Calas a customer of yours?'

'She comes in every morning. Is it really her husband who . . . ?'

When it came to putting such a grisly question into words, she baulked, and could only look towards the canal.

'It looks like it.'

'What's to become of her?'

And before Maigret could fob her off with an evasive answer, she went on:

'Not everyone would agree with me, I know, and there are plenty of grounds for fault-finding, but I think she's a poor, unhappy creature, and, whatever she's done, she was driven to it.'

A few minutes later, Maigret and Judel were in the Rue des Récollets, waiting for a break in the stream of lorries leaving the depot, to cross over safely to the forecourt of Roulers and Langlois. They went to the glass box on the right, on which the word 'Office' was inscribed in block letters. All round the forecourt were raised platforms, like those in a railway goods yard, piled high with boxes, sacks and crates, which were being loaded on to the lorries. People were charging about, heavy packages were being roughly manhandled. The noise was deafening.

Maigret had his hand on the door knob when he heard Judel's voice behind him:

'Sir!'

The Superintendent turned round to see a red-haired man standing on one of the platforms, with a narrow log-book in one hand and a pencil in the other. He was staring intently at them. He was broad-shouldered, of medium height, and wearing a grey overall. He was fair-skinned with a high colour, and his face, pitted with small-pox scars, had the texture of orange-rind. Porters loaded with freight were filing past him, each in turn calling out a name and number, followed by the name of a town or village, but he did not seem to hear them. His blues eyes were fixed upon Maigret.

'See that he doesn't give us the slip,' said Maigret to Judel.

He went into the office, where the girl at the enquiry desk asked him what she could do for him.

'I'd like to speak to someone in authority.'

There was no need for her to reply. A man with close-cropped, grey hair came forward to find out what he wanted.

'Are you the manager?'

'Joseph Langlois. Haven't I seen you somewhere before?'

No doubt he had seen Maigret's photograph in the papers. The Chief Superintendent introduced himself, and Langlois waited in un-easy silence for him to explain his business.

'Who is that red-haired chap over there?'

'What do you want him for?'

'I don't know yet. Who is he?'

'Dieudonné Pape. He's been with us for over twenty-five years. It would surprise me very much if you'd got anything against him.'

'Is he married?'

'He's been a widower for years. In fact, I believe his wife died only two or three years after their marriage.'

'Does he live alone?'

'I suppose so. His private life is no concern of mine.'

'Have you his address?'

'He lives in the Rue des Ecluses-Saint-Martin, very near here. Do you remember the number, Mademoiselle Berthe?'

'Fifty-six.'

'Is he here all day, every day?'

'He puts in his eight hours, like everyone else, but not always in the day time. We run a twenty-four-hour service here, and there are lorries loading and unloading all through the night. This means working on a three-shift system, and the rota is changed every week.'

'What shift was he on last week?'

Langlois turned to the girl whom he had addressed as Mademoiselle Berthe.

'Look it up, will you?'

She consulted a ledger.

'The early shift.'

The boss interpreted:

'That means, he came on at six in the morning and was relieved at two in the afternoon.'

'Is the depot open on Sundays as well?'

'Only with a skeleton staff. Two or three men.'

'Was he on duty last Sunday?'

The girl once more consulted her ledger.

'No.'

'What time does he come off duty today?'

'He's on the second shift, so he'll be off at ten tonight.'

'Could you arrange to have him relieved?'

'Can't you tell me what all this is about?'

'I'm afraid that's impossible.'

'Is it serious?'

'It may be very serious.'

'What is he supposed to have done?'

'I can't answer that.'

'Whatever you may think, I can tell you here and now that you're barking up the wrong tree. If all my staff were like him, I shouldn't have anything to worry about.'

He was far from happy. Without telling Maigret where he was going or inviting him to follow, he strode out of the glass-walled office and, skirting the lorries in the forecourt, went over to Dieudonné Pape.

The man stood motionless and expressionless, listening to what his boss had to say, but his eyes never left the glass box opposite. Langlois went to the storage shed, and seemed to be calling to someone inside, and indeed, within seconds, a little old man appeared, wearing an overall like Pape, with a pencil behind his ear. They exchanged a few words, and then the newcomer took the narrow log-book from the red-haired man, who followed the boss round the edge of the forecourt.

Maigret had not moved. The two men came in, and Langlois loudly announced:

'This is a Chief Superintendent from Police Headquarters. He wants a word with you. He thinks you may be able to help him.'

'I have one or two questions to ask you, Monsieur Pape. If you'll be good enough to come with me.'

Dieudonné Pape pointed to his overall.

'Do you mind if I change?'

'I'll come with you.'

Langlois did not see the Superintendent out. Maigret followed the storeman into a sort of corridor that served as a cloakroom. Pape asked no questions. He was in his fifties, and seemed a quiet, reliable sort of man. He put on his hat and coat, and, flanked on the right by Judel and on the left by Maigret, walked to the street.

He seemed surprised that there was no car waiting for them outside, as though he had expected to be taken straight to the Quai des Orfèvres. When, on the corner opposite the yellow façade of *Chez Popaul*, they turned not right towards the town centre, but left, he seemed about to speak, but then apparently thought better of it, and said nothing.

Judel realized that Maigret was making for the Calas bistro. The door was still locked. Maigret rapped on the glass. Moers came to let them in.

'In here, Pape.'

Maigret turned the key.

'You know this place pretty well, don't you?'

The man looked bewildered. If he had been expecting a visit from the police, he had certainly not expected this.

'You may take off your coat. We've kept the fire going. Take a seat, in your usual place if you like. I suppose you have your own favourite chair?'

'I don't understand.'

'You're a regular visitor here, aren't you?'

'I'm a customer, yes.'

Seeing Moers and his men in the kitchen with their cameras, he peered, trying to make out what was going on. He must have been wondering what had happened to Madame Calas.

'A very good customer?'

'A good customer.'

'Were you here on Sunday?'

He had an honest face, with a look in his blue eyes that was both gentle and timid. Maigret was reminded of the way some animals look when a human being speaks sharply to them.

'Sit down.'

He did so, cowering, because he had been ordered to do so.

'I was asking you about Sunday.'

He hesitated before answering: 'I wasn't here.'

'Were you at home all day?'

'I went to see my sister.'

'Does she live in Paris?'

'Nogent-sur-Marne.'

'Is she on the telephone?'

'Nogent three-one-seven. She's married to a builder.'

'Did you see anyone other than your sister?'

'Her husband and children. Then, at about five, the neighbours came in for a game of cards, as usual.'

Maigret made a sign to Judel, who nodded and went to the telephone.

'What time was it when you left Nogent?'

'I caught the eight o'clock bus.'

'You didn't call in here before going home?'

'No.'

'When did you last see Madame Calas?'

'On Saturday.'

'What shift were you on last week?'

'The early shift.'

'So it was after two when you got here?'

'Yes.'

'Was Calas at home?

Again, he hesitated.

'Not when I came in.'

'But he was, later?'

'I don't remember.'

'Did you stay long in the café?'

'Quite a time.'

'How long would that be?'

'Two hours, at least. I can't say exactly.'

'What did you do?'

'I had a glass of wine, and we talked for a bit.'

'You and the other customers?'

'No, I talked mostly to Aline.'

He flushed as he spoke her name, and hurriedly explained:

'I look upon her as a friend. I've known her for a long time.'

'How long?'

'More than ten years.'

'So, you've been coming here every day for ten years?'

'Almost every day.'

'Preferably, when her husband was out?'

This time he did not reply. He hung his head, troubled.

'Are you her lover?'

'Who told you that?'

'Never mind. Are you?'

Instead of replying, he asked anxiously:

'What have you done with her?'

And Maigret told him outright:

'She's with the examining magistrate at the moment.'

'Why?'

'To answer a few questions about her husband's disappearance. Don't you read the papers?'

As Dieudonné Pape sat motionless, lost in thought, Maigret called out:

'Moers! Take his prints, will you?'

The man submitted quietly, appearing more anxious than frightened, and his fingertips, pressed down on to the paper, were steady.

'See if they match.'

'Which ones?'

'The two in the kitchen. The ones you said were partly rubbed out.'

As Moers went out, Dieudonné Pape, gently reproachful, said:

'If all you wanted to know was whether I had been in the kitchen, you only had to ask me. I often go in there.'

'Were you there last Saturday?'

'I made myself a cup of coffee.'

'What do you know about the disappearance of Omer Calas?'

He was still looking very thoughtful, as though he were hesitating on the brink of some momentous decision.

'Didn't you know he'd been murdered, and his dismembered corpse thrown into the canal?'

It was strangely moving. Neither Judel nor Maigret had been prepared for it. Slowly, the man turned towards the Superintendent, and gave him a long, searching look. At last he said, gently reproachful still:

'I have nothing to say.'

Maigret, looking as serious as the man he was questioning, pressed him:

'Did you kill Calas?'

And Dieudonné Pape, shaking his head, repeated:

'I have nothing to say.'

CHAPTER SEVEN

The Cat

Maigret was finishing his meal, when he became aware of the way his wife was looking at him, with a smile that was maternal and yet, at the same time, a little teasing. At first, pretending not to notice, he bent over his plate, and ate a few more spoonfuls of his custard. But he could not help looking up in the end:

'Have I got a smut on the end of my nose?' he asked grumpily.

'No.'

'Then why are you laughing at me?'

'I'm not laughing. I'm smiling.'

'You're making fun of me. What's so comical about me?'

'There's nothing comical about you, Jules.'

She seldom called him 'Jules'; only when she was feeling protective towards him.

'What is it, then?'

'Do you realize that, during the whole of dinner, you haven't said a single word?'

No, he had not realized it.

'Have you any idea what you've been eating?'

Assuming a fierce expression, he said:

'Sheep's kidneys.'

'And before that?'

'Soup.'

'What kind of soup?'

'I don't know. Vegetable soup, I suppose.'

'Is it because of that woman you've got yourself into such a state?'

Most of the time, and this was a case in point, Madame Maigret knew no more about her husband's work than she read in the newspapers.

'What is it? Don't you believe she killed him?'

He shrugged, as though he was carrying a burden and wished he could shake it off.

'I just don't know.'

'Or that Dieudonné Pape did it with her as his accomplice?'

He was tempted to reply that it was of no consequence. Indeed, as he saw it, this was not the point. What mattered to him was understanding what lay behind the crime. As it was, not only was this not yet clear to him, but the more he knew of the people involved, the more he felt himself to be floundering.

He had come home to dinner instead of staying in his office to work on the case, for the very reason that he needed to get away from it, to return to the jog-trot of everyday life, from which he had hoped to go back with sharpened perceptions to the protagonists in the Quai de Valmy drama. Instead, as his wife had teasingly pointed out, he had sat through dinner without opening his mouth, and continued to think of nothing but Madame Calas and Pape, with the boy, Antoine, thrown in for good measure.

It was unusual for him to feel at this stage that he was still a long way from a solution. But then, in this case, the problems were not amenable to police methods.

Murders in general can be classified under a few broad headings, three or four at most.

The apprehension of a professional murderer is only a matter of routine. When a Corsican gangster strikes down a gangster from Marseilles in a bar in the Rue de Douai, the police have recourse to standard procedures, almost as though tackling a problem in mathematics.

When a couple of misguided youths commit robbery with violence, injuring or killing an old woman in a tobacconist's shop, or a bank clerk, it may be necessary to pursue the assailants through the streets, and here too there is a standard procedure.

As to the *crime passionnel*, nothing could be more straightforward. With murder for financial gain, through inheritance, life assurance or some devious means, the police know themselves to be on solid ground as soon as they have discovered the motive.

Judge Coméliau, for the present, was inclined to the view that financial gain was the motive in the Calas case, perhaps because he was incapable of accepting the idea that anyone outside his own social sphere, especially people from a neighbourhood like the Quai de Valmy, could have any but the crudest motives.

Given that Dieudonné Pape was the lover of Madame Calas, Dieudonné Pape and Madame Calas must have got rid of the husband, partly because he was an encumbrance, and partly to get hold of his money.

'They have been lovers for ten years or more,' Maigret had objected. 'Why should they have waited all that time?'

The magistrate had brushed this aside. Maybe Calas had recently come into possession of a substantial sum of money. Maybe the lovers had been waiting for a convenient opportunity. Maybe there had been a row between Madame Calas and her husband, and she felt she had put up with enough. Maybe...

'And suppose we find that, except for the bistro, which isn't worth much, Calas had nothing?'

'The bistro is something. Dieudonné may have got fed up with his job with Zenith Transport, and decided that he would prefer to end his days dozing in front of the fire in his carpet slippers in a cosy little café of his own.'

Here, Maigret had to concede, was a possibility, even though remote.

'And what about Antoine Cristin?'

The fact was that the judge was now lumbered not with one suspect but two. Cristin too was Madame Calas's lover, and if anyone was likely to be short of money, it was he rather than Pape.

'The other two were just making use of him. You'll find that he was their accomplice, mark my words.'

This, then, was the official view—or at least the view prevailing in one examining magistrate's office—of the Quai de Valmy affair. Meanwhile, until the real facts were brought to light, all three of them were being kept under lock and key.

Maigret was the more disgruntled in that he reproached himself for not having stood up to Coméliau. Owing to indolence perhaps, or cowardice, he had given in without a struggle.

At the outset of his career, he had been warned by his superiors always to be sure of his ground before putting a suspect through a rigorous cross-examination, and experience had confirmed the wisdom of this advice. A properly conducted cross-examination did not consist in drawing a bow at a venture, or hurling accusations at a suspect for hours on end, in the hope that he would break down and confess.

Even a half-wit has a kind of sixth sense, which enables him to recognize at once whether the police are making accusations at random or have solid grounds for suspicion.

Maigret always preferred to bide his time. On occasion, in cases of real difficulty, he had even been willing to take a risk rather than arrest a suspect prematurely.

And he had been proved right every time.

'Contrary to popular belief,' he was fond of saying, 'being arrested can be something of a relief to a suspected person, because, from then on, he does at least know where he stands. He no longer has to ask himself: "Am I under suspicion? Am I being followed? Am I being watched? Is this a trap?" He has been charged. He can now speak in his own defence. And, henceforth, he will be under the protection of the law. As a prisoner, he has his rights, hallowed rights, and nothing will be done to him which is not strictly in accordance with the rules.'

Aline Calas was a case in point. From the moment she had crossed the magistrate's threshold, her lips had, as it were, been sealed. Coméliau had got no more out of her than if she had been the gravel in the hold of the Naud brothers' barge.

'I have nothing to say,' was all she would utter, in her flat, expressionless voice.

And, when he persisted in bombarding her with questions, she retorted:

'You have no right to question me, except in the presence of a lawyer.'

'In that case, kindly tell me the name of your lawyer.'

'I have no lawyer.'

'Here is the membership list of the Paris Bar. You may take your choice.'

'I don't know any of them.'

'Choose a name at random.'

'I have no money.'

There was therefore no choice but for the Court to nominate counsel for her, and that was a slow and cumbersome process.

Late that afternoon, Coméliau had sent for Antoine who, having held out against hours of questioning by Lapointe, saw no reason to be more forthcoming with the magistrate.

'I did not kill Monsieur Calas. I didn't go to the Quai de Valmy on Sunday afternoon. I never handed in a suitcase at the left luggage office of the Gare de l'Est. Either the clerk is lying or he's mistaken.'

All this time, his mother, red-eyed, clutching a crumpled handkerchief, sat waiting in the lobby at Police Headquarters. Lapointe had tried to reason with her, and, after him, Lucas. It was no good. She was determined to wait, she repeated over and over again, until she had seen Chief Superintendent Maigret.

She was a simple soul, who believed, like many of her kind, that it was no good talking to underlings. She must, at all costs, see the man at the top.

The Chief Superintendent could not have seen her then, even if he had wanted to. He was just leaving the bar in the Quai de Valmy, accompanied by Judel and Dieudonné Pape.

'Don't forget to lock up, and bring the key to Headquarters,' he said to Moers.

The three men crossed by the footbridge to the Quai de Jemmapes, only a few yards from the Rue des Ecluses-Saint-Martin, behind the Hospital of Saint-Louis. It was a quiet neighbourhood, more provincial than Parisian in character. Pape was not handcuffed. Maigret judged that he was not the man to make a run for it. His bearing was calm and dignified, not unlike that of Madame Calas herself. He looked sad rather than shocked, and seemed withdrawn, or was it resigned?

He said very little. He had probably never been a talkative man. He answered, when spoken to, as briefly as possible. Sometimes he did not answer at all, but just looked at the Chief Superintendent out of his lavender-blue eyes.

He lived in an old five-storey building, which had an appearance of respectability and modest comfort.

As they passed the lodge, the concierge got up and peered at them through the glass. They did not stop, however, but went up to the second floor. Pape went to a door on the left, and opened it with his key.

There were three rooms in the flat, bedroom, dining-room and kitchen. There was also a large store-cupboard converted into a bathroom. It surprised Maigret to see that there was a proper fitted bath. The furniture, though not new, was less old-fashioned than that of the house in the Quai de Valmy, and everything was spotlessly clean.

'Do you have a daily woman?' Maigret asked in surprise.

'No.'

'You mean you do your own housework?'

Dieudonné Pape could not help smiling with gratification. He was proud of his home.

'Doesn't the concierge ever give you a hand?'

There was a meat-safe, fairly well stocked with provisions, on the kitchen window-sill.

'Do you do your own cooking as well?'

'Always.'

Above the sideboard in the dining-room hung a large gilt-framed photograph of Madame Calas, so much like those commonly to be seen in the houses of respectable families of modest means that it lent an air of cosy domesticity to the room.

Recalling that not a single photograph had been found at the Calas's, Maigret asked:

'How did you come by it?'

'I took it myself, and had the enlargement made somewhere in the Boulevard Saint-Martin.'

His camera was in the sideboard drawer. On a small table in a corner of the bathroom, there were a number of glass dishes and bowls and several bottles of developing fluid.

'Do you do much photography?'

'Yes. Landscapes and buildings, mostly.'

It was true. Going through the drawers, Maigret found a large number of views of Paris, and a few landscapes. There were a great many of the canal and the Seine. Judging from the striking effects of light and shade in most of the photographs, it must have cost Dieudonné Pape a great deal in time and patience to get the shots he wanted.

'What suit were you wearing when you went to your sister's?'

'The dark blue.'

He had three suits, including the one he was wearing.

'We shall need those,' Maigret said to Judel, 'and the shoes.'

Then, coming upon some soiled underclothes in a wicker basket, he added them to the rest.

He had noticed a canary hopping about in a cage, but it was not until they were leaving the flat that it occurred to him that it would need looking after.

'Can you think of anyone who might be willing to take care of it?'

'The concierge would be only too pleased, I'm sure.'

Maigret fetched the cage, and took it to the lodge. The concierge came to the door before he had time to knock.

'You're surely not taking him away!' she exclaimed in a fury.

She meant her tenant, not the canary. She recognized Judel, who was a local man. Possibly she recognized Maigret, too. She had read the newspapers.

'How dare you treat him like a criminal! He's a good man. You couldn't hope to find a better.'

She was a tiny little thing, of gipsy complexion and sluttish appearance. Her voice was shrill, and she was so enraged that it would not have surprised him if she had sprung at him and tried to scratch his eyes out.

'Would you be willing to look after the canary for a short time?'

She literally snatched the cage out of his hand.

'Just you wait and see what the tenants and all the other people round here will have to say about this! And for a start, Monsieur Dieudonné, we'll all be coming to see you in prison.'

Elderly working-class women quite often hero-worship bachelors and widowers of Dieudonné Pape's type, whose well-ordered way of life they greatly admire. The concierge followed the three men on to the pavement, and stood there sobbing, and waving to Pape.

Maigret turned to Judel:

'Give the clothes and the shoes to Moers. He'll know what to do. And I want the bistro kept under supervision.'

In giving instructions that a watch should be kept on the bistro, he had nothing particular in mind. It was just to cover himself if anything were to go wrong. Dieudonné Pape waited obediently on the edge of the pavement, and then fell into step with Maigret, as they walked alongside the canal in search of a taxi.

He was silent in the taxi, and Maigret decided not to question him further. He filled his pipe, and held it out to Pape.

'Do you smoke a pipe?'

'No.'

'Cigarette?'

'I don't smoke.'

Maigret did, after all, ask Pape a question, but it had, on the face of it, nothing to do with the death of Calas.

'Don't you drink either?'

'No.'

Here was another anomaly. Maigret could not make it out. Madame Calas was an alcoholic. She had been drinking for years, presumably even longer than she had known Pape.

As a rule, a compulsive drinker cannot endure the companionship of a teetotaller.

The Chief Superintendent had encountered couples very like Madame Calas and Dieudonné Pape before. In every case, as far as he could remember, both the man and the woman drank.

He had been brooding abstractedly over this at dinner, unaware that his wife was watching him. And that was not all, by any means. Among other things, there was Antoine's mother, whom he found waiting in the lobby at the Quai des Orfèvres. Handing Pape over to Lucas, he had taken her into his office.

He had not forgotten to instruct Lucas to let Coméliau know that Pape had been brought in:

'If he wants to see him, take him there. Otherwise, take him to the cells.'

Pape, poker-faced, had gone with Lucas into an office, while Maigret led the woman away.

'I swear to you, Superintendent, that my son would never do a thing like that. He couldn't hurt a fly. He makes himself out to be a tough guy because it's the done thing at his age. But I know him, you see. He's just a child.'

'I'm sure you're right, madame.'

'In that case, why don't you let him go? I'll keep him indoors from now on, and there won't be any more women, I promise you. That woman is almost as old as I am! She ought to know better than to take up with a lad young enough to be her son. It's shameful! I've known for some time that there was something going on. When I saw he was buying hair-cream, brushing his teeth twice a day, and even using scent, I said to myself . . .'

'Is he your only child?'

'Yes. And I've always taken extra care of him, on account of his father having died of consumption. I did everything I could for him, Superintendent. If only I could see him! If only I could talk to him! Surely, they won't try to stop me? They wouldn't keep a mother from her son, would they?'

There was nothing he could do but pass her on to Coméliau. He knew it was cowardly, but he really had no choice. Presumably she had been kept waiting all over again, up there in the corridor, on a bench. Maigret did not know whether or not the judge had finally granted her an interview.

Moers had got back to the Quai des Orfèvres just before six, and handed Maigret the key of the house in the Quai de Valmy. It was a heavy, old-fashioned key. Maigret put it in his pocket with the key to Pape's flat.

'Did Judel give you the clothes and the shoes?'

'Yes, I've got them in the lab. It's blood we're looking for, I suppose?'

'Mainly, yes. I may want you to look over his flat tomorrow morning.'

'I'll be working here late tonight, after I've had a bite to eat. It's urgent, I imagine?'

It was always urgent. The longer a case dragged on, the colder the scent, and the more time for the criminal to cover his tracks.

'Will you be in tonight?'

'I don't know. In any case, you'd better leave a note on my desk on your way out.'

He got up from the table, filling his pipe, and looked uncertainly at his armchair. Seeing him so restless, Madame Maigret ventured:

'Why not give yourself a rest for one night? Put the case out of your mind. Read a book, or, if you'd rather, take me to the pictures. You'll feel much fresher in the morning.'

With a quizzical look, he said:

'Do you want to see a film?'

'There's quite a good programme at the Moderne.'

She poured his coffee. He could not make up his mind. He felt like taking a coin out of his pocket and tossing for it.

Madame Maigret was careful not to pursue the subject, but sat with him while he slowly sipped his coffee. He paced up and down the dining-room, taking long strides, only pausing from time to time to straighten the carpet.

'No!' he said at last, with finality.

'Will you be going out?'

'Yes.'

He poured himself a small glass of sloe-gin. When he had drunk it, he went to get his overcoat.

'Will you be late home?'

'I'm not sure. Probably not.'

Perhaps because he had a feeling that he was about to take a momentous step, he did not take a taxi or ring the Quai des Orfèvres to order a police car. He walked to the underground station, and boarded a train for Château-Landon. He felt again the disturbing night-time atmosphere of the place, with ghostly figures lurking in the shadows, women loitering on the pavements, and the bluish-green lighting in the bars making them look like fish-tanks in an aquarium.

A man standing a few yards from the door of *Chez Calas* saw Maigret stop, came straight up to him, and shone a torch in his face.

'Oh! Sorry, sir. I didn't recognize you in the dark.'

It was one of Judel's constables.

'Anything to report?'

'Nothing. Or rather there is one thing. I don't know if it's of any significance. About an hour ago, a taxi drove past. It slowed down about fifty yards from here and went by at a crawl, but it didn't stop.'

'Could you see who was in it?'

'A woman. I could see her quite clearly under the gas-lamp. She was young, wearing a grey coat and no hat. Further down, the taxi gathered speed and turned left into the Rue Louis-Blanc.'

Was it Madame Calas's daughter, Lucette, come to see whether her mother had been released? She must know, from the newspaper reports, that she had been taken to the Quai des Orfèvres, but no further details had been released.

'Do you think she saw you?'

'Very likely. Judel didn't tell me to stay out of sight. Most of the time, I've been walking up and down to keep warm.'

Another possible explanation was that Lucette Calas had intended going into the house, but changed her mind when she saw that it was being watched. If that were the case, what was she after?

He shrugged, took the key out of his pocket, and fitted it into the lock. He had some difficulty in finding the light switch, which he had not had occasion to use until now. A single light came on. The switch for the light at the far end of the room was behind the bar.

Moers and his assistants had put everything back in its proper place before leaving, so that there was no change in the little café, except that it felt colder, because the fire had been allowed to go out.

On his way to the kitchen, Maigret was startled to see something move. He had not heard a sound, and it took him seconds to realize that it was the cat, which he had left with the butcher earlier in the day.

The creature was rubbing its back against his legs now, and Maigret, bending down to stroke it, growled:

'How did you get in?'

It worried him. The back door, leading from the kitchen to the courtyard, was bolted, and the window was closed too. He went upstairs, turned on the light, and found that a window had been left open. There was a lean-to shed, with a corrugated iron roof, in the back yard of the house next door. The cat must have climbed on to it, and taken a flying leap over a gap of more than six feet.

Maigret went back down the stairs. Finding that there was a drop of milk left in the earthenware jug, he poured it out for the cat.

'What now?' he said aloud, as though he were addressing the animal.

They certainly made an odd pair, alone in the empty house.

He had never realized how deserted, even desolate, a bar could look with no one behind the counter and not a customer in sight. Yet this was how the place must have looked every night after everyone had gone, and Monsieur and Madame Calas had put up the shutters and locked the door.

There would be just the two of them, man and wife, with nothing left to do but put out the lights and go upstairs to bed. Madame Calas, after all those nips of brandy, would be in her usual state of vacant torpor.

Did she have to conceal her drinking from her husband? Or did he take an indulgent view of his wife's addiction to the bottle, seeking his own pleasures elsewhere in the afternoons?

Maigret suddenly realized that there was one character in the drama about whom almost nothing was known, the dead man himself. From the outset, he had been to all of them merely a dismembered corpse. It was an odd fact that the Chief Superintendent had often noticed before, that people did not respond in the same way to parts of a body found scattered about as to a whole corpse. They did not feel pity in the same degree, or even revulsion. It was as though the dead person were somehow de-humanized, almost an object of ridicule.

He had never seen Calas's face, even in a photograph, and the head had still not been found, and probably never would be.

The man was of peasant stock, short and squat in build. Every year he went to the vineyards near Poitiers to buy his wine. He wore good suits, and played billiards in the afternoon, somewhere near the Gare de l'Est.

Other than Madame Calas, was there a woman in his life, or more than one perhaps? Could he possibly have been unaware of what went on when he was away from home?

He had accidentally encountered Pape, and, unless he were crassly insensitive, he must have seen how things stood between Pape and his wife.

The impression they created was not so much of a pair of lovers as of an old married couple, united in a deep and restful contentment, born of mutual understanding, tolerance, and that special tenderness which, in the middle-aged, is often a sign that much has been forgiven and forgotten.

Had he known all this, and accepted it philosophically? Had he turned a blind eye or, alternatively, had there been scenes between him and his wife?

And what about the others who, like Antoine, were in the habit of slinking in to take advantage of Aline Calas's weakness? Had he known about them too, and if so, how had he taken it?

Maigret was back behind the bar, his hand hovering over the bottles on the shelf. In the end he took down a bottle of Calvados, reminding himself that he must leave the money for it. The cat had gone over to the stove, but instead of dozing as it usually did, was restless, bewildered to find no heat coming from it.

Maigret understood the relationship between Madame Calas and Pape. He also understood the role of Antoine and the casual callers.

What he did not understand at all was the relationship between Calas and his wife. How and why had those two ever come together, subsequently married, and lived with one another for so many years? And what about their daughter, in whom neither of them seemed to have taken the slightest interest, and who appeared to have nothing whatever in common with them?

There was nothing to enlighten him, not a single photograph or letter, none of those personal possessions which reveal so much about their owners.

He drained his glass, and grumpily poured himself another drink. Then, with the glass in his hand, he went and sat at the table where he had seen Madame Calas sitting, with that settled air which suggested that it was her usual place.

He tapped out his pipe against his shoe, refilled it and lit it. He stared at the bar counter, the glasses and bottles, and the feeling came over him that he was on the brink of a revelation. Maybe it would not answer all his questions, but it would answer some of them at least.

What kind of a home was this, after all, with its kitchen where no food was served, since the Calas's ate their meals at a table in a corner of the café, and its bedroom which was only used to sleep in?

Whichever way you looked at it, this was their real home, this bar, which was to them what the dining-room or living-room is to an ordinary family.

Was it not the case that on their arrival in Paris, or very soon after, they had settled here in the Quai de Valmy, and remained ever since?

Maigret was smiling now. He was beginning to understand Madame Calas's relationship with her husband, and more than this, to see where Dieudonné Pape came into it.

It was very vague still, and he would not have been able to put it into words. All the same, there was no denying that he had quite shaken off his earlier mood of indecision. He finished his drink, went into the call box, and dialled the number of the Central Police Station.

'Chief Superintendent Maigret speaking. Who is that? Oh! it's you, Joris. How is your new arrival getting on? Yes, I do mean the Calas woman. What's that? Oh! What are you doing about it?'

It was pitiful. Twice she had called for the guard, and each time she had begged him to get her something to drink. She was willing to pay anything, anything at all. Maigret had not foreseen the terrible suffering that this deprivation would cause her.

'No, of course not . . .'

It was not possible for him to suggest to Joris that he should give her a drink in breach of the regulations. Perhaps he himself could take her a bottle in the morning, or have her brought to his office and order something for her there?

'I'd like you to look through her papers for me. She must have been carrying an identity card. I know she comes from somewhere round about Gien, but I can't remember the name of the village.'

He was kept waiting some time .

'What's that? Boissancourt-par-Saint-André. Boissancourt with an "a"? Thanks, old man. Goodnight! Don't be too hard on her.'

He called Directory Enquiries, and gave his name.

'Would you be so kind, Mademoiselle, as to find the directory for Boissancourt-par-Saint-André—between Montargis and Gien—and read out the names of the subscribers.'

'Will you hold on?'

'Yes.'

It did not take long. The supervisor was thrilled at the prospect of collaborating with the celebrated Chief Superintendent Maigret.

'Shall I begin?'

'Yes.'

'Aillevard, Route des Chênes, occupation not stated.'

'Next.'

'Ancelin, Victor, butcher. Do you want the number?'

'No.'

'Honoré de Boissancourt, Château de Boissancourt.'

'Next.'

'Doctor Camuzet.'

'I'd better have his number.'

'Seventeen.'

'Next.'

'Calas, Robert. Cattle-dealer.'

'Number?'

'Twenty-one.'

'Calas, Julien, grocer. Number: three.'

'Any other Calas?'

'No. There's a Louchez, occupation not stated, a Piedboeuf, blacksmith, and a Simonin, corn-chandler.'

'Will you please get me the first Calas on the list. I may want the other later.'

He heard the operator talking to the intermediate exchanges, then a voice saying:

'Saint-André Exchange.'

Boissancourt-par-Saint-André 21 was slow to answer. At last, a woman's voice said:

'Who's speaking?'

'Chief Superintendent Maigret here, from Police Headquarters, Paris. Are you Madame Calas? Is your husband at home?'

He was in bed with influenza.

'Have you a relation of the name of Omer Calas?'

'Oh, him! What's happened to him? Is he in trouble?'

'Do you know him?'

'Well, I've never actually met him. I don't come from these parts. I'm from the Haute-Loire district, and he left Boissancourt before my marriage.'

'Is he related to your husband?'

'They're first cousins. His brother is still living here. Julien. He owns the grocer's shop.'

'Can you tell me anything about him?'

'About Omer? No, I don't know any more. What's more I don't want to.'

She must have hung up, because another voice was asking:

'Shall I get the other number, Superintendent?'

There was less delay this time. A man's voice answered. He was even more uncommunicative.

'I can hear you perfectly well. But what exactly do you want from me?'

'Are you the brother of Omer Calas?'

'I did have a brother called Omer.'

'Is he dead?'

'I haven't the least idea. It's more than twenty years, nearer twenty-five, since I last heard anything of him.'

'A man of the name Omer Calas has been found murdered in Paris.'

'So I heard just now on the radio.'

'Then you must have heard his description—does it fit your brother?'

'It's impossible to say after all this time.'

'Did you know he was living in Paris?'

'No.'

'Did you know he was married?'

Silence.

'Do you know his wife?'

'Now, look here, there's nothing I can tell you. I was fifteen when my brother left home. I haven't seen him since. He's never written to me. I just don't want to know. I'll tell you who might be able to help you: Maître Canonge.'

'Who he is?'

'The notary.'

When, at last, he got through to Maître Canonge's number, a woman's voice, that of Madame Canonge, exclaimed:

'Well, of all the extraordinary coincidences!'

'I beg your pardon?'

'That you should ring at this moment! How did you know? Just now, when we heard the news on the radio, my husband was in two minds whether to get in touch with you by telephone or go to Paris and see you. In the end, he decided to make the journey, and he caught the eight-twenty-two train, which is due in at the Gare d'Austerlitz shortly after midnight. I'm not certain of the exact time.'

'Where does he usually stay in Paris?'

'Until recently the train went on to the Gare d'Orsay. He always stayed at the Hôtel d'Orsay, and still does.'

'What does your husband look like?'

'Good-looking, tall and well-built, with grey hair. He's wearing a brown suit and overcoat. He has his brief-case with him, and a pigskin suitcase. I still can't imagine what made you think of ringing him!'

Maigret put down the receiver with an involuntary smile. Things were going so well that he considered treating himself to another drink, but thought better of it. There would be plenty of time to have one at the station.

But first, he must ring Madame Maigret, and tell her that he would be late getting home.

CHAPTER EIGHT

The Notary

Madame Canonge had spoken no more than the truth. Her husband really was a fine-looking man. He was about sixty, and in appearance more like a gentleman farmer than a country lawyer. Maigret, waiting at the end of the platform near the barrier, picked him out at once. He stood head and shoulders above the other passengers on the 12.22 train, and walked with a rapid stride, his pigskin suitcase in one hand and his brief-case in the other. His air of easy assurance suggested that he knew his way about, and was probably a regular traveller on this train. Maigret noted all this when he was still quite a long way off.

Added to his height and impressive build, his clothes set him apart from the other passengers. He was almost too well-dressed. To describe his coat as brown was to do less than justice to its colour, which was a soft, subtle chestnut such as Maigret had never seen before, and the cut was masterly.

His fresh complexion was set off by silvery hair, and even in the unflattering light of the station entrance he looked well-groomed, smooth-shaven, the kind of man whom one would expect to complete his toilet with a discreet dab of Eau de Cologne.

When he was within fifty yards of the barrier, he caught sight of Maigret among the other people meeting the train, and frowned as though trying to recapture an elusive memory. He, too, must often have seen the Chief Superintendent's photograph in the newspapers. Even when he was almost level with Maigret, he was still too uncertain to smile or hold out his hand.

It was Maigret who stepped forward to meet him.

'Maître Canonge?'

'Yes. Aren't you Chief Superintendent Maigret?'

He put down his suitcase, and shook Maigret's hand.

'It can't be just a coincidence that I should find you here, surely?'

'No. I telephoned your house earlier this evening. Your wife told me that you were on this train, and would be staying at the Hôtel d'Orsay. I thought it advisable, for security reasons, to meet the train rather than ask for you at your hotel.'

The notary looked puzzled.

'Did you see my advertisement?'

'No.'

'You don't say! The sooner we get out of here the better, don't you think? I suggest we adjourn to my hotel.'

They got into a taxi.

'The reason I'm here is to see you. I intended to ring you first thing tomorrow morning.'

Maigret had been right. There was a faint fragrance of Eau de Cologne blended with the lingering aroma of a good cigar.

'Have you arrested Madame Calas?'

'Judge Coméliau has signed the warrant.'

'What an extraordinary business!'

It was a short journey along the quayside to the Hôtel d'Orsay. The night porter greeted Maître Canonge with the warmth due to a guest of long standing.

'The restaurant is shut, I suppose, Alfred?'

'Yes, sir.'

The notary explained to Maigret, who knew the facts perfectly well:

'Before the war, when the Quai d'Orsay was the terminus for all trains on the Paris—Orléans line, the station restaurant was open all night. It was very convenient. A hotel bedroom isn't the most congenial place in the world. Wouldn't it be better if we talked over a drink somewhere?'

Most of the brasseries in the Boulevard Saint-Germain were closed. They had to walk quite a distance before they found one open.

'What will you have, Superintendent?'

'A beer, thanks.'

'And a liqueur brandy for me, waiter, the best you have.'

Having left their coats and hats in the cloakroom, they sat at the bar. Maigret lit his pipe, and Canonge pierced a cigar with a silver pen-knife.

'I don't suppose you know Saint-André at all?'

'No.'

'It's miles from anywhere, and there are no tourist attractions. If I'm not mistaken, according to the afternoon news-bulletin, the man who was carved up and dropped in the Saint-Martin Canal was none other than that swine Calas.'

'Finger-prints of the dead man were found in the house in the Quai de Valmy.'

'When I first read about the body in the canal, although the newspapers hadn't much to say about it then, I had a kind of intuition, and I toyed with the idea of ringing you even then.'

'Did you know Calas?'

'I knew him in the old days. I knew her better, though—the woman who became his wife, I mean. Cheers! The trouble is, I hardly know where to begin, it's all so involved. Has Aline Calas never mentioned me?'

'No.'

'Do you really think she's mixed up in the murder of her husband?'

'I don't know. The examining magistrate is convinced of it.'

'What has she to say about it?'

'Nothing.'

'Has she confessed?'

'No. She refuses to say anything.'

'To tell you the truth, Chief Superintendent, she's the most extraordinary woman I've ever met in my life. And, make no mistake, we have our fair share of freaks in the country.'

He was clearly accustomed to a respectful audience, and he liked the sound of his own voice. He held his cigar in his elegant fingers in such a way as to show off his gold signet ring to the best advantage.

'I'd better begin at the beginning. You'll never have heard of Honoré de Boissancourt, of course?'

The Superintendent shook his head.

'He is, or rather was until last month, the "lord of the manor". He was a rich man. Besides the Château de Boissancourt, he owned some fifteen farms comprising five thousand acres in all, plus another two and a half thousand acres of woodland and two small lakes. If you are at all familiar with country life, you can visualize it.'

'I was born and brought up in the country.'

And what was more, Maigret's father had been farm-manager on just such an estate.

'Now I think you ought to know something of the antecedents of this fellow, Boissancourt. It all began with his grandfather. My father, who, like myself, practised law in Saint-André, knew him well. He wasn't called Boissancourt, but Dupré, Christophe Dupré, son of a tenant-farmer whose landlord was the former owner of the château. Christophe began by dealing in cattle, and he was sufficiently ruthless and crooked to amass a considerable fortune in a short time. You know his sort, I daresay.'

To Maigret, it was as though he were re-living his own childhood, for his village had had its Christophe Dupré, and he too had amassed great wealth, and had a son who was now a senator.

'At one stage, Dupré gambled heavily in wheat, and the gamble paid off. With what he made on the deal, he bought one farm, then a second and a third, and by the end of his life the château and all the land attached to it, which had been the property of a childless widow, had passed into his hands. Christophe had one son and one daughter. The daughter he married off to a cavalry officer. The son, Alain, came into the property on his father's death, and used the name of Dupré de Boissancourt. Gradually the Dupré was dropped and, when he was elected to the County Council, he changed his name by deed poll.'

This, too, evoked memories for Maigret.

'Well, so much for the antecedents. Honoré de Boissancourt, the grandson of Christophe Dupré, who was, as it were, the founder of the dynasty, died a month ago.

'He married Emilie d'Espissac, daughter of a fine old family who had fallen on hard times. There was one daughter of this marriage. The mother was killed in a riding accident, when the child was only a baby. I knew Emilie well. She was a charming woman, though no beauty. She sadly under-rated herself, and allowed her parents to sacrifice her, without protest. It was said that Boissancourt gave the parents a million francs, by way of purchase price one must assume. As the family lawyer, I am in a position to know that the figure was exaggerated, but the fact remains that a substantial sum of money came into the possession of the old Comtesse d'Espissac as soon as the marriage contract was signed.'

'What kind of a man was Honoré?'

'I'm coming to that. I was his legal adviser. For years, I have been in the habit of dining at the château once a week, and I've shot over his land ever since I was a boy. In other words, I know him well. In the first place, he had a club foot, which may explain his moody and suspicious disposition. Then again, his family history was known to everyone, and most of the county families refused to have anything to do with him. None of this was exactly calculated to bring out the best in him.

'All his life he was obsessed with the notion that people despised him, and were only out to cheat and rob him. He was for ever on the defensive.

'There is a turret-room in the château, which he used as a kind of office. He spent days on end up there, going through the accounts, not only those of his tenants, but all the household bills as well, down to the last farthing. He made all his corrections in red ink. He would poke his nose into the kitchen at meal-times, to make sure that the servants weren't eating him out of house and home.

'I suppose I owe some loyalty to my client, but it's not as if I were betraying a professional secret. Anyone in Saint-André could tell you as much.'

'Was he the father of Madame Calas?'

'Exactly.'

'What about Omer Calas?'

'He was a servant at the château for four years. His father was a drunken labourer, a real layabout.

'Which brings us to Aline de Boissancourt, as she was twenty-five years ago.'

He signalled to the waiter as he went past the table, and said to Maigret:

'Join me in a brandy this time, won't you? Two *fines champagnes*, waiter.'

Then, turning back to the Superintendent, he went on:

'Needless to say, you couldn't possibly have any inkling of her background, seeing her for the first time in the bistro in the Quai de Valmy.'

This was not altogether the case. Nothing that the notary had told Maigret was any surprise to him.

'Old Doctor Petrelle used sometimes to talk to me about Aline. He's dead now, unfortunately, and Camuzet has taken over the practice. Camuzet never knew her, so he wouldn't be any help. And I myself am not qualified to describe her case in technical terms.

'Even as a very young child, she was different from other little girls. There was something disturbing about her. She never played with other children, or even went to school, because her father insisted on keeping her at home with a governess. Not one governess, actually, but at least a dozen, one after the other, because the child somehow contrived to make their lives a misery.

'Was it that she blamed her father for the fact that her life was so different from other children's? Or was there, as Petrelle believed, much more to it than that? I don't know. It's often said that girls worship their fathers, sometimes to an unnatural degree. I can't speak from my own experience. My wife and I have no children. But is it possible, I wonder, for that kind of adoration to turn into hatred?

'Be that as it may, she seemed prepared to go to any lengths to drive Boissancourt to distraction, and at the age of twelve she was caught setting fire to the château.

'She was always setting fire to things at that time, and she had to be kept under strict supervision.

'And then there was Omer. He was five or six years older than she was, tough and strong, a "likely lad" as country-folk say, and as insolent as you please as soon as the boss's back was turned.'

'Did you know what was going on between them?' enquired Maigret, looking vaguely round the brasserie, which was now almost empty, with the waiters obviously longing for them to go.

'Not at the time. I heard about it later from Petrelle. According to him, when she first began taking an interest in Omer she was only thirteen or fourteen. It's not unusual in girls of that age, but as a rule it's just calf-love, and nothing comes of it.

'Was it any different in her case? Or was it just that Calas, who wasn't the kind to allow his better feelings to stand in his way, was more unscrupulous in taking advantage of her than most men would be in a similiar situation?

'Petrelle, at any rate, was convinced that their relationship was suspect right from the start. In his opinion, Aline had only one idea in her head, to defy and wound her father.

'It may be so. I'm not competent to judge. I'm only telling you all this, because it may help you to understand the rest of the story.

'One day, when she was not yet seventeen, she went to see the doctor in secret, and asked him to examine her. He confirmed that she was pregnant.'

'How did she take it?' asked Maigret.

'As Petrelle described it, she gave him a long, hard look, clenched her teeth, and spat out the words:

'"*I'm glad!*"

'I should tell you that Calas, meanwhile, had married the butcher's daughter. She was pregnant too, of course, and their child was born a few weeks earlier.

'He carried on with his job at the château, not being fitted for any other work, and his wife went on living with her parents.

'It was a Sunday when the news burst upon the village that Aline de Boissancourt and Omer Calas had vanished.

'It was learnt from the servants that, the night before, there had been a violent quarrel between the girl and her father. They could hear them in the breakfast-room, going at it hammer and tongs for over two hours.

'Boissancourt, to my certain knowledge, never made any attempt to find his daughter. And, as far as I know, she never communicated with him.

'As for Calas's first wife, she suffered from fits of depression. She dragged on miserably for three years. Then, one day, they found her hanging from a tree in the orchard.'

The waiters by now had stacked most of the chairs on the tables, and one of them was looking fixedly at Maigret and the notary, with a large silver pocket-watch in his hand.

'I think we'd better be going,' suggested Maigret.

Canonge insisted on paying the bill, and they went out into the cool, starlit night. They walked a little way in silence. Then the notary said:

'What about a nightcap, if we can find a place that's still open?'

Each wrapped in his own thoughts, they walked almost the whole length of the Boulevard Raspail, and eventually, in Montparnasse, found a little cabaret which appeared to be open, judging from the bluish light shining into the street, and the muffled sound of music.

'Shall we go in?'

They did not follow the waiter to a table, but sat at the bar. The fat man next to them was more than a little drunk, and was being pestered by a couple of prostitutes.

'The same again?' asked Canonge, taking another cigar out of his pocket.

There were a few couples dancing. Two prostitutes came across from the far end of the room to sit beside them, but they melted away at a sign from Maigret.

'There are still Calases at Boissancourt and Saint-André,' remarked the notary.

'I know. A cattle-dealer and a grocer.'

Canonge sniggered:

'Suppose the cattle-dealer were to grow rich in his turn, and buy the château and the land for himself. What a laugh that would be! One of Calases is Omer's brother, the other is his cousin. There is a sister as well. She married a policeman in Gien. A month ago, just as he was sitting down to his dinner, Boissancourt dropped dead of a cerebral haemorrhage. I went to see all three of them in the hope that one or other might have news of Omer.'

'Just a moment,' interposed Maigret. 'Didn't Boissancourt disinherit his daughter?'

'Everyone in the district was convinced that he had. There was a good deal of speculation as to who would inherit the property, because, in a village like ours, most people are more or less dependent on the château for their livelihood.'

'You knew, I daresay.'

'No. Boissancourt made several wills over the past few years all different, but he never deposited any of them with me. He must have torn them up, one after another, because no will was found.'

'Do you mean to say his daughter inherits everything?'

'Automatically.'

'Did you put a notice in the papers?'

'In the usual way, yes. There was no mention of the name Calas, because I couldn't assume that they were married. Not many people read that kind of advertisement. I didn't think anything would come of it.'

His glass was empty, and he was trying to catch the barman's eye. There had evidently been a restaurant car on the train, and he must have had a couple of drinks before reaching Paris, because he was very flushed, and his eyes were unnaturally bright.

'The same again, Superintendent?'

Maigret too, had perhaps had more to drink than he realized. He did not say no. He was feeling fine, physically and mentally. It seemed to him, in fact, that he had acquired a sixth sense, enabling him to penetrate the mysteries of human personality. Had he really needed the notary to fill in the details? Might he not, in the end, have worked the whole thing out for himself? He had not been far from the truth a few hours earlier. Why else should he have put that call through to Saint-André?

Even if he had not dotted the 'i's and crossed the 't's, the impression he had formed of Madame Calas had been very close to the truth. All that he had been told confirmed this.

'She's taken to drink,' he murmured, prompted by a sudden urge to have his say.

'I know. I've seen her.'

'When? Last week?'

This was another thing that he had worked out for himself. But Canonge would not let him get a word in edgeways. In Saint-André, no doubt, he was used to holding forth without interruption.

'All in good time, Superintendent. I'm a lawyer, remember, and in legal circles matters are dealt with in their correct order.'

He guffawed at this. A prostitute sitting at the bar leaned across the unoccupied stool between them, and said:

'Won't you buy me a drink?'

'If you like, my dear, but you mustn't interrupt. You might not think it, but we are discussing weighty matters.'

Mightily pleased with himself, he turned to Maigret.

'Well, now, for three weeks there was no answer to my advertisement, other than a couple of letters from cranks. And, in the end, it wasn't the advertisement that led me to Aline. It was pure chance. I had sent one of my guns to a firm in Paris for repair, and last week I got it back. It came through a firm of long-distance road hauliers. I happened to be at home when it was delivered. In fact, I opened the door myself.'

'And the hauliers were Zenith Transport?'

'How did you know? You're quite right. I invited the driver in for a drink, as one does in the country. Calas's grocery store is just opposite my house in the Place de l'Eglise. We can see it from our front windows. The man was having his drink, when he suddenly noticed the name over the shop:

' "Would that be the same family as the people who have the bistro in the Quai de Valmy?" he said, half to himself.

' "Is there a Calas in the Quai de Valmy?"

' "It's a funny little place. I'd never set foot in it until last week, when I was taken there by one of the storemen." '

Maigret was willing to take a bet that this storeman was none other than Dieudonné Pape.

'He didn't happen to say whether the storeman had red hair?'

'No. I asked him if he knew the Christian name of this Calas. He thought about it for a bit, and then said he vaguely remembered seeing it over the door. I asked, could it be Omer, and he said yes, that was it.

'At any rate, next day, I left by train for Paris.'

'The night train?'

'No. The morning train.'

'What time did you go to the Quai de Valmy?'

'In the afternoon, shortly after three. The bistro is rather dark, and when I first saw the woman, I didn't recognize her. I asked her if she was Madame Calas, and she said she was. Then I asked her Christian name. I got the impression that she was half-drunk. She does drink, doesn't she?'

So did he drink, not as she did, but enough, all the same, to make his eyes water now.

Maigret had an uneasy feeling that they had just had their glasses refilled, but he was not too sure. The woman had moved to the stool next to the notary, and was lolling against him with her arm through his. For all the expression on her face, she might not have heard a word of what he had said.

' "Your maiden name was Aline de Boissancourt, is that right?" I said.

'She didn't deny it. She just sat there by the stove, staring at me, I remember, with a great ginger cat on her lap.

'I went on:

' "Your father is dead. Did you know?"

'She shook her head—no sign of surprise or emotion.

' "As his lawyer, I am administering his estate. Your father left no will, which means that the château, the land, and all he possessed come to you."

' "How did you get my address?" she asked.

' "From a lorry driver who happened to have been in here for a drink."

' "Does anyone else know?"

' "I don't think so."

'She got up and went into the kitchen.'

To take a swig from the brandy bottle, of course!

'When she got back, I could see that she had come to some decision.

' "I don't want anything to do with the money," she said, as though it was of no importance. "I suppose I can refuse it if I want to?"

' "Everyone has the right to renounce an inheritance. Nevertheless . . ."

' "Nevertheless what?"

' "I would advise you to think it over. Don't make up your mind here and now."

' "I've thought it over. I refuse it. I imagine I also have the right to insist that you keep your knowledge of my whereabouts to yourself."

'All the while she was talking she kept peering nervously into the street, as though she was afraid someone would come in, her husband perhaps. That's what I thought, at any rate.

'I protested, as I was bound to do. I told her I hadn't been able to trace anyone else with a claim to the Boissancourt estate.

' "Perhaps it would be best for me to come back another time and talk things over again," I suggested.

' "No. Don't come back. Omer musn't see you here. I won't have it." 'She was terrified.

' "It would be the end of everything!" she said.

' "Don't you think you ought to consult your husband?"

' "He's the very last person!"

'I tried to argue with her, but it was no use. As I was leaving, I gave her my card. I said that, if she changed her mind in the next few weeks, she could telephone or write, and let me know.

'A customer came in then. He looked to me very much at home in the place.'

'Red-haired, with a pock-marked face?'

'Yes, I believe he was!'

'What happened?'

'Nothing. She slipped my card into her apron pocket, and saw me to the door.'

'What day was it?'

'Last Thursday.'

'Did you see her again?'

'No. But I saw her husband.'

'In Paris?'

'In my study at home, in Saint-André.'

'When?'

'On Saturday morning. He arrived in Saint-André on Friday afternoon or evening. He first called at the house on Friday evening, about eight. I was out, playing bridge at the doctor's house. The maid told him to come back next day.'

'Did you recognize him?'

'Yes, although he had put on weight. He must have spent the night at the village inn, where, of course, he learnt that Boissancourt was dead. He must also have heard that his wife was heir to the property. He lost no time in throwing his weight about. He insisted that, as her husband, he was entitled to claim the inheritance in the name of his wife. As there was no marriage contract in this case, the joint-estate system applies.'

'So that, in fact, neither could act without the consent of the other?'

'That's what I told him.'

'Did you get the impression that he had discussed the matter with his wife?'

'No. He didn't even know that she had renounced the inheritance. He seemed to think she'd got hold of it behind his back. I won't go into the details of the interview, it would take too long. What must have happened is that he found my card. His wife probably left it lying around. Very likely, she forgot I'd given it to her. And what possible business would a lawyer from Saint-André have in the Quai de Valmy unless it were to do with the de Boissancourt estate?

'It was only while he was talking to me that the truth gradually dawned on him. He was furious. I should be hearing from him, he said, and stormed out, slamming the door.'

'And you never saw him again?'

'I never heard another word from him. All this happened on Saturday morning. He went by bus to Montargis, and caught the train to Paris from there.'

'What train would that be, do you think?'

'Probably the one that gets in to the Gare d'Austerlitz just after three.'

Which meant that he must have arrived home at about four, or earlier if he took a taxi.

The notary went on:

'When I read about the dismembered body of a man recovered from the Saint-Martin Canal, right there next to the Quai de Valmy, it shook me, I can tell you. I couldn't help being struck by the coincidence. As I said just now, I was in two minds about ringing you, but I didn't want to look a fool.

'It was when I heard the name Calas mentioned in the news this afternoon, that I made up my mind to come and see you.'

'Can I have another?' asked the girl next to him, pointing to her empty glass.

'By all means, my dear. Well, what do you think, Superintendent?'

At the word 'Superintendent', the prostitute started, and let go of the notary's arm.

'It doesn't surprise me,' murmured Maigret, who was beginning to feel drowsy.

'Come now, don't tell me you've ever known anything like it! Things like that only happen in the country, and I must say that even I . . .'

Maigret was no longer listening. He was thinking of Aline Calas, whom he was now able to see in the round. He could even imagine her as a little girl.

He was not surprised or shocked. He would have found it hard to explain what he felt about her, especially to a man like Judge Coméliau. On that score, he had no illusions; he would be listened to tomorrow with amazement and disbelief.

Coméliau would protest:

'They killed him just the same, she and that lover of hers.'

Omer Calas was dead, and he certainly had not taken his own life. Someone, therefore, had struck him down, and subsequently dismembered his body.

Maigret could almost hear Coméliau's acid voice:

'What can you call that but cold-blooded? You can't imagine, surely, that it was a *crime passionnel*? No, Maigret, you've talked me round before, but this time . . .'

Canonge held up his brimming glass:

'Cheers!'

'Cheers!'

'You look very thoughtful.'

'I was thinking about Aline Calas.'

'Do you think she took up with Omer just to spite her father?'

Even to the notary, even under the influence of several glasses of brandy, he could not put his feelings into words. For a start, he would have to convince him that everything she had done, even as a kid in the Château de Boissancourt, had been a kind of protest.

Doctor Petrelle, no doubt, would have been able to express it better than he could. To begin with, the fire-raising; then, her sexual relations with Calas, and finally, her flight with him in circumstances where most other girls would have procured an abortion.

This too, perhaps, had been an act of defiance? Or revulsion?

Maigret had often tried to persuade others, men of wide experience among them, that, of all people, those most likely to come to grief, to seek self-abasement and degradation with morbid fervour, almost with relish, are the idealists.

To no avail. Coméliau would protest:

'If you said she was born wicked, you'd be nearer the truth.'

At the bistro in the Quai de Valmy, she had taken to drink. This, too, was in character. And so was the fact that she had remained there without ever attempting to escape, allowing the atmosphere of the place to engulf her.

Maigret believed he understood Omer too. It was the dream of so many country lads to earn enough money in domestic service, or as a chauffeur, to become the proprietor of a bistro in Paris. For Omer the dream had come true.

It was a life of ease, lounging behind the bar, shuffling down to the cellar, going to Poitiers once or twice a year to buy wine, spending every afternoon playing billiards or *belote* in a brasserie near the Gare de l'Est.

There had not been time to investigate his private life. Maigret intended to go into that in a day or so, if only to satisfy his own curiosity. He was convinced that, when he was not indulging his passion for billiards, Omer had had a succession of shameless affairs with local servant girls and shop assistants.

Had he counted on inheriting the Boissancourt property? It seemed unlikely. He must have believed, like everyone else, that de Boissancourt had disinherited his daughter.

It had taken the notary's visiting-card to arouse his hopes.

'I've had to do with all sorts in my time,' Canonge was saying, 'but what I simply can't understand—indeed, I confess it's quite beyond me, my dear fellow—is how, with a fortune landing in her lap out of the blue, she could bring herself to turn it down. '

To Maigret, however, it seemed perfectly natural. As she was now, what possible use could she make of the money? Go and live with Omer in the Château de Boissancourt? Set up house with him in Paris or elsewhere—the Côte d'Azur for instance—in the style of the rich landowners?

She had chosen to stay where she was, in the place where she felt safe, like an animal in its lair.

Day had followed day, all alike, punctuated by swigs of brandy behind the kitchen door, and Dieudonné Pape's company in the afternoons.

He too had become a habit, more than a habit, perhaps, because he knew. She need not feel ashamed with him. They could sit side by side in companionable silence warming themselves by the stove.

'Do you believe she killed him?'

'I don't think so.'

'It was her lover, then?'

'It looks like it.'

The musicians were putting away their instruments. Even this place had to close some time. They found themselves outside in the street, walking in the direction of Saint-Germain-des-Prés.

'How far have you to go?'

'Boulevard Richard-Lenoir.'

'I'll walk with you part of the way. What could have induced the lover to kill Omer? Was he hoping to persuade her to change her mind about the estate?'

They were both unsteady on their feet, but quite up to roaming the streets of Paris, which they had to themselves but for an occasional passing taxi.

'I don't think so.'

He would have to take a different tone tomorrow with Coméliau. At the moment, he suddenly realized, he was sounding quite maudlin.

'Why did he kill him?'

'What would you say was the first thing Omer would do when he got back from Saint-André?'

'I don't know—lose his temper, I imagine, and order his wife to accept the inheritance.'

Maigret saw again the table in the bedroom, the bottle of ink, the blotter, and the three sheets of blank paper.

'That would be in character, wouldn't it?'

'No doubt about it.'

'Supposing Omer ordered her to write a letter to that effect, and she still refused?'

'He'd have thrashed her. He was that sort—a real peasant.'

'He did resort to violence on occasion.'

'I think I can see what you're getting at.'

'He doesn't bother to change when he gets home. This is Saturday afternoon, round about four. He marches Aline up to her room, orders her to write the letter, uses threatening language, and starts knocking her about.'

'At which point the lover shows up?'

'It's the most likely explanation. Dieudonné Pape knows his way about the house. He hears the row in the bedroom, and rushes upstairs to Aline's rescue.'

'And does the husband in!' finished the notary, with a snigger.

'He kills him, either deliberately or accidentally, by hitting him on the head with something heavy.'

'After which, he chops him up!'

Canonge, who was distinctly merry, roared with mirth.

'It's killing!' he exclaimed. 'I can't help laughing at the thought of anyone carving up Omer. I mean to say, if you'd known Omer . . .'

Far from sobering him up, the fresh air, on top of all he had drunk, had gone to his head.

'Do you mind walking back with me part of the way?'

They faced about, walked a little way, and then turned back again.

'He's a strange man,' murmured Maigret, with a sigh.

'Who? Omer?'

'No, Pape.'

'Don't tell me he's called Pape, on top of everything else!'

'Not just Pape, Dieudonné Pape.'

'Killing!'

'He's the mildest man I've ever met.'

'No doubt, that's why he chopped up poor old Omer!'

It was perfectly true. It took a man like him, self-sufficient, patient, meticulous, to remove all traces of the crime. Not even Moers and his men, for all their cameras and apparatus, had been able to find any proof that a murder had been committed in the house in the Quai de Valmy.

Had Aline Calas helped him scrub the place from top to bottom? Was it she who had got rid of the sheets and clothes, with their tell-tale stains?

Pape had slipped up in one particular: he had not foreseen that Maigret would be puzzled by the absence of dirty linen in the house, and would make enquiries of the laundry. But how could he have foreseen that?

How had those two imagined their future? Had they believed that weeks, possibly months, would elapse before any part of Calas's body was found in the canal, and that by then, it would be beyond identification? That was what would have happened if the Naud brothers' barge had not been weighed down by several extra tons of gravel, and scraped the bottom of the canal.

Where was the head? In the river? In a drain? Maigret would probably know the answer in a day or two. Sooner or later, he was convinced, he would know everything there was to know, but it was of merely academic interest to him. What mattered to him was the tragedy and the three protagonists who had enacted it, and he was certain he was right about them.

Aline and Pape, he felt sure, once all traces of the murder had been eradicated, had looked forward to a new life, not very different from the old.

For a while, things would have gone on as before, with Pape coming into the little café every afternoon for a couple of hours. Gradually, he would have spent more and more time there. In time, the neighbours and customers would have forgotten Omer Calas, and Pape would have moved in altogether.

Would Aline have continued to receive Antoine Cristin and the other men in the kitchen?

It was possible. On this subject, Maigret did not care to speculate. He felt out of his depth.

'It really is goodnight, this time!'

'Can I ring you tomorrow at your hotel? There are various formalities to be gone through.'

'No need to ring me. I shall be in your office at nine.'

*

Needless to say, the notary was not in Maigret's office at nine, and Maigret had forgotten that he had said he would be. The Superintendent was not feeling any too bright. This morning, in response to a touch on the shoulder from his wife, he had opened his eyes, with a feeling of guilt, to see his coffee already poured out for him on the bedside table.

She was smiling at him in an odd sort of way, with unusual maternal tenderness.

'How are you feeling?'

He could not remember when he had last woken up with such a dreadful headache, always a sign that he had had a lot to drink. It was most unusual for him to come home tipsy. The annoying thing was that he had not even been aware that he was drinking too much. It had crept up on him, with glass after glass after glass of brandy.

'Can you remember all the things you were telling me about Aline Calas in the night?'

He preferred to forget them, having an uneasy feeling that he had grown more and more maudlin.

'You talked almost like a man in love. If I were a jealous woman...'

He flushed, and was at some pains to reassure her.

'I was only joking. Are you going to say all those things to Coméliau?'

So he had unburdened himself about Coméliau as well, had he? Talking to Coméliau was, in fact, the next item on the agenda—in somewhat different terms, needless to say!

'Any news, Lapointe?'

'Nothing, sir.'

'I want you to get an advertisement into the afternoon edition of the newspapers. Say that the police wish to interview the young man who was given the job of depositing a suitcase at the Gare de l'Est last Sunday.'

'Wasn't that Antoine?'

'I'm sure it wasn't. Pape would realize that it had much better be done by a stranger.'

'The clerk says...'

'He saw a young man of about Antoine's age, wearing a leather jerkin. That could be said of any number of young men in the district.'

'Have you any proof that Pape did it?'

'He'll confess.'

'Are you going to interrogate them?'

'At this stage of the proceedings, I imagine, Coméliau will be wanting to do it himself.'

It was all plain sailing now, a mere matter of putting questions at random, or 'fishing', as they called it among themselves.

Anyway, Maigret was not at all sure that he wanted to be the one to drive Aline Calas and Dieudonné Pape to the wall. Both would hold out to the bitter end, until it was no longer possible to remain silent.

He spent nearly an hour upstairs in the judge's office. He rang Maître Canonge from there. The telephone bell must have woken the notary with a start.

'Who's there?' he asked, in such comical bewilderment that Maigret smiled.

'Chief Superintendent Maigret.'

'What time is it?'

'Half-past ten. Judge Coméliau, the Examining Magistrate in charge of the case, wishes to see you in his office as soon as possible.'

'Tell him I'll be right over. Shall I bring the Boissancourt papers?'

'If you will.'

'I hope I didn't keep you up too late?'

The notary must have got to bed even later. God knows where he landed up after I left him, thought Maigret, hearing a woman's sleepy voice asking: 'What's the time?'

Maigret returned to his office.

'Is he going to interrogate them?' Lapointe asked.

'Yes.'

'Starting with the woman?'

'I advised him to start with Pape.'

'Is he more likely to crack?'

'Yes. Especially as he was the one who struck Calas down, or so I believe.'

'Are you going out?'

'There's something I want to clear up at the Hôtel-Dieu.'

It was a small point. Lucette Calas was in the operating theatre. He had to wait until the operation was over.

'I take it you've read the papers, and know of your father's death and your mother's arrest?'

'Sooner or later, something of the kind was bound to happen.'

'When you last went to see her, was it to ask for money?'

'No.'

'What was it, then?'

'To tell her that, as soon as he gets his divorce, Professor Lavaud and I are going to be married. He might have asked to meet my parents, and I wanted them to be presentable.'

'Don't you know that Boissancourt is dead?'

'Who's he?'

She was genuinely bewildered.

'Your grandfather.'

Casually, as though the matter were of no importance, he said:

'Unless she's convicted of murder, your mother is heir to a château, eighteeen farms, and goodness only knows how many millions.'

'Are you quite sure?'

'Go and see Maître Canonge, the notary, at the Hôtel d'Orsay. He's administering the estate.'

'Will he be there all day?'

'I imagine so.'

She did not ask what was to become of her mother. As he walked away, he gave a little shrug.

Maigret had no lunch that day. He was not hungry, but a couple of glasses of beer settled his stomach more or less. He shut himself up in his office the whole afternoon. In front of him on the desk lay the keys to the bistro in the Quai de Valmy and Pape's flat. He polished off a mass of boring administrative work, which he usually hated. Today, he seemed to be taking a perverse delight in it.

Each time the telephone rang he snatched it off the hook with uncharacteristic eagerness, but it was after five o'clock before he heard the voice of Coméliau on the line.

'Maigret?'

'Yes.'

There was a note of triumph in the magistrate's voice.

'I have had them formally charged and arrested.'

'All three of them?'

'No. I've released the boy Antoine.'

'Have the other two confessed?'

'Yes.'

'Everything?'

'Everything that *we* suspected. I decided that it would be a good idea to start with the man. I outlined my reconstruction of the crime. He had no choice but to confess.'

'What about the woman?'

'Pape repeated his admissions in her presence. It was impossible for her to deny the truth of his statement.'

'Did she have anything else to say?'

'No. She just asked me, as she was leaving, whether you had seen to her cat.'

'What did you say?'

'That you had better things to do.'

Maigret could never forgive Judge Coméliau for that.

Maigret and the Saturday Caller

MAIGRET AND THE SATURDAY CALLER
(*Maigret et le Client du Samedi*)
was first published in France in 1962
and in Great Britain in 1964

Translated from the French by Tony White

CHAPTER ONE

Certain images, for no apparent reason, and without our having any hand in the matter, cling to us and stick obstinately in our memories, even though we are hardly aware of having recorded them and they do not bear on anything of importance. In this way, no doubt, years later, Maigret would be able to reconstruct, minute by minute, move by move, that uneventful late afternoon at the Quai des Orfèvres.

First, there was the black marble clock with bronze fittings. When he glanced at it, it said eighteen minutes past six, which meant that it was really just after six o'clock. In a dozen other offices at Police Head-quarters, in the Chief's office, as well as in those of the other Inspectors, identical clocks were flanked by candelabra and, from time immemorial, they too had been fast.

Why did this thought strike him today more than any other? For a moment he wondered how many administrations or ministries this F. Ledent, whose fine copperplate signature was on the pale dial, had supplied with a consignment of such clocks, and he imagined the bargaining, intrigue and petty bribery which must have gone on before such an important transaction.

F. Ledent had been dead for half a century, maybe a whole century, judging by the style of his clocks.

The lamp with the green shade was on because it was January. The lamps in the rest of the building were on, too.

Lucas was standing up, slipping the documents, which Maigret had just passed him one by one, into a yellow folder.

'Shall I leave Janvier at the Crillon?'

'Not too late. Send someone to relieve him this evening.'

There had been a series of jewel robberies, one on top of another, as is always the case, from the de luxe hotels on the Champs-Elysées, and a discreet watch was being kept on each one of them.

Maigret automatically pressed an electric bell. It wasn't long before old Joseph, the messenger with the silver chain, opened the door.

'Anyone else for me?' the Inspector asked.

'Only the madwoman.'

It was not important. For months, she had been coming two or three times a week to the Quai des Orfèvres, slipping, without a word, into the waiting-room and settling down to her knitting. She had never given her name. The first day, Joseph had asked her whom she wanted to see.

She had given him a wicked, almost saucy smile and replied:

'Inspector Maigret will send for me when he needs me.'

Joseph had given her a form. She had filled it in in a neat hand which suggested a convent education. Her name was Clémentine Pholien and she lived in the Rue Lamark.

That time, the Inspector had got Janvier to see her.

'Were you sent for?'

'Inspector Maigret knows about it.'

'Did he send you a summons?'

She smiled, a slight, graceful woman, in spite of her age.

'There's no need for a summons.'

'Have you something to tell him?'

'Perhaps.'

'He's very busy just now.'

'Never mind. I'll wait.'

She had waited until seven in the evening and then gone away. They had seen her again a few days later, with the same mauve hat, the same bit of knitting, and she had taken her seat, like a regular, in the glass waiting-room.

They had made inquiries just in case. She had been running a haberdasher's in Montmartre for some while, and she derived a comfortable income from it. Her nephews and nieces had tried several times to have her put in a home but, each time, they had discharged her from the psychiatric hospital saying she was not dangerous.

Where had she got hold of Maigret's name? She didn't know him by sight, because he had passed the glass cage several times while she was there and she hadn't recognized him.

'Right, Lucas, we'll shut up shop!'

They were packing up early, especially for a Saturday. The Inspector filled his pipe, and went and fetched his coat, hat and scarf from the cupboard.

He passed the glass cage, carefully looked away and, down in the yard, ran into the somewhat yellowish fog which had descended on Paris during the afternoon.

He was in no hurry. His coat-collar turned up and his hands in his pockets, he circled the Palais de Justice, passed under the big clock, and crossed the Pont-au-Change. As he got half-way across the bridge, he had the feeling that someone was following him and he turned sharply round. There were lots of people going in both directions. Because of the cold, nearly all of them were walking quickly. He was almost sure that a man in dark clothes, about ten yards away, suddenly turned round.

He didn't pay much attention to it. In any case, it was only an impression.

A few minutes later, he was waiting for his bus in the Place du Châtelet, and he found room on the platform where he could go on smoking his pipe. Had it really got an unusual taste? He could have sworn it had. Perhaps it was because of the fog, or of some quality in the air. A very pleasant taste.

He wasn't thinking of anything in particular. He was daydreaming and vaguely studying his neighbours' bobbing heads.

Then he took to the pavement again, along the almost deserted Boulevard Richard-Lenoir, to the lights of his flat, which he could pick out from a distance. He started up the familiar staircase, saw the bright strips of light under the doors, and heard muffled voices and the sound of radios.

The door opened, as usual, before he had touched the handle. Madame Maigret, framed against the light, was holding a finger mysteriously to her lips.

He looked at her questioningly, trying to see behind her.

'There's someone . . .' she whispered.

'Who?'

'I don't know. He's peculiar.'

'What did he tell you?'

'That he simply had to speak to you.'

'What's he like?'

'I can't explain, but his breath smells of drink.'

There was *quiche lorraine* for supper, he could tell by the odours coming from the kitchen.

'Where is he?'

'I showed him into the living-room.'

She helped him off with his coat, hat and scarf. He felt the flat was less brightly lit than usual, but no doubt it was only an impression. With a shrug, he pushed open the door of the living-room where, for just over a month, a television set had held pride of place.

The man had remained standing in one corner, in his coat, holding his hat. He seemed in a state and hardly dared to look at the Inspector.

'You must forgive me for following you home . . .' he stammered.

Maigret immediately noticed his hare-lip. He did not mind finding himself face to face with the man at last.

'You've been to see me at the Quai des Orfèvres, haven't you?'

'Several times, yes.'

'Your name's . . . Just a minute. Planchon.'

'Léonard Planchon, that's right.'

He repeated, even more humbly:

'You must forgive me.'

His glance travelled round the small living-room and halted at the door, which was still half-open, as if he wanted to run away again. How many times had he already gone away like that without meeting the Inspector?

At least five. It was always a Saturday afternoon. In the end, they had nicknamed him the Saturday caller.

It was like the madwoman, but with a difference. Police Headquarters, like newspaper offices, attracts all sorts of rather weird people. In the end, you come to know their faces well.

'I wrote to you first . . .' he murmured.

'Sit down.'

Through the glass door a laid table was visible. The man glanced in its direction.

'Isn't it your supper-time?'

'Sit down,' the Inspector repeated with a sigh.

He had got back early for once, yet his dinner would still be late. So much for the *quiche*! And the television news! For some weeks, he and his wife had acquired the habit of watching the television as they ate, and they had changed their places round at table.

'You say you've written to me?'

'At least ten letters.'

'Signed with your name?'

'The first weren't signed. I tore them up. I tore up the others, too. That's when I decided to go and see you.'

Maigret, too, recognized the smell of alcohol, but his visitor was not drunk. On edge, yes. His fingers were so tightly clenched that they were white at the joints. He only gradually dared to look at the Inspector, with an almost pleading expression.

What age was he? It was hard to say. He was neither young nor old, and he looked as if he never had been young. Thirty-five?

It wasn't easy, either, to work out which social class he belonged to. His clothes were poorly cut, but good quality, and his hands, though very clean, were those of a manual worker.

'Why did you tear up those letters?'

'I was afraid you might think I was mad.'

Then, looking up, he added, as if he needed to convince Maigret:

'I'm not mad, Inspector. I beg you to believe that I'm not mad.'

This is usually a bad sign, yet Maigret was already half-convinced. He could hear his wife moving about in the kitchen. She must have taken the *quiche* out of the oven. It would be spoilt now, anyway.

'So you wrote me several letters. Then you turned up at the Quai des Orfèvres. A Saturday, I think?'

'It's the only day I'm free.'

'What do you do for a living, Monsieur Planchon?'

'I own a decorating firm. Oh, in a very small way. When it's fine, I sometimes employ five or six men. Do you understand?'

Because of his hare-lip, it was difficult to tell if he was smiling shyly or pulling a face. His eyes were very pale blue and his fair hair slightly reddish.

'This first visit was about two months ago. You wrote on the form that you wanted to see me personally. Why?'

'Because you're the only person I can trust. I've read in the papers . . .'

'Right! That Saturday, instead of waiting, you went off after about ten minutes.'

'I was afraid.'

'Of what?'

'I thought you wouldn't take me seriously. Or that you'd stop me from doing what I'd planned.'

'You came back the following Saturday.'

'Yes.'

Maigret had been in conference that day with his Chief and two of the other Inspectors. When he had come out, an hour later, the waiting-room was empty.

'You were still afraid?'

'I didn't know.'

'What didn't you know?'

'If I still wanted to go through with it.'

He wiped his forehead.

'It's all so complicated. You see, there are times when I don't know where I am.'

On another occasion, Maigret had sent Lucas to him. The man had refused to disclose the purpose of his visit, insisting that it was personal, and he had literally fled.

'Who gave you my address?'

'I followed you. Last Saturday, I nearly went up to you in the street. Then I decided that it wasn't a suitable place for the sort of conversation I wanted with you. Or in your office. Perhaps you'll understand now.'

'How did you know I was coming home tonight?'

Maigret suddenly remembered his impression on the Pont-au-Change.

'You were hiding on the Quai, weren't you?'

Planchon nodded.

'Did you follow me to the bus?'

'That's right. Then I took a taxi and I arrived here a few minutes ahead of you.'

'Are you in trouble, Monsieur Planchon?'

'Worse than trouble.'

'How many drinks did you have before you came here?'

'Two. Maybe three. Before, I never used to drink, hardly even a glass of wine at meals.'

'And now?'

'It depends which day it is. Or rather, which evening, because I don't drink in the daytime. Except, just now, I drank three brandies to give me courage. Are you angry with me?'

Maigret was puffing slowly at his pipe, his eyes fixed on his visitor, trying to make up his mind about him. He had not yet succeeded. He suspected that there was a pathetic side to Planchon and it baffled him. He gave the feeling of suppressed, overwhelming misery and, at the same time, of extraordinary patience.

He would have staked his last penny that Planchon had few contacts with his fellow-men, and that everything went on inside him. For two months, he had been tortured by the need to speak. He had tried, Saturday after Saturday, to see the Inspector and, each time, he had cleared off at the last moment.

'Supposing you just tell me your story?'

Another glance at the dining-room, where two places were laid opposite the television set.

'I feel awful keeping you from eating. It'll take some time. Your wife'll be cross with me, I know! If you don't mind, I'll wait here until you've eaten. Or I'll come back later. That's it! I'll come back later.'

He made as if to get up and the Inspector had to force him to keep his seat.

'No, Monsieur Planchon! You've made it this time, haven't you? Tell me what's on your mind. Tell me straight out what you wrote in all those letters you tore up.'

Then, suddenly, staring at the red-patterned carpet, the man stammered:

'I want to kill my wife . . .'

Suddenly, he looked up at the Inspector who had, with some difficulty, managed not to give a start.

'You intend to kill your wife?'

'I must. There's no other way out. I don't know how to explain. Every evening I tell myself that it'll happen, that it's impossible for it not to happen one day or other. So I thought that, if I told you about it . . .'

He pulled a handkerchief out of his pocket and wiped the lenses of his glasses, feeling for his words. Maigret noticed that one of his coat buttons was hanging on by a thread.

In spite of his nervous state, Planchon caught Maigret's quick glance, and gave a smile or pulled a face.

'Yes. That's another thing,' he muttered. 'She doesn't even pretend to . . .'

'Pretend to what?'

'Look after me. Be my wife.'

Was he sorry he had come? He was fidgeting on his chair and occasionally glancing at the door, as if he might suddenly dash through it.

'I wonder if I wasn't wrong. Yet you're the only man in the world I trust. I feel I've known you ages. I'm almost sure you'll understand.'

'Are you jealous, Monsieur Planchon?'

Their eyes met directly. Maigret sensed complete honesty in the face of the man opposite him.

'I don't think I am any more. I was. No! It's all over, now.'

'Yet you still want to kill her?'

'Because there's no other solution. Then I thought that, if I warned you, by letter or in person . . . Firstly, it was more honest. Then, perhaps, if I did that, I might change my mind. Do you understand? No! You can't understand if you don't know Renée. Forgive me if I seem muddled. Renée's my wife. My daughter's called Isabelle. She's seven. She's all I have left in the world. You don't have any children, do you?'

He looked around him once again to make sure there were no toys lying about, or any of those thousand and one things that reveal a child's presence in a house.

'They want to take her away from me, too. They're doing everything they can. They make no secret of it. I wish you could see how they treat me. Do you think I'm off my head?'

'No.'

'Mind you, it'd be better. I'd be put away immediately. Just as if I killed my wife. Or if I killed him. The best thing would to be kill the pair of them. But then, if I was in prison, who'd look after Isabelle? Do you see the problem?

'I've thought up complicated plans. I've hit on at least ten, and carefully worked them out down to the last detail. It's a question of not being found out. People would think they'd gone away together. I read in a paper that thousands of women in Paris disappear every year, and that the police don't bother to look for them. All the more unlikely, if he disappeared at the same time as her.

'Look, I've even decided, on one occasion, where I'd hide the bodies. I was working on a site way up above Montmartre. Where they precast concrete. I'd have driven them away at night in my van, and no one would ever have found them.'

He was getting worked up, but was now talking fairly freely, though he kept a close watch on the Inspector's reactions.

'Has anyone ever come and told you he intended to kill his wife or anyone else before?'

This was all so unexpected that Maigret caught himself racking his brain.

'Not like this,' he finally admitted.

'Do you think I'm lying or making up a story to seem interesting?'

'No.'

'Do you believe I really want to kill my wife?'

'You obviously intend to.'

'And that I'll do it?'

'No.'

'Why not?'

'Because you came to see me.'

Planchon got up, too on edge, too tense to remain seated. He raised his arms to the ceiling.

'That's what I think, too!' he almost sobbed. 'That's why I went away, each time, before seeing you. That's why I needed to talk to you, too. I'm not a criminal. I'm an honest man. And yet ...'

At this point, Maigret got up, went and fetched the decanter of plum brandy from the cupboard, and poured out a glass for his visitor.

'Aren't you having any?' the latter murmured, ashamed.

Then he glanced towards the dining-room:

'Of course, you haven't had supper yet. And I'm talking hot air. I want to explain everything all at once and I don't know where to begin.'

'Would you rather I asked you questions?'

'It might be easier.'

'Sit down.'

'I'll try.'

'How long have you been married?'

'Eight years.'

'Did you live alone?'

'Yes. I've always been alone. Ever since my mother died when I was fifteen. We lived in the Rue Picpus, not far from here. She used to go out cleaning.'

'And your father?'

'I never knew him.'

He had blushed.

'Did you become an apprentice?'

'Yes. I became a painter-decorator. I was twenty-six when my boss, who lived in the Rue Tholozé, found out he had a disease of the heart and decided to retire to the country.'

'Did you take over the firm?'

'I had some savings. Even so, it took me six years to pay off the capital.'

'Where did you meet your wife?'

'Do you know the Rue Tholozé, which leads into the Rue Lepic, just in front of the Moulin de la Galette? It's a blind alley which ends in a few steps. I live at the foot of the steps, in a small house in a yard, which is handy for ladders and materials.'

He was calming down. His speech was now more measured, flatter.

'About half-way along the street, on the left-hand side going up, there's a little dance hall, the *Bal des Copains*, where I sometimes used to spend an hour or two on a Saturday evening.'

'Did you dance?'

'No. I used to sit in a corner and order a lemonade, because I didn't drink then. I used to listen to the music and watch the couples.'

'Did you have any girl-friends?'

He answered bashfully:

'No.'

'Why not?'

He pointed to his lip.

'I'm not good-looking. Women have always scared me. I feel my infirmity must repel them.'

'Then you met one called Renée?'

'Yes. There was a big crowd that evening. We were put at the same table. I didn't dare speak to her. She was as frightened as I was. You could tell she wasn't used to . . .'

'Dances?'

'Dances, everything, Paris. In the end, she spoke to me, and I found out that she'd only been in town a month. I asked her where she came from. She came from Saint-Sauveur, near Fontenay-le-Comts in the Vendée, which happens to be my mother's village. When I was a child, I went there several times with her to see my aunts and uncles. That's what made things easy. We kept mentioning names we both knew.'

'What was Renée doing in Paris?'

'She was general help at a dairy in the Rue Lepic.'

'Was she younger than you?'

'I'm thirty-six and she's twenty-seven. That makes nearly ten years' difference. She was barely eighteen at the time.'

'Did you get married very quickly?'

'It took about ten months. Then we had a baby, a little girl, Isabelle. All the time my wife was pregnant, I was very frightened . . .'

'Of what?'

Once again he pointed to his hare-lip.

'They had told me it was hereditary. Thank heaven my daughter's normal! She's like her mother, except that she's got my fair hair and pale eyes.'

'Is your wife dark?'

'Like lots of people from the Vendée because, apparently, of the Portuguese sailors who used to go and fish there.'

'So now you want to kill her?'

'I don't see any alternative. We were happy, the three of us. Renée wasn't much of a housewife, perhaps. I don't want to run her down. She spent her childhood on a farm where no one bothered about tidiness or cleanliness. Down there in the marshes, they call the houses cabins and sometimes, in the winter, the water flows into the rooms.'

'I know.'

'Have you been there?'

'Yes.'

'I often used to do the housework at the end of the day. At that time, she was crazy about the cinema and, in the afternoon, she used to leave Isabelle with the concierge so she could go there.'

He spoke without bitterness.

'I didn't grumble. I musn't forget that she was the first woman to treat me as a normal man. You understand that, too, don't you?'

He no longer dared to turn towards the dining-room.

'Here, I am keeping you from your supper! What will your wife think?'

'Carry on. How many years were you happy?'

'Just a minute. I've never counted. I don't even quite know when it all began. I had a nice little firm. I spent what I earned putting the house into shape, repainting it, modernizing it, fixing up an attractive kitchen. You should come and ... But you won't. Or if you do, it'd mean that ...'

Once again he gripped his fingers, which were covered with red hairs.

'You presumably won't know the trade. At times, you've plenty of work and, at others, hardly any. It's difficult to keep the same workers. Except for old Jules, the one we call Pépère, who worked before for my old boss, I changed them almost every year.'

'Until the day ...'

'Until the day that Roger Prou joined the firm. He's a good-looking fellow, strong and shrewd, who knows what he's doing. At first, I was delighted to have got hold of a fellow like him, because I could trust him completely, on a job.'

'Did he make advances to your wife?'

'I don't honestly think so. He could have had as many women as he wanted, even customers, sometimes. I can't say because, to start with, I didn't notice anything, but I'm almost sure it was Renée who began it. It's not merely that I'm disfigured, but I'm not the sort of man a woman enjoys herself with.'

'What do you mean?'

'Nothing, really. I'm not very cheerful. I don't care for going out. What I like in the evenings is to stay at home and, on Sundays, go for a walk with my wife and daughter. For months, I didn't suspect anything. When we were out on a job, Prou used to slip back to the Rue Tholozé to go and fetch materials. Once, when I returned unexpectedly —it was two years ago—I found my daughter alone in the kitchen. I can still see her. She was sitting on the ground. I asked her: "Where's Maman?"'

'She answered, pointing to the bedroom: "There!"'

'She was only five at the time. They hadn't heard me coming and I caught them half-naked. Prou seemed embarrassed. Whereas my wife looked me straight in the face.

'"Well, now you know!" she said.'

'What did you do?'

'I left. I didn't know where I was going or what I was going to do. I found myself leaning on a bar and I got drunk for the first time in my life. I was thinking mainly of my daughter. I promised myself I'd go and take her away. I kept saying to myself: "She's yours! They've no right to keep her."'

'Then, after wandering about half the night. I went home. I'd been very ill. My wife was giving me black looks and, when I was sick on the carpet, she muttered: "You disgust me."'

'There you are! That's how it all began. The day before I was a happy man. All of a sudden.'

'Where's Roger Prou?'

'In the Rue Tholozé,' Planchon stammered, looking down.

'For the last two years?'

'Just about, yes.'

'Does he live with your wife?'

'All three of us live . . .'

He tried to wipe his glasses again and he blinked.

'Does it seem incredible to you?'

'No.'

'Do you understand why I couldn't leave her?'

'Leave your wife?'

'At first, I stayed on for her. Now, I don't know. I think it's only for my daughter, but maybe I'm wrong. You see, I couldn't bear the thought of life without Renée. Or the idea of being on my own again. And I had no right to throw her out. I was the one who took her and begged her to marry me. I was responsible for it, wasn't I?'

He sniffed and glanced sideways at the decanter. Maigret helped him to a second glass which he downed at a gulp.

'You'll be thinking I'm a drunkard. Mind you, I nearly became one. They don't like seeing me around the house in the evenings. They practically shove me out. You've no idea how unkind they are to me.'

'Prou settled in at your place from the very day you caught them?'

'No. Not straightaway. The next morning, I was surprised to see him carry on work as if nothing had happened. I didn't dare ask him what he had in mind. I was afraid of losing her, as I told you. I no longer knew where I stood. I trod carefully. I'm sure they went on seeing each other and, before long, they stopped taking any precautions. I was the one who hesitated before I came back, who made a noise to warn them I was there.

'One evening, he stayed to dinner. It was his birthday and Renée had cooked a superb meal. There was a bottle of champagne on the table. During the sweet, my wife asked me: "Don't you want to go out for a bit? Don't you realize you're in the way?"

'So I went out. I went out drinking. I asked myself questions. I tried to answer them. I told myself stories. I wasn't thinking of killing them then, I promise you. Tell me you believe me, Inspector. Tell me you don't think I'm mad. Tell me I'm not the loathsome creature my wife makes out I am!'

Madame Maigret's silhouette passed to and fro on the other side of the glass door of the dining-room. Planchon whined:

'I'm keeping you from your supper. Your wife will be cross. Why don't you go and eat?'

It was too late for the news, anyway.

On two or three occasions, Maigret had been tempted to pinch himself, to make sure that the man gesturing in front of him was real, that the scene was actually taking place, and that they were both living people.

At first sight, he was an ordinary man, one of the modest, striving millions you rub shoulders with every day in the Métro, in buses or on the pavement, heading for some unknown task and fate soberly and with dignity. Paradoxically, his hare-lip made him more impersonal, as if the blemish gave all those afflicted with it identical faces.

For a second, the Inspector wondered if Planchon had not, as some kind of diabolical ploy, deliberately chosen to come and wait for him in the Boulevard Richard-Lenoir, instead of being seen in his prosaic office at the Quai des Orfèvres. Was it not, in fact, intuition which had made him leave the glass waiting-room and its walls adorned with the photographs of police officers killed during the execution of their duties?

At Police Headquarters, where he had heard thousands of confessions, and where he had trapped so many people into heart-rending disclosures, Maigret would have seen his visitor in a sort of cold light.

But here, he was at home, in a familiar atmosphere, with Madame Maigret at hand, the smell of waiting supper, the furniture, the ornaments, the tiniest reflections of light in the same place that they had been for years and years. He would hardly be through the door, before it all enveloped him, like an old jacket you put on when you get home, and he was so used to the setting that, even after a month, he still resented the television set installed opposite the glass door of the dining-room.

Would he conduct as clear and detached an interrogation in this atmosphere as in his office, one of those interrogations which sometimes lasted hours, sometimes the whole night, and which used to leave him as exhausted as the victim?

For the first time in his entire career, a man had sought him out here, after putting it off for weeks, after following him in the street, after writing to him, so he made out, after tearing up his letters, and after waiting for him for hours in the waiting-room. A man, unremarkable in dress and appearance, had entered his home, humbly yet obstinately, to say in so many words:

'*I intend to kill two people: my wife and her lover. To this end, I have planned everything, worked it out to the last detail so as to avoid being caught ...*'

But now, instead of reacting sceptically, Maigret was listening to him with feverish concentration, not missing one of his changes of expression. He had almost stopped regretting the variety show he had planned to watch on television that evening, side by side with his wife, because they were still new to it and everything that happened on that little screen fascinated them.

What was more, just as the man indicated Madame Maigret moving about in the dining-room, he had almost said:

'Come and have a bite with us . . .'

He was hungry and he thought it might take some time.

He needed to know more, to ask questions, and to make sure he was not mistaken.

Twice or three times, his visitor, racked with doubt, had asked him:

'You don't think I'm mad, do you?'

He had thought of this possibility, too. There are varying degrees of madness, he knew by experience, and the tired haberdasher who came smiling into the waiting-room, to knit away until he needed her, was just one example.

The man had been drinking before he had appeared. He admitted that he drank every evening and the Inspector had given him a drink because he needed it.

Alcoholics plunge readily into a world of their own, one similiar to the real world, but with certain aberrations which are not always easy to detect. And they are sincere, too.

All these ideas had flashed through his head as he was listening, but none of them satisfied him. He was trying to understand better how to force his way into Planchon's bewildering little world.

'That was how I started to feel out of it,' said the man, still looking at him with his pale eyes. 'I don't know how to explain. I loved her. I think I still do. Yes, I'm almost sure I still love her, and I shall go on loving her, even if I have to kill her.

'Apart from my mother, she's the only person who took an interest in me and didn't worry about my infirmity.

'Besides, she's my wife. Whatever she does, she's my wife, isn't she? She gave me Isabelle. She carried her in her womb. You've no idea the months I went through while she was pregnant. I used to kneel down in front of her, thanking her for . . . I don't know how to say it. Part of my life was in her, do you understand? And Isabelle is part of both of our lives.

'Before, I was alone. No one looked after me. No one waited for me in the evenings. I worked without an object.

'Then, all of a sudden, she'd taken a lover, and I couldn't really blame her. She's young. She's attractive.

'Then, Roger Prou's more vigorous than I am. He's like an animal, bursting with health and strength.'

Madame Maigret had given up and returned to the kitchen. Maigret slowly filled another pipe.

'I kept arguing with myself. I kept on telling myself that it wouldn't last, that she'd come back to me, and that she'd realize that we were tied to each other, whatever she did. Am I boring you?'

'No. Go on.'

'I don't quite know what I'm saying. I think it was clearer in my letters, and not half so long.

'If I'd still been going to church, as when my mother was alive, I'd definitely have gone to confession. I don't remember how I came to think of you. At first, I didn't believe I'd have the courage to come and see you.

'Now that I'm here, I want to get it all off my chest. I promise you that I'm not talking so much because I've been drinking. I worked out everything I was going to say.

'Where was I?'

He was blinking and fiddling with a small brass ashtray which he had idly picked up from a small table.

'On the evening of Prou's birthday, they slung you out . . .'

'Not exactly, because they knew I'd come back. They sent me out so that they could spend the evening alone together.'

'Were you still hoping it would only be a phase?'

'Do you think I'm so naïve?'

'What happened after that?'

He gave a sigh and shook his head, like a man who has lost track of his thoughts.

'So much! Some days after his birthday, when I was home, about two or three in the morning, I found a camp-bed fixed up in the dining-room. At first, I didn't realize it was for me. I half-opened the door of the bedroom. They were both in the one bed, asleep, or pretending to be.

'What could I do? Roger Prou's stronger than I am. Besides, I wasn't very steady on my legs. I was convinced he might have struck me.

'Then, again, I didn't want Isabelle to wake up. She doesn't yet understand. In her eyes, I'm still her father.

'I slept on the camp-bed. When they got up, in the morning, I was already at work.

'My workmen gave me some odd leers. Only old Jules, the one with the white hair we call Pépère, reacted differently. He was in the firm before me, I think I told you. He calls me by my Christian name. He came and found me in the workshop and muttered: "Look here, Léonard, it's about time you slung that bitch out. If you don't act now, it'll end in disaster."

'He realized that I hadn't the courage. He looked me in the eyes, one hand on my shoulder, and concluded with a sigh: "I didn't realize you were as sick as all that . . ."

'I wasn't sick. It was just that I still loved her, needed her, her company, even if she was sleeping with someone else.

'I must ask you to answer me frankly, Monsieur Maigret.'

He didn't say Inspector, as he would have at the Quai des Orfèvres, but Monsieur Maigret, as if he wanted to underline the fact that it was the man he had come to see.

'Have you ever run across a case like mine?'

'Are you asking me if other men stay with their wives even though they know they have lovers?'

'Something of the sort.'

'Lots do.'

'Only I suppose their place is kept in the home, or at least there's some pretence made that they matter. Not me. For almost two years now, they've been slowly pushing me out. They hardly even lay my place at table. It's not Prou who's the stranger, it's me. During meals, they chat together, laugh, and talk to my daughter as if I were some sort of ghost.

'On Sundays, they take the van and go for a drive in the country. At first, I used to stay with Isabelle and always used to find some way of amusing her.

'If it weren't for Isabelle, I might have gone away. I don't know.

'In any case, my daughter goes more often with them now, because it's more fun to go for a car-ride.

'I've asked myself every question you can think of, not only in the evenings, when I've had a few drinks, but in the mornings, and all day while I'm working. I still work hard.

'Emotional questions and practical questions. Three months ago I even went and saw a lawyer. I didn't tell him as much as I've told you, because I felt he wasn't really listening to me, and that he was getting impatient.

' "So what do you really want?" he asked me.

' "I don't know."

' "A divorce?"

' "I don't know. The thing I want most is to keep my daughter."

' "Have you any proof of your wife's misconduct?"

' "I've told you that, every night, I sleep on a camp-bed while the two of them are in my room . . ."

' "It'd have to be checked by a police inspector. Under what code were you married?"

'He explained to me that, as we hadn't signed a marriage contract, Renée and I were married under the joint estate system, which means that my business, my house, my furniture, everything I own, including the clothes I have on, are just as much hers as mine.

' "What about my daughter?" I went on. "Would they give me my daughter?"

' "That depends. If misconduct is proved and if the judge . . ." '

He gritted his teeth.

'He told me something else,' he went on, after a moment. 'Before I went to see him, like before I came here, I had a drink or two to set me up. He noticed it straightaway. I realized this by the way he treated me.

' "The judge will decide which of you is better able to provide your daughter with a normal life."

'My wife said the same thing in other words. "What's stopping you from going away?" she said several times. "Haven't you any self-respect? Don't you realize that you're not wanted here?"'

'Each time I answered stubbornly: "I shall never abandon my daughter."

' "She's mine, too, isn't she? Do you think I'd let her go off with a drunkard like you?"'

'I'm not a drunkard, Monsieur Maigret. I beg you to believe me, in spite of appearances. I never drank before all this, not even the odd drop. But what could I do in the evenings, all alone in the streets?

'I started going into bistros and leaning on the bars, just to feel people around me, and hear people talking, human voices.

'I have one drink, then another. Then I start thinking, and that makes me want to drink another and another.

'I tried to stop and I felt so ill that I wanted to go and throw myself in the Seine. I thought about it a lot. It was the easiest way out. It was Isabelle that stopped me. I don't want to leave her to them. It's the thought that one day she might call him Papa.'

He was now crying quite unashamedly. He pulled his handkerchief out of his pocket. Maigret kept watching him stolidly.

There was obviously some aberration. Whether drunk or not, the man was becoming hysterical, purposely giving way to despair.

From the strict police angle, there was nothing to be done. The man had done nothing wrong. He intended to kill his wife and her lover, at least so he made out. But he had not even informed them of his intention, so there was no question of a threat of death.

From the legal point of view, all the Inspector could have said to him was:

'Come back afterwards.'

When at last he was guilty! He could have added, with little fear of correction:

'If you tell your story to the jury as you've just told it to me, and if you have a good lawyer, you'll probably be acquitted.'

Was this the solution that Planchon had, in some sense, come to wheedle out of him? For a few seconds, Maigret suspected him. He did not like men who gave way to tears. He was suspicious of men who confessed easily and this display of feelings, exaggerated by drink, certainly irritated him.

He had already missed his dinner and the television show. Planchon showed no signs of going. He seemed to be enjoying the warm atmosphere of the flat, too. Was he going to be like one of those stray dogs you pat as you pass by and then cannot get rid of?

'I'm sorry,' Planchon stammered, wiping his eyes. 'You must think me absurd. It's the first time in my life I've confided in anyone.'

Maigret was tempted to reply:

'Why in me?'

It was because the papers had written so much about him, and the journalists had built him up as a humane policeman who could understand everything.

'How long ago is it,' he asked, 'since you wrote me the first letter?'

'It's more than two months. It was in a little café on the Place du Tertre.'

Maigret had been a lot in the news at the time, in connection with a crime committed by a young man of eighteen.

'So you wrote about ten letters, all of which you tore up? All in the space of about a week?'

'Yes, about that. I even used to write two or three the same evening and not tear them up till the next morning.'

'Then, for six or seven weeks, you came each Saturday to the Quai des Orfèvres?'

From the way he announced himself, waited in the glass cage, and disappeared before he was seen, he had become almost a legendary figure, like the ex-haberdasher and her knitting. Was it Janvier or Lucas who had christened him 'the Saturday caller'?

Yet, during this time, Planchon had not put his threat into action. He had gone back each night to the Rue Tholozé, lain down on his camp-bed, got up first in the morning and carried on with his work as if nothing had happened.

Yet the man was more subtle than might have been thought.

'I can guess what you're thinking,' he murmured sadly.

'What's that?'

'That I've accepted the situation for almost two years. That, for two months, I've been talking about killing my wife or killing the pair of them.

'Because I haven't done it yet. Admit that's it! You're thinking I'd never have the guts.'

Maigret shook his head.

'That wouldn't need any guts. Any fool can commit murder.'

'But what if there's no other way out? Put yourself in my place. I had a nice little business and a wife and child. It's all being taken from me. Not only my wife and child but my livelihood. Because they never discuss going away. In their eyes, I'm the one who's in the way, so it's up to me to go. That's what I'm trying to make you understand.

'Look, even with the customers. It's happened gradually. Prou was just one of my employees, an intelligent, hard-working employee, I grant you. He's got more of the gift of the gab than I have. He handles the customers better than I do, too, especially the women.

'Without my realizing it, he began to act the boss, and when people rang up about a job, they nearly always asked for him. If I disappeared tomorrow, my absence would hardly be noticed. It's possible my daughter would be the only one who asked after me. I can't tell. He's more cheerful than I am. He tells her stories, sings her songs, and gives her rides.'

'What does your daughter call him?'

'She calls him Roger, like my wife. It doesn't surprise her that they sleep in the same room. During the day, the camp-bed's folded up and pushed into a cupboard, so it's as if any trace of me was wiped out. But I've kept you too long already. I'd like to apologize to your wife, she must be cross with me.'

This time, it was Maigret, intent on understanding, who stopped him from going.

'Listen to me, Monsieur Planchon . . .'

'I'm listening.'

'For two months, you've been trying to come to me and say, in so many words: "I intend to kill my wife and her lover." That's right, isn't it?'

'Yes.'

'For two months, you've been living daily with this thought.'

'Yes. There's nothing else I . . .'

'Just a moment! I don't suppose you expect me to say: "Go ahead!"'

'You've no right to.'

'But you think I should share your point of view?'

A quick flash in the man's eyes told him that he was not far from the truth.

'It's one of two things. Forgive me if I'm brutal with you. Either you've no intention of killing anyone, only the desire, especially after a few drinks . . .'

Planchon shook his head sadly.

'Let me finish. Or else, it seems to me, you haven't really made up your mind and you want to find someone to dissuade you.'

The man came back again with his eternal argument:

'There's no alternative.'

'Did you expect me to find you a solution?'

'There isn't one.'

'Right! Now, supposing my theory's incorrect. I can only see one other. You really have planned to kill your wife and her lover. You've even gone so far as to think up a place where you could get rid of the bodies.'

'I've thought of everything.'

'Yet you've come to see me, and my job is to lay my hands on criminals . . .'

'I know.'

'What do you know?'

'That it doesn't make sense.'

His stubborn expression indicated that he was sticking to his guns. He had started off in life without money, without means, with hardly any education. As far as Maigret could tell, his intelligence was fairly low.

Though he had been left alone in Paris after his mother's death, he had, however, managed through sheer persistence, to become the boss of a small but prosperous firm.

Could it be said that this man lacked logic? Even if he had started to drink?

'You mentioned confession just now. You told me that, if you had continued to practise your religion, you would have gone and confided in a priest.'

'I think so.'

'What do you think the priest would have told you?'

'I don't know. I suppose he would have tried to persuade me to drop my plan.'

'And what about me?'

'You, too.'

'In other words, you want someone to restrain you, to stop you making a fool of yourself.'

Planchon suddenly seemed lost. A moment earlier, he had still been looking at Maigret with confidence, with hope. Suddenly, it was as if they were no longer talking the same language, as if all the words they had exchanged up till then had been pointless.

He shook his head, and there was a sort of reproach in his eyes. Disappointment, anyway. He muttered very quietly:

'It's not that.'

Was he on the point of taking his hat and leaving, sorry he had wasted his time coming?

'Just a moment, Planchon. Try and listen to me, instead of following your own train of thought.'

'I am trying, Monsieur Maigret.'

'What benefit, what comfort would your confession to a priest have given you?'

He replied, still in a whisper:

'I don't know.'

He was still only half there. He was already beginning to withdraw into his shell, and to hear the Inspector's voice only as those anonymous voices he heard in the evenings when he was propping up bars.

'Would you still have killed afterwards?'

'I suppose so. It's time I went away.'

Maigret, apparently annoyed at disappointing him, kept on at him, searching for a glimmer of truth which he thought, at times, he could perceive.

'You don't like being stopped from doing what you've decided?'

'No.'

He added with an odd smile:

'Unless I'm put in prison, it isn't possible. And so long as I haven't done anything, I can't be put in prison.'

'So what you came here for was a sort of absolution? You had to know that you would be understood, that you weren't a monster, and that your plan was the only solution left to you.'

Planchon repeated:

'I don't know.'

He was so lost in the clouds that Maigret felt like shaking him, yelling at him, face to face, staring him in the eyes.

'Look, Planchon . . .'

He kept on saying the same thing, too. It was probably the tenth time that he had repeated the same words.

'As you've just said, I've no right to lock you up. But I can have you watched, even if it doesn't prevent anything. You'll be arrested immediately. It won't be me who tries you, but a court, and they won't necessarily try to understand, and they may be chiefly concerned with premeditation.

'Didn't you tell me that you had no family in Paris?'

'I haven't any anywhere.'

'What will become of your daughter, even during the months while the case is being prepared? And afterwards?'

Once again came the same old 'I don't know'.

'What then?'

'Nothing.'

'What are you going to do?'

'I don't know. I've no idea. I'll try.'

'What?'

'To get used to it.'

Maigret felt like yelling at him that this was not what he was asking him.

'What is there to stop you leaving?'

'With my daughter?'

'You're still head of the family.'

'What about her?'

'Is it your wife you're thinking of?'

Planchon nodded ashamedly. Then he added:

'And what about my business?'

This showed that it wasn't just a question of feelings.

'I'll see.'

'Will you come back and see me?'

'I've told you everything. I've taken up too much of your time as it is. Your wife . . .'

'Never mind my wife, this concerns you. Don't come back and see me, all right. But I want to keep in touch. Don't forget it was you who came to see me.'

'I'm sorry.'

'You're to ring me up every day.'

'Here?'

'Here or at my office. All I ask you is to ring me.'

'Why?'

'No special reason. To keep in touch. You'll say: "It's me!" And that will be enough.'

'I'll do it.'

'Every day?'

'Every day.'

'And supposing, at some point, you feel you're about to put your plan into action, will you ring me?'

He hesitated, and seemed to be weighing the pros and cons.

'That'd mean that I wouldn't do it,' he finally got out.

He was haggling, like a peasant at a fair.

'You realize that, if I ring you up to say that ...'

'Answer my question.'

'I'll try.'

'That's all I'm asking. And now, go home.'

'Not yet.'

'Why not?'

'It's not time. They'll both still be in the dining-room. What would I do?'

'Are you going to hang round the bistros again?'

He gave a resigned shrug and glanced at the decanter of plum brandy. Maigret, irritated, poured him a last glass.

'You might as well get drunk here as elsewhere.'

The man hesitated, glass in hand, a little ashamed.

'Do you despise me?'

'I don't despise anyone.'

'But supposing you did despise someone?'

'It certainly wouldn't be you.'

'Are you saying that to encourage me?'

'No. Because it's what I think.'

'Thank you.'

This time, he was holding his hat and glancing round him, as if he were looking for something else.

'I'd like you to explain to your wife ...'

Maigret edged him gently towards the door.

'I've spoilt your evening. And hers, too.'

He was on the landing now, more anonymous even than in Maigret's flat, a small, very ordinary man that no one would have looked at twice.

'Goodbye, Monsieur Maigret.'

Phew! The door closed and Madame Maigret shot out of the kitchen.

'I thought he'd never stop and you'd never get rid of him. I almost came in to give you an excuse.'

She stared at her husband.

'You seem preoccupied.'

'I am.'

'Is he mad?'

'I don't think so.'

She rarely asked him any questions. But this had happened at home. As she was bringing in the soup, she even went so far as to murmur:

'What did he come for?'

'To confess.'

She did not turn a hair, but sat down at table.

'Aren't you going to switch on the television?'

'The programme must be nearly over.'

In the old days, on Saturday evenings, when he was not held up at the Quai des Orfèvres, they used to go to the pictures together, not so much for the entertainment as to be out together. They would stroll, arm in arm, towards the Boulevard Bonne-Nouvelle. They felt at ease like that, with no need to talk.

'Tomorrow,' said Maigret, 'we'll go for a walk round Montmartre.'

Arm in arm, like Sunday strollers. He wanted to see the Rue Tholozé again, and look for a small house at the far end of a yard, where Léonard Planchon, his wife, his daughter and Roger Prou lived.

Was he right? Was he wrong? Had he said the right things?

Had Planchon got what he was after in the Boulevard Richard-Lenoir?

At that moment, he would be drinking somewhere, presumably chewing over all he had said.

It was impossible to tell if this conversation, so much longed for and so often postponed, had brought him any relief or if, on the contrary, it was going to start something.

It was the first time that Maigret had said goodbye to a man on the landing at his home, wondering if the same man might not, a little later on, kill two people.

It could happen that very night, at any time, possibly at the very moment that Maigret was thinking about it.

'What's the matter?'

'Nothing. I don't like this business.'

He thought of telephoning the Police Station in the 18th arrondissement, to have a watch kept on Planchon's house. But how could you put a policeman on point duty in the bedroom?

A police officer in the street would not be any use, either.

It was a typical Sunday morning, lazy, empty and a bit flat. If Maigret happened to be at home on that day, he would lie in, even if he was not sleepy, knowing that his wife did not like him 'getting under her feet', until she had done most of the housework.

He nearly always heard her get up quietly about seven o'clock, slip out of bed and cross to the door on tiptoe; then he would hear the click of the switch in the next room and a strip of light would appear at floor level.

He would go back to sleep again, without having really woken up. He knew that this was how things happened and the knowledge entered into his sleep.

It was a different kind of sleep from other days, a Sunday morning sleep. It had a different quality, and a different feel, too. For instance, every half-hour, he would hear the bells and he would be aware of the emptiness of the streets, the absence of lorries and the lack of buses.

He also knew that he had no responsibilities, and there was nothing hurrying him or waiting for him outside.

Later would come the muffled hum of the hoover in the other rooms; later still, the smell of coffee, which he specially liked.

All families have their traditions, to which they cling and which give a bit of colour to even the gloomiest of days.

He dreamt of Planchon. It was not really a dream. He saw him, as he had on the previous day, in their small living-room, but his attitude was different. Instead of being confused with emotion and despair, his features, disfigured by his hare-lip, conveyed malice and irony. Although the man was not moving his lips, Maigret had the impression that he was saying:

'Admit that you agree with me, that I've no alternative but to kill her. You don't dare to say it, because you're an official and you're afraid of blotting your copybook. Yet you're not trying to restrain me. You're waiting for me to be done with her and with him . . .'

A hand shook his shoulder gently and a familiar voice spoke the ritual words:

'It's nine o'clock.'

His wife handed him his first cup of coffee, which he always drank before he got up.

'What's the weather like?'

'Cold. And windy.'

Already fresh and neatly dressed in a pale blue overall, she drew the curtains. The sky was white, and the air looked white, too, an icy white.

Maigret, in his dressing-gown and slippers, went and sat down in the dining-room, which had been cleaned. The morning would now consist of certain rites which had gradually been established over the years.

Presumably it was the same in the flats which he could see on the opposite side of the Boulevard Richard-Lenoir, as well as in most homes in Paris and elsewhere. Presumably these little humdrum habits answered some need.

'What are you thinking about?' she asked.

She had noticed that he was preoccupied, sullen.

'About that fellow yesterday.'

Planchon's wife did not wake up her husband with hot coffee. When he opened his eyes, after a drunkard's restless sleep, he found himself on a camp-bed in the dining-room, and he was the one who got up first, hearing regular breathing from the next room, perhaps, and imagining two warm and relaxed bodies drowsing in the bed.

The picture affected him more than his visitor's long speech of the previous day. Planchon had really only mentioned weekdays. But what happened on Sundays? His employees would not be waiting for him in the yard or in the shed. He had nothing to do, either. It was probably Renée and her lover who were lying in at his place.

Did Planchon make coffee for them all, and lay the table in the kitchen? Did his daughter, in her nightdress, barefoot, her face puffy with sleep, go and join him there?

The man had told him that she did not ask any questions, but that would have not have stopped Isabelle from keeping her eyes open and wondering. What impression did she have of family life and of her father's?

Maigret ate his croissants while Madame Maigret began to get lunch ready. Now and then, they exchanged a few words through the kitchen door. The evening papers, which they had not read the day before, were on the table, with the weeklies which he kept for Sunday mornings.

Another tradition was a telephone call to Police Headquarters. Only, feeling slightly worried, he may have made it a little earlier.

Torrence was on duty. He recognized his voice, and imagined him in the near-empty offices.

'Anything new?'

'Nothing special, Chief, except that there was another jewel robbery last night.'

'At the Crillon again?'

'At the Plazza, in the Avenue Montaigne.'

Yet he had posted an inspector in each of the big hotels in the Champs-Elysées and the surrounding area.

'Who was there?'

'Vacher.'

'Didn't he see anything?'

'No. The same technique again.'

Naturally they had studied the records of all jewel-thieves, including Interpol records. But this one's methods didn't tally with any of the known experts, and he was working non-stop as if, in the space of a few days, he wanted to pile up a big enough fortune to retire on.

'Did you send someone to help Vacher?'

'Dupeu's gone to join him. There's nothing they can do for the moment. Most of the guests are still asleep.'

Torrence must have found the next question an odd one.

'No incidents in the 18th arrondissement?'

'Nothing I can recall. Hang on while I look at the reports. Just a moment. *Bercy* . . . *Bercy* . . . I'll skip all the *Bercys* . . .'

These, in police jargon, were the drunk and disorderly who were hauled off to spend the rest of the night in the Station.

'A fight at 3.15 a.m. in the Place Pigalle. Robbery. Another robbery. Stabbing, after a dance, in the Boulevard Rochechouart.'

The normal Saturday evening tally.

'No murders?'

'I don't see any.'

'Thank you. Have a good day. Give me a ring if there's any news from the Plazza.'

As he hung up, Madame Maigret asked him from the door:

'Are you worrying about that fellow yesterday?'

He looked at her like a man lost for an answer.

'Do you think he'll kill them in the end?'

As he was going to bed, he had told his wife about Planchon's confession, light-heartedly, as if he did not take the matter seriously.

'You don't think he's off his head?'

'I don't know. I'm not a psychiatrist.'

'Why do you think he came to see you? As soon as I saw him on the landing, I knew it wasn't an ordinary visit. I must admit he frightened me.'

Why should he worry? Was it any of his business? Not yet, anyway. He answered his wife evasively, settled down in his armchair and buried himself in the papers.

He had only been sitting down ten minutes when he got up, went and fetched the telephone directory, and found the name Planchon, Léonard, painter and decorator, Rue Tholozé.

The man had not cheated over his identity. Maigret hesitated a moment before dailling the number, but finally did it. As the ringing tone echoed in a strange house, he felt something tighten in his chest.

At first he thought there was no one there, because the ringing went on a long time. Finally, there was a click and a voice asked:

'What is it?'

It was the voice of a woman who did not sound in a very good mood.

'I'd like to speak to Monsieur Planchon.'

'He's not here.'

'Is that Madame Planchon?'

'It is, yes.'

'Do you know when your husband will be back?'

'He's just gone out with his daughter.'

Maigret noticed that she had said *his* daughter, and not *my* daughter, or *our* daughter. He also realized that someone in the room was talking to the woman, presumably saying:

'Ask him his name.'

In fact, after a short pause, she inquired:

'Who is that?'

'A customer. I'll ring back.'

He hung up. Renée was alive, all right. Roger Prou was, too, presumably, and Planchon had gone out with his daughter, which proved that the Rue Tholozé, like other places, had its Sunday rites.

He hardly gave it another thought all morning. Once he had scanned the papers with little interest, he stood a while by the window, watching people coming back from Mass, walking briskly, leaning forward, their faces blue with cold. Then he had a bath and got dressed, as the smell of cooking spread into every corner of the flat.

At midday, they had lunch facing each other, because they did not put on the television. They talked about Doctor Pardon's daughter, who was expecting her second child, and then about other things which did not stick in his mind.

About three o'clock, the washing-up done and the flat straight again, he suggested:

'How about a walk?'

Madame Maigret put on her astrakhan coat. He chose his thickest scarf.

'Where do you want to go?'

'To Montmartre.'

'That's right. You said so yesterday. Shall we take the Métro?'

'It'd be warmer.'

They got out at the Place Blanche and began to walk slowly up the Rue Lepic. The shutters of the shops there were closed.

The Rue Lepic makes a big bend where it meets the Rue des Abbesses, while the Rue Tholozé climbs straight up a steep slope, and rejoins it up by the Moulin de la Galette.

'Is this where he lives?'

'A little further up. Just at the foot of the steps.'

Almost half-way up on the left, Maigret noticed a house with violet-painted letters which lit up at night: *Bal des Copains*. Three youths were standing on the pavement, apparently waiting for someone. From inside came the sound of an accordion. No one was dancing yet. The accordionist, at the end of the near-dark room, was rehearsing.

It was here that, nine years before, the lonely Planchon had accidentally met Renée, because there was a crowd, and because a harassed waiter had sat the young girl down at his table.

The Maigrets, slightly out of breath, kept on walking. Between some five or six-storey blocks of flats, there were still a few low houses which went back to the time when Montmartre was a village.

They eventually came to an iron gate opening on to a cobbled yard, at the end of which was a small flintstone house, the kind you generally see in the suburbs. It was a single-storey building, already dingy, old-fashioned, with alternating red and yellow bricks round the windows. The woodwork was freshly painted blue, which clashed with the general scheme.

'Is this where he lives?'

They did not dare stop, but merely took in as much as they could as they passed slowly by. Madame Maigret later remembered that the curtains were very clean. Whereas Maigret noticed the ladders in the yard, a hand-cart, and a wooden shed. Through its windows drums of paint were visible.

The van was not in the yard. There was no garage. The curtains did not move. There was no sign of life. Were they to assume that Planchon, his wife, Isabelle and Prou had all gone out together for a car-ride?

'What shall we do?'

Maigret did not know. He had had the urge to see and, now he had seen, he had no plans.

'Why don't we go up to the Place du Tertre while we're here?'

They drank a carafe of vin rosé, and a long-haired artist offered to do their portraits.

The Maigrets were home by 6 p.m. He rang the Quai des Orfèvres. Dupeu was back. He had not found anything at the Plazza. Some of the guests, who had spent the night out, had not yet rung for their breakfasts.

He did not miss his television this time, although there was a thriller on which made him grumble all evening.

In fact, while he enjoyed the boredom of Sunday, he enjoyed still more the moment, on Monday morning, when he took charge of his office again. He checked in and shook hands with his colleagues.

They all discussed current business but Maigret preferred to keep quiet about the visit he had had on Saturday evening. Was he afraid he would seem absurd because he attached so much importance to it?

It was the only day of the week on which everyone shook hands. Lucas, Janvier, young Lapointe and all the rest were there, except for those who had been on duty. All of them had, like himself, spent their Sunday at home.

He finally picked on Lapointe and Janvier and took them into his office.

'Have you kept the cards we made for the Rémond affair?'

This went back several months, to early autumn. It had been a question of collecting evidence against a man called Rémond, with many aliases, suspected of having pulled off swindles in most European countries. He lived in a furnished flat in the Rue de Ponthieu and, to get into it without arousing the owner's suspicions, Janvier and Lapointe had turned up one morning with some official-looking cards from a fictitious office for revaluating building space.

'We have to measure every room, every passage,' they said.

They carried brief-cases, stuffed with papers, under their arms. Young Lapointe took notes solemnly while Janvier unrolled his steel tape-measure.

It was not entirely legal; still, it was not the first time they had used the trick, and it would serve again.

'Go to the Rue Tholozé. At the very top, on the right, there's a small house at the far side of a yard.'

Maigret would have given a lot to go there himself and sniff round the corners of the house, about which he wanted to know everything.

He gave detailed instructions and, once his colleagues had gone, settled down to routine business.

The sky was still white and hard and the Seine a nasty grey. It was nearly midday when Janvier and Lapointe returned. Maigret took his time signing some administrative papers before he rang for Joseph to go and fetch them.

'Well, lads?'

It was Janvier who spoke.

'We rang.'

'Naturally. And it was the woman who opened the door. What was she like?'

They exchanged a glance.

'Dark, quite tall, good figure.'

'Attractive?'

This time Lapointe chipped in:

'I'd describe her as a handsome female . . .'

'How was she dressed?'

'She was wearing a red dressing-gown and slippers. She hadn't done her hair. She had a yellow nightdress on under the dressing-gown.'

'Did you see her daughter?'

'No. She must have been at school.'

'Was the van in the yard?'

'No. And there wasn't anyone in the workshop.'

'How did she react to you?'

'Suspiciously. First of all, she watched us through the curtains. Then we heard footsteps in the passage. She half-opened the door and, showing only part of her face, asked: "What is it? I don't want anything."

'We explained what it was all about.'

'Wasn't she surprised?'

'She asked: "Are you doing this in the whole street?"'

'When we answered yes, she decided to let us in.

' "Will it take long?"

' "Half an hour at the very most."

' "Do you have to measure the whole house?" '

Then the two inspectors recorded their impressions. It was the kitchen that had struck them most.

'A magnificent kitchen, Chief, very bright and modern, with all the bits and pieces. You wouldn't expect to find a kitchen like that in an old house. There was even a dish-washer.'

Maigret was not surprised. Was it not typical of Planchon to provide his wife with every comfort?

'In fact, it's a very cheerful house. You can see straightaway it belongs to a decorator, because everything seems to have been freshly painted. In the girl's bedroom, the furniture's been painted pink.'

This detail, too, was typical of the Saturday caller.

'Go on.'

'Next to the kitchen is a fairly big living-room which is used as a dining-room, with country furniture.'

'Did you find the camp-bed?'

'In the cupboard, yes.'

Janvier added:

'I remarked casually: "That's handy, for putting up friends." '

'She didn't flinch?'

'No. She followed us everywhere, watching what we did, not too convinced that we'd really been sent by an official agency. At one point, she asked: "What's the point of all these measurements you're taking?"

'I handed her out the blarney: that, now and then, because of alterations to buildings, we had to revise the bases of property tax and that, if they hadn't added anything on, they stood to gain by it.

'I don't think she's very bright, but she's not the sort of woman who's taken in easily, and I could see the moment coming when she'd pick up the 'phone and ring up our imaginary office.

'That was why we got through it as quickly as possible. There are two other rooms on the ground floor: a bedroom and a smaller room which is used as an office and where the 'phone is.

'The bedroom, which is cheerful, too, hadn't yet been done out and was in chaos. The office was a typical small firm's office, a few files, bills stuck on a hook, a twenty-four hour stove and samples blocking up the fireplace.

'The bathroom isn't on the ground floor, but on the first floor, next to the girl's bedroom.'

'Is that all?'

Lapointe came in:

'There was a 'phone call while we were there. She made the caller repeat the name twice, wrote it down on a note-pad and said: "No, he's not here at the moment. He's on a site. What? Monsieur Prou, yes. I'll pass on your message and he'll come and see you, this afternoon probably."

'Now, Chief, if you want to know the size of each room . . .'

They had completed their job. Though Maigret was not much further on than before, at least he had a clearer idea of the house, and it was just as he had imagined it.

Did the two men, the husband and the lover, work at the same place or, on the contrary, did they prefer to work on different jobs? Didn't they have to talk to each other for their work? What tone did they use?

Maigret went home to lunch and asked if anyone had rung him up. No, they had not, and it was not until just after six that the call he was expecting was put through to his office.

'Hullo! Monsieur Maigret?'

'Speaking, yes.'

'Planchon here.'

'Where are you?'

'In a café on the Place des Abbesses, a few steps from a house where I've been working all day. I've kept my word. You asked me to ring you.'

'How do you feel?'

There was a pause.

'Do you feel calm?'

'I always feel calm. I've been thinking a lot.'

'You went for a walk with your daughter, yesterday morning, didn't you?'

'How did you know? I took her to the Flea Market.'

'And in the afternoon?'

'They took the car.'

'All three of them?'

'Yes.'

'Did you stay at home?'

'I had a sleep.'

So he was in the house when Maigret and his wife were passing the gate.

'I've been thinking a lot.'

'What conclusions have you come to?'

'I don't know. There aren't any. I'm going to try and hang on as long as possible. Deep down, I wonder if I'm all that keen on a change. In any case, as you said yesterday, I might lose Isabelle.'

Maigret could hear the clink of glasses, a distant murmur of voices, and the ring of a cash register.

'Will you ring me tomorrow?'

The man at the other end of the line hesitated.

'Do you think there's any point?'

'I'd rather you called me every day.'

'Don't you trust me?'

How could he answer that question?

'I'll hang on, don't worry!'

He gave a sad little laugh.

'I've stuck it out for two years. I'm enough of a coward to go on indefinitely. Because I am a coward, aren't I? Admit that's what you're thinking. Instead of doing something about it, like a man, I came snivelling to you.'

'You had reason to come and you didn't snivel.'

'You don't despise me?'

'No.'

'Did you tell your wife all about me, after I'd gone?'

'No, I didn't.'

'Didn't she want to know who that maniac was who spoilt your supper?'

'You ask too many questions, Monsieur Planchon. You're too self-conscious.'

'I'm sorry.'

'Go home now.'

'Home?'

Maigret was at a loss to know what to say to him. He didn't remember ever having been so embarrassed in his life.

'But, damn it all, man, it's your house, isn't it? If you don't want to go back there, go somewhere else. But do avoid hanging round the bistros, because you'll only get more and more worked up.'

'I feel you're annoyed.'

'I'm not annoyed. I merely want you to stop chewing over the same ideas again and again.'

Maigret was annoyed with himself. Perhaps he had been wrong to speak like that. It is difficult, especially on the telephone, to find the right words to say to a man who is planning to kill his wife and his foreman.

It was an absurd situation and, to crown it all, it was as if Planchon had feelers. Though Maigret was not really annoyed, he resented being saddled with this affair which he would not have dared to tell his colleagues about for fear they would think him a fool.

'Keep calm, Monsieur Planchon.'

He could find only the sort of stupid formulas you use to comfort people.

'Don't forget to call me tomorrow. And keep telling yourself that what you've got in mind won't settle anything, quite the contrary.'

'Thank you.'

It was not convincing. Planchon was disappointed. He had only just left work, and presumably he had not drunk enough for it to make any difference or for him to see things a certain way, as on Saturday evening, for instance.

He must have been stone-cold sober and without illusions. How did he see himself, in the absurd or loathsome role that he was playing in his own house?

His 'Thank you' had been bitter. Maigret wanted to go on talking, but he had to give up because his caller had rung off. There was another solution, which the man had scarcely mentioned on the Saturday and which suddenly worried the Inspector.

Now that Planchon had defined his problems by telling them to someone, and now that he could not foster any more illusions about himself, might he not be tempted to settle things by doing away with himself?

If Maigret had known where he had rung from, he would have telephoned him back straightaway. But what could he say?

Damn and blast it! It was not his business. He did not have to interfere. It was not his job to sort out people's lives, but to lay hands on those who had committed crimes or offences.

He worked for another hour, almost savagely, at the jewel robbery case, which would probably keep him going for weeks. It seemed obvious that the thief had, on each occasion, been a guest at the hotel from which the jewels had disappeared. The thefts had taken place in four different hotels, at two or three day intervals.

In this case, it seemed simple enough to study the list of guests in the hotels and to lay hands on the man or men on the various lists. But this did not work. And little more was gained from the descriptions supplied by the hall-porters.

Weeks? It might take months, and it was possible that the story might end in London, Cannes or Rome, unless they found signs of the jewels at some dealer's in Antwerp or Amsterdam.

Yet it was less depressing than dealing with a Planchon. Maigret went home by taxi, because it was late. He had dinner, watched the television, went to sleep and was woken by the familiar smell of coffee.

At the office, he growled:

'Get me the 18th arrondissement Police Station. Hullo, is that the 18th? Is that you, Bernard? Anything interesting last night? No. No murders? No missing persons? Look, would you keep a discreet watch on a small house at the top of the Rue Tholozé, just below the steps. Yes. Not a twenty-four hour watch, of course. Only at night. Just a glance on each round. Check, for instance, that a decorator's van is in the yard. Thank you. Oh yes, if it's not there at night, ring me at home. Nothing special. Just an idea. You know how it is. Thanks, old boy!'

Just another routine day, people to question, not only about the jewels, but about two or three matters of lesser importance.

From six o'clock onwards, he kept an eye on the 'phone. It rang twice, but it was not Planchon. At half-past six, he still had not telephoned, nor at seven, and Maigret grew annoyed with himself for feeling anxious.

Nothing could have happened during the daytime. It seemed inconceivable, for instance, that Planchon could have taken advantage of his daughter's being at school and come back and killed his wife, and then waited for Prou to return and done away with him, too.

In fact, Maigret had not asked him what weapon he had intended to use. Had not the decorator told him that he had worked out his double crime down to the last detail?

He was unlikely to have a revolver and, even if he had, it was hardly likely that he would use it. Men of his kind and most manual workers normally tend to use a tool with which they are familiar.

What tool would a house-painter . . .?

He could not help laughing at himself when he thought of a paintbrush.

At a quarter past seven, he still had not rung, so Maigret went home. The telephone did not ring during supper or during the evening.

'Still thinking about him?' his wife asked.

'Not all the time, of course, but it worries me.'

'You told me once that people who talk a lot rarely do anything.'

'Rarely, I agree. But it does happen.'

'Have you caught a cold?'

'Maybe on Sunday, in Montmartre. Do I sound thick?'

She went to fetch him an aspirin and he slept right through the night. When he woke up, he saw the rain streaming down the windows.

He waited until ten before he phoned the 18th.

'Bernard?'

'Yes, Chief.'

'Nothing from the Rue Tholozé?'

'No. The car hasn't left the yard.'

It was only at seven in the evening, still without news, that he made up his mind to telephone the Rue Tholozé. A man's voice, which he did not recognize, replied:

'Planchon? Yes, that's right. But he's not here. He won't be here this evening, either.'

CHAPTER FOUR

Maigret got the impression that his caller had tried to hang up on him and that, at the last moment, he had hesitated, as if he were suspicious. The Inspector quickly asked:

'How about Madame Planchon?'

'She's gone out.'

'Won't she be back this evening, either?'

'She should be back any minute. She's gone shopping locally.'

Another pause. The instrument was so sensitive that Maigret could hear Prou's breathing.

'What do you want her for? Who are you?'

He almost passed himself off as a customer and told him some story. After a pause, he decided to ring off.

He had never seen the man to whom he had spoken at the other end of the line. The little he knew about him was through Planchon, who had reason to be prejudiced.

Yet as soon as he heard the sound of his voice, Maigret immediately felt antipathetic towards Renée's lover and resented him. His antipathy did not stem from the decorator's story. It was the voice itself, its drawling, aggressive tone. He would have sworn that, at that end, Prou was glaring suspiciously at the instrument, and that he never answered questions directly.

He was a type of man he knew well, the sort who isn't easily thrown, who leers at you and who, at the first awkward question, knits his bushy eyebrows.

Did he, in fact, have bushy eyebrows? And hair growing low on his forehead?

Maigret sorted through his papers bad-temperedly, and carried on with his routine. First he called in Joseph.

'Isn't there anyone else for me?'

Then he poked his head into the duty room.

'If anyone wants me, I'm at home.'

Out on the Quai, he opened his umbrella. On the platform of the bus, he found he was squeezed up against someone in a dripping raincoat.

Before he sat down to supper, he again rang the Rue Tholozé. He was in a bad mood with everything and everybody. He was annoyed with Roger Prou, heaven knows why, and he was annoyed with himself. He was almost annoyed with his wife who was eyeing him anxiously.

Was it a habit, at the other end, not to answer straight off? It was

as if the 'phone were ringing in a void. Then he remembered that
the instrument was in the office. They probably had their meals
in the kitchen, not the dining-room, so there was some distance to
cover.

'Hullo!'

Someone at last! A woman.

'Madame Planchon?'

'Yes. Who is it?'

She spoke naturally, in a rather serious but not unpleasant voice.

'I was hoping to speak to Léonard.'

'He's not here.'

'Do you know when he'll be back? I'm a friend of his.'

This time, as with Prou, there was a silence. Was Roger Prou beside
her? Were they exchanging looks?

'Which friend?'

'You don't know me. I was supposed to be meeting him this
evening.'

'He went out.'

'For long?'

'Yes.'

'Can you tell me when he'll be back?'

'I've no idea.'

'Is he in Paris?'

Another hesitation.

'If he isn't, he hasn't left me his address. Does he owe you money?'

Maigret rang off once again. Madame Maigret, who had been
listening to what he was saying, asked, as she was serving the soup:

'Has he disappeared?'

'It looks like it.'

'Do you think he's killed himself?'

He muttered:

'I don't think anything.'

He could see his visitor once again in the living-room, his knuckles
white from gripping his fingers and, above all, his pale eyes, which
fixed him pleadingly.

Planchon had been drinking and was under a strain. He had talked
a lot. Maigret had let himself get involved and there were scores of
leading questions he should have asked himself and which he had
not.

After dinner, he rang the Information Room. It was the time when
the men on duty took a snack, one eye on their telephones. The man
who answered had his mouth full.

'No, Chief. No suicides since I've been on. Hang on while I look at
today's reports. Just a moment. An old lady threw herself through a
window on the Boulevard Barbès. A corpse was taken out of the Seine,
shortly before five o'clock, at the Pont de Saint-Cloud. It looks from its

condition as if it had been in the water a fortnight. I don't see anything else.'

It was Wednesday evening. The next morning, in his office, Maigret started scribbling on a sheet of paper.

It was on the Saturday evening he had found Planchon waiting at his home on the Boulevard Richard-Lenoir.

On the Sunday morning, the Inspector had telephoned the Rue Tholozé for the first time, and Madame Planchon had replied that her husband had just gone out with his daughter.

It was true, and the decorator had later confirmed it. Isabelle and her father had gone off, hand in hand, to the Flea Market in Saint-Ouen.

On the afternoon of the same Sunday, Maigret and his wife had walked past the little house. The van had not been in the yard. There had been no one visible through the curtains, but he had found out later, again through Planchon, that he had been asleep in the house.

Monday morning: Janvier and Lapointe, using questionably legal means, had called at the Rue Tholozé and, under Renée's suspicious gaze had visited all the rooms, on the pretence of measuring them.

In the afternoon, Léonard Planchon had telephoned the Quai des Orfèvres, from a café on the Place des Abbesses, so he said. Apart from a murmur of voices and the clink of glasses, he could hear the ring of a cash register.

The fellow's last words had been:

'*Thank you!*'

He had not mentioned a journey or, for still better reason, a suicide. It was on the Saturday that he had made a vague reference to this solution, which he had rejected so as not to leave Isabelle in the hands of Renée and her lover.

Tuesday, no telephone call. Even so, to set his mind at rest, Maigret had asked the police in the 18th to keep an eye on the house in the Rue Tholozé by night. Not a constant watch. The police officers, during their rounds, merely glanced to make sure nothing unusual was going on and that the van was still in the yard. It was.

Finally, Wednesday. Nothing. No call from Planchon. And when the Inspector telephoned, about seven in the evening, Roger Prou had answered that the decorator would not be back that evening. He sounded vague, as if on his guard. Renée was not in the house just then, either.

But, as her lover had said, she was there an hour later and he gathered from his answers that she did not expect to see her husband for a long while.

He attended the conference, as he did every morning, still not mentioning the case, which did not officially exist. Shortly after ten, he left Police Headquarters in an icy drizzle, took a taxi and drove to the Rue Tholozé.

He did not yet know what he was going to do. He had no definite plan.

'Shall I wait?' asked the driver.

He decided to pay him off, because there was a chance he might be there some while.

The van was not in the yard, but an employee in a white overall, spotted with paint, was moving around in the shed. Maigret made his way towards the little house and rang the bell. A window opened on the first floor, just above his head, but he did not move. Then he heard footsteps on the stairs, the door half-opened, as it had to Janvier and Lapointe, and he saw some untidy dark hair, an almost equally dark look, a chalk-white face, and a splash of red dressing-gown.

'What is it?'

'I'd like to speak to you, Madame Planchon.'

'What about?'

The door remained open about six inches.

'About your husband.'

'He's not here.'

'That's why I want to talk to you. Because I need to see him.'

'What do you want him for?'

He eventually decided to say:

'Police.'

'Have you got a warrant?'

He showed her his badge. Her attitude changed. She opened the door wider and stood aside to let him pass in.

'I'm sorry. I'm alone in the house and there have been some mysterious 'phone calls the last few days.'

She was watching him closely and wondering if perhaps he was the person who had telephoned.

'Come in. The house is still in chaos.'

She showed him into the living-room. There was a hoover in the middle of the carpet.

'What has my husband done?'

'I have to get in touch with him so I can ask him some questions.'

'Has he been in a fight?'

She showed him a chair. She hesitated to sit down herself and held her dressing-gown crossed in front of her.

'Why do you ask me that?'

'Because he spends his evenings and part of his nights in the bistros and, when he's been drinking, he tends to get violent.'

'Has he ever struck you?'

'No. Anyway, I wouldn't have let him. But he has threatened me.'

'Threatened you with what?'

'To have done with me. He didn't say how.'

'Did this happen several times?'

'Several times, yes.'

'Do you know where he is now?'

'I've no idea and I don't want to know.'

'When was the last time you saw him?'

She stopped to think for a moment.

'Hold on. Today's Thursday. Yesterday was Wednesday. The day before that, Tuesday. It was Monday evening.'

'What time?'

'Late in the evening.'

'You don't remember the exact time?'

'It must have been around midnight.'

'Were you in bed?'

'Yes.'

'Alone?'

'No. I don't need to lie to you. Everyone round here knows the set-up, and I may add that everyone approves of us, Roger and me. If my husband wasn't so stubborn, we'd have been married years ago.'

'You mean you have a lover?'

Looking him straight in the eyes, she answered, not without some pride:

'Yes.'

'Has he been living in this house?'

'So what? When a man like Planchon digs his toes in and refuses a divorce, you have to . . .'

'For long?'

'It'll soon be two years.'

'Did your husband accept the situation?'

'He's only been my husband on paper for a long time now. He hasn't been a real man for years. I don't know what you want him for. It's no concern of mine what he does away from here. What I can safely say is that he's a drunk and you can't expect anything of him. If it wasn't for Roger, the firm would no longer exist.'

'I'd like to get back to Monday evening. You slept in this bedroom?'

The door was half-open. On the bed was an orange eiderdown.

'Yes.'

'With this man you call Roger?'

'Roger Prou, a good man, who doesn't drink and works hard.'

She referred to him proudly, as if she would have flown at the throat of anyone who dared to malign him.

'Did your husband have supper with you?'

'No. He hadn't got back.'

'Did that often happen?'

'Fairly often. I'm getting to know how drunkards carry on. For a while, they preserve a certain amount of self-respect and decency. Then, in the end, they drink so much, they stop feeling hungry, and have a few drinks instead of meals.'

'Had your husband gone that far?'

'Yes.'

'Yet he went on working? Mightn't he have fallen off a ladder or some scaffolding?'

'He didn't drink during the day, or hardly ever. As for his work, if we had to rely on him . . .'

'You've a daughter, I believe?'

'How did you know? I suppose you've been questioning the concierge. I don't mind, we've nothing to hide. I have a daughter, yes. She'll soon be seven.'

'So, on Monday, you had your supper together, this Roger Prou, you and your daughter?'

'Yes.'

'In this room?'

'In the kitchen. I can't see that it matters. We nearly always have our meals in the kitchen. Is that a crime?'

She was puzzled by the line the interrogation was taking, and was beginning to get impatient.

'I take it your daughter went off to bed first?'

'Of course.'

'On the first floor?'

She was obviously surprised to find him so well informed. Had she already connected his visit with the two men who had come to measure up the rooms of the small house?

However, she did not lose her composure, but went on studying her visitor, not ever looking away. Then suddenly she asked him a question.

'By the way, you wouldn't happen to be the famous Inspector Maigret?'

He nodded and she frowned. It was not so unusual for an ordinary police officer, a local inspector, for instance, to come and make inquiries about her husband's actions and movements, considering the life that Planchon led in the evenings. But for Maigret in person to take the trouble . . .

'In that case, it must be important.'

Then she said with a touch of irony:

'You're not going to tell me he's killed someone?'

'Do you think he's capable of it?'

'He's capable of anything. When a man goes that far . . .'

'Was he armed?'

'I've never seen a weapon in the house.'

'Did he have any enemies?'

'I was his only enemy, as far as I know. At least, to his mind. He hated me. He insisted on staying here on conditions which no man would have accepted, out of pure spite. He ought to have understood, if only for his daughter's sake.'

'Let's get back to Monday. What time did you and Roger Prou go to bed?'

237

'Hang on . . . I went to bed first.'

'What time?'

'About ten. Roger was working in the office, making out the bills.'

'Was he the one who saw to the accounts and financial matters?'

'First of all, if he hadn't done it, no one would have, because my husband wasn't capable of it any more. Then he put enough of his own money into it.'

'You mean he and Planchon were in partnership?'

'Practically. There was nothing in writing between them. Or rather they signed a paper only about a fortnight ago.'

She broke off, went into the kitchen, where something was boiling on the stove, and came back almost immediately.

'What else do you want to know? I've my housework to do, my lunch to cook. My daughter will be back from school shortly.'

'I'm afraid I'll have to keep you a moment or two longer.'

'You still haven't told me what my husband's done.'

'I hope your answers will help me to find him. If I've understood right, your lover put money into the business?'

'Every time there wasn't enough to pay the bills.'

'And a fortnight ago, they signed a paper? What sort of paper?'

'A paper saying that, on payment of a certain sum, Prou would become owner of the business.'

'Do you know how much the sum was?'

'I typed the document.'

'Can you type?'

'Sort of. There's been an old machine in the office for years. Planchon bought it before I was pregnant, a few months after our marriage. I was bored. I wanted something to do. So I started typing out accounts with two fingers, and then letters to the customers and tradesmen.'

'Do you still do it?'

'When necessary.'

'Have you got this paper?'

She looked at him more attentively.

'I wonder if you've the right to ask me. I even wonder if I have to answer you.'

'You don't have to, for the time being.'

'For the time being?'

'I can always call you in to my office as a witness.'

'As a witness to what?'

'Your husband's disappearance, shall we say?'

'It's not a disappearance.'

'What is it, then?'

'He's gone away, that's all. He should have gone a long time ago.'

All the same, she got up.

'I don't see why I should hide anything from you. If the paper interests you, I'll go and get it.'

She made her way into the office. There was the sound of a drawer being opened. She came back a few seconds later, holding the sheet of paper. It was a sheet of paper headed Léonard Planchon, painter and decorator. The words had been typed with a purple ribbon, the typing was uneven, some of the letters were higgledy-piggledy, and there were gaps between two or three of the words.

I, the undersigned, Léonard Planchon, transfer to Roger Prou, on payment of a sum of thirty thousand new francs (thirty thousand), my share in the decorating firm situated in the Rue Tholozé in Paris, which I hold in conjunction with my wife Renée, née Babaud.

This transfer includes the lease of the building, materials and furniture, but excludes my personal possessions.

The document was dated the 28th of December.

'Normally,' Maigret remarked, looking up, 'agreements of this sort are signed in the presence of a lawyer. Why didn't you do this?'

'Because there was no point in paying any fees. When people are honest...'

'Was your husband honest, then?'

'We were, anyway.'

'This paper was signed three weeks ago. From then on, Planchon was out of the business. I wonder why he went on working for it.'

'And why he went on living in this house when he had been finished with it for still longer?'

'In fact, he worked as an employee?'

'More or less.'

'Was he paid?'

'I suppose so. That was up to Roger.'

'Were the three million old francs paid by cheque?'

'In notes.'

'Here?'

'Not in the street, anyway.'

'In front of witnesses?'

'All three of us were witnesses. Our private affairs were nothing to do with anyone else.'

'Weren't there any conditions to this arrangement?'

The idea seemed to strike her and she remained silent for a moment.

'There was one, but he hasn't observed it.'

'What was that?'

'That he should go away and give me my divorce at last.'

'Still, he's gone.'

'It took three weeks!'

'Let's get back to Monday.'

'Again? Is this going to take long?'

'I hope not. You were in bed. Prou came and joined you. Were you awake when he went to bed?'

'Yes.'

'Did you look at the time?'

'If you must know, we had other things to do ...'

'Were you both asleep when your husband came in?'

'No.'

'Did he open the door with his key?'

'Not with a biro, anyway.'

'He could have been too drunk to open the door himself.'

'He was drunk but, even so, he found the keyhole.'

'Where did he normally sleep?'

'Here. On a camp-bed.'

She got up once again, opened a cupboard and showed him a folded camp-bed.

'Was it already fixed up?'

'Yes. I fixed it myself before I went to bed so that he wouldn't bang about for half an hour.'

'And he didn't go to bed on Monday?'

'No. We heard him go up to the first floor.'

'To go and kiss his daughter?'

'He never went and kissed his daughter in that state.'

'What did he go and do?'

'We were wondering. So we listened. He opened the cupboard on the landing where his things were. Then he went into the little room we use as an attic, because there isn't one in the house. Then there was a noise on the stairs and I had to stop Roger from going to see what was happening.'

'What was happening?'

'He was fetching down his suitcases.'

'How many suitcases?'

'Two. We only had two in the house, anyway, because we never really travelled.'

'Didn't you speak to him? Didn't you see him go?'

'Yes. When he came down into the dining-room, I got up and motioned to Roger to stay where he was, so as not to cause a scene.'

'Weren't you afraid? You told me that, when your husband had been drinking, he was violent and that, once or twice, he'd threatened you.'

'Roger was in earshot.'

'How did your last conversation go?'

'I could hear him talking to himself before, through the door, and he seemed to be sniggering. When I went in, he looked me up and down and started laughing.'

'Was he very drunk?'

'Not the same way as usual. He didn't make any threats. He didn't strike any poses and he didn't cry, either. Do you see what I mean? He seemed pleased with himself. It was as if he were going to play a trick on us.'

'Didn't he say anything?'

'The first thing he came out with was: "There you are, my dear!"'

'He showed me the two suitcases proudly.'

She never once took her eyes off Maigret and he, in turn, was carefully watching for the slightest flicker on her face. She must have noticed, but it did not seem to worry her.

'Is that all?'

'No. He also came out with a tortuous phrase which more or less amounted to: "You can look in them to make sure I'm not taking away anything that belongs to you."

'He was swallowing half his words, as if he was talking to himself rather than me.'

'Did you say he seemed pleased with himself?'

'Yes, I keep telling you. As if he was playing some trick on us. I asked him: "Where are you going?"'

'And he swung his arm round so hard that he nearly lost his balance.

' "Have you got a taxi at the door?"'

'He looked at me, sniggered again, but didn't answer. He picked up the suitcases and I caught him by the overcoat.

' "It's not all that important, but I must have your address for the divorce proceedings." '

'What did he answer?'

'I can remember exactly, because I repeated what he said, a little later on, to Roger: "You'll get it, my love. Sooner than you think . . ." '

'Didn't he mention his daughter?'

'He didn't say anything else.'

'Didn't he go and kiss her in her bed?'

'We would have heard him, because Isabelle's room is just over our heads and the floorboards creak.'

'So he went over to the door with his two suitcases. Were they heavy?'

'I didn't pick them up. Quite heavy, but not all that, because he only took his clothes, underclothes and his washing things.'

'Did you go with him to the door?'

'No.'

'Why not?'

'Because it would have looked as if I was showing him out.'

'Didn't you see him cross the yard?'

'The shutters were closed. All I did, a bit later on, was go and bolt the front door.'

'Weren't you afraid he'd go off with the van?'

'I would have heard the sound of the engine.'

'Didn't you hear the sound of any engine? Wasn't there a taxi alongside the kerb?'

'I've no idea. I was too delighted to know he was out of the house at last. I ran into the bedroom and, if you must know the whole story, I flung myself into Roger's arms. He had got up and had heard everything through the door.'

'That happened on Monday evening, didn't it?'

'Yes, Monday.'

It was only on the Tuesday that Maigret had asked the police station in the 18th to keep a discreet watch on the little house. According to Renée Planchon, it was already too late.

'You've no idea where he could have gone?'

Maigret imagined he could once again hear the last words Planchon had spoken to him over the telephone that same Monday, about six in the evening, from a bistro in the Place des Abbesses.

'*Thank you . . .*'

He had felt, at the precise moment, that the man's voice conveyed a touch of bitterness, or even slight irony.

However, if he had known where to ring him up, he would have done so immediately.

'Didn't your husband have any relations in Paris?'

'Neither in Paris nor anywhere else. I know that, because his mother was from the same village as mine, Saint-Sauveur, in the Vendée.'

She obviously did not know that Planchon had seen Maigret and had confided in him. Yet everything she said confirmed what the Inspector already knew.

'Do you think he's gone back there?'

'What for? He'd scarcely know the place. He only went there two or three times with his mother when he was little and, if there's any family left, they're vague cousins who've never taken any interest in him.'

'You don't know if he has any friends?'

'Even when he was still all right, he was so shy and uncouth that I still wonder how he ever came to speak to me.'

Maigret tried a little experiment.

'Where did you first meet him?'

'A little down the street, at the *Bal des Copains*. I'd never set foot in it. I'd just arrived in Paris and I was working locally. I should have been on my guard against . . .'

'Against what?'

'A man who had something wrong with him.'

'What was that to do with his character?'

'I don't know. But I understand it. People like that think about it the whole time, they feel different from others. They make out that everyone's looking at them and laughing at them. They're more sensitive than the rest, they're envious, bitter . . .'

'Was he already bitter when you married him?'

'I didn't notice it straightaway.'

'How long after?'

'I don't remember. He didn't want to see anyone. We hardly ever went out. We lived here like prisoners. He liked that. He was happy.'

She stopped and looked at him as if to say that they had gone on long enough.

'Is that all?' she asked.

'That's all for the moment. I'd be obliged if you'd let me know as soon as you have some news. I'll leave you my 'phone number.'

She took the card he handed her and put it on the table.

'My daughter will be back in a few minutes.'

'Wasn't she surprised when her father went?'

'I told her he was on a journey.'

She showed him to the door, and Maigret felt that she was worried and that she now wanted to delay him and ask him questions. But what?

'Goodbye, Inspector.'

He did not feel too satisfied, either. Hands in pockets and coat-collar up, he went back down the Rue Tholozé, passed a small girl with fair, tight pigtails, turned to watch her, and saw her go into the yard.

He would have liked to ask Isabelle some questions too.

Planchon's wife had not asked him to take off his coat, so Maigret had remained nearly an hour that way in the overheated house. Out now in the fine drizzle, which seemed to be composed of invisible ice-crystals, the coldness gripped him. Ever since his Sunday walk in the same district, he had felt that he was starting a cold, and this was what gave him the idea, instead of going down the Rue Lepic to find a taxi in the Place Blanche, of turning left towards the Place des Abbesses.

This was where the decorator had telephoned him from on the Monday evening. It was the last time they had been in touch.

The Place des Abbesses, with its Métro station, the Théâtre de l'Atelier, which looked like a toy or a stage set, and its bistros and small shops, seemed to the Inspector far more the genuine working-class Montmartre than the Place du Tertre, which had become a tourist trap, and he remembered that when he had first discovered it, shortly after his arrival in Paris, one chilly morning in spring sunshine, he had felt he had been transported into a picture by Utrillo.

It was swarming with ordinary people, people from the surrounding areas, coming and going, like a big town on market day, and it was also as if there were some family link between them, as if in some village.

He knew, from experience, that some of the older people had never in fact set foot outside the area and that there were still shops that had been handed down from father to son for several generations.

He looked through the windows of several bistros before he noticed, on a tobacco counter, a small cash register which seemed new.

Remembering the noises he had heard during his conversation with Planchon, he went in.

It was nice and warm inside, with a homely smell of wine and cooking. The tables, seven or eight at the most, were covered with paper table-cloths, and a slate announced that there were sausages and mash for lunch.

Two builders in overalls were already eating at the far end. The proprietress, dressed in black, was sitting at a desk against a background of cigarettes, cigars and lottery tickets.

A waiter, his sleeves rolled up to the elbows and wearing a blue apron, was serving wine and apéritifs at the counter.

There were about ten people drinking and they all turned to look at him. There was a fairly long silence before they started talking again.

'A hot rum,' he ordered.

Madame Maigret had confirmed that his voice was a different pitch from usual. He would probably become hoarse.

'Lemon?'

'Yes, please.'

At the far end, near the kitchen, he could see a telephone box with a glass door.

'Excuse me. Do you have a customer with a hare-lip?'

He knew that his neighbours were listening, even those with their backs to him. He was almost sure they had guessed that he was from the police.

'A hare-lip,' repeated the man in shirt-sleeves. He had put the hot rum down on the bar and was pouring wine from one bottle into another.

He paused before he replied, as if through a kind of solidarity.

'A small bloke. With fair, slightly reddish hair.'

'What's he been up to?'

One of the customers, who looked like a commercial traveller, broke in:

'Don't kid yourself, Léon! You don't think Inspector Maigret's going to tell you . . .'

There was a roar of laughter. Not only had they guessed he was from the police, but they had recognized him.

'He's disappeared,' Maigret muttered.

'Popeye?'

Léon went on to explain:

'We call him Popeye, because we don't know his name, and he's like the cartoon character.'

He raised his hands to his lips, as if to cut them in two and added:

'The hole looked as if it had been specially made to stick a pipe in.'

'Is he a regular?'

'Not really a regular, because we don't know who he is, or even if he's really a local. But he used to come a lot, almost every evening.'

'Did he come in on Monday?'

'Hang on. Today's Thursday. On Tuesday, I went to see old Nana buried. She used to sell papers on the corner. Monday . . . Yes. He came on Monday.'

'He even asked me for a coin for the 'phone,' broke in the proprietress from her desk.

'About six?'

'It was just before supper-time.'

'Did he speak to anyone?'

'He never spoke to anyone. He used to stand at the end of the counter, about where you are, and order his first brandy. He would stay there, lost in his thoughts. They couldn't have been very cheerful ones, because he always looked rather depressed.'

'Were there many people here on Monday evening?'

'Less than now. We don't do meals in the evenings. Some of the customers were playing *belote* at that table on the left.'

It was the one where the two builders were eating grilled sausages, which the Inspector would have liked. Some dishes always seem better in restaurants, especially in small bistros, than at home.

'How many brandies did he drink?'

'Three or four, I can't remember. Do you know, Mathilde?'

'Four.'

'About his normal ration. He used to stay quite a while. Sometimes, he'd turn up about nine or ten, in which case he wouldn't look too good. I suppose he'd been round all the local bars.'

'Did he ever join in the conversation?'

'Not that I know of. Did anyone ever speak to him?'

The commercial traveller broke in again.

'I tried once, but he looked through me. Mind you, he was well away by then.'

'Did he ever cause a disturbance?'

'He wasn't the sort. The more he drank, the calmer he got. I swear I've seen him crying, all by himself, at his end of the counter.'

Maigret had a second hot rum.

'Who is he?' asked the waiter in the blue apron.

'Just a decorator from the Rue Tholozé.'

'I told you he was a local. Do you think he's committed suicide?'

Maigret did not think anything, especially now, after his long talk with Renée. As Janvier had said—or was it Lapointe?—she reminded you more of a female than a woman, a female who clings on to her male and who will, if necessary, defend him ferociously.

She had not got flustered. She had answered all his questions and, though she had sometimes hesitated, it was because she was not very intelligent and was trying very hard to grasp their meaning.

The less cultivated people are, the more suspicious they appear and she had not changed much since she had left her village in the Vendée.

'What do I owe you?'

When he went out, they all looked at him, and they would no doubt start to talk about him, almost before the door was shut. He was used to it. He found a taxi almost straightaway and drove home.

He ate his roast veal unhungrily and his wife wondered why he suddenly said:

'Make some sausages tomorrow.'

He was at the Quai des Orfèvres at two o'clock. Before going up to his office, he stopped at the Hotels Section.

'I want you to try and trace a certain Léonard Planchon, a decorator, thirty-six years old, living in the Rue Tholozé. It's possible he may have moved into a hotel, probably a small hotel, also probably in the Montmartre area, with two suitcases, fairly late on Monday evening.

He's on the small side, with fair, slightly reddish hair, and a hare-lip . . .'

They would examine hotel forms and visit boarding-houses.

A few moments later, he was sitting down, unable to decide which pipe to smoke. He called in Lucas.

'Circulate all taxi-drivers. I want to know if any of them picked up a fare carrying two suitcases, on Monday about midnight, near the Rue Lepic or the Place Blanche.'

He repeated the description, including the famous hare-lip.

'While you're at it, inform the railway stations, just in case.'

It was all routine and Maigret did not seem to have much faith in it.

'Has your Saturday caller disappeared?'

'Looks like it.'

He was so busy with other things that he did not think about him for a whole hour. Then he got up to switch on the lights, because the sky was growing darker and darker.

Suddenly he decided to go and see his Chief.

'I must have a word with you about something that's on my mind.'

He felt slightly absurd for attaching so much importance to it and, as he described the conversation he had had at his house on the Saturday, he felt that his story was not very convincing.

'Are you sure he's not mad or a bit touched?'

His Chief also came across such people because some of them, either through obstinacy or cunning, managed to get interviews with him. Sometimes it was only at the end of the story that he realized it did not hold water.

'I don't know. I've seen his wife.'

He summed up his conversation of the morning with Renée.

His Chief, as he had expected, did not see things in the same light, and appeared surprised at Maigret's concern.

'Are you afraid he's committed suicide?'

'It's a possibility.'

'You've just told me that he talked to you about doing away with himself. What I can't understand, in that case, is why he took the trouble to go and fetch his things, and saddle himself with two suit-cases.'

Maigret sucked at his pipe but did not say a word.

'Perhaps he wanted to get away from Paris. Perhaps he went and moved into the nearest hotel,' his Chief continued.

The Inspector shook his head.

'I should like to know more about it,' he said with a sigh. 'I wanted to ask your permission to call the lover in to my office.'

'What sort of man is he?'

'I haven't seen him but, from what I know, he can't be a very easy type. Then there are the employees. I'd like to question them.'

'In view of how things stand with the Examining Magistrates, I'd rather you had a word or two with the Director of Public Prosecutions.'

The same old antagonism still existed, though fairly well disguised, between Police Headquarters and the gentlemen at the Palais de Justice. Maigret could remember the time when he could carry out an investigation without reference to anyone, and when he got in touch with the Examining Magistrate only after the matter had been wound up.

Since then there had been new laws and no end of decrees and, to keep the right side of the law, you had to watch what you did. Even his morning visit to the Rue Tholozé could, if Renée Planchon had decided to make a complaint, have brought on him severe censure.

'Aren't you going to wait for the result of your inquiries?'

'I have a feeling that they aren't going to produce anything.'

'Go ahead if you must. I wish you good luck.'

So it was that, about five o'clock in the afternoon, Maigret went in through the little door which cuts off Police Headquarters from a very different world in the Palais de Justice.

On the other side were the Public Prosecutors, the judges, the courtrooms and vast corridors, with lawyers in black gowns who looked as if they were flapping their wings.

The Public Prosecutor's offices were stately and opulent compared with those of the police. Strict etiquette was observed there and everyone spoke in whispers.

'I'll show you in to Deputy Prosecutor Méchin. He's the only one free at the moment.'

He waited a long while, just as others waited to see him in the glass cage at Police Headquarters. Then a door opened into an Empire-style office and he found himself walking on a red carpet.

The Deputy Prosecutor was tall and fair, and his dark suit was immaculately cut.

'Please take a seat. What's the trouble?'

He glanced at the platinum watch on his wrist, like a man whose time is precious. He looked as if he ought to be sipping tea in some aristocratic drawing-room.

It seemed vulgar, almost bad taste, to bring up the little decorator from the Rue Tholozé, his long story, interrupted two or three times to swallow a glass of plum brandy, his tears and his passionate outbursts.

'I still don't know whether it's a simple disappearance, a suicide or a crime...'

He summed up the situation as best he could. The Deputy Prosecutor listened to him, studying his hands with their manicured nails. They were very fine hands, with long slender fingers.

'What do you intend to do?'

'I should like to hear what the lover, Roger Prou, has to say. Possibly also the three or four employees at the Rue Tholozé.'

'Is he the sort of man who's likely to object or be a nuisance?'

'I'm afraid so.'

'Do you think it's necessary?'

The affair took on a different light, even more than in his Chief's office, and Maigret was tempted to give up and erase from his memory the little man with the hare-lip who had burst so indecently into his life on the Boulevard Richard-Lenoir.

'What's at the back of your mind?'

'Nothing. It's all in the air. I've got to see Prou to start me going.'

Then, when he had given up hope of consent, the Deputy Prosecutor again glanced at the time and got up.

'Serve him with a summons for questioning. But be careful. As for the employees, if you really must . . .'

A quarter of an hour later, Maigret was in his office, filling in the spaces on an official form. Then he called Lucas up.

'I'd like the names and addresses of the men employed at Planchon's firm in the Rue Tholozé. You can apply to Social Security. They must have the lists in their files.'

An hour later, he was filling in three other forms because, apart from Roger Prou, there were only three employees, including an Italian called Angelo Massoletti.

After this, until nine in the evening, he heard witnesses about the jewel thefts, especially members of the staffs of the hotels where these thefts had been committed. He had some sandwiches, went home, and drank another hot rum, with two aspirins, before going to bed.

At nine o'clock in the morning, a well-built man, with white hair and a fresh complexion, was already in the waiting-room and, five minutes later, he was shown into Maigret's office.

'Is your name Jules Lavisse?'

'I'm known as Pépère. Some people call me St. Peter, because, I suppose, they think my white hair's a halo . . .'

'Have a seat.'

'Thanks. I'm more often up a ladder than on a chair.'

'Have you been working for Léonard Planchon long?'

'I was working for him when he was still a youngster and when the boss's name was Lempereur.'

'So you know what's been going on in the Rue Tholozé?'

'That depends.'

'On what?'

'On what you do with what I say.'

'I don't follow.'

'If you want to mention it afterwards to the boss's wife or Monsieur Roger, I just work there and don't know anything. Especially if I have to repeat what I say in court.'

'Why in court?'

'Because when you have people along here, it means that something funny's going on, doesn't it?'

'Do you think there's something funny going on in the Rue Tholozé?'

'You haven't answered me.'

'There's every chance that this conversation will remain between these four walls.'

'What do you want to know?'

'How were things between your boss and his wife?'

'Didn't she tell you? I saw you crossing the yard yesterday and you stayed over an hour with her.'

'Has Prou been her lover long?'

'I don't know anything about him being her lover. But he's been sleeping in the house for two years.'

'And how has Planchon taken it since then?'

The old house-painter gave a wry smile.

'Like a cuckold.'

'You mean he accepted the situation in good part?'

'Good part or not, he hadn't much choice.'

'But it was his home.'

'Maybe he was under the illusion that it was his, but it was really hers.'

'When he married her, she had nothing.'

'I remember. It doesn't alter the fact that, as soon as I saw her, I knew he wouldn't have any more say in things.'

'Do you think Planchon's a weak man?'

'In a sense. I'd say more that he's a good bloke who's been unlucky. He could have been happy with any woman. And he had to pick that one . . .'

'Yet they were happy for some years.'

The old man shook his head doubtfully.

'I suppose so.'

'You don't agree?'

'Maybe he was happy. Maybe she was happy, too. But they weren't happy together.'

'Was she unfaithful to him?'

'I think she was unfaithful to him even before she moved into the Rue Tholozé. Mind you, I didn't see her. But since she's been Madame Planchon . . .'

'With whom?'

'Anything in trousers. With nearly all the employees who worked there. If I'd been a bit younger . . .'

'So Planchon didn't suspect anything?'

'Do husbands ever suspect anything?'

'How about Prou?'

'She ran into a tough customer there, a man with ideas. It wasn't enough for him to have his fun up against a wall, like the rest.'

'Do you think he meant to take over from his boss from the beginning?'

'In his bed, first of all. Then as head of the firm. Now look, if you repeat what I'm telling you, I may just as well go and look for another job. Apart from which, he might be waiting for me one day round a corner.'

'Does he get violent?'

'I've never seen him strike anyone, but I wouldn't like him for an enemy.'

'When did you last see Planchon?'

'Right! We're there at last. You've taken your time. I had the answers all ready when I came, because I thought that would be the first thing you would ask me. Monday evening, at half-past five.'

'Where?'

'In the Rue Tholozé. I wasn't on the same job as him. I had to repaint an old lady's kitchen in the Rue Caulaincourt. The boss and the others were working on a new house in the Avenue Junot. A big job. At least three weeks. I went by the Rue Tholozé about half-past five, as I told you, and I was in the shed when the van came back into the yard. The boss was driving, with Prou next to him, and Angelo and Big Jef behind him.'

'Did you notice anything special?'

'No. They unloaded some gear and the boss, as usual, went into the house to change. He always used to change after work.'

'Do you know how he spent his evenings?'

'I sometimes used to meet him.'

'Where?'

'In the bistros. Ever since Prou moved in, he's been boozing it up, especially in the evenings.'

'Have you ever had the feeling he might commit suicide?'

'It never occurred to me.'

'Why?'

'Because when you stick a situation like that for two years, there's no reason why you shouldn't accept it the rest of your life.'

'Did you ever hear that he wasn't the boss any more?'

'He hadn't been for ages. They let him believe it but, in fact ...'

'Didn't anyone ever tell you that Prou had bought the firm?'

The man nicknamed Pépère stared at him out of his beady little eyes and shook his head.

'Did they get him to sign a paper?'

Then, as if he were talking to himself, he said:

'They're even smarter than I thought.'

'Didn't Prou mention it?'

'First I heard of it. It doesn't surprise me. Is that why he left? Have they finally slung him out?'

It seemed to upset him, though.

'What I can't really understand is why he didn't take his daughter with him. I was convinced he was sticking it out for her sake.'

'Didn't they say anything on Tuesday?'

'Prou told us that Planchon had left.'

'He didn't tell you how and why?'

'Only that he was dead drunk when he came and fetched his things.'

'Did you believe him?'

'Why not? Isn't that how it happened?'

A look of curiosity came into his eyes.

'You've got something at the back of your mind, haven't you?'

'How about you?'

'I'm not that clever . . .'

'Weren't you surprised?'

'I told my wife, when I got back that evening, that Planchon probably wouldn't last much longer. If anyone loved his wife, he did. To the point of absurdity. And his daughter, well, she was the world to him.'

'Did you take the van on the Tuesday morning?'

'We all got in it. Prou was driving. He dropped me off in the Rue Caulaincourt, opposite my old lady.'

'Did you notice anything out of the ordinary?'

'There were the usual tins of paint, some rolls of wallpaper, some brushes and sponges and all the rest of it.'

'Thank you, Monsieur Lavisse.'

'Is that all?'

The old man seemed disappointed.

'Would you like me to ask you some more questions?'

'No. I thought it would take longer. It's the first time I've been here.'

'If you remember anything, don't hesitate to come and see me or telephone.'

'Prou will ask me what we talked about.'

'Tell him I checked up on Planchon, how he behaved, whether it's likely he committed suicide . . .'

'Do you think it is?'

'I know no more than you.'

He went out and, a few moments later, the young Italian, whose Christian name was Angelo, took his seat, which was still warm. He had only been in France six months and Maigret was forced to repeat each question two or three times.

One of them seemed to surprise him.

'Has your boss's wife ever made advances to you?'

He was a good-looking young fellow with soft, melting eyes.

'Advances?'

'Did she try and get you into the house?'

This made him laugh.

'And what about Monsieur Roger?' he objected.

'Is he jealous?'

'I think he ...'

He went through the motions of sticking a dagger in his chest.

'Have you seen Monsieur Planchon since Monday?'

That was all for him and the third employee, called for eleven o'clock, the one his mates knew as Big Jef, answered most of the questions by merely saying:

'I don't know.'

He didn't want to get involved in other people's business and he did not seem to have any great affection for the police. However, Maigret was to find out later that he had been arrested two or three times for creating a disturbance and, on one occasion, for assault and wounding, after breaking a bottle over the head of one of his neighbours in a bar.

Maigret had lunch at the Brasserie Dauphine with Lucas, though the latter had nothing to report. The circular to the taxi-drivers had produced no results. This meant nothing, because some of them avoided contact with the police as much as they could. They were all well aware that it meant time wasted, interrogations at the Quai des Orfèvres, then with the Examining Magistrates, and finally, sometimes, two or three days hanging about in the witnesses' ante-room at court.

Though the Hotels Section was one of the most efficient, they had found no trace of Planchon. As far as could be judged, he was not the sort of man to obtain false papers. If he had landed up at a hotel or boarding-house, it would have been under his own name.

The last picture he had of him was that of a little man, weighed down with two suitcases, walking along the Rue Tholozé at midnight. Of course, he might have taken a bus and gone to a station, where he would not necessarily have been noticed.

'What do you think of it, Chief?'

'He promised to 'phone me every day. He didn't on Sunday, but he rang me on Monday.'

He had not killed Renée and her lover. Had he decided to leave on the spur of the moment? About eight o'clock, he had left the cigarette counter in the Place des Abbesses and, by then, he had already drunk several brandies. The chances were that he had been into several other drinking haunts. A thorough search of the neighbourhood would no doubt reveal his tracks.

Once he was drunk, what ideas had passed through his head?

'If he threw himself in the Seine, it might be weeks before he's fished out,' Lucas muttered.

It was obviously absurd to imagine the man with the hare-lip filling his suitcases with all his private belongings and lugging them through the streets, just so as to go and throw himself in the Seine.

Maigret, who was still nursing his cold, though it had not actually come into the open, had a brandy with his coffee. At two o'clock, he was back in his office.

Roger Prou made him wait a good ten minutes and so the Inspector, in turn, as if for revenge, let him stew in the waiting-room until a quarter to three. Lucas went and had a look at him two or three times through the glass.

'How does he look?'

'Not easy.'

'What's he doing?'

'He's reading a paper, but he keeps glancing up at the door.'

Joseph finally showed him in. Maigret remained seated, bent over his papers, which seemed to demand all his attention.

'Sit down,' he growled, pointing to one of the chairs.

'I haven't all afternoon to waste.'

'I'll be with you in a moment.'

Even so, he went on reading, underlining certain phrases in red pencil. This took another good ten minutes, after which Maigret got up, opened the door of the duty room, and spent some time muttering instructions.

Only then did he really look at the man sitting in one of the green velvet upholstered chairs. He went back to his place at his desk and, when he spoke, his voice was quite expressionless:

'Is your name Roger Prou?'

'Roger Etienne Ferdinand Prou,' he answered, isolating the syllables. 'Born in Paris, in the Rue de la Roquette.'

Half-rising from his chair, he pulled out a wallet from his hip-pocket and took from it an identity card. He laid it on the desk and said:

'No doubt you want proof?'

He was freshly-shaved and was wearing a blue suit, presumably the one he wore on Sundays. Maigret had not been far wrong in imagining him with very dark, wiry hair, growing low down on his forehead, and dark eyebrows.

He was a handsome male, in the same way that Renée was a handsome female. Their calm yet aggressive manner made you think of wild beasts. Though Prou had been awkward on principle, because he was being made to waste his own and his employees' time, he was not letting himself be put off by the Inspector's time-honoured little ploy. His expression was mainly ironical.

In the country, he would have been cock of the walk, the one who, on Sundays, persuades his mates to go and antagonize the lads of the neighbouring village and who cynically puts the girls in the family way.

In a factory, he would have been the trouble-maker, crossing swords with the foreman and casually provoking incidents to establish prestige over his mates.

With his build and with the character Maigret suspected he had, he could have been a ponce, too. Not at the Etoile, but in the Porte Saint-Denis or Bastille areas. You could easily imagine him playing cards all day in the bistros, and keeping a sharp look-out along the street.

He could even have been the leader of a mob of gangsters, probably not a thug, but the organizer, for instance, of warehouse burglaries around the Gare du Nord or in the neighbouring suburbs.

Maigret pushed him back his identity card, which was in order.

'Have you brought the paper I asked for?'

Prou had kept hold of his wallet. Still calm, with thick, confident fingers, he pulled out the sheet of paper, signed Léonard Planchon, which made him co-owner, with his mistress, of the decorating firm.

He handed it to the Inspector, with the same calm and disdain.

Maigret got up, moved over once again to the duty room, stood there between the two rooms so as not to lose sight of his visitor.

'Lapointe!'

Then he whispered:

'Take this up to Monsieur Pirouet. He knows all about it.'

This was upstairs in the Forensic Laboratory, in the roof of the Palais de Justice. Monsieur Pirouet was a comparatively recent acquisition to the Force, a curious fellow, fat and hearty, who had been looked on with some mistrust when he had joined as an assistant chemist, because he looked more like a commercial traveller. They had got into the habit of referring to him ironically as Monsieur Pirouet, with the accent on the Monsieur.

Yet he had turned out to be a first-rate colleague, versatile and inventive, who had already built several ingenious machines with his own hands. They had also found out that he was an astonishingly good graphologist.

Well before Prou's visit, Maigret had sent an inspector to Social Security to obtain some pay-sheets with Planchon's signature on them.

The weather was dull. Fog was descending on the streets, as on the previous Saturday.

The Inspector regained his seat leisurely, as if in slow motion. Prou, in spite of his calm, spoke first:

'I take it you called me in to ask me some questions?'

Maigret gave him a friendly, almost unironical look.

'Certainly,' he murmured. 'I still have some questions to ask, but I don't quite know what.'

'I warn you that if you're making a fool of me . . .'

'I have no intention of making a fool of you. Your ex-boss, Planchon, has disappeared, and I should like to know what's become of him.'

'Renée told you.'

'She told me that he left on Monday evening with his two suitcases. You saw him go, too, didn't you?'

'Just a minute! Don't you go putting words in my mouth. I *heard* him. I was behind the door.'

'So you didn't see him go?'

'All but. I heard them talking. I also heard him going upstairs to fetch his things. Then his footsteps in the passage, the front door shutting again, and then his footsteps again in the yard.'

'Since then, he's vanished.'

'How do you know? A man doesn't disappear just because he leaves home.'

'It so happens that Planchon should have 'phoned me on Tuesday.'

Maigret had not planned his interrogation, and this apparently harmless remark was an inspiration of the moment. Naturally, he did not once take his eyes off his companion. Did Prou's reaction disappoint him? He definitely gave a slight start. His thick eyebrows knitted. He seemed to sum up the situation in a matter of seconds, foreshadowing all that these few words implied:

'How do you know he should have 'phoned?'

'Because he promised to.'

'Did you know him?'

Maigret avoided making a reply and filled his pipe with fussy little

256

prods which would have driven anyone mad. Yet Roger Prou gave no
sign of nervous tension.

'Let's talk about you. You're twenty-eight?'

'Twenty-nine.'

'You were born in the Rue de la Roquette? What was your father?'

'A carpenter. He had and still has his workshop at the end of a blind
alley. Since you must know everything, he specializes in repairing
antiques.'

'Have you any brothers or sisters?'

'Sisters.'

'So you were the only boy in the family? Didn't your father try to
teach you his trade? It's a dying craft, I understand, and there's a good
living to be made at it.'

'I worked with him until I was sixteen.'

He was purposely talking as if he were reciting a school lesson.

'After which?'

'I got fed up with it.'

'You preferred being a house-painter?'

'Not straight off. My aim was to be a professional cyclist. Not long-
distance. Not the Tour de France. A track cyclist. I raced two years as
a junior at the Vélodrome d'Hiver.'

'Did that earn you enough to feed yourself?'

'No, it didn't. That's why, when I realized that I was too heavy and
that I'd never be a star, I packed it in. Do you want to know the rest?'

Maigret nodded, drew slowly on his pipe and toyed with a pencil.

'I got my call-up brought forward so as to get my military service
over.'

'You already had something in mind.'

'Exactly. There's no reason why I shouldn't tell you. To earn enough
money to be a free agent.'

'What did you do when you got back to Paris?'

'First of all I worked in a garage, but it was too boring for my taste.
On top of which, I had the boss constantly breathing down my neck,
and we more often used to work ten or twelve hours a day than eight.
Then I was an apprentice-locksmith for a few months. Eventually, one
of my mates got me into the decorating business.'

'With Planchon?'

'Not yet. With Desjardins and Brosse, on the Boulevard Rochechouart.'

They were getting nearer Montmartre and the Rue Tholozé.

'Were you saving any money?'

Prou got the message.

'Of course.'

'Much?'

'As much as I could.'

'When did you start with Planchon?'

'Just over two years ago. I had a row with one of the bosses. Anyway, it was too big a firm. I wanted to work for a small boss.'

'Were you still living with your parents?'

'For some while I'd been living alone in rooms.'

'Where?'

'At the end of the Rue Lepic. In the Hôtel Beauséjour.'

'I suppose you met Planchon in a café and he told you he was looking for a good worker?'

Prou again looked at him with a frown. Maigret was not surprised to discover that his reactions were almost identical to Renée's.

'What are you trying to make me say?'

'Nothing. I'm collecting facts. Planchon used to go round the local drinking places. It's only natural to assume . . .'

'You assume wrong.'

'Of course, you could have met Madame Planchon either when she was doing her shopping or . . .'

'Is that why you're wasting my time, just to hand me out all this chat?'

He looked as if he were going to get up and make for the door.

'For one thing, I didn't meet Renée before I went to work at the Rue Tholozé. And for another, it wasn't her who who put me on to her husband. Right?'

Maigret replied with an odd sort of a smile:

'All right! Did you answer an advertisement? Did you see a notice outside the gate asking for a worker?'

'There wasn't any notice. I went in on the off chance, and it so happened that just then they needed someone.'

'How long afterwards did you become Madame Planchon's lover?'

'Now, look here, what right have you to poke into people's private lives?'

'Planchon has disappeared.'

'That's what you say.'

'You don't have to answer.'

'Supposing I don't?'

'I shall be free to draw my own conclusions.'

Prou muttered disdainfully:

'About a week.'

'In fact, it was love at first sight?'

'She and I clicked straightaway.'

'Did you know that she had also clicked, as you put it, with most of your friends?'

At this, Prou went red in the face and momentarily gritted his teeth.

'Did you know?' Maigret went on.

'That's nothing to do with you.'

'Do you love her?'

'That's my business.'

'How long was it before Planchon caught you?'

'He didn't catch us.'

Maigret feigned surprise.

'I thought he'd caught you red-handed and that it was, as a result of that, that . . .'

'That what?'

'Just a minute. Let's get things straight. You were one of Planchon's employees and, when you got the chance, you slept with his wife. Were you still living in the Rue Lepic?'

'Yes.'

'Then, one fine day, you moved into the little house in the Rue Tholozé and you more or less shoved Planchon out of bed and took his place.'

'Have you seen him?'

'Who?'

'Planchon? You told me just now that he was supposed to 'phone you. So he must have been in touch with you. Did he come and see you? Did he complain about us?'

At such moments, Maigret's expression grew vague and his entire personality became maddeningly passive. He did not seem to have heard the question, but gazed limply in the direction of the window and, still drawing on his pipe, muttered, as if to himself:

'I'm trying to visualize the scene. Planchon comes back home, one night, and finds a camp-bed fixed up for him in the dining-room. The man's no doubt astonished. Until then, he knew nothing of what was going on behind his back and then, within the space of an hour, he discovers that he no longer has the right to sleep in his own bed.'

'Do you find that funny?'

Though still outwardly calm, Prou's eyes were hard and bright. Now and again, he could be heard gritting his teeth.

'Do you love her all that much?'

'She's my wife!'

'Legally, she's still Planchon's. Why hasn't your mistress got divorced?'

'Because it takes two to get a divorce and he keeps stubbornly refusing.'

'Did he love her, too?'

'I've no idea. It's nothing to do with me. Go and ask him yourself. If you've seen him, you know as well as I do he isn't a man. He's a nonentity. He's a write-off. He's a . . .'

He was getting worked up.

'He's Isabelle's father.'

'And do you imagine Isabelle doesn't prefer having me in the house to a bloke who gets drunk every evening, and who sometimes goes and cries on the girl's bed?'

'He didn't drink before you went to work for him.'

'Is that what he told you? And you believed him? In that case, there's no point in talking and we're wasting our time. Give me back my paper, ask me the questions you still have to ask, and get it over and done with. I'm not worried if you've cast me as the villain . . .'

'There's only one thing I don't understand.'

'Only one?' he asked ironically.

Maigret then said slowly and expressionlessly, as if he hadn't heard:

'It's now just over a fortnight since Planchon handed you over his share in the firm. Your mistress and yourself thereby became the owners. I don't suppose Planchon ever intended to stay on and work under your orders?'

'The proof is that he left.'

'But he stayed two weeks.'

'That surprises you because you seem to think that people have to act one way or another, according to your own logic. It so happens that this man didn't act logically. Otherwise, he wouldn't have slept for two years on a camp-bed while his wife was sleeping with me in the next room. Don't you understand that?'

'So, ever since he signed the transfer document, he'd resigned himself to going away?'

'It was agreed between us.'

'You had a sort of right to sling him out?'

'I don't know. I'm not a lawyer. The fact remains we were patient enough to wait two weeks.'

As he was listening, the Inspector could see the little man with the hare-lip making his confession in the living-room of the Boulevard Richard-Lenoir, while behind the glass door the table was being set for dinner. Of course, Planchon had been drinking to give himself courage, as he said, and Maigret, feeling him weaken, had poured him out a glass of plum brandy. What he had said, though, rang true.

Yet . . . Hadn't Maigret already felt slightly uneasy on the Saturday night? Hadn't he doubted Planchon and looked at him two or three times, his eyes suddenly hardening?

His long story contained traces of passion.

Yet Renée, that morning, though calmer, had been no less passionate.

And Prou was trying to control himself by gritting his teeth.

'Why do you think he came to this sudden decision on Monday evening?'

The other shrugged indifferently.

'Did he have the three million francs on him?'

'I didn't ask him.'

'When you gave them to him, two weeks before, what did he do with them?'

'He went up to the first floor. I suppose he hid them somewhere.'

'Didn't he take them to the bank?'

'Not that day, because it was in the evening, straight after supper.'

'In the office?'

'No. In the living-room. We waited until the girl had gone to bed.'

'Had you already discussed it together? Was everything agreed between you, including the amount? I suppose you kept the notes in the office?'

'No. In the bedroom.'

'For fear he might go off with them?'

'Because the bedroom was our place.'

'You're twenty-nine. You haven't really had time to save, except after your military service. How had you been able to put so much money aside in so short a space of time?'

'I only had part of it. Exactly a third.'

'Where did you find the rest?'

He did not seem at all disconcerted. On the contrary! It was as if he had been waiting for the Inspector at this turn in events. He went on, with ill-concealed satisfaction:

'My father lent me a million francs. He's worked long enough to save a mint. And my sister's husband lent me the other million. His name's Mourier, François Mourier, and he has a butcher's shop on the Boulevard de Charonne.'

'When did you fix up these loans?'

'On Christmas Eve. We'd hoped to settle with Planchon the next day.'

'Settle with?'

'Give him the money and see him out of the house! You know quite well what I meant.'

'I suppose you signed some receipts?'

'I like things done properly, even in the family.'

Maigret passed him a note-pad and pencil.

'Will you write me down the exact addresses of your father and brother-in-law?'

'You really trust me, don't you?'

However, he wrote down the two addresses. His writing was deliberate but neat, almost scholarly. Just as the Inspector took back the pad, the telephone rang.

'Pirouet here. I've finished. Do you want to come and see, or would you rather I came down?'

'I'll be up.'

Then he said to Prou:

'Will you excuse me a moment?'

He went through the next office, left the door open and told Lapointe:

'Go in and keep an eye on him.'

A few moments later, he was up under the roof-top, shaking Moers' hand and brushing past the dummy used for reconstructions into the laboratory.

Monsieur Pirouet, his face shiny with sweat, was standing in front of two dripping photographic enlargements held up by clothes-pegs.

'Well?'

'There's something I must ask you, Chief. Does the fellow who signed these papers drink a lot?'

'Why?'

'Because that would explain the difference in the writing. Look first at the signature on the Social Security return. The writing isn't very steady. I'd say it belonged to an unstable man who, even so, knows what he's doing. Do you know him?'

'Yes. I had him with me for almost a whole evening.'

'Do you want me to give my impressions of him?'

Maigret nodded, and he went on:

'He's a man who's only had a primary education, but who's always tried hard. He's almost congenitally shy, yet has flashes of pride. He tries to appear calm and self-controlled, whereas in fact he's very emotional . . .'

'Not bad!'

'There's something wrong with his health. He's ill or thinks he is.'

'How about the signature on the transfer document?'

'That's why I asked you if he drank. The writing's somewhat different. It's maybe the same hand, in which case whoever signed it was either drunk or under great stress. See for yourself. Compare them. The strokes here are regular, if a bit shaky, as they would be with a man who wasn't actually drunk when he was writing. On the transfer document, however, all the letters are jerky.'

'Do you think it could be the same man?'

'In the circumstances I've just mentioned, yes. If not, it's a forgery. You often find the same unsteadiness and the same signs of stress in forgeries.'

'Thank you. Now, has this writing anything in common with that?'

He showed him the two addresses which Roger Prou had written down a few moments before on a sheet of paper. Monsieur Pirouet only had to glance at it.

'No connection. I'll explain.'

'Not just now. Thank you, Monsieur Pirouet.'

Maigret took the original documents and went down to his own floor. He found Prou still sitting on his chair and Lapointe standing in front of the window.

'You can go now.'

'Well?' Renée's lover asked.

'Nothing. I'll give you back the transfer document. I take it that it was typed by Madame Planchon?'

'She told you, didn't she? There's no mystery about it.'

'Was her husband drunk when he signed it?'

'He knew what he was doing. We didn't take advantage of him. That doesn't mean he hadn't drunk several glasses of brandy. He always had by that time.'

'Is your father on the 'phone? Do you know his number?'

Still looking disdainful, Prou gave him the number. The Inspector proceeded to dial it.

'His name's Gustave Prou. Don't be afraid to speak up because he's got a bit deaf.'

'Monsieur Gustave Prou? I'm sorry to trouble you. I'm here with your son. He tells me that, in the month of December, you lent him the sum of a million old francs. Yes. I'm with him. What? Do you want a word with him?'

The old man was suspicious, too. Maigret handed the receiver to Prou.

'It's me, Papa. Do you recognize my voice? Good! You can answer the questions. No, it's just a formality. I'll explain later on. See you soon. Yes, everything's all right. Yes, he's gone. Not now. I'll drop by on Sunday.'

He handed back the receiver to the Inspector.

'Can you answer my questions now? Did you lend him a million francs? Right! In notes? You drew them from the bank the previous day? From the Savings Bank? Yes, I can hear you. Did your son sign a receipt? Thank you. Someone'll be calling on you. Just a check-up. All you have to do is show the receipt. Just a moment. What day was it? Christmas Eve?'

Prou's eyes conveyed more irony and contempt than ever.

'I suppose you're going to ring my brother-in-law?'

'There's no hurry. I don't doubt he'll confirm what you say.'

'Can I go?'

'Unless you want to make a statement.'

'What statement?'

'I don't know. You might have some idea where Planchon went when he left the Rue Tholozé. He's not particularly strong. What's more, he was drunk. He couldn't have gone far, weighed down with two large suitcases.'

'That's up to you, isn't it? Or am I expected to find him, too?'

'I'm not asking you to do that. Simply, if you get an idea, to let me know, so as to save time.'

'Why didn't you ask Planchon himself when you saw him or when he 'phoned? He's in a better position to answer than I am.'

'Oddly enough, he had no intention of leaving the Rue Tholozé.'

'Did he say so?'

It was Prou's turn to fish.

'He told me a lot of things.'

'Did he come here?'

In spite of his composure, he was looking slightly uncomfortable.

Maigret was careful not to answer and to look as blank as possible, as if he had ceased to attach any importance to the conversation.

'There's one thing that surprises me,' the Inspector murmured, however.

'What?'

'I don't know if he still loved his wife or if he had begun to loathe her.'

'I suppose it varied from time to time.'

'How do you mean?'

'According to how drunk he was. He was a different person at different times. Sometimes, we'd stay awake listening to him muttering in the next room, wondering if he wasn't planning to spring some lousy trick on us.'

'What sort of trick, for instance?'

'Do you want me to spell it out for you? I'll tell you something else. I always arranged to be on the same job so as to keep an eye on him. If, during the day, he mentioned he was going to slip back to the Rue Tholozé, I went along with him. I was afraid for Renée.'

'Do you think he would have been capable of killing her?'

'He went so far as to threaten her.'

'With death?'

'Not in so many words, perhaps. When he'd been drinking, he used to talk to himself knowingly. I couldn't repeat his exact words. They were always a bit muddled.

' "*I'm just a coward. All right! Everyone laughs at me. But one day, they'll see that . . .*"

'Get the idea? His eyes would glint with malice. He was like a man who knew what he was doing. Sometimes, he'd suddenly burst out laughing.

' "*Poor Planchon! A poor, little, insignificant man, with a repellent face. Yet perhaps the little man isn't such a coward as all that . . .*" '

Maigret was listening carefully, with a slight constriction of the chest, because it did not sound made up. The Planchon he had seen at the Boulevard Richard-Lenoir, and the man whom Prou was now taking a cruel delight in imitating, were one and the same person, with barely any exaggeration.

'Do you think he really meant to kill his wife?'

'I'm sure that he'd thought about it and that, at a certain stage of drunkenness, he kept harking back to it.'

'What about you?'

'Me, too, perhaps.'

'And his daughter?'

'He probably wouldn't have touched Isabelle. And yet . . . If he could have blown up the house with a bomb . . .'

Maigret got up with a sigh and walked hesitantly over to the window.

'Hasn't the same idea ever occurred to you?'

'To kill Renée?'

'Not her. Him!'

'It would certainly have been the quickest way of getting rid of him. But I must ask you to believe that, if I'd intended to, I wouldn't have waited two years. Can you imagine what those two years have been like with that man constantly around?'

'How about him?'

'He should have realized earlier and gone away. When a woman stops loving you, when she loves someone else, and when she tells you so to your face, you know what to do . . .'

He had got up, too. He had lost a little of his calm. His voice was growing angrier.

'That didn't stop him from poisoning our lives, or you from going to question Renée at home, or sending for my employees, or trying to make me say various things for more than an hour. Have you any more questions to ask me? Am I still a free man? Can I go?'

'You can.'

'Goodbye, then.'

As he went out, he slammed the door behind him.

That evening, Maigret was able to watch television in the warm, wearing his bedroom slippers, and his wife knitting beside him, but he would have liked to be in Janvier or Lapointe's place. They were in the Montmartre he knew so well, in streets familiar to him, each going his own way, from bistro to bistro, from a yellowish light to a whiter one, from an old-fashioned décor to a more modern one, from the smell of beer to the smell of Calvados.

He had, of course, been happy when he had been promoted and finally become Chief Divisional Inspector of the Criminal Branch. Even so, he felt nostalgic about certain beats on which you shivered during winter nights, and about some of the concierges' offices, with their different smells which you visited for days on end, forever asking the same, apparently futile questions.

Up at the top, they reproached him for being too ready to leave his office and go off on his own like a retriever. How could he explain, especially to the magistrates, that he had to see things, sniff around, and get the feel of a place?

Ironically enough, they were showing a tragedy by Corneille. On the little screen, costumed kings and warriors took it in turns to declaim noble lines, reminiscent of schooldays, and it was odd being interrupted every half-hour by the telephone ringing and hearing Janvier's voice—he was the first to ring—saying much less emphatically:

'I think I'm on the track, Chief. I'm ringing you from a bar in the Rue Germain-Pilon, two hundred yards from the Place des Abbesses. It's called *Au Bon Coin*. The owner's already gone to bed. His wife's serving at the bar, and keeps going and sitting by the stove. All I did was mention a man with a hare-lip and she remembered.

' "Has something happened to him?" she asked.

'He often used to come and have a couple of drinks about eight o'clock at night. Apparently, the cat was fond of him and used to rub up against his legs. He'd lean down and stroke it.

'It's a small, ill-lit bar, with dark walls. I don't know why it stays open at night, because there's no one there except an oldish man drinking a hot rum over by the window.'

'Has she seen Planchon since Monday?'

'No. She's pretty sure Monday was the last time he came in. In any case, she mentioned to her husband yesterday that they hadn't seen the customer with the hare-lip and she wondered if he was ill.'

'Did he ever confide in her?'

'He hardly ever spoke. She felt sorry for him, thought he looked unhappy, and tried to cheer him up.'

266

'Carry on looking.'

Janvier took the plunge into the cold and dark and, a little further on, went into another café, and then another. Lapointe was doing the same, too.

Maigret returned to Corneille's characters on the screen. From her armchair, his wife looked at him questioningly.

At half-past nine, it was Lapointe's turn to ring up. He was telephoning from the Rue Lepic, from another, larger, brighter bar, where the regulars were playing cards and where he was on to Planchon's scent.

'Still on the brandy, Chief! They knew who he was here, and that he lived in the Rue Tholozé, because they'd seen him pass by, in the daytime, driving a large van with his name on it in big letters. They felt sorry for him. When he arrived, he was already half-drunk. He never spoke to anyone. One of the *belote* players remembered that the last time he came in was on Monday. He ate two hard-boiled eggs which he took from the wire holder on the counter.'

Janvier must have chosen the wrong route because, soon after, he telephoned that he had had no luck in five bistros. They had never heard of the man with the hare-lip.

Singers, male and female, had taken over from Corneille's heroes on the screen when, about eleven o'clock, Lapointe rang up for the second time. He seemed excited.

'I've news, Chief. I wonder if we mightn't do better to meet at the Quai des Orfèvres. I'm watching a woman through the door of the kiosk, and I'm afraid she'll slip away.

'I'm in a brasserie on the Place Blanche. The terrace is glassed in and heated by two braziers. Are you still there?'

'I'm listening.'

'The first waiter I spoke to knows Planchon well by sight. Apparently, he always used to come along fairly late in the evening and, more often than not, wasn't too steady on his legs. He used to sit on the terrace and order a beer.'

'Presumably to chase down all the brandies he had drunk elsewhere?'

'I don't know if you know the place. There are two or three women on the terrace the whole time, watching the passers-by. They work mainly at the exit of the cinema next door.

'The waiter pointed one of them out to me.

' "Here! You have a word with Clémentine. That's her name. She'll tell you more than I can. I've seen them go off together a few times."

'She immediately guessed I was from the police and, at first, she didn't want to say anything.

' "What has he done?" she merely asked. "Why are you looking for him? Why do you think I should know him?"

'Bit by bit, she began to talk, and I think what she said will interest

267

you. I even think it would be as well to take a written statement from her while she's in a good mood. What shall I do?'

'Bring her to H.Q. I'll be there about the same time as you.'

Madame Maigret went resignedly to fetch him his shoes.

'Do you want me to call a taxi?'

'Yes.'

He put on his overcoat, not forgetting his scarf. He had just drunk a hot rum, because he still felt he was in for a good bout of 'flu.

At the Quai des Orfèvres, he saluted the lone officer on duty, climbed the broad, grey, ill-lit staircase, walked along the empty corridor, switched on the light in his office, and pushed open the door of the duty room.

Lapointe was there, still wearing his hat, and a woman got up from the chair on which she was sitting.

At the same moment, all over Paris, hundreds of people, who might have been her sisters, were walking the streets in the shadows, not far from furnished hotels with their front doors discreetly ajar.

She was wearing exaggeratedly high stiletto heels and her legs were thin. The entire lower half of her body was long and slender. She broadened out only at the hips, and the disparity was all the more striking, because she was wearing a short coat, made of some long-haired fur which looked like goat.

Her face was like a doll's, bright pink, with coal-black eye-lashes.

'Mademoiselle was good enough to accompany me,' said Lapointe pleasantly.

She replied ironically but unmaliciously:

'As if you wouldn't have carted me off anyway!'

She seemed impressed by the Inspector and looked him up and down.

He took off his overcoat and motioned to her to sit down again. Lapointe had settled himself in front of a typewriter, ready to take down her statement.

'What's your name?'

'Antoinette Lesourd. I'm usually called Sylvie. Antoinette sounds old-fashioned. It's my grandmother's name and ...'

'Do you know Planchon?'

'I didn't know his name. He used to come to the brasserie every evening, and he was always well-oiled. At first, I thought he was a widower drowning his sorrows. He seemed so unhappy.'

'Did he speak to you first?'

'No. I did. The first time, I was quite sure he was going to run away. Then I said: "I've got troubles, too. I know what it's like. I was married to a layabout who went off one fine day with my daughter."'

'It was when I mentioned my daughter that he suddenly softened.'

Then, turning to Lapointe, she said:

'You're not putting all that down?'

'Only the essentials,' Maigret put in. 'Since when have you known each other?'

'Months. Let's see. In the summer, I went to work in Cannes, because the American fleet was in. I came back in September. I must have met him about the beginning of October.'

'Did he follow you the first evening?'

'No. He bought me a drink. Then he told me he had to get home, that he got up early because of his work, and that it was late. He only followed me two or three days later.'

'Back to your place?'

'I never have anyone back to my place. Anyway, the concierge wouldn't allow it. It's a respectable house. In fact, there's a judge living on the first floor. I usually go to a hotel in the Rue Lepic. Do you know it? Whatever you do, don't make it awkward for them. With all the new regulations, you never quite know where you are.'

'Did Planchon often go along with you?'

'Not often. Possibly a dozen times in all. And even then he didn't always do anything.'

'Did he talk?'

'He once said: "You see! They're right. I'm not even a man." '

'Didn't he mention any details about his life?'

'I spotted his wedding ring, of course. One evening I asked him: "Is it your wife who's giving you hell?" '

'And he answered that his wife hadn't deserved to meet a man like him.'

'When did you last see him?'

Maigret could tell from the way Lapointe, still at his typewriter, winked that he had got to the interesting bit.

'Monday evening.'

'How can you be sure it was Monday?'

'Because on Monday I got pinched and spent twenty-four hours in the nick. You can ask your colleagues. My name must be down on the list. They went off with a Black Maria full.'

'What time on Monday did he arrive at the brasserie?'

'It was just before ten. I'd just come out, because there's no point in starting early in Montmartre.'

'What state was he in?'

'He could hardly walk. I saw straight off that he'd had more to drink than usual. He came and sat next to me on the terrace near the brazier. He couldn't even raise his arm to call the waiter. He stammered: "A brandy. And a brandy for Madame."

'We almost fell out. I didn't want him to drink spirits, in the state he was, but he kept on.

' "I'm ill," he kept saying. "Nothing like a large brandy to put you right." '

'Did he say anything else that struck you?'

Another wink from Lapointe.

'Yes. A few words that I didn't understand. He said, two or three times: "He won't believe me, either." '

'Didn't he explain?'

'He muttered: "Don't worry. I know what I'm doing. And you'll understand, too, one day." '

Maigret remembered the tone in which Planchon, the same Monday, a few hours before this scene, had spoken to him over the telephone, while he was still in the Place des Abbesses:

'Thank you.'

He hadn't merely sensed the bitterness and disillusion but some kind of a threat, too.

'Did you go to the hotel together?'

'He wanted to. But when we got outside, he fell flat on the pavement. I helped him to get up. He was humiliated.

' "I'll show them I'm a man," he moaned.

'I had to hold him up. I knew that the hotel manager wouldn't let him in as he was, and I didn't want him to be sick in the room, either.

' "Where do you live?" I asked him.

' "Up there."

' "Where's up there?"

' "Rue Tho... Rue Tho..."

'He could hardly get his words out.

' "Rue Tholozé?"

' "Yes. Straight along... Straight along..."

'It isn't always funny, I can tell you. I was afraid a copper might spot us and think I was trying to rob him. They'd obviously have made out that I'd forced him to drink. I don't want to malign the police, but you must admit they sometimes...'

'Go on. Did you call a taxi?'

'Are you joking? I was skint. I helped him walk along. It took us almost half an hour to get to the end of Rue Tholozé, because he kept stopping, his legs kept buckling and he kept telling me at every bistro that a large brandy would put him right. In the end, he stopped in front of an iron gate and fell down again. The gate wasn't shut. There was a van in the yard and a name on it that I couldn't make out in the dark. I didn't leave him till we reached the door.'

'Were the lights on in the windows?'

'There was some light filtering through the blinds on the ground floor. I wedged him up against the wall, hoping he'd stay on his feet for a while, rang the bell and ran off.'

All the while she was talking, the typewriter kept tapping away.

'Has something happened to him?'

'He's disappeared.'

'I hope they're not going to think it's me?'

'Don't you worry.'

'Do you think they'll send me up in front of the judge?'

'I hope not. And even if they did, you'd have nothing to worry about.'

Lapointe removed the sheet of paper from the typewriter and handed it to the woman.

'Am I to read it?'

'And sign it.'

'I shan't have any trouble?'

She eventually signed her name in her large, clumsy handwriting.

'What shall I do now?'

'You're free.'

'Do you think I'll still get a bus?'

Maigret took a note from his pocket.

'Here's the money for a taxi.'

She had hardly left when the 'phone rang. It was Janvier, who had rung the Boulevard Richard-Lenoir. Madame Maigret had told him that her husband was at the Quai des Orfèvres.

'Nothing else, Chief. I've done the Boulevard Rochechouart as far as the Place d'Anvers. I've been up at least a dozen side-streets.'

'You can go to bed now.'

'Has Lapointe found something?'

'Yes. We'll tell you tomorrow.'

When Maigret got home, there was one thing he was afraid of: waking up with a temperature. He still had an unpleasant tickling sensation in his nostrils, and he felt as if his eyelids were burning. What was more, his pipe did not taste the same.

His wife made him another hot rum. He sweated all night. At nine o'clock in the morning, he was sitting, somewhat light-headed, in the Magistrates' ante-room, where he waited a good twenty minutes for the Deputy Prosecutor.

The Inspector must have looked depressed, because the Magistrate asked him:

'Well, did the fellow you called in make any trouble?'

'No, but there are developments.'

'Have you found your decorator? What was his name again?'

'Planchon. No, we haven't found him. We've been able to reconstruct how he spent his time on Monday evening. When he got back home shortly before eleven o'clock at night, he was so drunk that he couldn't stand up, and he fell down on the pavement several times between the Place Blanche, where he had a last drink, and the Rue Tholozé.'

'Was he alone?'

'A prostitute, with whom he'd gone several times, was holding him up.'

'Do you believe her?'

'I'm sure she's telling the truth. She rang the bell of the house before she went away, leaving Planchon more or less propped up against the wall. It's impossible that the same man, a few minutes later, could have gone upstairs to the first floor, filled two suitcases with his things, then come downstairs carrying them, and finally gone out into the street.'

'He might have taken something to sober himself up. Such things exist.'

'His wife and Prou would have mentioned it.'

'Prou's the lover, isn't he? Isn't he the one you called in? What does he say?'

Slowly and patiently, still dizzy, Maigret told the story of the three million francs and the receipts. First of all there was the receipt signed Planchon.

'Monsieur Pirouet, our handwriting expert, isn't certain. In his opinion, the paper could have been signed by Planchon when drunk, but the result would have been similiar if the signature had been copied by someone else.'

'Why do you mention several receipts?'

'Because, since December 24th, Prou has borrowed two million old francs, one million from his father and the other from his brother-in-law. One of my men went and photographed the receipts. The one held by the brother-in-law states that the sum is to be repaid in five years, and that Prou is to pay interest at six per cent. The father's, on the other hand, provides for repayment in two years and doesn't mention any interest.'

'Do you think they're goodwill receipts?'

'No. My assistants have checked up. On the 23rd of December, the day before payment, Prou's father drew a million francs in notes from his Savings Bank account in which he holds just over two million. As for the brother-in-law, Mourier, he drew out the same amount, on the same day, from his postal cheque account.'

'But I thought you mentioned three million francs?'

'The third million was drawn by Roger Prou from his account with the Crédit Lyonnais. So that, on that date, there were three million old francs legal tender in the house on the Rue Tholozé.'

'On what date was the transfer document signed?'

'December 29th. It all took place as if Prou and his mistress had planned everything well before Christmas, and were waiting for an opportunity to get the husband to sign the document.'

'In that case, I don't see . . .'

As if to make things more difficult, Maigret added:

'Monsieur Pirouet has analysed the ink of the signature. He can't date it precisely, but he's sure it's more than two weeks old.'

'What do you intend to do? Drop the case?'

'I've come to ask you for a search warrant.'

'After what you've just told me?'

Maigret nodded, not too proud of himself.

'What do you expect to find in the house? Planchon's corpse?'

'It's hardly likely.'

'The banknotes?'

'I don't know.'

'Must you really?'

'Planchon was incapable of walking at eleven o'clock on Monday.'

'Wait here a moment. I can't take the responsibility. I'll have a couple of words with the Public Prosecutor.'

Maigret waited alone for about ten minutes.

'He doesn't care for it much, either, especially just now when the police aren't having a very good press. Still . . .'

Anyway, the answer was yes and, a moment or two later, the Inspector went off with the signed warrant. It was ten to ten. He whipped open the door of the duty room, could not see Lapointe but spotted Janvier.

'Get a car from the yard. I'll be right down.'

Then he rang the Crime Squad and gave instructions to Moers.

'Get them there as quickly as you can. And pick out the best.'

Then he went downstairs and sat beside Janvier in the little black car.

'Rue Tholozé.'

'Did you get the warrant?'

'I dragged it out of them. I'd rather not think what's in store for me if there's nothing here, and if the wife or her lover kick up the dust.'

He was so deeply plunged in thought that he hardly noticed that the sun had just come out for the first time in several days. Janvier went on talking, as they dodged in and out between buses and taxis.

'People like him don't work on Saturdays, as a rule. I think it's forbidden by the Unions, unless they get double pay. There's a chance we may find Prou at home.'

He was not there. It was Renée who came and opened the door, after glancing at them through a window. She was more suspicious and disagreeable than ever.

'You again!' she exclaimed.

'Isn't Prou here?'

'He's gone to finish off an urgent job. What do you want this time?'

Maigret took the warrant from his pocket and gave it to her to read.

'So you're going to search the house? Well, really, that's the limit!'

A Crime Squad van, full of men and equipment, drove into the yard.

'And who are that lot?'

'My colleagues. I'm sorry but it'll take us some time.'

'Will you make a mess?'

'I'm afraid so.'

'Are you sure you're in your right?'

'The warrant's signed by the Deputy Public Prosecutor.'

She shrugged.

'That's a great help. I don't even know what he is.'

However, she let them in, giving them all black looks.

'I hope it'll be over by the time my daughter's back from school.'

'That depends.'

'On what?'

'On what we find.'

'If you'd only tell me what you're looking for.'

'Your husband definitely left with two suitcases on Monday evening, didn't he?'

'It was I who told you.'

'I suppose he took away the three million francs which Prou paid him on December 29th?'

'I've no idea. We gave him the money but it wasn't our business what he did with it.'

'He didn't pay them into his bank account.'

'Did you check up?'

'Yes. You said yourself he had no friends. So it's unlikely that he trusted the sum to anyone.'

'What are you driving at?'

'He couldn't have been walking round with that sum on him all the time ever since December 29th. Three million francs is a big load.'

'So?'

'Nothing.'

'Is that what you're looking for?'

'I don't know.'

The experts were already at work, beginning with the kitchen. It was a job they were used to, and they went about it methodically, leaving no stone unturned, searching tins containing flour, sugar and coffee as well as the dustbins.

It all went so smoothly that it looked like some kind of ballet, and the woman watched them with surprise, almost bewilderment.

'Who's going to clear it all up?'

Maigret didn't answer.

'Can I make a 'phone call?' she asked.

She rang up a flat in the Rue Lamark, a Madame Fajon, and asked to speak to the house-painter who was working there.

'Is that you? They've come back. The Inspector, yes, and a crowd of men who are turning the house upside down. Some of them are even taking photographs. No, apparently they've got a warrant. They showed me a paper supposed to have been signed by a deputy something. Yes. I'd rather you came back.'

She gave Maigret an ugly look, which contained a hint of defiance.

One of the men was scratching at some stains on the floor of the dining-room and collecting the dust that he obtained in little bags.

'What's he doing? Doesn't he think my floor's clean enough?'

Another man was tapping the walls with an upholsterer's hammer.

Photographs and reproductions of pictures were taken down one after another, and then replaced somewhat crookedly.

Two men had gone up to the first floor where they could be heard pacing about.

'Are they going to do the same in my daughter's room?'

'I'm afraid so.'

'What shall I tell Isabelle when she gets back?'

It was the first time that Maigret had joked:

'That we've been playing treasure-hunts. Haven't you got a television?'

'No. We should have bought one next month.'

'Why "should have"?'

'Should have, shall, what's the difference? If you think I'm in any state to choose my words...'

She had apparently recognized Janvier.

'When I think that he came and measured up all the rooms in the house on some excuse...'

They heard a car entering the yard, a car door slamming, and some rapid footsteps. Renée must have recognized them because she immediately moved towards the door.

'Look!' she said to Roger Prou. 'They're going through everything, including my saucepans and linen. They're upstairs in the girl's room, too.'

Prou's lips quivered with fury as he looked the Inspector up and down.

'Do you have the right to do this?' he asked, his voice trembling.

Maigret handed him a warrant.

'How if I 'phoned a lawyer?'

'It's your right. But all he could do is be present at the search.'

About midday, there was a rattle at the letter-box and, through the window, Maigret saw that it was Isabelle who had arrived back. Her mother rushed off and shut herself in the kitchen with her, where the Crime Squad men had finished their work.

No doubt some interesting things would have come to light if he had questioned the little girl but, except in cases of absolute necessity, Maigret loathed interrogating children.

The office had been searched without result. A group of men moved towards the shed at the end of the yard, and one of them climbed into the van.

It was a tooth-comb search by men of long experience.

'Will you come up, Inspector?'

Prou, who had also heard, followed Maigret up the stairs.

A child's bedroom, with a teddy bear still on the bed, looked as if removals were going on. The wardrobe and mirror had been shoved into a corner. None of the furniture was in its place and they had taken up the reddish linoleum which covered the floor.

One of the floor-boards had been prised up.

'Look here.'

But Maigret first looked at Prou's face. He was standing in the frame of the door. His face had grown so hard that the Inspector yelled:

'Watch out, down there.'

But Prou did not make a bolt for it, as might have been expected. He did not move into the room, or even bother to bend over the hole in the floor, down at the bottom of which was a package wrapped in newspaper.

Nothing was touched until the photographer came. Then fingerprints on the greyish boards were taken.

At last Maigret was able to bend down, pick up the package and open it. There were some bundles of ten thousand franc notes, three of them, and one of the bundles was crisp and new.

'Have you anything to say, Prou?'

'I know nothing about it.'

'Wasn't it you who put the money in this hiding-place?'

'Why should I have?'

'Do you still maintain that, on Monday evening, your former employer left here with two suitcases containing his things, yet didn't take the three million francs?'

'I've nothing to add.'

'Wasn't it you who raised the linoleum, prised up a floorboard and hid the ten thousand franc notes?'

'I know no more than what I told you yesterday.'

'Was it your mistress?'

He gave a rather hesitant look.

'What she may or may not have done is no concern of mine.'

CHAPTER EIGHT

What she may or may not have done is no concern of mine ...

These words, the tone in which they were said, and the look which accompanied them lingered in Maigret's mind during the months that followed.

That Saturday, there were lights at the Quai des Orfèvres until the small hours of the morning. The Inspector, acting warily, had advised both the two lovers to designate a lawyer. As they did not know any, they had been given a list of members at the Bar and they had chosen at random.

In this way, the regulations had been strictly observed. One of the lawyers. Renée's, was young and fair-haired and she immediately began, in spite of herself, to turn the charm on him. Prou's, by contrast, was middle-aged, with a clumsily knotted tie, grubby shirt and dirty finger-nails, who could be seen touting for clients all day long in the corridors of the Palais.

Ten, twenty, a hundred times, Maigret repeated the same questions, sometimes to Renée Planchon alone, sometimes to Prou, sometimes to both together.

At first, when they were confronted, they seemed to consult each other's faces. Then, as the questioning went on, and when they were separated for some while before being brought together again, their looks grew more suspicious.

When he had seen them the first time, Maigret had been reminded, not without some admiration, of a couple of wild animals.

The couple no longer existed. They remained two wild animals, though, and it did not look as if it would be long before they tore each other to pieces.

'Who struck your husband?'

'I've no idea. I don't know that he was struck. I went upstairs before he left.'

'You told me ...'

'I know no more than I've said. You've confused me with all your questions.'

'Did you know that the three million francs were in your daughter's bedroom?'

'No.'

'Didn't you hear your lover shift the furniture, raise the lino and prise up a strip of parquet?'

'I'm not at home the whole time. I keep telling you I don't know

277

anything. You can question me as long as you like, I've nothing else to say.'

'And you didn't hear the van leave the yard on the night of Monday to Tuesday?'

'No.'

'Yet the neighbours heard it.'

'Good for them.'

It was not true. Maigret had resorted to a somewhat crude trick. The concierge in the building opposite had not heard anything. Of course, his office was on the side opposite the yard. They had questioned the tenants without any success.

Meanwhile, Prou repeated obstinately what he had told the Inspector during his first interrogation at the Quai des Orfèvres.

'I was asleep when he came in. Renée got up and went into the dining-room. I heard them talk for quite a while. Someone went up to the first floor.'

'Weren't you listening behind the door?'

'I've told you the truth.'

'Did you hear everything that was going on next door?'

'Not very well.'

'Could your mistress have knocked down Planchon without your knowing it?'

'I went back to bed and straight to sleep.'

'Before your ex-boss left?'

'I've no idea.'

'Didn't you hear the yard door close again?'

'I didn't hear a thing.'

The lawyers agreed and each one adopted his client's attitude. At five in the morning, Prou and his mistress were taken away separately to the cells. Meanwhile, Maigret went to bed for only an hour, drank five or six cups of black coffee, and then went along once again to the Magistrates' offices, too solemn for his taste. This time, although it was a Sunday, he was permitted an interview with the Public Prosecutor himself and he remained closeted with him nearly two hours.

'The body still hasn't been discovered?'

'No.'

'No bloodstains in the house or the van?'

'Not so far.'

With no corpse, it was still not possible to charge the couple with murder. There remained the notes which, as the receipts proved, belonged to Planchon. There was no reason why they should be hidden under Isabelle's floorboards.

She had been taken to a children's home.

Maigret was allowed another three hours' questioning, on the Monday morning, once again in front of the lawyers, after which an

Examining Magistrate took the case in hand. This was the new method to which he had got used.

Was the Magistrate any happier about it than he was? He had no idea because they did not bother to keep him in touch.

Only a week later, a body was pulled out of the Seine at the Suresnes Dam. About a dozen people, and, in particular, the owners of the Montmartre bars, which Planchon went to every evening, and the girl called Sylvie identified him.

Prou and Renée, taken separately to see the decomposed body, kept their jaws clenched.

According to the police doctor, Planchon had been killed by several blows on the head with a heavy instrument probably wrapped in a cloth.

He had then been tied up in a sack. Later, there was a battle between the experts about the sack and the cord round it. They had, in fact, found similar sacks in the shed at the end of the yard, as well as some cord used to support ladders, which semed to be made of the same stuff.

Maigret knew nothing about all this for several months. Spring had been around long enough for the chestnut-trees to burst into flower. Men were going about in their jackets. A young Englishman was identified as the jewel-thief in the big hotels, and Interpol got on to his tracks in Australia, while a few stones, removed from their settings, were recovered in Italy.

The Planchon affair only reached the courts a few days before the judicial holidays, and Maigret found himself closeted in the witnesses' room with a certain number of people he knew and others he did not.

When it was his turn to go into the witness-box, he realized, from his very first glance at the accused, that Renée Planchon and Prou's passion had been transformed into hatred.

They defended themselves to save their own skins, ready to let suspicion rest on the other. They glared viciously at each other.

'Do you swear to tell the truth, the whole truth and nothing but the truth?'

With his hand, Maigret repeated the gesture that he had made so often in the same surroundings.

'I do!'

'Tell the jury what you know about the case.'

The two accused were once again staring at him resentfully. Wasn't it he who had started the investigation, and didn't they owe their arrest to him?

It was obvious that the act had been premeditated and had been worked out some time before. Prou had been clever enough to borrow the two million francs on December 24th from his father and his brother-in-law.

Wasn't it natural enough to buy the firm he was working for from a drunkard who was no longer able to cope?

The receipts were genuine. The money had been paid all right.

But Planchon had never known anything about it. He had never had any idea what was being hatched up in his own house. Even though he had felt that they wanted to turn him out, he had never dreamed that the process had already begun or that, on December 29th, or at any rate about that time, his wife was typing out a fake transfer document at the bottom of which someone would forge his signature.

Who? Renée or her lover?

The experts were to have interminable discussions and some bittersweet exchanges about that, too.

'On the Saturday evening . . .' began Maigret.

'Speak up.'

'On the Saturday evening, when I returned home, about seven, I found a man waiting for me.'

'Did you know him?'

'I didn't, but I guessed who he was straightaway because of his harelip. For almost two months, in fact, a man answering to his description had been coming to see me at the Quai des Orfèvres on Saturday afternoons, but used to disappear before I had a chance to see him.'

'Do you solemnly swear that it was Léonard Planchon?'

'Yes.'

'What did he want?'

As he faced the jury, the Inspector turned his back on the two accused, so that he could not see their reactions.

They must have been flabbergasted when they realized that he was going to help them out.

In complete silence, followed by such an uproar that the judge had to threaten to clear the court, Maigret said clearly:

'He wanted to tell me that he intended to kill his wife and her lover.'

In theory, he would have liked to say sorry to poor old Planchon. But a few moments before he had just sworn to tell the truth, the whole truth and nothing but the truth.

Once order was restored, he was able to answer the judge's detailed questions and, his evidence concluded, he did not really have time to hang around the courtroom, because he had just been told that a crime had been discovered in a luxury flat in the Rue Lauriston.

There were no confessions. Yet the charges were overwhelming enough for the jury to answer the first question in the affirmative.

Ironically enough, it was Maigret's statement that saved Roger Prou's neck and won him extenuating circumstances.

'You have heard the Inspector's statement,' the lawyer pleaded. 'It was one man or the other. Even though my client killed, it was, in a sense, a legal self-defence.'

Antoinette, the girl with the long legs and broad hips they called Sylvie, was in court when the foreman of the jury read out the verdict.

Twenty years for Roger Prou and eight for Renée Planchon, who glared at her ex-lover with such loathing that a shiver passed through the courtroom.

'Did you read this, Chief?'

Janvier showed Maigret a recent edition of a newspaper with the verdict on the front page.

The Inspector glanced at it and merely growled:

'Poor wretch!'

He felt he had betrayed the man with the hare-lip, whose last words on the telephone had, however, been:

'*Thank you ...*'

Noland
February 27, 1962